THE THIRD MAGPIE

M S CLEMENTS

PUBLISHED BY PGUP BOOKS

PgUp Limited
18 King Street
Maidenhead
SL6 1EF

ISBN 978-1-9160638-0-8

Printed and bound in Great Britain by Clays Ltd, Elcograf S.p.A.

For my family,

John, Susana and Julia

'It isn't what we say or think that defines us,
but what we do.'

Sense and Sensibility
Jane Austen

CONTENTS

A SHORN HEART

'The shorn moon trembling indistinct on her path,
Frail as a scar upon the pale blue sky,
Draws towards the downward slope: some sorrow hath
Worn her down to the quick, so she faintly fares
Along her foot-searched way without knowing why
She creeps persistent down the sky's long stairs.'

from 'Brother and Sister'

D H Lawrence

EVIE

Insomnia has a way of opening the void, filling it with illusion and voices from long ago. Even Maya's soft puffs of righteous sleep cannot distract my brain from flooding with scenes from that summer holiday. My teen-self echoes inside me, *'Jump, Finn. Jump!'*

Even if I could erase that memory, I won't. I crave it. That chilled water lapping against me as swimmers power through lengths of the pool. Untamed hair escaping the sodden scrunchie, tickling the edge of my mouth as the locks stick to my cheek. I need to be that young woman again. I need to be able to say one more time, *'Don't be scared, Finn. I'm right here.'*

I lie in bed hankering for my youth, but these flesh and bones must creep forward. With the irritating heat of maturity passing, I curl up once more against my wife's comforting body.

And now I'm thirsty. Hopeful water will end my restlessness and conscious not to awaken her, I roll on to my side and begin a finger-tip search of the bedside table. I pause. The silver picture frame is cold against the heat of my skin. I spread out my palm, reaching for that young man, a captive of time and place, make-believing I can push through, touch him, and bring him back to safety. It doesn't work. I find the tumbler and take a sip. And still, I miss him.

I flip over my pillow and lie back down, mentally listing all of the day's jobs; a new vet starts today, bake some cakes; change these sheets, night sweats create so much washing; is it parents' evening tonight? I think so. They'll be teenagers soon. I ought to organise a party. How old would Finn be?

No. How old is Finn now? Definitely 'is'. I should know that. I should. I really should.

I shuffle around, trying to get comfortable. My nightie rucks under me and the straps are cutting. I fling it off. My body relaxes, and Finn waits for me in that in-between world, where dreams and nightmare sit on the horizon. Today he is the seven-year-old boy, frightened and uncertain. There is an angry bruise on his shin, and his feet shift back from the edge. Ball-like fists pound his thighs and those eyes, his vibrant blue eyes, brimming with childhood fear. My memory calls out to him, *'Come on, darling, jump. You can do it. I'll catch you; I promise.'*

This time will be different. This time he'll jump, I know he will. He'll jump and skinny arms will envelope me. I'll clamp him to my chest. His heartbeat, his panic and joy, they'll thump against my skin, just like it did before.

Downstairs in the kitchen, Petra whines. Perhaps she misses her sibling too. I squint at the pile of clothes flung onto the bedroom chair, morphing those fabric peaks and valleys into the mountain range that loomed behind the holiday resort. Dad's optimistic words reverberating off the rocky escarpment to haunt my days.

'Sometimes, these things happen. He'll grow out of it in time.'

I slide out of bed, and Maya slips her arm onto the empty space. I am grateful she doesn't wake. I'd only sink back into her embrace, wallowing in the comforting lies she'd gently whisper into my ear. Lies that bar my desired recollections from gate-crashing my life. And I want those memories. I want them to become real again. I want to hear those children running riot, screeching, laughing and plunging into the pool from every angle. I want the goose bumps that race down my arms with the chattering of my teeth.

Downstairs, the AGA warms me while Petra noses my bare feet, slowing our exit. I step into the pre-dawn air, heavy with the scent of Angel's Trumpet. With all the ungainliness of a puppy, Petra sits obediently on top of my foot, unsure where to put her legs, her attentive marble-brown eyes watching me. I clip on the leash and banish all self-indulgent thoughts. I must allow heartache to exist inside the mundane.

We emerge from the sombre cover of the woods and wait, catching our breath. Petra chewing her saliva-soaked tennis ball, and me on the wooden stile. Dawn claws away the night sky, splitting its darkness with grey and tangerine scars. In the village, blinking lights announce that the lives of others must also continue.

Velvet pads of infant excitement drum past me, injecting a dose of brief happiness to soothe my life of work, parenthood and loss. I delude myself. I make excuses, replaying the scene expecting a different outcome, but Andy is always there dictating the conclusion regardless of my actions. He'll ring on Wednesday. He always does. My stomach tightens at the prospect of his call. Insincere enquiries followed by complaints about Mum, her eccentricities and cyber activism. He'll demand I return to Melborough. As though I'd ever convince her to tone down the protests and letter writing. I can't change her, no one can. If she refused to listen to me when Finn was little, why change now? No, Andy will have to deal with her himself. What about his friends in Foreign Affairs? All those useful government contacts. God forbid one of them should make inquiries on our behalf. No, Andy won't push them for an answer, can't annoy them, that's bad for business. Andy, the businessman, the firm and steady hand of Finlay Communications. Andy, the bully, the sadistic shit determined to terrify our little brother.

I don't understand it. Why that pool? Why that day and

that incident. There are so many others to decipher, yet my head chooses to repeat Finn struggling under Andy's tight grip, tears dripping into the pool. Andy is savouring the torture, his hissing threats carrying over poolside noise.

'Sink or swim, weirdo? I say sink, just like before.'

Dad's feeble censure drips off his muscular back along with the chlorinated water. I intervene, make my threats, and whisper his sordid little secrets back into his ear. He concedes defeat and releases Finn with foul-mouth insults.

Where's the mystery? Andy was Andy and I dealt with it. There was nothing to warrant a lifetime of anger and mistrust. Besides, Finn's difficulties were nobody's fault, not really. The accident at the brook, his silence, the illness, none of that had anything to do with Andy. We all made mistakes. It's my mind playing tricks on me again. Just early morning misgivings conjuring conspiracies where none exist. He's my brother and he loves us. We should go home. We should move on. I'll tell Andy on Wednesday. We will go back. Christmas, yes, the perfect opportunity. Dad will be thrilled. He hates the December gloom. It's the rain against the sitting-room window. And it's the way he goes cold if the mobile rings just after relaxing with his evening drink. Seeing the twins will make all the difference. We've never had a Christmas together at home. Yes, we'll go at Christmas. I'll tell Maya as soon as I get back. We'll return to Melborough. Cara and Mikey will enjoy it, decorating the house and opening the abandoned cards, even if Mum hides in her study, re-fuelling her unhappiness with gin.

But what if Mum had listened to me, or to Dad? What if my phone had been charged when Finn tried to call? What if we had got help earlier? What if?

Oh for goodness sake, this isn't healthy. Everyone else can see it, even me.

Determination marches me across the wheat field, morning light giving it a creamy apricot hue. I am hungry at the thought of it becoming fresh bread. My stomach rumbles in anticipation while I ruminate on holiday plans.

I stop.

Hot sweat rises within to accompany the revelation. What am I thinking? I must protect them. We can't go back at Christmas. It's not the right time. The children will remind them of Finn, and Mikey might ask questions. Mum and Dad are too old to go through that again. No, we'll go another time, when it's easier to organise cover vets. Perhaps we'll go in the Spring. I'll think about it, there's no rush.

Petra pants with fulfilled exhaustion, her ears prick up with the tolling church bell ringing out with the precision of a funeral mass. By the verge, a magpie pecks at the remnants of a mouse. I shudder with irrational superstition.

'Good day, Mr Magpie,' I say over Petra's barks. Our way is cleared of the malevolent corvid, and we trot along the path to the backdoor of the bakery where our usual mug of tea and bowl of water awaits us.

If the lives of others must continue, then I suppose, so must mine.

NEW
ALBANY

NORMALITY IS HARD WORK

Life is exhausting, but stop for a moment, even for a second, and allow the absurdity of our behaviour to cloud our thoughts, then all will disintegrate. This hard-won illusion of a normal life will disappear, revealing the extent of our own deception.

SOPHIE

After sixteen years of marriage, every nuance of Finn's arrival was imprinted deep within her. The click of the garden gate, that huff when he lifted his bike onto the hooks, and the frustrated jangling of the stubborn door handle.

Sophie was already filling the kettle by the time she heard the anticipated thud of his bag hitting the table. Warm hands caught her waist, followed by an affectionate kiss brushing her cheek. That oft-repeated routine always ending with a request to satisfy his innocent addiction.

'Any chance of a cup of tea?'

Finn dragged out a chair and emptied his bag of exercise books. Elbows on the table and his shoulders hunched with resigned compliance, he stared forlornly at the pile before him. Another year trapped in a job he did not choose, but for Sophie's sake, content to fulfil his allocated role.

'How did the meeting go?' she asked, mustering as much fake cheer as possible.

'Austen, again.' Finn plucked a book from the pile, closing the conversation down with his deliberate flicking through the pages.

Sophie gently patted his shoulder in silent commiseration as she passed him to fetch a couple of mugs from the opposite cupboard. He'd cheer up with a cup of tea, but when she looked back at him, a barely audible expletive escaped her mouth. His fingers were splaying out, filling the screen with the bold headline of the Daily Briefing. He didn't hear her. Sophie watched him nudge his glasses to the top of his head, all the while her teeth nervously nibbled away the tender flesh of her bottom lip. She should have closed the tab the minute he arrived. Finn squinted, and in Sophie's shoulders, muscles contracted, developing another knot of pain. She rubbed her neck. At some point he would find out, it was inevitable, but even rational thought could not soothe her angst. Finn's back rose and fell with his breaths, gaining pace and catching up with her own rising unease.

'You should get your eyes tested, I'm sure your sight is getting worse. I'll make an appointment.' She had used the same tactics countless times. But this time her distraction technique failed. Finn frowned. There was no reply, only the scrape of a chair as he left the table to seek the solitude of the sitting-room. Behind her, the kettle whistled with piercing urgency to warn of the pressures that lurked beneath the surface of normality. She knew how he'd react. And what did she offer him in exchange for her guilt? A hand to hold and a cup of tea.

Sophie followed her husband through to the sitting-room, pushed his legs off the sofa and sank her miniature frame into his warmth. She searched his face for a forgiving smile. It came, then disappeared like a mirage in the desert. His arm had dropped onto her, so she snuggled in closer. With her fingers entwined in his, she lifted his hand to her mouth, placing a delicate kiss on each knuckle.

'Why do they keep doing this to me? To us?' said Finn.

All affection dissolved away with his question. Wary of the inevitable argument, she removed his arm from her shoulder. Criticism was counterproductive. The permanence of decisions made by New Albany's elite must remain unchallenged by dissent. It is the will of the people.

'It's not personal, darling. It's not against you and me.'

'Not against you. No, you're right.'

She reached for his arm, trying to recreate ordinary

happiness. 'It's just the situation. After all, the article said it would only be a temporary measure. That's something at least.'

Sophie was well aware that there were never temporary measures. New regulations would be adhered to just like all the previous ones; yet one more inconvenience, nothing more. 'The article said it's in response to the terrorist attacks in AZ Twelve. Apparently insurgents are hiding in the other Area Zones. It's only until they are caught. It is for our safety, after all.' Sophie parroted the official line, hopeful her reassuring smile would diminish his worries and disguise her fear.

Finn tugged his arm from her grasp. 'Well, if that's what they say, then of course it must be true. Silly me!' His sarcastic reply stabbing back at her.

Sophie handed him his tea, shuddering when his heavy metal bangle struck the porcelain, producing a bell-like ring to announce who he was, and what he was, the Digitally Interned Alien, obliged to keep that bangle permanently locked onto his wrist. Finn instinctively slid it back up his arm and pulled down his sleeve. Out of sight, but never far from their consciousness.

'I'd better start re-reading those wretched books. I just wish there were something else to study for a change. As much as I love Jane's work, six years is quite enough.'

'Why don't you suggest something else?' asked Sophie, grateful for the new topic of conversation.

'And what influence can I have over the curriculum? Even if I were allowed to make a recommendation, I can hardly be seen to corrupt the girls. Let's face it, what's the point? There's barely a decent novel left on the approved list.'

With nothing more to add, Finn pushed himself off the sofa and retreated to the kitchen. In the corner of the sitting-room the digital assistant, THEO, bleeped, its green light reverting to red. Sophie glowered, wishing she had the courage to destroy it. Instead, she clutched the fragile china cup and sipped her herbal tea.

Twenty-two, nineteen. Her eyes were watering from the undisturbed vigilance of the oven clock. Twenty-two, twenty, the red digits blinked back at her. Twenty-two, twenty-one, and another minute slipped past. She shut her eyes, willing time to stop. Twenty-two, twenty-two, all the twos, like ducks in a row. She laughed. Was it the caffeine that was sending her to that place of contorted sanity? She rarely drank coffee, yet there she was, supping on that bitter black stimulant. Her hand trembled with the weight of the cup. A reaction to the drink or the fear of uncertainty? She no longer knew nor cared. Finn wasn't home.

In the hallway the antique clock mocked her further. Its rhythmic tick-tock verbalising, *'Finn's gone, Finn's gone.'* She fought to ignore it, forcing herself to tune into the surrounding silence beyond the kitchen door. Not even the outside world could drown out the pessimism consuming her.

Mini whirlwinds spiralled leaves up into the air, their dry, brittle edges becoming ghostly fingernails scratching against the panes in the door, demanding entry. In the distance came the rattle of car tyres jouncing on pitted lanes. It was so faint, almost imagined. But it wasn't. Other sounds were hushed. Only the turning wheels existed. They stopped. Then came the silence. Her accelerating heartbeat anticipated the knock at their front door. Deep within her, guts twisted and cowered beneath the rising screams of her inner voice, *'How will you cope? How will you cope?'* A car door opened and slammed shut and then another. Two of them. They always came in pairs.

She put the cup down and gripped the edge of the table,

steadying herself as she rose from the chair. *'How will you cope without him?'* That was when she heard it; the click of the garden gate. Sophie raced to the back door in time to see the red lights of a departing vehicle and a thin shadow hurling a bicycle onto the ground.

'Finn! Thank God. Where have you been?'

His hug felt tighter than usual. Pushing him back, she saw his tired and drawn face lit up by the kitchen light. There was so much she wanted to say, but anger and relief could wait. 'Where were you? I've been sick with worry,' she whispered, avoiding the known trigger words in case THEO might activate.

'Sorry darling. I got a puncture. I was trying to fix it, but it got late, and I just didn't realise the time.'

'Finn, it's half ten!' Sophie swallowed back the urge to yell at her husband's apparent nonchalance. His eyes told her a different story. He was frightened. The heartbeat pounding its drum inside her ears became louder, faster. He was acting, saying it was just one of those things. Except it wasn't. He was hiding the truth. *Just one of those things* was not an option for the likes of Finn.

Free of her grip, he squeezed past her and sat down at the kitchen table. He appeared engrossed by the little flowers of the oil-skin tablecloth. This was Finn, he always told her the truth. Neither spoke. Sophie remained in the open doorway, a queasy unease making her cling onto the frame. She put it down to the sickly scent of the Nicotiana instead of all the more likely explanations that were bombarding her brain. At the table, Finn lay his head down onto his arms, his face turned towards her. And there they were, those simple words, uttered in his soft voice. The truth she dreaded. The truth that kept her awake at night.

'They arrested me.'

THEO's light illuminated the kitchen, distorting the space with its spectral green. She didn't give Finn time to say another word, yanking him up by his arm, directing him back outside. By the dim light of the torch, she dragged him down the garden until they reached the steamer chairs, beneath the apple trees.

'I think you had better tell me everything. Don't leave anything out in case I need to get Dad involved.'

Finn slumped back into the chair. 'You won't need to call your father. I'm pretty certain there won't be a follow up or any charges.'

Too agitated to sit, Sophie paced about. Above her, the little beam of light vaulted from branch to branch as the torch bounced on his restless leg. He was nervous. He was bending the truth. She stopped moving. 'No, you can't be arrested for a puncture, what happened?'

'Violation of the curfew.'

'What?'

'I told you, it got late. I'm subject to the new curfew laws, or have you forgotten?'

'I...I..., no Finn, there must be more to it. Work finished hours ago.'

'It was just...well...I don't know how it happened.'

'You need to tell me, Finn. I need the details.'

'There's nothing to tell. There was a meeting, you know, the usual. Something about curriculum changes, and Frank Harrison just wouldn't stop rambling on about lack of sports priority. The head was trying to sort stuff out. I remember thinking I had plenty of time to get home despite the over-run but then Carl wanted to chat. He seemed upset and I couldn't just walk off. There was still time, but I guess fate had other ideas. I did get a puncture on the way home. I'm sorry, darling. I honestly didn't realise the time.'

Sophie sat in the neighbouring chair shaking her head in disbelief. This was not what Finn had signed up for. Nobody had.

'I know. It isn't your fault.' Her eyes were adjusting to the dark and she watched him wrap his arms around himself. It was mild for September, yet he was shivering. She searched out his hand, vigorously rubbing the back of it to warm him as she spoke, 'I don't get it. It can't have been that late, and even with those delays, the guys in the guardhouse know you. They wouldn't have arrested you for that. Are you sure there was nothing else?'

'Temporary security measures to fight the insurgency,' said Finn mimicking the Daily Briefing newsreader, 'and I am the unfortunate collateral damage.'

'Even so.'

'New recruit; he spotted the bangle. His chance to shine, I suppose.'

'What about Sergeant Mason? He'd have sorted it.'

'He was out, drunks fighting at The Packers' Inn. The guy was on his own and didn't have a clue who I was.' Finn stifled a small chuckle. 'The lad couldn't even figure out how to turn on the computer.'

'Really? How can you not know that?'

'I blame the teachers.'

'Yeah, they're the route of all incompetence.' She gave his arm an affectionate punch. 'What else?'

'He took so flipping long and I just wanted to get the whole thing over and done with, get charged, then go home. I even had to show him how to use the microchip reader. God knows what they do teach them.'

'Not computer skills,' muttered Sophie under her breath.

'Possibly not. Anyway, by the time we got to the charges page on my file, Sergeant Mason walked in. When he saw

21

me, he gave that recruit such a filthy look, I almost felt sorry for the boy. Almost.'

There was mirth underlying his words, the revenge of a powerless man. Sophie smiled too. 'So, was that Sergeant Mason's car in the lane?'

'Yeah, he brought me and the bike back, but not before shutting me in a cell and putting the fear of God into me. I was loudly reminded of my unique privileges and that they can be removed as easily as they are given. I am the model alien, the Alien of Ministerial Importance. That shining example of how well the system works. A credit to New Albany, proving that the DIA programme is a magnificent success. But above all, it's my duty not to be a disappointment to my father-in-law.'

Sophie bit her lip at his sarcasm. The faint humour that appeared barely seconds earlier had been banished with the cracking pretence of the model alien. Her sticky tape of lies would not be up to holding him together for much longer.

Work demanded that the other night's inconvenience should be forgotten, just like all the others. Sergeant Mason had poked his head into the surgery to apologise to Sophie. As usual, she was friendly and brushed off the arrest as if it meant nothing to them, wishing the new recruit well and hoped he might find a use for the unexpected bonus in his pay packet.

That day, her life continued much like any other, a monotonous routine of pointless paperwork and complaining teens. She finished late, her list of ladies growing like their expanding wombs. The last bus home was punctual for a change. The driver, a dog-tired man who returned her smile with indifference, gave her bus pass a cursory glance before accelerating away, jolting Sophie into her usual seat. One more day ticked off the calendar.

The ever-recurring scenes of her slow journey home drifted past the window. Colourful displays of hanging baskets distracted shoppers from the disappointing reality behind the shop front. Outside The Packer's Inn, young guardsmen gathered for an after-work drink, chatting and smoking while vocally rating the flirting schoolgirls. One girl stopped to accept an offered smoke. The medic in Sophie sighed as the girl inhaled the noxious toxins, a sign of her loyalty to the nation's economy.

On the opposite side of the square, a second group of recruits relaxed on a low wall, joking with each other. In front of them, a middle-aged lady was struggling with her shopping, her metal bangle repeatedly slipping down her upper arm. Not wanting to stop, she tried to nose it back behind her sleeve. Her efforts were fruitless. She shrugged and continued on her way. That was when the recruits jumped off the wall as one, barging past her. Her shopping bag spilt its contents across the pavement, the clattering tins accompanying the young men's laughter. The recruits sauntered away, pleased with their cruel comedy act. No one helped the woman gather her groceries. Commuters side-stepped neatly out of her way so as not to dirty their shoes with the broken eggs. She was an inconvenience, nothing more.

Forty minutes later, the bus deposited Sophie at the edge of town. The half mile lane up to the cottage was no more than a muddy track these days. Lack of passing traffic had allowed nature to reclaim her stolen territory. Late blackberries dotted the overgrown hedgerow, providing tasty treats for the tired nurse. She licked the juice off her stained finger then groaned with backache when she stooped to pick up the shopping. From the corner of her eye she spied her only neighbour, Mrs Carter, standing guard at her window, watching and waiting. Already fed-up, Sophie put her head down. *'Please don't let it be me.'* The persistent thumping against the wooden window frame made her heart sink.

'Yoo-hoo! Sophia dear, can you spare a minute?' called the elderly woman from the opened window.

'Of course, how can I help you?'

She daren't refuse Mrs Carter. The rumours abounded about her; she was a spy, an informant, an agent of the ASSU. They all laughed about it, but nobody was brave enough to risk her annoyance.

Even before she had time to cross the threshold, Mrs Carter announced her demand, 'I want to redecorate the bathroom and I need a tiler.'

'I'm afraid I don't know any,' Sophie replied, hoping ignorance would offer her an early escape.

Mrs Carter peered over her old-fashioned glasses, 'Of course, well you wouldn't, would you, my dear, they are far too expensive these days. Likewise, I've only my pension you see.'

Realisation hit Sophie like a slap in the face. 'Don't worry Mrs Carter, we are not going away this half term holiday. I'm sure my husband will be happy to help.'

'Would he, my dear? Oh, that would be lovely, I'm sorry I can't pay him that much, I'm only a pensioner you see.'

Dates and peppercorn pay settled; Sophie departed Mrs Carter's cottage with its all-pervasive stench of impending death. She distracted her anger with thoughts of the coming weekend and the prospect of enjoying every luxurious minute. They would be free to enjoy the Indian Summer, and her parents' garden would be spectacular. In the herbaceous border, late summer blooms would nod their heads loftily above the annuals below, and on the terrace, they would relax and savour

Anna's freshly made lemon and lavender shortbread.

The welcoming smell of dinner and the velvety tones of Finn singing in the kitchen greeted her on opening the front door. She lingered a while, her earlier complaints chastened by Puccini's lyrics.

'Oh, mia patria sì bella e perduta!'.

When she reached the kitchen, she saw him leaning on his arm, his face barely ten centimetres from the tablet screen. His back to her, she crept up unnoticed and deftly pulled his earphones away, 'What's for dinner?'

Finn jumped like a startled cat, his arm flicking up to wipe away a stray tear on his cheek. 'Christ Soph, don't do that! I'll have a heart attack one day.'

She laughed, and with his face cupped in her hands, Sophie kissed him loudly on his lips. 'I'm a nurse, I'll give you the kiss of life. Honestly, darling, with a voice like yours, the church would kill to have you in the choir.'

Finn waved his manacled wrist at her. 'Ten years of musical training, but this little bracelet says "No!". The Church of New Albany will have to look elsewhere for its next sacrificial lamb.'

'Their loss, my gain.' Sophie turned to unpack the shopping and Finn replaced the earphones. On the screen she noticed images of exotic blooms, dramatic coastlines and impossibly blue skies. Never one to miss out on programmes about gardening, she poked her husband in the ribs. 'Whatcha watching?'

'Huh?'

'What are you watching?' she mouthed slowly.

He took off the earphones. 'Oh, "The Planet's most Beautiful Gardens". They all appear to be in AZ Eight.'

'Well fancy that! Shame we live in AZ Five. Maybe we'll have a holiday there one day.'

'Or maybe we won't,' Finn replied, his glasses steaming over as he checked on the dinner.

On the table was yet another night's collection of neat books and papers waiting to be marked, ready to disappoint or delight their young owners. Sophie gathered them up and dropped the stack unceremoniously onto a chair. Tired, she wanted dinner and bed, but first she had to break the news to Finn about the weekend. Her inner actress was practised when it came to convincing shows.

'Good news, I have the whole weekend off. Henry said I was due some holiday, so he altered the rota without that miserable old git of an office manager spotting it. He'll go absolutely ballistic.' She chortled to herself, delighting at the thought of that vile bully being undermined.

'But, isn't Henry in charge?' asked Finn, while he dished out the casserole.

His innocence made Sophie smile. 'Technically, he is, but only technically. Anyway, I've already rung my parents and Christopher will drive up to collect us on Friday aft—,' her husband's expression stopping her mid-flow, 'Oh, Michael Finlay, don't you dare give me those puppy-dog eyes.'

Obvious dismay flashed across his face, reflecting his dread of an eternally long weekend with the in-laws.

'Can't we spend the time here, just the two of us?' he pleaded.

Sophie would not be swayed. 'No, Mum's promised me a trip to Greenhaugh's Nursery, there are some plants I'm after before the weather gets too cold. We'll have use of the car, so I can load up the boot.'

He looked sullen, more like a man facing the gallows than a weekend away. Stretching across the table, she caught hold of his hand. 'Oh, come on Finn! It'll be a break for both of us. No restrictions for forty-eight hours.'

He might complain but that scant freedom meant as much to him as it did for her. Forty-eight hours with the security guards locked outside the perimeter wall. Inside, at liberty to talk, laugh and argue. Nobody would be listening. That privilege was worth enduring her mother's grievances. Forty-eight hours imagining a different life. Forty-eight hours remembering having had a life.

The 'Bridge Tea Room' was famous for being a peaceful temple to gossip. It was *the place* for the well-groomed society ladies of New Albany to share their secrets with occasional shrill laughter denoting tasty morsels of information. Gloved hands waved to passing acquaintances ensuring their presence was noted. A couple of young ladies opposite Sophie were deep in whispers, their wide brimmed hats touching in conspiratorial communion. They leant back in the chairs grinning at the information. Sophie thought they might be talking about her, but she couldn't be sure. Like most of the women in that tearoom, their eyes were hidden by obligatory, expensive sunglasses. Women shaded from reality, just as Sophie might have been if she had accepted a different role in Albian life.

She looked down at her feet, and the bag sitting next to her leg. It was from one of the smartest shops in Area Zone Five. She only went in on her mother's insistence. The pearl bead handles stood to attention and its blue velvet ribbon had been tied into a neat bow. An expensive carrier that was destined for the rubbish tip. She undid the ribbon and pulled out the parcel, touching the blue tissue, momentarily lost in thought.

'Would you like some of my passion fruit gateau? It really is lovely, but the calories!' said her mother.

Sophie nodded but didn't stop looking at the tissue parcel.

She unfolded the delicate paper. 'Perhaps I should take it back.' Her nose wrinkled with indecision as she examined the blouse more closely.

Michelle replaced the teacup on the saucer and bent forward, mimicking her daughter's expression as she scrutinised the blouse. 'It's a lovely colour. Well, I think it suits you to a tee. That shade of green really brings out the colours in your eyes. Hold it up against your face.'

Sophie obliged her mother and unfurled the blouse. The fabric felt as soft as baby's skin next to her cheek. She instantly lowered it again.

'Oh yes,' enthused Michelle, 'definitely the right shade. No, that one's a keeper.'

Sophie's uncertainty sought a reason to return the blouse. 'A bit dressy though, and far more than I'd ever spend. When on earth would I wear it? We never go out.'

Her mother fiddled with a button on her dress, turning her gaze away from her daughter. If only it were possible to turn back time, rephrase those few words? It had been a surprisingly pleasant shopping trip up to the point when Sophie reminded Michelle of her self-imposed privations. Simple statements that lead to rows and recriminations. Pricked with guilt, she attempted to stave off the descent into argument. 'It is pretty though.'

'Yes, and so are you,' replied Michelle, returning her daughter's smile.

Sophie sipped her tea, relieved to have saved the situation with such relative ease. Her relief was short lived.

'A beautiful young woman who should have her pick of successful men. It's not too late.' Each of her mother's words were beautifully enunciated with razor sharp intent. The 'discussion' had begun. Her mother was an expert in twisting any situation into finding fault with Sophie's marriage.

'Have we started already? We settle this nonsense each time we meet. I am with a successful man whom I love utterly and completely.'

'He's a schoolteacher, hardly successful, but I suppose you probably do love him by now. It's not our place to interfere, we just want the best for you.'

Of course, she wanted to interfere. That was the whole point of the ridiculous discussions. Sophie's inner resentment rose with her mother's meddling.

'I hear Admiral Carter's son is looking for a wife. You know, he's a professor and such a clever chap.'

Sophie seethed. 'Oh, bloody hell, Mum, why don't you just shut up!'

Michelle, startled by her daughter's outburst, replaced her floral teacup on the saucer and put a finger to her daughter's lips. 'Don't swear, Sophia.'

Sophie backed off, reaching for her tea, but Michelle hadn't finished.

'The law of the land is clear. Foreigners cannot teach our sons.' She turned her cup on the saucer, then suddenly stopped, pushed it aside and leant across the table. 'At least Daddy was able to help,' she whispered.

'You'll never get it will you? Finn loved lecturing, but some nut-job in gov—'

'Sophia! Stop it.' Her mother looked about the room, concerned Sophie's comments might be overheard. Her red lips were almost touching the flesh of her daughter. 'I hear what you are saying, but we can't, not here. That wasn't my fault. You must see that, darling. It wasn't our fault.'

Michelle shifted back into her chair, the volume control on her voice turned up to an acceptable comment level. 'There were decisions taken by greater men to ensure the well-being of the country. It was a difficult period. We live in dangerous times.'

Sophie saw through her mother. Michelle, the Albian devotee, always suitably loyal to the lawmakers. Deference where deference was due. But that didn't change anything. As far as Sophie was concerned the blame lay with her parents' generation, and there would be no forgiveness or forgetting their role in her husband's polite dismissal. Her mother was as guilty as all the rest of her peers. They gave tacit approval for the injustice. That crime was theirs to own, but the life sentence must be served by others.

Sophie tugged at her hat, her cheeks flushed with anger and her forehead itchy from the hat band.

'Do you want me to help? It's much easier to wear correctly with longer hair. You should let it grow.'

'No, thank you, I can cope perfectly well, even with short hair,' Sophie snapped back. Her hat straightened, she returned to her tea, studiously avoiding eye-contact with her mother. Sophie flipped over her phone to glance at the screen; it was early. Christopher was not due to collect them until later. Two more dragging hours to search her brain for uncontroversial subjects. She returned the phone to her handbag. It would be a quiet mother and daughter lunch.

To avoid the vacuous inanities of New Albany's idle elite, Sophie stared out of the window. The late afternoon sun shone brightly but the temperature was dropping. Some passing shoppers had dispensed with their summer hats and were sporting the soft felt ones of winter warmth. Muted colours, almost sombre. Why did fashion dictate that the autumn should be so colourless, so bland? Sophie decided she would wear her scarlet hat and coat to church the following Sunday. And her scarlet gloves too, whatever the temperature.

About to pour herself another cup of tea, Sophie noticed

her mother glaring at a young woman's uncovered knees. 'Do you want some more, Mum?' she said, before her mother could make a snide comment.

Michelle rolled her eyes. 'Thank you, darling. I'm parched. Oh, I have some news about Auntie Emma's eldest.'

'Why on earth do you insist on calling her "Auntie Emma"? She's no relation to us.'

'I've known Auntie Emma all my married life, she is my dearest friend.'

Sophie, her anger still simmering, asked, 'As dear to you as Anna? Or have you forgotten the woman currently cooking in your house?'

Visibly hurt by Sophie's comment, Michelle's lips tightened into a pout before answering, 'This is not the time and definitely not the place.'

Sophie apologised. Her mother was right. The diners might appear engrossed in trivia, but some ears were always attuned to comments that could harm the innocent. The last thing that Sophie wanted was for Anna to be endangered because of her goddaughter's antipathy towards her own mother.

'Emma's eldest, Jack, is expecting his sixth son. Emma's eighth grandchild, isn't that fantastic?' She paused to allow her daughter to acknowledge the change of subject. Sophie said nothing. 'Well, once the baby's born they are all going to be invited to AZ One for a medal ceremony. Six healthy boys. We're thinking of taking a girls' trip to the Capital to visit the shops. She wants it to be a special outfit. We'll probably go next time Daddy's out of the country. Stay in the flat, get tickets to a concert or two. Why don't you come? It will give you an excuse to wear that blouse.'

Sophie had already lost interest in her mother's wittering. Outside the tearoom window, an ancient mulberry tree spread its branches lazily across the green. Its yellowing leaves reflected the sun's rays. A life span, centuries long, oblivious to the unknown faces in unknown places. Nature, unbending to the whims of fickle politicians and their arbitrary codes of conduct.

'Sophia, are you listening to me?'

'Sorry, what did you say?'

'Honestly darling, away with the fairies again. Would you like to come with us to the Capital, shopping? My treat.'

'No, Mum. I can't keep taking time off. Henry will sack me, and we certainly can't live on Finn's salary.'

Michelle nodded her head in reluctant acceptance. 'You know it was funny, Emma and I used to imagine you marrying their younger son, Adam, you remember Adam, don't you?'

'Of course, I remember Adam.' It was Sophie's turn to roll her eyes as she recalled that annoying child. A bully, just like his brother, he would chase her into the copse at the bottom perimeter of the garden and demand his prize. Her bile rose with the recollection of her long hair being yanked to the ground, then he'd sit astride her chest. His back to her, he would lift her skirt *'to take a good look'*. Later, she wore trousers whenever he was due to visit. He responded by teasing her, telling her to cut her hair short if she wanted to dress like a boy.

'I would have rather gouged my eyes out with forks than marry that disgusting twerp.'

'Sophia Elle, what a vile thing to say!'

Vile and true. Draining her tea-cup, she thanked her lucky stars that she had married Finn.

MICHELLE

She wandered the house in post lunch apathy, examining the evidence of her ownership. Over the years she had erased all trace of her mother and stepfather. All, except for the piano.

The days of diamonds sparkling by candlelight as manifestos were discussed were long gone. When was the last time a crisis meeting was held in her drawing room? And when was the last time she brokered a convenient alliance with nothing more than polite conversation and good cheer? In the sixteen years since Sophie's wedding, nothing. There had been no urgent call for her to arrange a light buffet for twenty, or any reason to call the caterers for a lavish garden party. Tim conducted his work in the office. She had been shut out. Her role had been diminished from magnificent hostess to who? Who exactly was Michelle Smith?

Out in the garden, her daughter was chatting with Christopher and his wife, Anna. She didn't need to hear the conversation to know the topic. Animated hands waved towards the herbaceous borders and broad smiles filled their faces. Acquaintances would complement Michelle on the beauty of the garden, yet she could barely identify a daisy. It would be pointless to head outside to join them, there was nothing she could add. Snatching up a magazine, she licked her forefinger and was ready to flick through the pages, when the music began. Anyone else would hear the delicacy and feeling of the playing, but Michelle merely recoiled as those bullet-like notes fired into her. She should have sold it, got rid of it, but Tim liked the idea of owning a prestigious grand piano, even though he couldn't play. But he could.

Finn could play it almost as well as her mother.

People like Finn were not her equal. They lacked her strength and determination. There would be no one to hear. Tim was ensconced in his den, and Sophie, the only one who'd intercede, was with Anna and Christopher. Unconsciously and in time with the music, she tapped her teeth with manicured nails, planning her attack. She would do it.

From the library door, she stood observing the interloper, engrossed with the rise and fall of the music. The late afternoon sun was shining through the French windows, bouncing off the gleaming burr walnut of the piano. Most of the time it was abandoned, almost lonely, much like Finn, yet under his gentle command, her mother's treasure sang.

Anger swelled at the sight of him. Finn, a gentleman, but as far as Michelle was concerned, he was a dangerous man. A man capable of using the deadly weapons of gallantry and sensitivity to steal Sophie away from her. A man whose gifts could only be sadness and despair.

Michelle brushed past him and sat on the small armchair beside the piano. The music ceased, and Finn's hands retreated to his lap.

'I hope you don't mind me playing,' he said.

Michelle shrugged. She turned in the seat to stare out of the window. 'Not at all.' Glancing over her shoulder, she saw him straighten his back, ready to play again. 'I really ought to sell it as no one else ever plays the thing. Tell me, what was that tune?'

'Chopin's Étude number nine, in F minor.'

Michelle turned back to the piano, and irritated by the absence of a score said, 'You appear to have a good memory.'

He smiled and thanked her.

The desire to throw a vase at him made her catch her breath. Her loathing stemmed from fear. Fear and loathing, so often found hand in hand, gaining strength from the malignancy of the other. She had won before and would do it again.

'Why don't you leave her, be free once more, and go back to your own people. Is it spite that keeps you from freeing Sophie?' Michelle paused to take pleasure in his reaction.

Finn lowered his eyes, focusing on the patterns of the rug, his face reddening beneath her scrutiny. Sophie was not there to argue for her timorous husband, and he would have no choice but to hear the words spat at him. Michelle's eyes closed with pleasure, arming herself for another assault on the tethered victim, so she did not see his chest rising, and with his mask of civility dropped, he countered her attack.

'Free her? Free her? Who exactly is the prisoner? Tell me, which of us wears the curse of imprisonment? I signed that contract because I love Sophie. She is the only reason I am here. She loves me, and I love her. I will never do anything to hurt her.'

Michelle smirked. He was such an amateur. 'You say you love her, but are you so sure she loves you?'

'I am. Nothing, absolutely nothing can change our love for each other.'

'How sweet. You believe love is set in stone. It isn't. Love, just like life itself, is subject to change. Surely you of all people should understand that.'

Finn turned on the stool, gently lowered the lid on the piano keys, before departing the room without another word. Once more she was victorious, and yet, alone in the library, there was no one to see the tears working their way down Michelle's cheek.

SOPHIE

'Did you have to buy every single bulb in Greenhaugh's?' complained Finn, after Sophie tossed him yet another bag of daffodil bulbs.

'Yes, Mum was paying, my birthday treat, remember.' Rolling back onto her ankles, she marvelled at her husband, her shy, devoted knight. Sophie walked over to him and massaged his shoulders, sensing his body relaxing with her touch.

'And is it your birthday wish to have me on my knees all day?' he said, bending forward to brush the dirt from his trousers.

'Treat 'em mean, keep 'em keen.'

Finn recoiled in mock horror. 'You evil woman, I can see we are going to have words later tonight.'

Tiny laughter lines had developed around his eyes and, hiding within his fair hair were rogue grey ones. The young student that had rescued her was gone, but his enticing mouth remained. She wrapped her arms around his waist and lifted herself up onto her tiptoes, inviting a kiss. 'Is that what they call it these days? There will be no *words* nor anything else if you don't get these daffs planted.' Sophie nodded towards the bank behind the bench. 'Plant those over there. I'll sort out this bramble.'

'Yes, Miss Sophia. Your word is my command.'

Sophie giggled and gently punched his arm, 'Work now, *word* later.'

They planted and cleared the garden in contented silence until Sophie let out an annoyed squeak. She caught Finn's grin as he anticipated dealing with her mini drama. With her middle finger held high, and her bottom lip curled down, Sophie moved towards him until that finger was up by his nose. 'Thorn!'

'You don't half make a fuss. Come on then, let's have a look.'

He began the futile attempt to find the thorn. Sophie sighed, he definitely needed new glasses. Thoughts of the expensive necessity was obliterated by the sensual pleasure of his finger tracing along her skin.

'Ow!'

'I can feel it,' he said, excited by his discovery.

'Yeah, and so can I.'

Finn squeezed his thumb and forefinger together, thinking to use his stubby nails as tweezers. Bored by his failure, Sophie pulled her hand away, curling her fingernails into her palms. Once Finn went in search of the first aid box, she unfurled her fingers and examined her own nails. They were grubby, worn down and chipped, an accurate reflection of how she felt.

'Got the tweezers, let's have another go,' he called as he returned from the house.

Sophie screwed her eyes shut and put out her hand. Moments later, Finn held up the thorn, triumphant. 'My beautiful mistress has been rescued from the evil thorn monster.'

Before Sophie had a chance to finish cleaning the wound with antiseptic, he had grabbed her hand, smothering her injured finger with kisses.

She giggled. 'Bet that tastes disgusting now.'

'Nothing about you could ever be disgusting. Are we still doing *words* later, or have we graduated to full blown *row*?'

Sophie wasn't listening to her husband's obvious

innuendo. She was staring at a tiny speck of blood at the tip of her finger. It reminded her of the fairy tales she adored as a child. Was she Snow White's mother, or maybe she was Aurora, that Sleeping Beauty? That thorn had revived a melancholic memory. The fear and sadness of a predetermined destiny that lay beyond the princess's control.

PLAYING HOSPITALS

MELBOROUGH MANOR HOUSE, AGED FIVE

Today Kitty is the doctor, telling teddy that Little Panda is perfectly fine. Nothing wrong, just a normal Little Panda in his blue dress. Evie's laughter disturbs our playing, so Kitty and I run to the door and drag her in.

'Play with us.'

'Are you playing hospitals, Sweetie?'

I nod, holding the giant syringe to Dr Kitty's paws.

'And will that make Panda better?' says Evie, her fingers tickling my side.

'Stop it, Evie,' I say through my giggles, 'Kitty says it will, but Teddy is cross now.'

'Why is Teddy cross?'

'Because Teddy thinks it will make Little Panda poorly. Will it make Panda sick?' I cuddle up on to her lap.

Evie stops tickling me and hugs me close. 'No, darling, the injection won't make you ill. It's to protect you.'

'But what about Panda?' I don't want her to talk about me. I want to know about Panda.

'Panda will be just fine,' she says, popping a kiss on my nose, 'and so will you.'

'I'm not having any injections, Mummy says so.' I wriggle to get off her, but she holds me.

'We'll see.' She sniffs Kitty's fur and pretends to be sick. 'Maybe it's time for Kitty to have a bath before she makes you poorly.'

I snatch her out of my sister's hand. I don't care how

grubby she is, no one is allowed to take her from me, not even for one day. I love her.

'It's OK, no one is taking her from you tonight. It's bedtime. Are you ready?'

Evie doesn't pick a book from the shelf. She has read my favourites so many times that she can say them off by heart. So, I close my eyes and listen.

FINN

A creak from the kissing gate alerted him to Carl's arrival. His friend always knew where to find him whether or not Finn wanted his company. He returned his attention to the tarnished plaque on the back of the memorial bench, giving it a little wipe.

'You'll wear that plaque out one day,' Carl called out, making his way towards the bench. Finn slid his legs off the seat, opening a space for him.

'Then I'll replace it,' he replied, touching the name. 'It's been sixteen years this year. Can you believe it? Sixteen years without them. It still hurts when I think of Evie.'

'Understandable, you guys were close,' said Carl, wriggling his bottom on the bench to warm the wood before relaxing into his customary position. Even though it wasn't that cold, Carl flicked up his jacket collar and tugged it closer around his large frame.

'Anything nice?' he asked, already fingering through the contents of Finn's lunch box. Finn said nothing, so Carl picked out the cheese from the sandwich and ate what was left.

'Did you have a good half term?' His words mumbled by the fresh bread.

'Fine, we stayed at home as usual. Soph took on some extra shifts to help out the guys with children.'

'Aw, now that's kind.'

'Not really, it's expected of her as she is childless.' He paused, then added, 'As we are childless. What about you?'

'Um, well I went away, AZ Eight. Just three days, mind.' Carl turned away, embarrassed by his answer.

41

An almost imperceptible raised eyebrow betrayed Finn's surprise. 'Sun, sea and surf. Who did you bribe?'

'Weather wasn't great to be honest, anyhow I was visiting my little brother.'

'Isn't he in AZ Twelve? Did he get transferred?'

'You could say that, but no, not transferred. He got caught. Turns out arrest is the fastest route to AZ Eight.'

Finn gaped at his friend, astounded by the revelation. Questions tumbling out of his mouth with no consideration as to whether they could or should be answered. 'Why didn't you tell me? When did this happen? What did he do?'

Carl shrugged his shoulders and pointed out that having a brother caught for people smuggling was not something you brag about. In fact, you positively keep it a secret, especially when you are an ageing bachelor teacher whose best friend is a DIA.

Unnerved by Carl's comment, Finn pulled his arms tight across his body, his foot tapping the earth and a slight stammer delaying his response. 'I… I…I'm sorry. How is he?'

'Well, there's the positive, he's lost weight and gained a tan. On the flip side, he's depressed and won't speak to me. I've no connections, you see. Guess I'm pretty useless as a brother.'

Finn knew what Carl was implying, even though it was not unkindly meant. Being the son-in-law of New Albany's Foreign Minister had its advantages. A father-in-law who would call in favours when necessary. Tim Smith was Albian elite, a man with friends and connections, people who would overlook some foreigner teaching girls in a mediocre school. Rules can be easily manipulated when someone senior enough orders it so.

'I wasn't getting at you, Finn. I'd never do that. You're my only mate in this dump. Come on lad, what did you get up to? Can't imagine you keeping house while Sophie worked?'

Finn admired Carl's ability to mind read. Relaxing slightly, he recounted Sophie's never-ending lists of little jobs, ending with the three days tiling for Mrs Carter.

'Mrs Carter? Not the one from the Culverhouse Surgery? I thought she was long dead, busy terrifying the poor devil and demons of hell.'

They shuddered at the mental image of Mrs Carter, a gorgon of unique ability. Unfortunate patients would pray for a miraculous recovery rather than plead beneath her stony scowl for an elusive appointment. Finn laughed as he told Carl about the old woman monitoring him the whole time he tiled, reminding her tiler at ten-minute intervals that she was only a pensioner and had to look after the pennies. Carl's round tummy bounced with silent chortling when Finn described the old woman waving a broomstick at him, just in case he displayed any amorous intentions towards her virtue.

'Sounds like wishful thinking on her part, or maybe it's just one more element of her torture routine,' Carl said, wiping a laughter tear from his eye.

'Oh God, Carl, imagine it, being arrested and when the interrogation officer walks in, it's Mrs Carter. You'd tell them everything, immediately.'

'If ASSU nab you, believe me, they don't need Mrs Carter to make you tell them everything. Those bastards are a dab hand at interrogation.'

Humour and dreams of normality were mere fleeting moments in their world, and Carl's response flung Finn back to within the sight of his accompanying demon, a man always on the verge of arrest.

The two men sat side by side on the bench, each wondering if or when they would find themselves in a Secret Service cell. Carl kicked at the dry earth beneath the bench, fine dust rising and settling on their shoes. He wiped them on the back of his trousers. Finn poured some water from his bottle onto a couple of napkins and handed one to his companion.

'As if anyone cares?' he said, dabbing his lips with the damp paper.

'I do. I'm still allowed that luxury. They haven't taken that away from me just yet,' said Finn, cleaning the dirt off his shoes.

Carl harrumphed. 'Talking about our dear leaders, did you get wind of the latest news?'

'Soph keeps me away from it as much as possible. What new indignation am I due?' Finn continued polishing the shoe-leather with the dry part of the paper napkin. His shoes shone, reflecting the man in the black leather. Shoes that were cared for, treasured, re-soled and re-heeled at the start of every academic year. An expensive relic from years gone by when Finn was free to choose the best. He looked back up at Carl. 'Well?'

'Nah, nothing to do with you, well a bit, but not really.'

'Did you get hit on the head today? You're not making sense.'

'We've a new Commandant for our Area Zone, and his darling daughter is joining the school.'

Finn blinked in surprise. 'Why would he send her to School House 87? That doesn't make sense.'

'No idea, perhaps she fancies playing poor girl for a change.' Carl paused, engrossed by a phone message.

'That's admirable, I think.' Finn watched him tap away on the phone. It appeared new, but given he was banned from owning one, he had long since given up on latest trends and fashions on the mobile phone industry.

Carl slipped the phone back into his pocket and grinned. 'Ok, so this new girl, she's been allocated to your class this term; transfer notes are in your pigeon-hole.'

'My class?' The shock made him choke on his own saliva. After Carl had thumped him a couple of times on his back, he managed to voice his concern. 'He does knows I am a DIA, doesn't he? I don't fancy a punishment beating just because of a clerical error.'

Carl gave Finn a reassuring pat on his leg, saying, 'That Commandant is known for his ability to extract information. Bet he already knows what you are, where you live and how many times you make love to the lovely Sophia Elle. Is that the time?' He brushed the breadcrumbs off his jacket and stood up to leave, 'Well, best head back, got a history lesson to give. Oh, I do love a bit of fiction, don't you?'

HE'LL BE JUST FINE

CARNDEAN HALL PREPARATORY SCHOOL, AGED SIX

Daddy and the headmaster chat about all the Sheehan connections to the school.

'Michael Finlay Sheehan, the seventh Sheehan and the fourth generation to attend Carndean,' boasts Daddy.

No one asked me if I wanted to go.

Daddy jokes about fees and the headmaster shifts in his seat. I stare at my new shoes, my first lace-ups. I'll have to learn how to tie my own laces now.

'So, Michael, what books do you like?' says the headmaster.

I don't reply.

'Oh, he's quite an avid reader, he's even started some Harry Potter,' says Mummy.

The headmaster continues to watch me, so I look at the floor.

'And do you like music, Michael? We have an orchestra and the boys choir go on tour after Christmas.'

Mummy answers his question, 'His piano teacher says he has a natural talent, and he has been singing in the church choir for the past year.'

The head's smile disappears as he reads the papers on his desk. 'Mrs Sheehan, my notes indicate that Michael has some learning issues. Our special needs—'

'Oh, yes. We did visit several consultants when Finn was younger, but nothing proved conclusive. He mispronounced certain sounds, that's all. We took him to a speech therapist,

and she dealt with it. He's grown out of that now. He does get fre—'

'Yes, that is in my notes, but it says you have other concerns.'

'Well you see, I believe—'

'Darling,' Daddy holds onto Mummy's arm, 'I think we can say he is just dreadfully shy, like many children of his age.' He turns to the head, 'He became quieter after his accident, but he's all better now, aren't you Finn?'

I nod and look away. I don't want to be here. They'll fight again, and Mummy will take me to another doctor in his funny front room clinic.

The headmaster gives me one of those smiles before returning his attention back to Mummy and Daddy.

'As you say Mr Sheehan, I am sure he will settle in just fine and will soon be as boisterous as any other Carndean boy. Although, preferably not as 'distracting' as his brother.'

'Andy is much better behaved these days, Headmaster.' Daddy says, tapping his foot. Mummy looks away.

'Glad to hear it. Anyway, our school matron studied child psychology prior to becoming a school nurse. She's wonderful. He'll be just fine here, won't you Michael?'

FINN

Check the lesson plan, check the books, check the equipment. Check it again. Finn hated standing in front of the girls giving a presentation on Mr Bennet and Elizabeth, or on Wickham's deceit. Like many pretending to be someone he wasn't, he suffered from stage fright. Frightened he'd get the facts wrong, frightened the girls would laugh at him, frightened it would become too much. He was terrified of the monsters of his past returning. Finn delved into his bag, was it there? What if he had mislaid it? His sudden panic was soothed by its smoothness, the comfort of its weight in his hand: his talisman. He placed the pen on the desk and stared at it. Matt black, with an engraved gold clip, just like the nib hidden within its cap. His last gift from Evie. He went through his checks once more, his hands balling into fists and his fingernails cutting into his palms. There had to be positive reasons for standing in that classroom, instead of the comfortable study in Melborough Manor House. The answer never altered: Sophie.

The girls sauntered into the classroom, chatting about boys and marriage arrangements. One girl was showing off her engagement ring. A simple silver band, the fiancé's initials etched into a tiny heart. She would not be returning after Christmas. Her role in life as a happy teenager would cease. Soon to be a wife, within a year a mother, the devoted, obedient ideal of New Albany. Envied by her classmates, pitied by her teacher. Finn disguised his feelings with a murmur of congratulations. He would be left with yet another empty seat in his dwindling class.

The Commandant's daughter was the last to enter,

accompanied by the head. The girls stood in respectful unison, something their own teacher rarely experienced. He lopped towards Finn, waving his arm, simultaneously acknowledging the pupils while releasing them from their homage. Noise erupted in the classroom with scraping chairs, emptying bags, and audible murmurs about the new girl. That girl was twisting a loose lock of hair between delicate fingers, aware of the whispers but not looking to see who was responsible.

'Mr Michael, may I introduce our new pupil, Miss Fry. Miss Fry, Mr Michael will be your English teacher for this term.'

Finn bowed his head in polite greeting, repeating the words expected of a subordinate, 'An honour, Miss Fry.'

She did not reply, turning her back on him and taking her seat at the front of the class. Finn was struck by how mature she appeared. Tall and elegant, with her blonde ponytail flowing down to the middle of her back, she exuded a confidence the other girls lacked. Even the head seemed intimidated.

Miss Fry stared at him, as though examining a strange specimen, before giving the teacher a look of practiced contempt. That, he was used to receiving, what unnerved him was her continued observation of him throughout the lesson. It was clear she was intelligent, briefly transporting him to his lecturer days and the rare exceptional student. However, this girl was only seventeen. Regardless of the information on her transfer notes, her prior education had not been courtesy of a mediocre girls' school.

* * *

Monday 26th October

I started School House 87 today. Another of Daddy's

social experiments. A girl spoke to me, Carly? Carol?
Who cares? We have nothing in common. English
teacher's odd. Weather - dry.

* * *

Finn threw down his coat on to the leaf strewn ground. It was so enticing, like a beautiful throw of bright dying colours, an autumnal riposte to the dull tones of the season. He stretched out and studied the cloud formations in the sky. One of these bright, sunny days would be the last of the year and Finn would take advantage of each and every one.

By the time Carl had reached his recumbent friend, Finn had closed his eyes, lost in his own world of memories.

'Wakey wakey, you lazy git!' he said, giving Finn a gentle shove with the tip of his shoe. Carl's black silhouette shaded him, blocking out the sun. 'Anything nice?' he asked. The shadow followed him to the bench where he immediately began rummaging through the napkins and waxed paper.

'I ate the steak before you arrived, along with the Cabernet Sauvignon and the tarte aux cerises.'

'Let me guess, cheese sarnies?'

He replaced the lunch box in disgust. With his hands behind his head, he closed his eyes and tipped his face skywards, breathing in deeply. 'You smell that, lad, that's the delightful aroma of decay. I just love the autumn. The grey skies, the wind and rain, shorter days and a sense of approaching death.'

Finn shook the leaves and mud off his coat and joined Carl on the bench. 'You make the world so cheery. It's a wonder the girls don't troupe behind you singing their little hearts out, and besides, it's a beautiful blue sky today.'

'I'm not here for a philosophical discussion about the

joys and disappointments of the seasons. The head wants to see you. That old bat of a secretary is currently running around the school in a mild state of panic. Surprisingly, she didn't think to look for you in the graveyard.'

With those few words Finn's whole body tensed with the anticipation of impending doom. He did not thank his friend for the message, but instead rapidly gathered his things together. New Albany teachers knew urgent calls from the school head were never a good sign, but for someone like Finn, it might mean instant dismissal or worse. Another polite request for his resignation so that the son of a middle ranking officer's son might play teacher to some teenage girls.

Carl shouted to Finn as he sped off in the direction of the school, 'I'll drop by yours later. You can tell me everything then.'

From his sanctuary beneath the apple trees, Finn heard the gate click. It was too early to be Sophie. Even without glancing up, he knew it was Carl. Few other guests ventured out to their cottage, and those that did, knocked at the front door, all except for Carl.

He interrupted Carl's purposeful walk towards the house, and with his hand lifted in greeting, he wandered in Finn's direction, his head turning to admire the autumn colour. The sole reason Sophie bought the cottage was because of its garden. It wasn't particularly wide by the house, but fanned out into a generous plot, overlooked by no one and allowing them the rare luxury of privacy. Sophie's garden was her pride and joy; her surrogate child.

'Garden looks stunning!' Carl said, making himself comfortable on the neighbouring chair. He picked up a small pillow, embroidered with delicate forget-me-nots.

'One of Soph's? Pretty.'

Finn nodded and held out a wine glass for his friend. 'I'm drinking, do you want some? I thought I'd enjoy the last of the sun with some wine, it's elderflower?'

Carl shook his head in disgust.

'Are you sure? I am on my second glass already,' said Finn, reaching for the half empty bottle at his side. His speech was more measured than usual. His father-in-law's homemade wine was notoriously strong as well as unpalatable. He rarely succumbed.

'Is that to celebrate the end of your teaching career? I hear that the tobacco factory needs a cleaner. I could put a word in for you?'

'Oh, that's so kind, but I didn't have to resign. The head, well you see, he was offering me an extra job instead.'

'Has Mrs Carter been extolling the greatness of your tiling skills?'

It was Finn's turn to shake his head. He giggled before replying, 'Well, you're not going to believe this. Guess what? I am the new private tutor for Miss Fry, the Commandant's daughter.'

Carl stared at his friend in disbelief, giving the bottle a quick check. 'Let me make you some tea. You are obviously drunk; I can hear your accent.'

Finn put his hand out to stop him. 'Don't go.'

Carl removed Finn's half-drunk glass of wine from his hand and sat back down, taking a sip of the pale liquid. 'Good God that's foul! You realise I am only doing this to save you. Go on lad, what happened?'

'He ordered the head to the mansion and asked for me by name. By name!'

'Who?'

'The Commandant, silly. He said his daughter deserved

the best and that's me, apparently. And, he is going to pay me above the DIA rank limit. Tuesdays, Wednesdays and Thursdays until the end of the school year. Sophie is going to be so thrilled.'

'Bet there's a catch?'

'None that I can tell,' replied Finn, retrieving his glass and finishing off what remained of the wine.

'You're telling me he breaks his own employment rules to take you on as a tutor? And you say there isn't a catch. I'm sorry, if it smells of rotten fish then you can be damn sure it is a rotten fish.' The pitch of Carl's response rose in disbelief.

'Honestly, no catch. I was sceptical too, but the head said all the paperwork would be approved. I'll have a late pass on tutoring nights and permission to be alone in the house with Miss Fry.'

'What? Alone? Are you fucking crazy? Why on earth did you agree to that?'

Finn laughed again. 'I won't really be alone, there are all the household staff for one, and the security outside too. Even if she were in a room of twenty, she'd probably consider herself alone.'

'What does Sophie say?'

'Soph's at work. I'll surprise her once she gets back. This extra pay, well it means we'll have money to save.'

Finn was reluctant to say it out loud, but he knew Carl understood. Six years of saving and maybe the chance of a child would be within their grasp.

Carl looked directly to the teacher. 'Watch your back, Finn. There is always a catch.'

DO WE EVER LEARN?

We seek to discover the mysteries of life yet fail to learn any lessons. Desirous of the precious and tempting bloom of knowledge, we complain when pricked by its barbed thorns.

LEARNING TO RIDE

MELBOROUGH MANOR HOUSE, AGED FIVE

'Close your eyes, Finn.'

I do as Daddy tells me and shut my eyes so tightly that my nose wrinkles up. I am so excited.

'Ta dah!' he says, just like the man on the dance show. 'Your first proper bike.'

Everything shines, the handlebars, the black padded seat, there is even a basket at the front for Kitty. It's bright green. Daddy waits for my cheers. I shiver. Was Dorothy's bike green in that scary film? I can't remember.

'It's your brother's old one. We took it to the body shop and well, look at it now. The basket is new though.'

Dad's large hand runs over the seat, patting it, encouraging me to approach it. I remember Grandmama telling me not to be afraid, time to be a big boy like Andy. I give a well-rehearsed grin. Pretending is far safer. Pretending keeps everyone else happy.

'Jump on,' says Daddy, and he helps me onto the bike. My toes just about touch the tarmac. I wobble and hold on tight to Daddy's arm.

'I won't let go, darling. But you'll be fine and soon be flying, just you wait and see,' he says.

I hold my breath and push down hard. The bike starts to move, my other foot finds the rising pedal. Daddy cheers and soon I am picking up speed. Unable to keep up with me, he lets go. I am riding a bicycle, just like my brother. I am flying. I am happy.

The farm gate is ahead, open onto the lane that leads down to the village. I'm not allowed on the lane. My parents, Mrs McManus, Evie, they have all told me. I must stay by the house and never wander off, so I never do. I pull on the brakes, but it's too hard. I keep pedalling and the lane gets closer. I must stop, I must pull harder, I mustn't go onto the lane.

I lie under the new bike. My glasses lost in the hedge. I am not Andy.

Daddy runs towards me. His hands are on his hips and he's out of breath. He lifts the bike off and bends down to check on me. 'No bones broken. Proud of you son, you were riding. Now let's get you cleaned up before Mummy sees you.'

He finds my glasses and pushes the little green bicycle back towards the house. I stand up to follow him. A throb stops me. The skin beneath my knee is all red and sore. I watch a fat bloody tear roll out from the dirty cut and slide down my shin towards my Superman sock.

FINN

The official residence of the Area Zone Commandant sat throne-like at the top of the hill. It was visible from most parts of the city and loomed over the inhabitants with domineering arrogance. It eschewed welcoming in favour of intimidation, the preferred architectural fashion for any New Albany building of note.

Anxious to be on time, Finn peddled faster. He loathed the growing sense of panic at the merest thought of being late. Giving a good impression could never be a bad thing, and if he found himself on the right side of the Commandant, who knew what favours might come his way. There were rumours about other trusted DIAs receiving help from Area Zone Commandants. He doubted comments surrounding the Commandant's temperament, after all, he asked for the best, and had contracted Finn.

The noise of the shifting gravel beneath his wheels alerted the guards to Finn's arrival. One stepped out of the guardhouse bringing the teacher to an abrupt halt. He was young, no older than the girl he was about to teach, a boy in a man's uniform. The gun he was carrying was prepped to be fired, and yet, as Finn looked into the guard's face, he only saw teenage acne spreading across the boy's forehead.

'Name?' the boy soldier barked.

Finn replied, quietly and respectfully, 'Hello, I am Mr Michael. You are expecting me. I am the new tutor for Miss Fry.'

'Leave your bike over there, then stand and face the wall,' he ordered, indicating with his gun to the far side of the gatehouse.

The other guard, accompanied by a black spaniel, joined his young companion. They examined him suspiciously, watching him push his bike towards the gatehouse and chain it up to the metal fence. They were diligent in their primary role, the protection of the Commandant and his family. All visitors must be considered a potential terrorist, including myopic schoolteachers.

Finn returned to the guards, smiling as he approached them.

'The wall! Face the wall!' the slightly older one ordered.

A little taken aback but not surprised, he faced the wall and stretched out his arms on the brickwork. He had never experienced a full security check but had witnessed other DIAs being frisked on his daily ride to and from work.

A wave of homesickness crashed through Finn. He imagined the black spaniel smearing the shine on his shoes was the ghost of Piper. Temptation tugged at him, and he fought against the desire to lower his hand to brush it through the dog's black coat and play with his soft ears.

'All clear, turn around and hold out your bangle for reading.'

Fear of accidental arrest over, he followed the orders without complaint. His file was read, permission and late pass codes were cross checked. Everything was in order.

'Follow me!' The guard was pointing his gun towards the entrance. The metal gate pulled back slowly, revealing the grandeur of the mansion's garden. He nodded towards Finn, prompting the teacher to walk through first, then followed close behind, the gun directed at Finn's back.

He knew there were others hidden in the shadows, watching and waiting, spying on him from behind trees, their guns trained onto his body. Even at his parents-in-law, there were half a dozen guards on duty at any one time, although Tim insisted they remained outside the perimeter.

The mansion garden was in full view, with coloured spotlights highlighting specimen trees and plants. In the distance he noticed the outline of an orangery and fairy lights twinkling a pathway to the pool house. There was a sweetness to the air. He stopped, trying to recognise the flowers' scent. From where he stood he had a clear view of the Commandant's Mansion. It was a fairly recent pastiche of an elegant house from a different but equally unequal past, displaying all the trappings of wealth. Despite the magnificence of the stone portico and large windows looking onto the grounds, it came across as lacking. His mother's laughter resonated through his head as she criticised the magazine articles on the rich and famous.

'Good taste is rarely bought'.

The guard poked him in the back with the tip of the gun, making Finn jump. 'Keep moving.' He was waving the gun towards the side of the house.

At the tradesman's door, the guard tugged the bell pull, its clanging echoing inside. Finn heard footsteps and then the turning of keys and bolts sliding back. A fragile silhouette against the harsh inner hall lights, the housekeeper flattened herself into the door letting the guard and Finn through. She flicked her fingers indicating that they should continue down the corridor to the kitchen. Behind him, he heard the guard slam the bolts back into place, locking him inside the mansion.

Once in the kitchen, he could see her more clearly. Her hair was grey, yet she was probably no older than Finn. According to Albian anthropological theorists, average DIAs were prone to the appearance of early aging, it was one of their many faults. She was skinny, with sharp angular bones pushing through her sallow skin. The maid's grey dress flapped about her frame and her bangle bounced on her wrist as she busied herself. Finn noted that her hand was small enough to slip out of the bangle. But what was once voluntary had become compulsory, and the fate of the non-compliant was enough to dissuade all but the most desperate to leave that bangle on their arm. He remembered an interview with a politician friend of Tim's on the Daily Briefing, banging a desk with his hand and repeatedly talking over the interviewer.

'Harsh punishment delivers results!'

It was unlikely she had always been a domestic, but that was what she was, with its low wages, long hours and no rights. The politicians had achieved their aim; cut the red tape and get people working. The servant complied with her lowly status, placing a cup of tea and a slice of cake before the expectant guard. There was not even an acknowledging nod from him. Finn stood by the wall, observing deference from one and institutional disdain from the other.

Even though she made no sounds, the kitchen was full of noise. On the hob, dishcloths boiled, brown bubbles of soap bursting as they skimmed the edge of the pot. The maid had retreated to a corner chair and was sewing a button on the Commandant's deathly black uniform. The other silver buttons rang against each other as she turned the jacket. The guard devoured his treat, scraping the cake fork across the porcelain plate. Overseeing it all was an enormous clock, its bronzed arms sprawling out across the wall, the minute hand visibly juddering with the passing time. It was three minutes to eight. The lesson was due to begin but there was no sign of the pupil, nor any indication if he were to go to another room. Anxious the lesson would begin late, Finn tried to summon up enough courage to speak to the guard. It proved unnecessary. Miss Fry had entered the kitchen.

She was dressed neither for comfort nor to shock. The dowdy navy school uniform had been abandoned in favour of a pale green floral dress, tailored to fit her perfectly. Her bodice seemed almost too tight, squeezing and emphasising her thin young waist. The skirt was wide and rested just below her knee in accordance with the Morality Code. A pale, pink cardigan completed the look. Her hair was loosely tied with a gossamer-thin, green ribbon, allowing her blond waves to flow softly over her shoulder.

The guard gulped the remaining tea on hearing the scraping door and stood to attention as quickly as his body allowed. Did she even notice the guard's deft wave of his hand to brush away the cake crumbs off his uniform?

'You can leave now,' said Miss Fry with the confidence that comes with privilege. She was used to delivering orders to the subordinates within her realm. Position trumps maturity.

Once the door closed she fixed her attention on the housekeeper. 'Mrs Fran, this is my tutor, Mr Michael. He will be here Tuesdays, Wednesdays and Thursdays. Make sure someone accompanies him to my sitting-room.'

'Yes, ma'am.' And then the maid was gone, scurrying away from the young mistress and her tutor.

He wondered if he should shake her hand, or maybe a little bow. What were the expected manners and behaviours of a domestic?

'Come!' she said.

'Obedience,' thought Finn, following his pupil into the mansion. He studied the excess of riches on display. There was artwork on every wall, oversized, modern, bleak. The furniture was the epitome of the latest Albian fashion. Too gaudy for Finn's taste. Once at the top of the wide stone staircase, she led him along a corridor. A deep pile rug silenced their footsteps and on the glass side tables, colourful objet d'art reflected the rich tones of the carpet. It reminded him of

the sumptuous hotels and luxuriously furnished suites of their family holidays, where two teens and a small child would play-fight. Andy once dared him to do forward rolls along the hotel corridors. He never did. And wouldn't here either.

Miss Fry stopped at a pair of double doors. 'This is my wing. We will have the lessons in my private rooms.'

The sitting-room could accommodate the entire ground floor of their cottage. Opposite was a fireplace and a wood burning stove, the logs inside glowing with intense orange heat. The room was warm, too warm. Two blue velvet sofas faced each other perpendicular to the stove and an array of colourful cushions were arranged on them. Dominating the furthest sofa was an oversized silver fur cushion. Behind the nearer sofa, and within the space of a bay window, stood a round table with her books already laid out. Finn headed towards it, until his pupil interrupted his passage.

'Oh, we needn't start quite yet. We should become better acquainted first, help us feel relaxed for the lesson. That way I'll get more out of it.'

Finn's uncertainty was increasing with each passing minute. Was Carl right? Had he made a mistake?

Miss Fry snatched the bag from his grip, and taking his arm, led him to the sofa. To his great relief she sat on the opposite one. He perched on the edge of the seat, his restless leg betraying his nervousness. 'Don't you think we should start, Miss Fry? It's already a quarter past eight.'

'My name is Catherine. Sometimes Daddy calls me Cat. Meow!' She started to laugh.

'Um, what should I call you?' He assumed it would be Miss Fry, as he did in the classroom.

'Miss Fry will do for the time being, maybe I'll change my mind later. We'll see how you behave.'

Finn attempted to ignore her comment, a teenager

trying to impress the older man, nothing more. She would bore of the dominating pupil act and serious study would be accompanied by rolled eyes and teen ennui. The normal state of affairs for a teacher, pupil relationship.

'You're my first DIA, but not my first tutor. It's quite a thrill, a DIA in my sitting-room.' She was curling a lock of her hair around her finger.

'Um, I... isn't Mrs Fran a DIA?' Finn wasn't really sure where the conversation was supposed to go.

'Obviously, and Mr Johan too. You haven't met him, have you?'

Finn shook his head.

'But it's different you see. They are just servants. Oh, but so are you.' She laughed again and Finn blushed. 'I suppose the difference is you are *my* servant, here for *my* benefit alone. Daddy chose you. Must be quite an honour.'

Finn knew the procedure, deference, always deference. He nodded his head. 'Yes, Miss Fry, a great honour.'

He wanted to ask her if he had got the lesson time incorrect, but as he looked up to speak, Catherine was leaning into the gap between the sofas.

'I watched you, you know, when you arrived. I can see pictures from the security cameras. You have a good bike.'

The heat of embarrassment rose up within Finn. Had she laughed at the humiliation of the security search, the sniffer dog and the surly guards?

'You are such a timid little man, aren't you? You remind me of a mouse, terrified of the slightest sound. I can understand it though, this house, this whole environment must be so alien to someone like you.'

'I...I...' Finn's stammered reply stopped short. She was not interested in his past. He was her servant and should know his place. 'Shouldn't we start the lesson now, Miss Fry?'

'We learn so much from first impressions, don't we? That was the original title of "Pride and Prejudice", you know.'

'Yes, I did know that. I hope I have given a good impression so far.'

'So far, and what impression do you have of me, your mistress?'

Finn hesitated, unsettled by her choice of words, this was a girl who held power and knew the extent of her control over him. A teenager whose whims would be satisfied without question. 'You strike me as a very intelligent young woman. I'm sure we will make excellent progress this year.'

She accepted the compliment with a broad smile, giving prominence to her high cheekbones and the deep dimples by her mouth.

'We should begin the lesson, start as we mean to go on,' he added.

'If you say so.' The smile dropped and with it her dimples. Miss Fry placed her fur pillow on the arm of the chair and gave it a gentle thump before flopping back against it. The fur was moulting, and tiny fibres lifted into the air before floating down and disappearing into her hair.

Finn rummaged through his bag. It had to be there, it just had to be. He had checked before leaving, but what if he had only dreamt about putting it in the bag, or maybe he was remembering a different day. Panic swirled inside. She was watching him, waiting. It had to be there. Relief came when he felt his fingers slip inside the leaves of the book. His copy was so old that he wondered how those pages hadn't turned to dust years ago. He ought to get a New Albian edition with all their helpful notes and commentary, but he didn't. He kept that decrepit edition of "Pride and Prejudice", comforted by its aged smell and fluorescent schoolboy underlining.

'I take it you have read the book, then?' he asked, sitting

up with his copy in hand. The front cover had sticky tape across the middle disfiguring the face of Elizabeth as she looked out to her audience.

She lifted her legs and tucked them underneath her, before smoothing her dress out over her knees. 'I have read lots of books. I like to read, it's one of my favourite pastimes.'

'Excellent, maybe we'll get onto further reading once we have completed the exam syllabus.'

Finn began to relax, thinking the tutoring might even be pleasurable. Finally, a pupil who understood the joy of reading instead of his usual uphill battle of book versus film.

* * *

Tuesday 3rd November

Had my first lesson with that DIA. He really is a strange little man. Daddy wants me to start thinking about marriage, says he'll be making enquiries.

* * *

SOPHIE

The flickering bicycle light was the signal for her lungs to fill and empty with relief. She kissed him on entering the kitchen, giving an involuntarily shiver when their lips touched. The night air had become so cold of late. By the time he had unpacked his bag, she had already made him a chamomile tea and heated up his supper.

'Come and eat in the sitting-room. The stove is lit, and you can warm up,' she said, carrying the supper tray for him.

Curled up in her corner chair, she watched him tuck into dinner. He was hungry and ate without saying a word.

'It's cold out tonight,' she said, hoping for conversation.

'Very.'

'I must ask Dad to smuggle in some cocoa on his next trip. I miss our hot chocolates in front of the fire.'

'Yes, lovely.'

Sophie's patience could wait no more. She needed to know. 'Well? Go on, tell me about it. How did it go?'

Finn put down his knife and fork, and took a sip of tea, grimacing in disgust the minute the liquid and scent entered his body, 'Chamomile? Really? Are you trying to poison me too? Isn't it enough I am forced to swallow your father's perverse version of wine?'

Sophie laughed at her husband's mock insult, 'It's to calm you. Now, tell me or I'll get the wine?'

Finn moved the tray off the sofa, and with puppy-like enthusiasm, she jumped at the chance to snuggle up, eager to hear his story.

'It was fine. I was nervous, who wouldn't be? Don't think

66

the guards like me, but then again I don't like them either.'

He described the house, the decorations, the opulence. Sophie wondered where the Commandant had got his money. Even with her father's elevated position, they certainly did not have that sort of wealth. She assumed it was inherited. The days of success through merit alone had long been debunked by the elite leaders of New Albany, a flawed ideology responsible for the mistakes of the past. And the past was somewhere she wanted to forget. She had Finn. Pushing herself in closer, she listened to his descriptions. His report of Miss Fry's sitting-room leaving her astounded. 'How old did you say she was?'

'Her file says seventeen, but I think more like going on thirty. I've never met a more confident girl.'

'More confident than me?'

'Oh yes, darling, more confident than you.' Finn kissed the tip of her nose.

'Is she pretty?' Her tone reflecting disappointment.

'I think striking is a better description. She'd stand out in a crowd, but I'm not sure if that's down to her looks or her demeanour. There is definitely something about her that demands attention.'

Sophie nibbled her lip. There was no doubt about his fidelity but even so, her insecurity pinched her confidence. Moving forward, she reached for her tea. Finn's arm caught her waist, and she let him draw her back. There was no peck on the nose this time, he took her left hand and kissed the base of her ring finger, where her engagement ring once lived. 'No one can compare to my Little Pixie. To be honest, I don't want others noticing you too much because I want you all to myself. If they look at you and see the treasure I have, they are bound to steal you away from me, and then where will I be? Without you, I cease to be.'

HELLO AND GOODBYE

MELBOROUGH MANOR HOUSE, AGED TWENTY-FOUR

I tell her it will be fine, they'll love her. But I am nervous too, this is a return to my safe and comfortable world. I need their approval, their consent. Above all, I want their support.

Melborough Manor House's strong, grey walls loom before me. It has been my sanctuary. It has been my prison. Smoke rises from the chimney before disappearing into the grey February sky. Inside, the sitting-room fire will be burning brightly, a glowing welcome for the student and his young bride-to-be.

I fiddle with her engagement ring. It's too big for her tiny hand, and the antique jewels are digging into her flesh. I twist it back for her.

We hardly cross the sitting-room threshold when Evie leaps out of her seat running to me, arms outstretched. I struggle to breathe inside her enveloping hug. Her approval will mean the most.

My fiancée is apprehensive, darting looks around the room. She is the interviewee waiting to be scrutinised by the Sheehan panel, who will evaluate her worthiness to become wife to their young, damaged son and brother.

A tentative kiss on Evie's cheek, before taking a step back, apparently confused by the woman standing behind my sister. She whispers to me, 'I thought it was only family.'

'It is,' I whisper back, but before I can add any more, Evie is pushing Maya forward, making the introductions.

'Delighted to meet you, Sophie. I have heard so much

about you through Finn's letters and calls to Evie,' says Maya.

Andy, no doubt irritated at not being introduced first, gets out of his armchair, tossing Dad's puppy off his lap. 'What about me? Surely I should get a chance to kiss my future sister-in-law?'

His temper softened while I was ill, genuine concern ensured he was more cautious around me back then, but now? Has his guilt served its time? My brother does not listen to his conscience readily.

A handshake and a cold awkward hug give me my answer. He indicates to the woman who has been sitting beside him. 'This is my girlfriend, Nisha. Nish, this is the idiot brother I've told you about.'

Mum had told me about Nisha, not the usual subservient girl Andy liked to dominate and betray. This time he had picked a woman, as determined and confident as any in my family.

'I shall ignore you,' she said, approaching to kiss us. 'We all know what a clever brother you have, what you didn't tell me was how charming and good looking he is too.'

Is she able to tame his outbursts, a raised eyebrow sufficient to silence his taunts, diffusing laughter to counter his temper? Will she be the glue to finally fix the brothers?

I sink down into the familiar cosiness of the sofa. Sophie seeks out my hand for reassurance and I squeeze it in return.

She is the last to enter, love written across her face, matched only by the emotion flooding my heart. I want to say how much I love her and miss her, instead I let tradition hold my tongue, using the bland words expected of a son of the Sheehan household.

'Sophie, let me introduce you to Mrs McManus, our housekeeper.'

She wipes her hands on her apron before shaking Sophie's, 'Pleased to meet you, Miss.' Turning back to me, she grabs my hand and kisses it. 'I have been baking like a lunatic all week for my Little One.'

I kiss her cheek to the sound of my brother's mocking laughter.

'Mrs McManus, he's a grown man now, well almost.'

She ignores my brother and kisses my forehead as she has done a thousand times before. 'He will always be my Little One.'

Finn

Scarlet leaves descended from the maple tree standing beyond the perimeter wall, that red rain illuminated by the security light. It was a welcome distraction for Finn, as it had been twenty-four hours before, meanwhile behind him every element of the humiliating security procedure was ticked off on the guard's tablet.

At the tradesman's door, it was Mr Johan, the Commandant's butler, who was waiting for the handover. He nodded to the guard and said nothing to Finn on the two flights up the service stairs to Miss Fry's sitting-room. She was never there when he arrived. Only after Mr Johan had exited would his pupil emerge from the door to the right of the fireplace. He presumed it was her bedroom. The strict rules of society protocol were followed rigidly, and Finn waited patiently for permission to sit down. Once at the table, she poured her tea, leaving the slice of cake to go stale in the stifling heat of the room.

Despite his initial nervousness, Finn was enjoying his tutor sessions with Miss Fry. He was right to suspect she was an extremely precocious young woman. They argued about Elizabeth. Did she marry Darcy out of genuine love or did the idea of marriage only become attractive after visiting Pemberley? Cat was adamant that love did not play any part in Elizabeth's decision. Simply put, Elizabeth's choice was that of a mercenary. Darcy had proved himself weak when he proposed while visiting Lady Catherine de Bourgh. From that point on Elizabeth was the one in control. Her teacher was not wholly convinced by her argument, but he

71

accepted the possibility generations may have misjudged Elizabeth Bennet.

The anxiety came later. Accompanied off the premises and his bangle checked, he was free to depart. That symbol of bondage would pinch his arm, but the pain was necessary to keep it hidden. Despite his late pass, the risk persisted of some young recruits hoping to prove themselves in front of a pretty girl by beating up a DIA, regardless of whether or not he had permission to be out. Relief came only after passing Mrs Carter's house and the safety of the cottage.

* * *

Saturday 21st November

I'm so bored of this rain. I'm bored with everything, rain, school, Daddy. Went downstairs today, there's more to life than Elizabeth bloody Bennet.

* * *

The autumn days ticked by, filled with bored schoolgirls and evenings either teaching Miss Fry or preparing for her lessons. If Sophie felt abandoned, then she said nothing. Their time together was brief, but it was her love that gave him the strength to continue to the next day.

At seven-forty-five on the dot, he stood outside the guardhouse, soaked through by the bitterly cold November rain. 'Bit wet tonight isn't it?' he commented politely to the dry guards.

'Place your bike over there, then stand and face the wall.'

Never a hello, a smile nor even recognition. The guards venturing out as little as possible in their waterproof coats. Finn's jacket was worse than useless in that driving rain. Once in the kitchen, he removed his sodden coat, and without a word, Mrs Fran took it from his dripping hand and hung it up near the perpetually hot stove, a pool of water gathering beneath it.

Wet to the skin, he shivered slightly while standing by the sitting-room door. The fierce heat of the room penetrated his damp clothes.

'Come and sit on the sofa, Mr Michael,' Cat said when she entered the room.

'Um, no, I don't think I should. I'm really quite wet. I might mark the furniture.'

Cat laughed and approached to examine him. 'You sound like a naughty puppy. Should I make you sit on a rug at my feet?' She squeeze the sleeve of his woollen jumper, the water oozing up between her fingers and dripping onto the floor. 'You should take off those wet clothes,' she said, wiping her hand on her skirt. She disappeared back to her bedroom, leaving him reddening through the heat of embarrassment. She returned moments later carrying thick, white towels and a bathrobe. 'Now you'll be able to sit on the sofa.'

He mumbled his thanks and dried his face. Cat snatched back the towel from her tutor and tossed it towards the stove. 'Well seeing as you are refusing my suggestion, then you should sit on the floor by the fire. I wouldn't want my furniture damaged.'

Before he could reply, she had thrown down some cushions for herself and was kneeling by the stove, adding more logs. Within seconds the flames inside the chamber had converted into dancing will-o'-the-wisps, hypnotising Finn. He wasn't sure if it was the heat of the stove, or the proximity of his pupil, that was making him feel dizzy. Cat had removed her cardigan, exposing her bare arms to him. Arms that were long and thin, with firm muscles becoming defined as she altered her position.

'If you are hot Miss Fry, then perhaps we should return to the table.'

'I am quite comfortable, but perhaps you should remove your jumper. Your face is positively scarlet.'

Finn caught Cat staring at his bare waist as he pulled the sweater over his head, untucking his shirt. Embarrassed, he quickly tugged it down.

'Mr Michael?' she asked, moving closer, her hand on his knee, 'What do you see when you look at me?'

Taken aback by her question, Finn shuffled away from her. 'I... well, it's not... I'm not sure this is appropriate.'

Cat leant back, sprawling her legs out in front of the stove, ankles crossed and her bare arms behind her, pushing forward her chest. 'Surely it's for me to say what is or isn't appropriate? Am I a child, a pupil or a woman? Who were you looking at when you noticed my naked arms?'

Stunned, Finn was lost for words.

'Cat got your tongue?' His pupil laughed, making a snipping gesture with her fingers. She continued studying his every movement like a zoologist investigating her captive creature. 'We are defined by our birth, aren't we? You're an Immi and I'm the Commandant's daughter. Here I am, your pupil but at the same time, I'm your mistress, doesn't that make me a woman?'

Finn remained silent. How could he reply under the circumstances? Every possible answer might be construed as an insult. She understood that as well as he did. He was trapped without an exit.

'It seems I am the adult in the room, but that is how it should be. How can a DIA ever be more worthy than an Albian? It's genetically impossible. Well, maybe we should continue, what do you think, Mr Michael?'

Finn stammered and stuttered his way through the lesson,

his nervousness increasing beneath her probing inspection. Suddenly she sat up, her interest in the marital strife of Mr and Mrs Bennet discarded. She inched forward, closing in on her prey, whispering, 'My father has a wonderful library. His collection of books is unparalleled. There are music collections and films too.'

He smiled at his pupil, relieved at the innocence of her statement after her previous comments. 'What a wonderful resource.'

Cat Fry pushed herself further towards him, her lips by his ears, with her warm conspiratorial breath brushing his cheek and said, 'Do you know why it is so wonderful? All the books, music, films, everything, they are all banned.'

'I beg your pardon?' said Finn, his face paling with uneasy thoughts.

She sat back onto her ankles, chuckling at his shocked reaction. 'Banned books, music, films, you name it. If it has been banned on grounds of morality, then I can guarantee there is a copy hidden in the basement library. None of the servants are allowed in there. Just Daddy and me, and he's away at the moment. Would you like to see it? I'll take you. We'll choose a book for our next session. Have you read Nabokov's "Lolita"?'

Finn reeled at the thought of the repercussions if he were found using banned material in a lesson. Not even his father-in-law would be able to prevent the severe punishment it would incur. Incapable of a suitable response, he took his usual tack in stressful situations, ignore it completely. He pushed himself up from the rug, escaping to the table. 'I'm sorry, I feel a bit unwell, would you mind if we sat here.'

Cat eyed him carefully, before getting to her feet and joining him. He continued with the lesson, but his train of thought was disjointed, lost in the prospect of arrest.

'You really have no need to worry, you are perfectly safe here,' she said. 'There are no hackable devices in my private rooms. No one can see nor hear us in my wing. We are alone, utterly and totally alone.'

Nonetheless, Finn did worry. He persisted in trying to change the subject, talking about Lady Catherine's role, but to no avail. She was equally persistent.

'Shall I lend you a copy? We could discuss Humbert Humbert. He's such a complex character don't you think. You might even say it ties in with "Pride and Prejudice". The Georgiana Darcy and Wickham storyline has certain similarities, don't you think?'

Finn's heartbeat sped up, drumming out the beat for a condemned man's walk. He needed to stop the conversation, stumbling out his reply, 'Miss Fry, I can't discuss banned novels, especially not Category Four material.'

'Are you frightened I'd tell. Scared they'd give you a punishment beating?'

'No, well yes, a bit. Please, Miss Fry, it's not available to read for good reason. We ought to continue.'

Cat lay her hand provocatively on his lap, her manicured fingers fanning out on his thigh, gently moving back and forth. False comfort designed to torment. 'I do mind. Austen can be so dull. We should widen our study. You forget that I'm free to do as I please while in the privacy of my rooms.'

Finn plucked up the courage to cross his leg, removing her hand at the same time. His heartbeat deafening all rational thought. Certain she was setting a trap, he posed an exam question to divert her attention. 'Did Jane Austen assume a woman's happiness can only be achieved through marriage?'

'Do men believe a women's happiness lies in marriage?' retorted Cat. 'The answer might lie in our basement library?'

He failed. Every innocent question answered with

another, perfectly poised to unnerve him. The panicked teacher glanced at the clock on the mantle. The seconds ticking down to another battle in what to do or say.

'This time next year I'll be married. Only slightly older than Jane's Lydia Bennet. Was she happier for being married to Wickham? Possibly, but Jane depicted her as a foolish girl. Am I a foolish girl, Mr Michael?'

'Not at all, you're an intelligent young lady,' he quickly replied.

'Maybe Jane was commenting on wealth and position in society. People seek a happy marriage, but there is an argument to say you are happier in an advantageous one.'

Finn began to sense a slight respite from the encroaching panic, interpreting her comment as a resumption of the topic. 'Go on.'

'My father will be arranging mine. Believe me, it will be highly advantageous to both parties. However, it is down to a father's skill to ensure his own offspring holds the greater share of the power.'

'Are we still talking about Jane's attitude to marriage?'

Cat got off the chair and rang the bell. It was nine o'clock. 'Let's continue this tomorrow.'

Before he left, Finn caught sight of Cat disappearing into her bedroom. She might be intelligent, but she was also very strange indeed.

WHISPERED TRUTHS

MELBOROUGH MANOR HOUSE, AGED FIVE

It's funny how adults can argue in whispers. They do it all the time, and it's always about me.

Safe and warm, I've curled up in her lap pretending to sleep. Evie's arms tighten around me, stopping Mummy from picking me up.

'You've got to stop doing this to him. It's not fair.' Evie's voice is quiet, but I know she is angry. She sounds like Andy.

'What exactly?' replies Mum. Her cold hands grab me, pulling me away. I don't want to leave Evie, but I mustn't let them know I'm listening.

'You know exactly what I mean. He's more likely to be made unwell by your behaviour than preventing any illness.'

'Don't be ridiculous, I am doing what is right for him. He's not like you and your brother.' Mummy takes Kitty from my hand.

'There's nothing wrong with Finn. He's shy, that's all.'

'You don't understand. Your father and you say it's in my head, but it's not. I won't risk it.'

'Oh, for God's sake, Mum, that's all bollocks. He won't get sick from the vaccine. How many times do we need to explain it?'

'Don't swear at me. Look, he'd be having a vaccine for a disease that is virtually extinct. Pointless to put him through it. I'm not discussing this anymore. Now, let go, I'll put him to bed.'

I am being lifted, soft shushing in my ear. She tucks Kitty back under my arm. 'Evie, sweetheart, one day you'll have a child and you will understand the constant fear that lives in a mother's head.'

'I think we both know that is unlikely,' says Evie.

FINN

Carl's lumbering walk through the graves alerted Finn to the imminent interruption of his peace.

'Your mum's birthday?' he said, watching Finn lay a small bouquet of garden flowers on the bench.

Finn nodded. Like funeral ushers, the men observed a moment of respectful silence before the little brass memorial dedicated to Eloise Philips, beloved mother and wife. If Finn couldn't give flowers to his own mother, then this would have to suffice. A dead stranger who happened to share the same first name.

'You OK, old boy?' Carl asked, placing his arm across Finn's shoulder.

Finn smiled. 'Given you are ten years older than me, then surely you're the old boy.'

Carl acknowledged the accurate observation prior to ending his friend's act of remembrance by sitting on the bench, obscuring the plaque. He delved into Finn's lunch box searching for anything more palatable than cheese. There wasn't.

'So, lad, not had a chance to catch up recently. Busy, busy, busy! What about you?'

'Are you reinventing the past again? One day someone will catch you out,' said Finn, sitting down next to Carl.

'Well, it's my only reward in this profession, apart from the pittance of a teacher's salary. Currently the girls are under the impression the Spanish Armada had fighter jets that were spectacularly downed by mosquito drones. Meanwhile, Sir Francis Drake is on Plymouth Hoe doing a line of coke before coming up with his cunning plan.'

'And the girls believe you?'

'Why wouldn't they? I'm their appointed history teacher. I must be approved by the Ministry, and therefore, everything I say must be true.'

Finn was genuinely astounded, and also somewhat scared for his friend. 'What about the devices. They can hear. You'll be arrested.'

'Ah, now that's the thing, spilt coffee on it this morning, short circuited it. The boffins can't fix it until next week, so I have one week of alternative history to impart to my little ladies. Remember Finn, History is always written by the victor. The defeated are relegated to become the comic book villain. This week, the victor and therefore dictator of facts, shall be the one and only Mr Farnborough.'

'Why not tell them the truth instead of your ridiculous stories?'

'So I amuse myself with my fantasies, what of it? What's the point of the truth? It only leads to heartache or worse, innocents recruited to become the doomed insurgents of the future. I like our girls too much for that. Talking of the little darlings, how are the tutor sessions with the Commandant's daughter?' He elbowed Finn in good humour.

Finn's cheeks warmed with the involuntary blushing of a blameless man. They both had heard the crude comments from the other members of staff, particularly Frank Harrison.

'Let me do a session alone with her and I'd show her what a true Albian can do. Doubt I'd be able to stand after drooling over those legs all evening?'

Finn paid far more attention than necessary to a conker at his feet, softly replying, 'She is an extremely intelligent student. Wasted in this school.'

* * *

Wednesday 25th November

Poor Mr Michael, such a frightened mouse. He does make me laugh though.

* * *

Cat was already waiting in the stiflingly, hot sitting-room when he entered, drinking her sweet mint tea. Finn hoped the disquiet of the previous lesson had passed, and there'd be no recourse to corrupting material. He'd strive to be the model alien, watched or not.

'Come,' she said, beckoning him to the table. 'You are quite the highlight of my evenings. These sessions make everything clearer for me.'

'Thank you.'

'Are you well, Mr Michael?' She peered at his face as he took his seat. 'You look rather pale.'

The headache he had been harbouring all day, increased its stabbing pain. 'I'm fine, just a headache.' Emboldened by her earlier compliment he added, 'Um, Miss Fry, I was wondering if I might have a glass of water?'

'Of course, or perhaps some tea? Mr Johan will bring up a fresh pot?'

'Just water but thank you.'

Within minutes of asking, Mr Johan had returned to the room with a jug of water, fresh lemons juggling for space among the ice-cubes. The citrus aroma filled him, awakening memories of a life before. Finn breathed in, wanting more. He watched the butler carefully fill the crystal glass, thanking him before Mr Johan left the room. Refreshed by the water, he turned back to Catherine who was staring at him quizzically.

'Why did you do that?'

'I'm sorry, do what?'

'Why did you thank him? You don't need to do that. It's his job to serve.'

'Oh, I see.' He picked up his pen, relieved he was not in trouble. 'I suppose my mother's drilling in good manners means I thank everyone, even the ones that punch me in the face.'

'You're such a funny little creature, aren't you Mr Michael?

* * *

Thursday 26th November

These lessons could prove helpful. Mr Michael seems surprisingly refined.

* * *

Catherine held up the silver teapot ready to pour. 'Do you like mint tea?'

There was only one answer, regardless of his actual feelings towards the drink. 'Thank you, yes very much so.'

'It was your comment about good manners,' she continued as the liquid gurgled into the delicate teacup.

Finn shut his eyes, trying to remember what he had said. Had it been taken as a slur against her? Was he now in trouble? When would the miserable guard come up the stairs to take him away for the justly deserved beating? What had he said?

'You said your mother drilled good manners into you. Without a mother, who is there to teach me how to be the perfect wife and companion? Daddy is busy and certainly not Mrs Fran.'

Finn was suddenly filled with panic. 'No, oh I'm sorry, Miss, I didn't mean to insult you, it was a reminiscence, nothing more.'

'If you say so.' Cat indicated to him to take his seat. 'However that's not what intrigues me. I've never met a DIA quite like you. You have grace and good manners, most peculiar.'

'My mother, it wasn't that she was strict, but she did have rules, and some were strange, I'll admit to that, but I suppose we accept the strangeness around us when there is no one to tell you otherwise,' replied Finn.

'Do you ever wonder what it must be like to be privileged?' Halted by a thought, she paused, then looked directly into his eyes. 'Of course you don't, how could you?' Catherine moved to open her book, 'And I wasn't insulted. These sessions should teach all the essential skills that the classroom cannot provide. If I pretend you are a middle ranking official, then I can practise my entertaining skills. Might I offer you a slice of cake?'

If Cat didn't bring up the subject of banned books again then he was happy to play along. To him she was Miss Fry, a confused child, seemingly abandoned to figure out her own way through life, rarely mentioning her father. Her bizarre games, merely a training ground. She was experimenting on him.

'That's most kind,' Finn answered, accepting the offered cake from her.

Cat soon tired of her little game, her focus reverting to the fate of Caroline Bingley. 'I still consider Caroline the better marriage prospect for Darcy. As I said before, it is the advantageous nature of marriage that is important. If you are liable to lose more by leaving a relationship than by staying, then inevitably you stay.'

'Darcy wasn't interested in Caroline.'

'That's beside the point. Caroline was of his class, wealthy and his social equal. It made sense.'

'What about Anne de Bourgh? She was wealthy too.'

Cat rolled her eyes. 'Oh God, no. Too sickly and she'd more than likely die in childbirth. No, Caroline matched Darcy. I'm sure of it. Elizabeth and Darcy's marriage would have soured. She'd only bring embarrassment to the marriage. How can that be advantageous to Darcy?'

'Isn't love more important?'

Cat studied her teacher, lifting her hand and moving it towards his face. He leant back to avoid her but too late. Her long fingers touched his skin, walked up to the bridge of his nose and firmly pushed his glasses back into position.

'There is something puzzling about you, for an older man, you are extremely naïve and yet, I don't believe it. You are like the story books of olden times, with all its uncut pages. Maybe I hold the blade that can slice you open, what do you think?'

Finn didn't think anything. Fear had gripped him. In his mind he was far away from Miss Fry's sitting-room. He was in a bathroom, and the floor was covered with blood.

LIFE ON THE FINE POINT OF PAIN

We are all Damocles, and love has become the single strand of hair by which the sword hangs. Its blade honed with those moments of affection, desire and purpose. The sharper the point the deeper it drives into you.

SOPHIE

Her needle punctured the silence. The stabbing of taut cotton followed by lilac silk singing its way through. Then came another stab, and another. Sophie lifted the embroidery hoop to her side lamp and admired the tiny viola. So delicate, almost as uplifting as the violas that would reappear in the spring. She rubbed her eyes with the back of her hand. Her last daylight bulb died weeks ago, and Bain's Hardware had no idea when they would be able to get any more. The weak yellow glow in her side lamp was no substitute.

Gentle tapping on the wooden floor broke into her thoughts. Finn's stockinged foot was moving rhythmically. He had his pen in his mouth, and in his hand was a sheet of paper, but he was not reading the words. An invisible scene somewhere in the middle distance held him in a trance. Sophie put away her sewing, determined not to say anything, he'd just get irritable again.

'Are you OK?' she said, ignoring herself.

Finn took a second or two to register her. Sophie was about to repeat her question when he answered, 'I'm fine, a little tired. I think these late nights are getting to me.'

That *"I'm fine"* again. If she persisted, the inevitable row would ensue. Sophie got out of her chair and picked up the tablet. He'd talk to her eventually, he always did. Alive with her fingers, she swiped the screen searching for some news or a comedy. Silence was becoming tedious.

'There've been more cases of influenza in AZ Twelve. Article reckons it came in through one of the smuggler routes,' Sophie commented, hoping to elicit some response.

All she got was his pen scratching across the paper and a nod of his head. Irritated, she resolved to get some conversation out of Finn before another silent night was over. 'The Health Ministry wants to start a vaccination campaign immediately. No doubt we'll be hearing about this in surgery. Henry will be furious, he hates bureaucracy. Bet there'll be some late nights helping him with the paperwork. You don't mind, do you?'

'No, why should I?'

Sophie sighed, blood and stone sprang to mind, but Finn was not the only stubborn one in that marriage.

'To be honest, mass vaccination programmes are a nightmare to administer.'

Finn raised his head. 'Mass vaccination programmes for patriots only,' he replied, correcting his wife.

Sophie's ears reddened. Votes and photo opportunity considered the only driving force when it came to health policy. Medical science played no role whatsoever. That discussion would only bring pain and guilt.

THE STUDENT PARTY

TOLBRIDGE UNIVERSITY, AGED EIGHTEEN

Students are meant to be slovenly, lazy and above all party animals. I am none of the above. I am supposed to mingle, meet and chat. My roommate, Marcus, he's good at that sort of thing. An ever-welcoming smile with a comforting drink for whomever finds their way to our student flat. Calm and good humoured, Marcus gets on with everyone.

The little sitting-room fills with strangers, each clutching a bottle. I slink further into the background. An armchair close to the curtain provides the ideal spot to sit out the party. The students chat and joke; all friends of Marcus, from his Geography course. He suggested I invite some guys from my tutor group. I nearly did invite one girl, but I don't know her number to send her a text.

A dark-haired girl sees me and pushes her way through the gossiping group, grabbing a bean bag as she passes. She drops the fluffy bag onto my feet, then sinks her lithe body into its embrace. 'You're Marcus' roommate, aren't you? The quiet one. Do you have a name?'

'Michael.'

'I'm Kaylie, by the way, pleased to meet you.' A skinny arm holds a glass of vodka up for me to take. Her wrist is covered with silver bangles, urgently jangling as I hesitate. There is no point telling her that I don't like vodka. I place the full glass on the windowsill.

'This is where you thank me and start asking about my course,' she says, curling up in the fur like some indulgent

cat. *My silence gives Kaylie the green light to talk incessantly, oblivious to my one-word replies.*

Chatter and laughter ricochet off every surface while she tells me about a fossil hunting trip out to the beach. I'm not sure if she wants me to join her or just relating another story. I really don't care. I shut my eyes and wish the room away. I should have gone home. Is it possible to miss something so much that it transforms into real physical pain?

The room is too hot. Opening a window, I let the cold air filter through the bodies around me.

'You idiot, can't you see it's bloody raining?' Kaylie jumps up, squealing at me. It hurts my head. I close the window and she returns to the beanbag. On the windowsill a paper napkin soaks up the rain. I watch the dark green blotches spread out. Tentacles that reach for the edge, an invisible creature invading the paper, consuming it.

I am the fool being devoured within this alien world. This party, one more torture to deepen my pain. What do I have to offer that might interest this vivacious girl at my feet? If I speak, I will reveal the actor hiding behind the mask of the diligent student. They will all see I don't belong in that room. I don't belong in that place.

The smell of sweat, perfume and alcohol curls around my neck, squeezing my throat. Young bodies move in time with the music, its volume pulsing upwards, louder and louder. The music is gone, and chaotic confusion fills my head.

A careless blonde drops crisps onto the floor, crushing the snack into the depths of the rug with her trainers. Kaylie blathers on, all the time my fingernails dig into my palms and my right leg bounces in time with rising fear. I push my glasses up and pinch the bridge of my nose. I have a headache. A wine glass has tipped over on my desk, soaking into the pages of the book I am studying. My "Tess" is bathed in the deep red liquid.

I have to escape. I have to breathe. I step over Kaylie's sprawling limbs, her arm holding up her empty glass towards me.

'I'll have another vodka, thanks.'

I take it and abandon the room, unnoticed by the other guests enjoying student rituals.

Marcus and his girlfriend, Katie, fill our tiny kitchen. They are locked to each other in passionate kissing. I leave them to it and head to my bedroom. I need to shut the party out, so I push a chair up against the door, seeking refuge on my bed. Opposite, the wardrobe door has opened, its black gap goading me. Here be monsters. It torments me on purpose because it can. I am its useless prey, caught in a trap, powerless to shut that monster out, incapable of turning away from its triumphant success. Sweat snakes down my face and mingles with tears. Behind the door I can hear Marcus' voice. He's looking for me, but the chair holds strong. Marcus is safe from my monsters.

FINN

The quiet of the room was only disturbed by the rain hitting the window and the constant ticking of the mantle clock. He had begun to anticipate her moves, so it came as no surprise when her hand lay across his, stopping his pen.

'A magpie landed in the garden this morning,' she said.

'I'm sorry, a magpie?' Finn was confused, unsure whether she was talking about magpies or if it was another cryptic statement he was yet to decipher.

'A single magpie is an evil omen. However, if someone else sees it with you it removes the bad luck. Mr Johan spotted it just before it flew away. I don't like magpies.'

'Then I'll remember not to gift you one,' he replied.

'Aren't you superstitious?'

'No, not at all. I even walk under ladders.' Finn returned to marking the paper, ignoring her eyes scrutinising him.

'And what about broken mirrors?' Catherine added.

Finn replaced the cap on his pen and set it down on the table. Most of the time, she was a highly literate, confident woman, but once more he was being confronted with the young seventeen-year-old girl searching for advice.

'A broken mirror is dangerous not for any wild superstitious reasons, but because of the shards of glass. Get one of those in your foot, well, you might get an infection and who knows, death possibly. I'd say that would constitute bad luck, but only if you don't clear up all the broken pieces.'

'And are you a broken mirror?'

Finn started to wonder if there had been something stronger than mint tea in the pot. Just as suddenly as her childish behaviour arrived so it would disappear.

Catherine examined a chipped nail and nibbled a loose bit. 'Tell me, are you a mere reflection of a broken man? When you see yourself, are you incapable of knowing if it is the real you? Are you a shattered individual, hoping one day for the right person to come along and collect up all the pieces? Someone who can glue you back together again?'

Finn hid his discomfort. The fragile veil of pretence was lifting with her words of truth, and he needed to pull it back down into its rightful place. 'Well... I... it's not that...I can't say I have. Do you?'

'Sometimes, but not often.' Cat abandoned her seat and wandered the room humming to herself. She loaded more logs onto the fire, picked up cushions and moved them to new places. Stopping by the mantle, she dragged her finger across the top, checking for dust. 'Do you know the whole rhyme?'

'Are we still discussing broken mirrors?' said Finn. His anxieties were elbowing their way into his head, demanding his attention despite his efforts to ignore them.

Catherine's eyes narrowed, focusing on Finn's tapping foot. 'No, magpies. Do you know the rhyme?'

'I think so. "One for sorrow, two for joy, three for a girl, four for a boy. Five for silver, six for gold, seven for a secret never to be told." Is that the one you mean?'

'Yes, that's the one. Yesterday I saw three magpies, but what news were they bringing? What does "Three for a girl" mean?'

Finn stared directly into her face, heart shaped and perfectly symmetrical. Her high cheeks glowing from youthful vigour and health. If he wasn't so scared of her, he'd even say she were beautiful.

'So? What do you think it means?' Cat pulled him out of his involuntary trance.

He had never considered the meaning of the rhyme, despite Evie repeating it to him at bedtime. He was confused yet relieved by the change in direction. 'Surely it means you will have a daughter, and four means you'll have a son.'

'I won't be having daughters. Medical science ensures I will give birth to the right sex. The likes of me only ever have sons, because that is what we pay for, and that is what society expects.'

'Your father had a daughter, I'm sure he loves you as much as he would if you were a boy.'

'No, I am a useful tool, nothing more. Perhaps I am the girl and you the boy, silver the money that pays for you, and gold? What's gold?'

Cat returned to her seat. Once more placing her hand over his, her fingers touching the simple gold band on his left ring finger. 'Gold represents your wedding vows. Seven, well that one is easy. All marriages have secrets, yours will be no different. Secrecy must always exist.'

'We shouldn't talk about my marriage. It is completely irrelevant to our lesson.'

'But that's all we have been talking about for the past month.'

Marriage was exactly what they had been discussing, Elizabeth and Darcy, Charlotte and the Reverend Collins, Lydia and Wickham. He tried to convince himself it was Cat wanting to bring real life experience to the debate, nothing sinister, purely teenage curiosity.

'There is a different version, older I believe,' she continued.

'Is there? That's the only one I've heard.'

Cat left him again and wandered to the window, tapping out a rhythm on the glass with her chipped nail. She intoned the rhyme out to the black night as though reciting a spell to ward off the evil that lay outside. 'One for sorrow, two for mirth, three for a funeral, four for a birth.'

Finn's anxieties broke free as adrenaline released into his bloodstream. Fight or flight; it could never be fight, not with someone like Miss Fry. Flight? It was nearly nine o'clock, the lesson would soon end, and he'd be free.

'If it wasn't "Three for a girl", maybe those magpies were warning me of a funeral, question is, whose?' Cat returned to his side, prodding him for an answer. He had nothing to say, his foot still tapping under the table, stoking up the panic held within him.

'Why do you always tap your foot? It is very annoying.' She pushed down on his knee.

'Don't know, it's just me I suppose. Rarely notice I'm even doing it.' he lied.

The mantle clock struck the hour. She took her hand off his knee but did not stop watching him. Finn burned beneath her glare as he collected up the papers and books. Snatching up his wrist, she held him tight. 'Sometimes I think we must be so different, you and I, but there are other times, like tonight when I wonder if that is true. It's as if we are opposite sides of the same coin.'

'I… it's…um… maybe everyone can find similarities in other people if they look hard enough.'

Catherine released his wrist. 'Perhaps you are right. I shall get Mrs Fran to put bread out, attract a few more magpies into the garden. "Eight for a wish, nine for a kiss."'

With that she left the table. Finn watched her, both terrified and captivated. The way she walked, her back straight, like the catwalk models Evie used to admire when he was a little boy. Catherine spun around and pressed her hand to her mouth. She gave each of her fingers a loud and provocative kiss, and then, with pursed lips, blew each kiss towards him.

* * *

Tuesday 1st December

A strange lesson tonight. Sometimes I wonder who exactly is the teacher? He was so scared, I'm certain he was, but why? He's hiding something. Then again, aren't we all.

* * *

It had been a frustrating day at school, after two of his pupils decided to release their pent-up jealousy with each other in the middle of his lesson. Both girls claimed a certain young guardsman had declared his love for them. Barbed remarks became increasingly vicious while his polite requests for calm remained ignored. The other girls didn't help, taking sides, adding their own array of insults. It was inevitable that words would become hair pulling and kicks. Prevented from intervening, he sent out one of his quieter pupils to fetch Mr Harrison, while he pointlessly refereed the spectacle before him. He was acquainted with the guardsman in question, a louche unpleasant youth in Sergeant Mason's guard house. He'd avoid him whenever possible on his obligatory registration days. Watching the girls fight, he pondered the loser's lucky escape.

Later, on his way to the mansion, he spotted both girls again. This time the loser was comforting the teary-eyed victor. Through her sobs, Finn overheard her say, 'I can't believe he did that! Bastard!'

He smiled. The girls' lucky escape had put him in a very good mood for his encounter with Miss Fry. It was going to be a productive lesson.

*

On the table lay a small parcel wrapped in pretty, green paper. Around it, a gold ribbon was tied into a bow.

'Aren't you going to open it?' Cat pushed the gift towards him, expectantly. 'It would be rude to refuse my present. Your mother would disapprove.' Hawk-like, she watched him.

He touched it with the tips of his fingers, a pulse of malevolent energy transferring from gift to body. He flinched, wincing slightly. His headache had returned.

'Open it!'

Finn recognised it was an order not to be countermanded. A slight tremor ran down his arm as he took hold of the trailing ribbon. He pulled and the bow unravelled. With slow and measured actions, he removed the band and placed it to one side, then unfolded the paper concealing the monster. The book cover showed the young legs of a girl on her tiptoes, her feet enclosed in pale pink bobby socks, "Lolita" written across the middle. The ramifications of the gift raced through his mind; arrest, sentence and labour camp.

Finn looked up at the beaming girl before him. 'You know I can't accept this book. Just having it carries a severe penalty.'

'It's an early edition, very valuable I believe.'

He shook his head. It was as though she didn't understand or worse, didn't care. 'My life and that of my wife might be destroyed by your *gift*. I'm sure you understand the dangers. You are condemning me.'

Miss Fry moved forward onto her elbows, resting her head on her hands. 'I am not condemning you. I don't expect you to take it home, nor read it openly in the street, I want you to read it to me. No one will be listening. I'm bored of the Bennets and the insufferable Darcy. I want to examine a totally different kind of relationship.'

'No, this can't happen. I don't have to tutor you. I'll

resign.' Finn was panicking, trapped by her caprice.

Her hands flat on the table, Cat pushed in towards Finn. 'Who are you to give me orders? She was calm, and undeniably in control. 'If I want you in my sitting-room three times a week, that is exactly where you will be.'

She left the table and threw herself down onto the sofa, indicating to the other seat with her outstretched arm. 'Sit!'

'I am not your puppy to be trained to your command.' Finn knew he was not obliged to teach her, it was extra work. He was entitled to turn it down, even as a DIA. Snatching up his bag, he went to the door, pushing down on the handle. It refused to budge. 'Is this door locked?'

'Of course, it is. Do you think you can just come and go as you please? Nobody's listening, nobody's watching and there is nowhere for you to go. Now sit!' Cat returned to the table, collected the book and placed it into Finn's hot hand. 'We'll start now.'

SOPHIE

It was the fourth time she had unpicked the flower. Her mind was elsewhere. A quarrel about bike lights from earlier in the week plagued her. Finn argued the lights drew attention to him cycling late at night, but Sophie remained unconvinced by his argument. Cycling blind along those pot-holed ribbons of tarmac, he was more likely to break an arm, or worse. It wasn't always guards who were responsible for broken bones. She knew of the lynchings, never mentioned in the Daily Briefing, but they happened all the same. Patriots taking offence at a DIA for no other reason than *'He looked at me. He was disrespectful.'* She would rest easy only once the gate had been flung open, followed by his customary greeting.

And there it was, that unmistakable click. The weight of worry lifted, she put away her embroidery and ambled into the kitchen expecting their usual routine. But there was no greeting, and no kiss either. He sat down heavily at the table. The air of exhaustion that he carried most days, hunched over his shoulders, pressing years onto him.

'Good lesson?' she asked, bending to kiss his cold cheek.

'Fine. I've a headache. I might go straight to bed.'

'Let me get you something. You've had quite a few recently.' Relieved the break in routine was merely due to a headache and nothing she had done or said, Sophie nipped to the sitting-room to grab her handbag. Moments later and with painkillers in her hand, she returned to an empty kitchen.

Outside the kitchen door an array of intricate webs covered

99

a rhododendron, frost converting those fragile traps into cloths of diamonds and silks. Sophie admired them through her yawns. Finn had slept badly, his efforts not to disturb her failing. It was the early hours before he eventually fell asleep. She wondered if she should wake him but soft footsteps behind her informed her that it would be unnecessary.

'How are you feeling this morning?' she asked as she returned to the table.

'I'm fine, I told you last night, it was just a headache. Don't fuss so much.'

For someone professing to be fine, he didn't look it. He looked even worse than the night before. Unhealthy shadows were developing under his eyes and although normally pale, his skin had taken on a green-grey pallor.

'Shall I ask Henry for an appointment?'

'No. Stop fussing, I'm fine.' Finn shied away from her rising hand.

Sophie searched her memory for something she might have said or done to cause upset? There was nothing that stood out, and she had been particularly careful in recent weeks. Sophie ignored Finn's mood and wrapped her arms around him in a comforting hug. 'I'm not working on Sunday. After church let's come home, snuggle in front of the stove and spend the day in glorious idleness. What do you think?'

Finn wriggled out of her embrace, 'I have reports to write. I'm going to work otherwise I'll be late.'

THE CHARLATAN

TOLBRIDGE UNIVERSITY, AGED EIGHTEEN

Raps of rain against the bedroom window remind me I am awake, and that once again, sleep has evaded me. I place a pillow over my head. Tap-tapping breaks the glass and tap-taps inside my skull. Rhythmically poking me if dare I close my eyes. The monster has joined me on the bed again and takes pleasure in my torment. With each vicious prod, the monster laughs at my inadequacies. The morning tutorial will show everyone that I am a fraud, undeserving of my place on the course. I will be forced to leave, return home a failure. My family, Evie, they would all see me for what I truly am, a charlatan, a pretender. I allow them to believe I am someone I'm not entitled to be.

The phone alarm beeps in the other room. Katie and Marcus are awake, their movements audible from my bed. I pull the pillow tighter trying to keep out their happiness. It doesn't work, their lovemaking is noisy and vigorous. I cannot possibly leave the room now. I'll wait until they leave for class. Once I am alone, I'll be able to get up. No reason for embarrassment.

Katie's in the bathroom, they'll both be out of the flat soon, it will be safe to leave the bedroom then. I try and close my eyes for a little bit while they have breakfast. At least get an hour's sleep before the tutorial. I'll be fit to climb out of the bed with a bit more rest. I'll be fine. But the monster prods me again, reminds me he hasn't left, and the tutorial will not be fine. It will be my unmasking, unveiling the conman for all to see.

The front door slams, they are gone. Now I can leave the room, no more excuses. If I get ready now, I'll have plenty of time to go over the essay. The duvet pins me down, I can't even lift the pillow from my face. I lie in the warmth of my bed and invent reasons why this is the safer option.

My hopeful logic is interrupted by a gentle knock at the door. They both left, I'm sure of it, the door slammed. My phone has beeped, it's nine o'clock, lectures have begun. The door opens, and Marcus walks in carrying a mug of steaming tea and a plate of toast and marmite.

'Come on Finn, you'll be late if you don't get up now.'

His face shows disgust. He turns his head back to the open doorway to take in some un-fetid air. Dirty clothes lie abandoned across the floor and he picks his way through, placing the breakfast tray on the chair, currently pushed up against the wardrobe. He moves the papers and books which share my bed and sits next to me, handing me a cup of tea.

'You need to get up, you can't stay in here anymore. You can't miss any more lectures,' *he says, but I don't answer. I sip the steaming tea.*

'You should eat something.'

He moves last night's uneaten pasta and replaces it with the plate of toast, but the sight and smell of food flips my stomach.

'I've got a stomach upset. It's probably best I stay away, just in case I give it to anyone else. You should go, you've got lectures this morning.'

'Katie is covering for me. Look, you haven't left this room in nearly a week and you've hardly eaten anything. I'm worried about you.'

'Not surprising given I have a stomach bug,' *I repeat, but Marcus isn't listening. He has left my bed and is opening a window. He searches my drawers for clean clothes and ignores my protestations.*

'Get up and stop me if it bothers you so much.'

I lie back and pull the duvet higher, hiding him from view.

'You should see a doctor, tell them what's up. They might give you something to make you feel better.'

'It's not serious, I'll be fine, I just need a bit of rest. There's no call for a doctor.'

Marcus listens to me calmly, before yanking back the covers from my grasp.

'You can either get dressed and go to the medical centre here, or I ring your parents and you can explain to them why you've been lying in your own filth for the last week.'

I'm not prone to losing my temper, I don't want to be like Andy, but I feel the explosion of anger building up inside of me. How dare Marcus interfere. It is none of his business. If I feel like staying in bed, then I will. He's a roommate, not my mother. If he doesn't want to share, perhaps he should leave. That way we can both be happy. I am blinded by anger. Marcus isn't listening, he has heard it all before, another place, another time. He calmly sits back down on the bed, oblivious to my rage, leaving me to row with myself. Marcus pulls out his phone from his pocket and starts scrolling down a list of names. 'Sheehan, Home' appears on the screen. He means it, he is calling my parents. Panic overtakes me. They mustn't see me like this. I must pretend for their sakes.

'Fine, I'll get up, waste a doctor's time. Perhaps you'll believe them when they say it's just a bug.'

FINN

The rising tension had become physical. Palpitations overtaking him each time he thought about that book lying on the green paper. Finn rubbed his face and looked up to see twenty pairs of young eyes staring back. He had been mid lesson when he suddenly stopped, petrified. That class of bored teenagers, eager to leave school had turned into neat rows of young girls, their feet clad in little bobby socks and their lips pursed to blow kisses at their teacher.

The 'Lolitas' disappeared but not the constant churning of his stomach, tightening with each jerky movement of the clock face hands. It hung on the wall facing him and its tick-tock echoed around the room, counting down the minutes until the end of the school day. Time edging him ever closer to that mansion sitting-room.

The door lock clicked with the turning key, but this time Finn remained impassive and waited by the door. She was lying on her sofa, her crossed feet resting on the arm. She was wearing bobby socks.

'I want you to sit here.' Catherine pointed to the opposite sofa. Her tutor obliged, attempting to squeeze into the farthest corner.

It took a few seconds before Finn could even formulate any words, but he knew he must begin the session.

'We should start on "Emma". We really do need to get on. We still have another book to complete before your exam in the summer.'

'Three books if you count the one we are working on right now.' Cat sat up, facing him. Her leg crossed over her knee, ensuring the little pink ankle sock was clearly visible.

Finn fought to ignore the visual distraction. He was confused by her answer. 'We have finished "Pride and Prejudice".'

'Then that makes four,' she replied.

There was little incident during the rest of the lesson. Finn was subdued, Cat triumphant. She had control. The soprano bell of the mantle timepiece chimed for attention. Catherine flicked her eyes at the gold clock, closed her book and smiled.

'I know so little about you, Mr Michael. You're married, is she an Immi like you?'

He couldn't look at her, that insult cutting through him like a newly sharpened blade.

'My wife is a loyal Albian.'

'A mixed marriage. How daring! Did her family disown her?' she was leaning forward, eager to know more.

Refusal of reply was not an option for Finn.

'We married before the Purity within Marriage Directive came into effect. Divorce is considered a crime against The Moral Code, so we are permitted to remain married.'

'Of course, but she is free to annul it at any time, isn't she? No reason necessary.'

'Yes.'

* * *

Thursday 3rd December

I read Mr Michael's DIA file tonight. He's not an ordinary Immi after all, he's a MI, complete with his unique number, 568216/2/MI.

*

Another evening, and another airless lesson inside the sumptuously furnished prison cell with his beautiful young torturer. He flinched when her arm stretched across the coffee table to shut his book. Emma Woodhouse was being banished back to Highbury in preparation for Cat's meddling.

'I read your file last night. I'm curious. So, Mr Michael isn't your name, is it? No one is interested in your name, are they? You're a Digitally Interned Alien, Number 568216/2/MI. A DIA of Ministerial Interest. How intriguing, numbers and letters forming your true identity. I shan't call you Mr Michael anymore. Your number is far more unique.'

If the sofa could swallow him, then that is what he would have wanted. He understood what he had signed. He was 568216/2/MI, he was a DIA, he was an alien, he was an Immi. Michael Finlay Sheehan, a name of no relevance. There existed no reason for anyone to call him Dr Sheehan, but they could call him Mr Nobody, if it meant he could stay with the woman he loved.

'It's a public file. I have no secrets.'

'It's a rather boring file, you've never been charged with anything, not even the mildest of misdemeanours. Nobody is that perfect. Where do you hide your evil picture? In the attic?'

'I abide by the rules set out by the programme. Are you saying I shouldn't? I should purposely break them because otherwise I might have a *boring* file?'

Cat fell back into the comfort of the sofa cushions.

'That's the thing, I don't think you are that boring.' She paused, examining another broken nail. Finn could only watch, tortured by the quiet nibbling of her front teeth.

'There, that's better.' She held up her finger to show him. 'So, what was I saying, honestly I'm so forgetful these days.

Oh yes, secrets.'

The room had disappeared, even Catherine had gone. The only thing Finn could see were her emerald eyes glinting back at him. Daring eyes that captured the very breath within him. Inquisitor eyes, reading his soul.

'There are secrets, aren't there? Secrets that are being withheld. A secret file where the true 568216/2/MI is hidden. Who is protecting you? Why are they protecting you? Are they actually protecting someone else? Your wife? There's no sign of her name on your file. I smell a conspiracy of silence.'

All thought deserted Finn. He was floundering, the netted prey desperate to return to safety. He was hot. His head hurt. He needed some air. He heard himself speak but barely remembered opening his mouth. Instinct had taken control.

'Miss Fry, it's too warm in here, please may I open a window?'

AN IMPROMPTU BARBECUE

MELBOROUGH MANOR HOUSE, AGED SIX

'It's hot enough for a barbecue,' Daddy says.

Evie's friends sit in a circle talking about University and exams, Mummy and Daddy lie on the sun loungers drinking wine. Andy chats to a girl called Jasmine. He plays with her long dark hair. I laze on the lawn, watching Andy and the girl laugh, whispering in each other's ears. He takes her by the hand and disappears down the path towards the summerhouse. Evie tells me that's where Andy likes to go to discuss biology. That's stupid. He hates school, and anyway, if he wants to talk about school work why does he need to go to the summerhouse. It makes no sense. Evie laughs when I tell her, then kisses my head.

'You'll understand one day, just not too soon I hope,' she says.

'Who wants ice-cream?' Daddy stands on the patio armed with his trusty scoop and tubs of his homemade ice-cream.

Mummy asks me what I'd like. The reply, as ever, chocolate.

'Finn, sweetheart, have you seen Andy anywhere?' she adds.

'Think he went to the summerhouse.'

'Oh, will you be a darling and tell him there's ice-cream?'

The door to the summerhouse is open and I hear Andy, breathless, as though he has been running. Jasmine keeps repeating 'Andy' and 'Oh God'. They are not at all alike, Andy and God, at least I hope not. I call from the path but get no reply. I want to go back but I promised Mummy, I call again, but they still don't hear me. Their funny talking just continues. I edge nearer and peer inside. I cannot take my eyes off my brother. His bare bottom moving back and forth. My laughter makes Andy turn.

'Where are your shorts, Andy?'

Jasmine screams and I run. I don't know why, but I do. I can hide among the trees by the brook. Andy's swearing he'll kill me. He is so angry. He's always angry with me.

My flip flops slide on the grassy slope that leads to the brook and I slip. I land heavily and roll down the slope. My arm hurts, I want to stop running, but Andy keeps shouting. What have I done? He grabs my tee-shirt and pulls me up. He doesn't care that I am crying. I tell him I'm sorry, and my arm hurts. I want Evie, but Andy is dragging me away. Away from Evie, down the slope, further and further down towards the water.

FINN

There was only one area where there existed no distinction between loyal Albian and a DIA; attendance at the Sunday church services. The Church of New Albany was fully integrated within the Ministry of Moral Conduct. The monitored sermons, a way of disseminating the latest beliefs to the faithful. Attendance was recorded, a means of checking on the DIA population within any given parish. Finn loathed it.

Even though there was no obligation to attend as a couple, Sophie always accompanied Finn to the early morning service. A steady stream of parishioners headed to their allocated place of worship. Mostly DIAs going to the first service after the end of their curfew. That extra early start to complete their obligations before heading off to their menial jobs, to clean, to cook, to serve.

The couple stood at the bottom of a flight of wide stone steps which led to the fairly new, purpose-built church. Finn was nervous. Every Sunday a repeat of the previous week. The same build-up of tension, the same pain radiating from the back of his neck. The same overwhelming desire to run away. Sophie's reassuring voice whispering words of gobbledygook.

'You might have to be here, but who cares if you are listening or not?'

He replied with his programmed weak smile. He needed her hugs, her touch, her kisses, but none of that would be possible, not there, not in front of the church. He watched her smile disappear as she spotted the absent flag pin on his lapel. The show of loyalty displayed proudly by patriots and DIAs alike. It was the fifth pin he had contrived to lose in as many months. While Sophie delved into her handbag to locate yet another spare, he thought up a devious plan to dispose of it. That pin would accidentally fall into a patch of hemlock growing off to the side of the lane by the cottage. That fleeting, pleasant thought was interrupted by Sophie.

'See you out here after, OK?'

He nodded before glancing over his shoulder towards the guard waiting at the DIA entrance. Finn's bangle read, he climbed the narrow staircase to the balcony that ran around the church, before taking up his usual position, close to a wooden screen. A display of patriotic workmanship, the screen consisted of wooden panels pierced with depictions of flora and fauna and served a useful purpose. Those behind the screen could be educated in the wisdom and supremacy of The Church through the mouthpiece of the officially appointed reverend, while at the same time, Albians channelled their patriotism without having the discomfort of viewing DIAs in their temple. Finn's favoured location gave him the advantage of being able to see Sophie through the little holes. Sophie knew where he would be and always glanced up to that panel, her husband remaining hidden from view.

The bell rang, and the choir filed out followed by the Reverend Peters. In Finn's opinion, that corpulent pastor of perverse piety conceivably held the record for the most tedious sermons on the planet. A man who would not think twice about spending two hours droning on about the need to eradicate dandelions from the garden. A weed infested lawn a sure sign of the owner's moral degeneration, whose own corruptive nature would spread like those weeds to the innocent souls surrounding him, victims of another's indolence. Finn had spent that sermon lost in his memories, a child playing with Evie in a beautiful dandelion filled meadow, the bright yellow heads lifting their spirits. They blew seed heads into the summer sky and made childish wishes for the seeds to carry away on the breeze.

The choir began to sing, and Finn let the music enter his body to transport it somewhere else, floating away like those dandelion seeds, somewhere beautiful, somewhere into his past.

Finn sat on a wall a short distance from the Church. Some passing DIA's acknowledged him but none had the time nor the courage to stop and chat. He watched Sophie walking towards him, talking to a tall man, Henry. Finn balled his fists when he saw the doctor place his hand on Sophie's arm, touching her, talking to her, smiling at her. He kissed Sophie on the cheek, sending surging jealousy and resentment coursing through Finn. When Henry sauntered off to the waiting car, there was no cheery smile for his employee's husband.

'Shall we go? I've a nice bit of chicken from the butchers. I think I'll do a casserole. It's getting so cold now.' Sophie stood by him, unaware of the turmoil that little scene had caused her husband.

'Why do you let him touch you?'

'Sorry darling, what did you say?'

'I said, "Why do you let him touch you?" Every week you come out of church together, chatting and then he kisses you. I'm your husband. I am not allowed to kiss you in public. I can't even hold your hand when we are out. Why should he be allowed to do that? It's not right.' Simmering anger giving his words a petulant edge.

Sophie gave him a resigned look, pulling on her scarlet gloves. 'We were just talking about work. Henry has a full day tomorrow with the vaccination programme. He's asked me to do an extra hour after my shift. He's my boss, I had to say yes. The kiss was just that, a goodbye peck on the cheek, meaningless. When we get home, I'll show you what a meaningful kiss is if you want.'

Finn pushed himself off the wall and walked away a few paces ahead of her. He was in no mood for any kisses, meaningful or otherwise.

* * *

Thursday 9th December

I think I shall add a little extra to the English lessons. I need to liven things up before I become as stale as everyone else.

* * *

'Good evening, 568216.'

Finn didn't care, Michael wasn't even his real name. For the authorities and paperwork, he was a mere number. At School House 87 he was Mr Michael. He had only been 'Michael' to his schoolteachers, doctors and hospital administrators. He was Finn, and the longer he kept her away from his real identity, the better.

Cat was distracted, swiping her finger across her tablet. He was used to being ignored but continued in his efforts to capture his pupil's attention.

'Um, er, Miss Fry, don't you think we should discuss Mr Knightley's reaction to Emma interfering with Harriet and Mr Martin's relationship?'

Cat stopped playing with her tablet and looked up, the

corners of her mouth rising upwards and her eyes widening. He had her, or so he thought. Seconds later, the room filled with music. Music engulfing him with memories of home. Music deemed to be corrupting and unacceptable by New Albany.

'Do you dance?' Cat was standing in front of him, her hand held out ready to be taken.

'Is that an order, am I obliged?' He didn't need to hear her answer. This was her world, her fiefdom. He put his hand on hers and she jerked him close. Her arms wrapped around his torso. She rocked him in time to the music, dissolving a past pleasure into another tormenting weapon.

'Why don't you have children?' she said, edging ever closer with each sway of her body.

Finn tensed, tightening his grip on the teenager's small hand.

'Ow, that hurts.'

'I'm sorry, I didn't mean to hurt you. I'm not used to dancing, sorry.' He hoped his excuse was enough to save him from answering her question.

'Then we should dance more often. I like dancing, it is liberating.' She pulled at him, using the toes of her shoes to nudge him in her desired direction. Her face was touching his and with her breath on his neck she whispered, 'Does she get rid of them? Sixteen years married and what do you have? Nothing.'

Tiny beads of sweat were developing on Finn's forehead. The room was spinning, his head was spinning; sofa, stove, sofa, table, door, sofa, stove, sofa, table, door.

'Does it disgust her to carry an alien's offspring? Is that why she gets rid of them?'

The fault lay with him and him alone. His breathing accelerated and perspiration rolled down into his eyes, blurring his vision. He tried to escape her grip, but she held onto him, vice-like. His chest tightened. He had to concentrate, willing himself not to lose his temper.

'Our sole purpose in this life is to breed little patriots, dutiful mini versions of our husbands, ready to serve New Albany, "In Nostra Patria Gloriam Uteri"'

Finn stopped moving and stared at his pupil. For New Albany, the female Albian, even the ones as elite as Catherine Fry, were nothing more than a womb for sale to the right ambitious officer. Her anger pierced out from furious eyes, harpooning and entwining him, drawing him into her.

He turned away, breaking the hold. 'I am sure you'll be more fortunate than us.'

'Is that how you see it? Misfortune? I doubt that's how your wife sees it? She has a life, she has freedom, she has choice, free of childbirth and screaming brats.'

Finn stood stock still. Sophie had no more freedom than him. Her life was bound to his, she had sacrificed freedom and choice to be with him. The princess in her tower had no concept of the reality of his wife's life.

'Do you think she is waiting for the day she can no longer bear children, officially declared a failed patriot, free to escape the bounds of New Albany, free to join you in your worthless Outer World? Repatriated together?' Cat's insults carried spitefulness. 'Are you her ticket to escape? Is this what it's all about? Escape. It's an illusion, they won't want her either. You can never leave. We are all prisoners, it's just that some of us are better treated.'

Her words were like the suffocating hold of a boa constrictor, compressing his lungs with her ominous warnings. He bent forward, trying to regain his composure, dwelling on the reasons why he should ignore her. If he lost his temper he'd be just the same as Andy, and he wasn't Andy.

Cat went over to a small cabinet next to the fireplace. The little cupboard contained a collection of bottles all filled with the same amber liquid, and a set of small tumblers. Pouring the liquid into two glasses, she handed one to her tutor.

'Drink?'

'I doubt I have a choice?'

She laughed and shook her head, watching him bring the glass to his mouth. He let the syrupy drink coat his lips, and like Cat, he did not turn away but stared straight back at her. She sat on the sofa, puckered her lips into a kiss then closed her eyes, savouring the caramel in her mouth. Finn took that brief opportunity to tip his drink into her mint tea, left to go cold on the side table. His hand shook and the crystal glass caught the edge with the porcelain, making a bell-like ring. Cat opened her eyes, sighing with mature disappointment and slid off the sofa. She was on all fours, each arm gracefully extended as she crawled across the gap between them, her head up, focused on him. One arm pushed down to the left of him, then the other to his right. The seat depressing beneath the weight of her strength. She pushed herself forward, her face getting closer and closer. Her nose touched his, and her lips rested on his mouth. He could taste the sweetness of strawberry lip salve mixed with caramel. Every nerve within him was poised for attack. His body had fired up a furnace inside him. He didn't need a mirror to know his face had gone red, and that his fringe was stuck to his forehead with globules of perspiration. Suddenly, she pulled back, returning to her seat.

'How did she do it?'

'What?'

'Stop the pregnancies, of course.'

'She did nothing. I mean, she did nothing wrong. We've just been unlucky. Sometimes that happens, no particular reason. We do want children.'

Cat filled the seat next to Finn, the heat of her body

adding to his misery.

'What about your illness?'

The blood in his flesh that moments before made his cheek flushed red, drained away, leaving his face chalky white. The guilty memory of past mistakes had caught up with him.

'Mumps wasn't it?' She was perfectly entitled to view his medical file. After all, he was a DIA and his past had been documented and placed on view for public scrutiny.

'It's a myth, mumps rarely causes total infertility; we've been unlucky, that's all.' An expensively organised clerical error keeping his forgotten past safe from her insinuations.

Catherine raised an eyebrow and poured another drink. The music played, and the ticking clock marked the minutes of the inquisition, plenty of time left for Cat Fry to pry.

'Do you know what else I found on your file, tucked away under miscellaneous notes? A request. You wanted to abandon your wife and start a new life. You requested a repatriation leaflet, didn't you?'

Finn looked down, replying quietly, 'I didn't know that was on my file. It was just a conversation.'

It had been years ago, just a trivial chat with Sergeant Mason. But it had happened, and it had been documented. It had become an irrefutable truth.

Cat lay her hand on his bouncing lap. Her long-manicured fingernails had found the crack and were prising open his box of anxiety and memories.

'I don't believe you. Something stopped you. Or someone else.'

Finn wiped away a bead of sweat rolling down the side of his face with the back of his hand. He needed to keep calm. She mustn't get to the truth. That box must be kept shut.

'You say you want children, but you endure the

117

restrictions, the humiliation, all for a barren wife? I don't believe you. There is more to this, there must have been a very strong reason for you not to go.'

His heart was thumping, panic surging inside him. She was opening the box.

'Was it because she was pregnant. It is amazing what a human will do for love of a child, isn't it?'

'Why do you say that? You can't know that. How would you know that?

'Because, 568216, you just told me. Where is it? What did your precious wife do with it?'

A brief moment of calmness overtook Finn's normal state of near panic. He no longer cared what would happen next.

'Bitch!' Finn sprung out of the seat spinning round to confront his bully. 'My wife did nothing wrong. It was your bloody country and people like you! I loathe you all.' Catherine tried to grab at him but was met by Finn's hand slapping her face. 'I am just a number to you, just another DIA to be tortured for your own sick pleasure.'

Finn's blind anger paused just long enough to see brief shock on Catherine's face. She touched the reddening cheek. He expected tears, he expected anger. He got a broad grin and long arms extending along the back of the sofa, basking in the glory of her triumph. She had goaded him into a fatal mistake, and once the mad calmness had disappeared, Finn knew it too.

'Oh dearie me, what shall we do with 568216? The Commandant's daughter brutally attacked by a DIA. There will be harsh punishment. They'll need to make an example of you. A DIA betraying the trust put in him. They'll take you away from that patriot wife, a woman disgraced by your immorality.'

Alarm bells were deafening all rational thought. Cat would

be believed without the inconvenience of proof. Who's to say she would stop at the accusation of crude language? He read a banned book. They danced to prohibited music. She had rested her lips against his. He had slapped her.

'Look at me, 568216. Look at what you did.'

Finn couldn't move. She was by him again, her fingers pressing into the flesh of his cheeks, forcing his face up. Her face was in his. The satisfaction in hers mirrored by his despair.

'You have privilege status. Why do you have Ministerial Importance? Who's protecting you? Why are they protecting you? Is that why you are such a perfect angel, you can't disgrace whoever it is, can you?'

Cat could accuse him of any crime, he'd be lucky with just a labour camp sentence. Sexual assault of an unmarried patriot girl by a DIA carried the death penalty. This was not a misdemeanour that a bribable guard would conveniently forget to add to his file.

Catherine released her grip and sat beside him, her hand running up and down his back like a mother comforting a fallen child.

'We will have to find a way to save you, won't we? If that's what you deserve. Do you deserve to be saved?'

'I'm sorry, I'm so sorry, truly I am. Please, I will not do it again. I am very, very sorry.'

She had trapped him. Her fingers were on the soft cotton of his trousers, tracing circles.

'Why don't you tell me about the baby? I want to know what happened. You can do that can't you? Tell me about your child, and your wife will avoid the ignominy of becoming a hanged man's widow.' She spread her fingers out and pushed down, keeping his leg still, waiting for his decision. The box had been forced open and he must answer her.

'She died. She came too early. There are so few premature baby units in this country, she wasn't a priority, even if I had been allowed to access my money. Molly lived for an hour. They recorded her as a miscarriage, but she was born alive, crying to be saved. We weren't even allowed to bury her. To them, she was human waste to be incinerated and not the child we mourned.'

'There, that wasn't so hard. Was it?' she spoke softly, soothingly, 'Would you like some water. You look rather pale.'

Finn said nothing. There was nothing left to say. He was silenced by the guilt of the failed parent. The daily guilt that he couldn't save his child. The guilt that he had caught mumps so soon after. The guilt they had not been able to conceive another baby.

New Albany's voluntary prisoner sat in the dark, his face illuminated by the tablet on his knee. Cat was right, under miscellaneous was the request for the Repatriation Information Booklet. Had Sophie known all along? Had Sergeant Mason told her that her own husband, who professed undying love, was preparing to leave her? The conversation between sergeant and alien had been a moment of madness, one too many bad days, an innocent bystander who became the focus of blame. The unfortunate embodiment of those distant and invisible strangers waging daily conflict with the Albian authorities. He missed his home, and he missed Evie. The restrictions were only ever meant to be temporary. Six months they said. They forced him to choose, family or wife, and they forced him to miss Evie's wedding.

Doubts beset his thoughts. Had the sacrifice of freedom been a price worth paying? Would his life have been bearable without the one woman who gave it reason and purpose?

Finn recoiled at his naïve younger self, in love, laughing at the peculiar rules and regulations of his adopted home. He was Michael Finlay Sheehan and she, Sophia Elle, daughter of an up and coming government minister. It wasn't the right time for a baby, they were too young. Contraception might have been illegal, but it was available all the same, as long as you had the money or the right connections. They had both. Apart from that minor transgression they were law abiding citizens, they weren't terrorists, saboteurs intent on bringing down the government. Sophie's own father was in that administration. Finn was the model foreign worker, dutiful and loyal. Restrictions existed, but not for people like them. Strong security was good, nobody could possibly want terrorist attacks, and if a few inconveniences and reductions in rights meant everyone was safe, so be it.

The descent from blissful naivety to bewildered reality had been a harsh and bruising one. They soon learnt that temporary meant permanent and blame requires a face and a name. The Daily Briefings reported a litany of rape and murder by marauding foreign workers. The economy was failing, responsibility attributed to all the invading aliens stealing the best jobs. They were thieves, they were perverts, they were cockroaches out to destroy the beautiful dawn of New Albany with their libertine practices. The identity card scheme was meant to be the safety net, a way to distinguish between the good foreign worker and those deemed a danger to society. Finn didn't have anything to hide. He was the model foreigner, the ideal alien. How could it all go wrong so fast?

Sat in Sophie's chair, Finn had become a ghostly figure caught in the blue light of the screen. He couldn't help but wonder about Cat's words, they were all prisoners of New Albany, all subject to its harsh reality.

The file closed and the tablet back on charge, Finn

returned to the kitchen table to mark essays. The past had happened, its details recorded. The fall from Dr Sheehan to 568216/2/MI was complete. New Albany owned him now, his body at least. His memories remained free, unchained, prodding its victim with sharp, painful stabs.

FALSE COMFORT

ST DYMPHNA'S HOSPITAL, AGED EIGHTEEN

It is the unmistakable malodour that betrays my exact location. Those regular trips to hospitals and clinics to soothe my mother's worries have left their mark on my sense of smell. They all have that same stomach-churning stench of antiseptic, fear and anxiety.

I am in a ground floor room and to my left a large window looks out onto a central square. Hospital staff and visitors hurry past to avoid the persistent rain. Umbrellas twirl, cheerfully bright as though to spite the December gloom. One lady's umbrella is red with glistening snowflakes. I imagine what she might choose for summer rain, something fresh, distorted flowers beneath giant raindrops perhaps. The lady exits the square and I am alone again.

On the windowsill there is a miniature Christmas tree, well, not really a Christmas tree, more a stick sprayed with white paint and daubed with glitter. It resembles one I made at school. Mum insists on putting it up in the dining room next to Evie's papier-mâché robin and Andy's toilet roll Santa. The tree in this room is covered with miniature baubles and fairy lights, flashing intermittently. Other ornaments attempt to transport me from here and trick my brain into believing that I could be at home. A normal, family home covered in garish decorations and lights. A house full of children and hassled adults waiting for the big day. This isn't my imitation home. I'll deny it, but lying here, in this hospital bed is where I will be spending Christmas.

The silence of the room is disturbed by a rustle of paper. I turn over to see a youngish man reading a magazine. A nurse judging from his uniform, sitting in one of those obligatory blue vinyl chairs that only seem to exist next to hospital beds. He folds up the magazine on noticing I am awake, greeting me with a friendly broad smile. His hand reaches forward to touch my arm. That electricity that comes with human contact, shocks me, and I jerk my arm back. He leans forward, grasping my hand in his, this time I only feel comfort and reassurance.

'Hello, my name is Mohammed, but everyone calls me Mo. How are you feeling now, Michael?'

FINN

Finn's world had descended into a grey melancholy, hushing all, even the birds. Beyond the gate, Carl's steps echoed within the frozen leaves snapping beneath his boots. The birds did not take flight, and Finn remained rigid.

'There you are. You do realise it's absolutely freezing out here.' Carl shuffled up beside his friend on the bench and began his usual examination of the lunch box. The search was rewarded, and he held up an apple in triumph. 'Are you going to eat this?'

Finn turned to see what Carl was scavenging, shook his head and returned his attention to a bare tree. His friend's teeth sank into the red skin of the apple. The crunch piercing the silence. He chewed the white juicy flesh and with greedy gulps, swallowed, ending with the licking lips of a hunger satisfied.

Finn exhaled, the cold air turning his breath into white wisps rising up into the clouds. He imagined each of those wisps carrying part of him back across the Albian Sea to his family and the safety of home.

Carl placed a mittened hand on Finn's back, drawing him back into the graveyard. 'You OK, Finn? You look like shit.'

'Thanks. I'm fine, I needed some fresh air.'

'Fresh air? Christ Finn, it's minus three at the moment, the only thing you'll be getting is pneumonia. Come on back to the staff room, we do have some heating you know.' Carl tugged at Finn's arm, but he jerked it back, frustrating his friend's attempt to encourage him indoors.

'Oh, come on Finn! You need to come in, this is ridiculous. You can't keep eating out here.'

Finn touched the brass plaque with his bare fingers, their heat producing circles of clarity on its iced surface.

'I like to share my lunch with Eloise Phillips, 1879 to 1956, beloved wife, mother and grandmother. She is a quiet lunch companion, never complains, never judges. A rotten corpse with no prejudices.'

Carl snorted. 'Don't be so sure, they were just as nasty then as they are today. They kept it undercover though, a veneer of kindness and tolerance to barely coat their true tendencies. She'd be as quick to judge and condemn you as any patriot today. As long as there is someone more miserable than them, then all is right with the world. I hope it's hot wherever she is. I hope she is fucking burning.'

Carl's anger captured Finn's attention. 'What's happened?'

'I got a notification letter about Si this morning. The fucking bastards have extended his re-education programme. Six months minimum. No visitation rights. I was going to see him at Christmas. He's my only family. It's not fair, it's just not fair.'

Carl's comedic release valve had failed him. How could there be comedy when dealing with the barbarism of New Albany.

'All he did was drive the family to the border. Nothing more. They were his friends, he wanted to help them. Instead he had to watch them being shot in the back of the head. All of them. Mum, dad and three children. Their only crime, wanting a better life for their kids. Wanting freedom.' Carl glared back towards the school and the girlish chatter from lunchtime gossiping. 'I'm so glad I don't have any, it's no life for them here, lad. Even if they are patriots.' He got up to leave, putting a hand on his friend's shoulder, squeezing it slightly. 'Are you so sure you want to bring a child into this disgrace of a world?'

A northerly wind bit away at any exposed flesh. The first five minutes of his lessons were taken up with girls unwrapping themselves from the various layers of scarves, hats, coats and gloves. Consequently, they ignored him during the last five when they began the laborious task of wrapping themselves up again. He didn't really mind, but he would have preferred it if they were able to do it quietly. The headaches were getting worse. For Finn, there wasn't a sound so torturous as the high pitch squeal of an over excited girl. The persistent cough didn't help either.

Finn longed for each day to end. The icy roads had made it too slippery to cycle to work, this meant an hour and a half's walk to get back. Fortunately, it being a Monday, he could relish an evening free of Miss Fry. Pushing the thought of her to the back of his mind, he tried to refocus on his lesson.

Finn surveyed the class before him, rows of teenage girls, dull with post lunch lethargy. One girl wiped the condensation off the window, and at the back another two were giggling, their phones springing to life every few seconds. They didn't need to know about Emma Woodhouse's matchmaking, they were busy with their own.

He coughed, both to clear his throat and gain their attention. 'Would you rather have freedom to make your own mistakes and learn from them, or have your life closely regulated by others, letting them take all the important decisions for you?'

The girls at the back of the class weren't interested, so Finn nodded to an eager girl at the front. 'Miss Taylor, what do you think?'

'I would much rather my father took the decisions. He has more experience and his choices are more informed. There are fewer chances of mistakes.'

'Don't you think that would be relinquishing your ability

to take decisions? In effect infantilising you.'

Before Miss Taylor had a chance to reply, Finn began to cough. He used his handkerchief to smother it, but to no avail, his lungs required him to cough. He was struggling to breathe, becoming increasingly light-headed. Waving a free hand behind him, he tried to locate a chair. School protocol ignored, he had to sit down.

'Are you OK, Mr Michael?' asked Miss Taylor.

Finn nodded, indicating she should continue. Resting an elbow on the desk, he leant his aching head against his hand listening to Miss Taylor drone on about the importance of obedience.

'Without it you'd end up with anarchy and the likes of Harriet are the sad result. Failure to follow the rules of society can only lead to social disgrace,' she said.

All energy to argue the point had deserted him. The child's assertions becoming white noise while he watched the hour hand on the classroom clock. He was as keen to end the lesson as the sleepy girls. The bell rang, muffled by the scramble to abandon his classroom. Two hats, three gloves and a scarf lay forgotten on the floor. He intended to tidy them up but wobbled as he bent to pick them. It was time to go home, someone else could clear up for a change.

Through the kitchen door he saw the cottage wait in silent darkness, he didn't mind, he had plans. Draw the curtains, light the stove, make a hot drink and curl up under a blanket with one of the books they kept hidden inside the sofa, each dog-eared and barely together. He was relishing the idea of the comforting evening ahead, he might even close his eyes and imagine being back in the lazy luxury of the Melborough sitting-room. Those blissful thoughts were shoved away by the incessant dripping from the outside tap. Finn picked up the torch from the windowsill and shone it on the culprit. A steady stream of droplets glistened in the light. He tried to turn the brass tap, but it refused to budge. It was frozen solid.

SOPHIE

Sophie shook her head at the shadow coughing in front of her. 'You should be inside, in the warm. Come on, that can wait.'

Finn was fumbling to fix the tap while balancing the torch between his chin and chest. 'I've nearly finished. If I don't do this now, we risk burst pipes. Then we'll be stuck. There, all done.'

'Clever boy. Now get inside.'

Sophie tried to guide her husband towards the kitchen door, but reluctant to abandon his task, he pulled back, shining the torch into a box by his feet. He bent double to peer more closely. 'I'm sure there's some lag—'

The hacking cough returned, violently shaking him. Sophie reached out, helping him to stand upright. 'It can wait until morning.'

'No, it's going to be…hmm…going to be... I don't feel so well.'

His initial vomiting over, Sophie sat him on the bench gently rubbing her hand along his back. He was still trembling, and his skin felt clammy. Ever prepared, she found a tissue in her uniform pocket and dabbed his mouth, wiping away the spittle that had gathered at the corners. The initial relief after being sick would soon disappear and she needed to get him into the house and into bed.

'How do you feel now?' Sophie asked when she returned from the kitchen.

'I'm sorry, I made your uniform dirty.'

She kicked away her clothes from the bedroom chair and lay down the tray of drinks. 'Don't be daft! Come on, let's get you into bed. You'll soon start to feel better after some rest. I've made elderberry tea, that will help.'

His trembling had upgraded to teeth chattering shivers, while he fumbled with the buttons on his shirt. Eventually, after pushing the little white disk through the hole, he let out a victorious sigh. That slightest of exertions making him pause before engaging in battle with the next button.

'Let me do that,' said Sophie, moving to sit by Finn. She undid each of the remaining buttons and helped him out of his clothes. Once in bed, Finn shut his eyes and lifted his hands over his ears, complaining about the noise in their bedroom. There was no noise. Sophie checked his pulse and pressed her fingers against his forehead. She didn't need the thermometer to tell her that Finn had a fever. A call to the guardhouse medical centre would mean the arrival of an unknown, minimally trained medical officer, his scant knowledge considered sufficient for the DIA Medical Service. Dr Thatcher would come at a high price, a price she accepted.

'I'll call Henry.'

Finn squeezed her wrist, preventing her from leaving his side. 'No, don't do that. It's only a cough. I stood up too quickly, that's all. I'll be fine in the morning. We don't need to go to the expense of Henry.'

'We both know it's not just a cough. You can't go to work like this. I've got to tell the guardhouse if you are sick, you know that. At least we'll have the advantage of a doctor we know.'

The green light on THEO caught her attention. Sophie was in no mood to deal with the spy in the bedroom. They hadn't said anything incriminating but even so, Sophie collected up the cushions from the bed and piled them over the wretched spy attached to the wall. If they must listen, then let it be muffled speech.

Henry unpacked his medical bag onto Sophie's dressing table, pushing aside her make-up bag and the framed wedding photo. The accoutrements of the modern Albian doctor were laid out; a tablet with a detachable microchip reader, a digital thermometer and a stethoscope. Not much change in thirty odd years.

Sophie had met Henry at university, and he was keen for her to join his practice after she qualified. There was virtually nothing that she didn't know about the man. A good doctor and dedicated patriot, he carried himself with the perpetual air of arrogance that came to those who believed themselves superior.

'First things first, we need to check you are who you say you are,' he said, pointing the reader at Finn's bangle. He waited for the long, G sharp whine, then plugged the reader into the tablet. The screen awoke with the security head-shots. Front view. Left view. Right view. 'Well that's you OK, 568216/2/MI, Michael Finlay.' Henry scrolled down the screen until he came to the section for medical details, tapping it to enter the file. 'This is such a fag but needs to be done. Ah here we go. Right, OK Michael, let's begin, shall we?'

It didn't take him long to examine Finn. He stood up and shot a look back at Sophie. 'Flu, no surprises there. You know the drill, plenty of fluids, paracetamol to bring down the fever. I really don't have to tell you your job, do I? You're my most experienced nurse.'

Sophie didn't reciprocate his smile, instead she pushed the chair next to the bed and held Finn's hand. A lock of damp hair was stuck across his eye. She lifted it away, quietly telling him to go back to sleep. Behind her, Henry gossiped on about co-workers and the next day's schedule. She looked over her shoulder, and not wanting to disturb Finn she whispered, 'Do you think they'll confine him to home for long?'

'Dunno,' he said. He had Sophie's wedding picture in his hand. Putting it down, he added, 'I don't have anything to do with DIA medical confinements. You need to speak to Captain Kendrick, down at his guardhouse in the morning. He'll give you all the details.' He walked over to the bed, peering at Finn from over Sophie's shoulder. 'Word is, this outbreak is nasty. Kendrick tells me that the fever tends to worsen as the illness develops. The authorities don't want it spreading and are being unusually tough. There's talk about emergency regulations and we'll all have to comply. There can be no exceptions where disease control is concerned.' She felt his hand on her shoulder, hot and firm. 'Shall we go downstairs to discuss matters? I expect you'll also need some time off. I'm sure we'll come to an arrangement.'

Henry was at the door, eager to depart. Normally so self-assured, he appeared uneasy, darting looks along the landing.

Sophie tucked Finn's hand back under the sheet and heaved herself off the chair. 'I'll show you out, we can discuss payment in the kitchen.'

There were a dozen or so people in the guardhouse waiting-room, each trying to avoid eye-contact with any of the others. Sophie tore a number off the roll and sat down on a plastic chair. It was going to be a long morning.

From her handbag, she pulled out a battered book, the front and back covers ripped off. It's yellowing pages released that distinctive old book smell, filling her head with pleasant memories. On the cover page, in neat schoolboy writing, *'Timothy Smith, 9P, St Jude's School.'* By rights the book should be on the banned list, but it had become unpopular long before the new regime took charge. Sophie pinged off the elastic band that held it together, momentarily catching the attention of a man opposite. He wasn't interested in her or her book, only how much longer he'd have to wait for his number to be called out by the desk clerk. These were not the people who would frown and holler at Heller's satirical world. Sophie was free to reacquaint herself with Captain Yossarian, but her guilty conscience still jumped when the shadow of a uniformed man fell upon her.

'Miss Sophie? I thought it was you. Is everything OK at home?' said the sergeant, his face alight with an endearing smile.

'Oh hello, Sergeant Mason. Finn's got the flu, I'm waiting to see Captain Kendrick,' she explained, slipping the book beneath her skirt.

'George, please. Yep, it's a nasty bug alright. It's causing a bit of disquiet up on high by all accounts, and it seems to be spreading, though patriots aren't being affected as far as I can tell.' He filled the empty seat next to her. 'Rumour has it they suspect this is the start of a new campaign by the insurgents. Infect DIAs with a new variety of flu and they go out purposely trying to infect us. They didn't bank on us having a vaccine, now did they?' He was laughing, Sophie was not. *Look after your own first,* that sacred doctrine of every loyal patriot.

An elderly lady in the corner of the room began to cry. George stopped laughing and took in the sullen faces surrounding him, all DIA spouses, all there for the same reason. He patted Sophie's knee with paternal reassurance. 'Don't you worry Miss Sophie, I'm sure Finn will be just fine.

He'll get the right help, they all will, just you wait and see.'

Sophie nodded, the large lump in her throat stifling all words. She looked down at Sergeant Mason's hand tapping her knee. There were age spots and wrinkles across the back of it and grey hairs poked out of his uniform cuff. He had known them for years, yet she still couldn't think of him as a friend, no matter how kind his demeanour towards her. She lifted her face, almost challenging him. 'You can't suspect Finn of purposely making himself ill, can you?'

His ears reddened with her accusation. 'No, not at all. It's the insurgents' fault, you know. They don't care who they infect. I guess most DIAs are innocent, just like Finn. Come on, let me see if I can speed things up for you. Captain Kendrick owes me a favour.'

'George, that's kind, but I am happy to wait my turn.'

'No, no, I insist, can't have Mr Smith's daughter waiting around.'

He disappeared behind a security door, leaving Sophie to scan the room. Anxious faces all hoping to see Captain Kendrick and learn the fate of their sick loved one. Confinement? For how long? No work meant no pay for a DIA. New regulations required those needing specialist care were to be sent to a DIA Treatment Centre, a good three hours bus ride from their home. Her gut instinct told her that was somewhere best avoided, especially given the rumours. In the corner the elderly woman wiped away her tears with a delicate handkerchief. Sophie imagined life without Finn. Beneath the cotton fabric of her blouse, goose bumps of fear chased up her arm.

It was mid-afternoon by the time Sophie made it back to the cottage. Through the window she spotted someone moving about in her kitchen. She sighed. Admittedly, Sophie had not expected the meeting to take five hours, but he really was not well enough to be stomping around the kitchen.

'Finn, why are you so stubborn? I told you to stay in bed,' she said, flinging open the kitchen door.

'Last time I checked he was asleep upstairs.' The man hiding behind the cupboard door closed it and faced Sophie.

'Sergeant Mason!'

'We've spoken about this before, please call me George.'

'What are you doing in my kitchen?'

The table was a complete mess, her largest pan was full of vegetables, with a whole chicken perched on top. Inside the carcass she saw a lemon and herbs from the garden. Was that lavender? Vegetable peelings were scattered across the work surface and the floor, and in the middle of the mess, George, brandishing a large chef's knife in his hand.

'Half day today and seeing how you wouldn't accept my help with Captain Kendrick, I thought I'd pop in to see if your husband needed anything. I knew you'd be a long time.'

Her surprised silence was interrupted by coughing from upstairs, reminding her of what was important. 'I should check on Finn.' She put the bag of medical supplies down on the table, leaving her intruder to chop onions.

Whatever George was cooking, it was bubbling on the hob when she returned to the kitchen, its tempting smell making her empty stomach rumble.

'How is he?' said George, holding the chair out for her.

She was genuinely worried. This flu was different, like nothing she had experienced before. All number of possible ailments sprang to mind. None reassuring. 'He's getting worse, delirious and his temperature has gone up. I need to call Dr Thatcher again.'

Once Sophie's call to Henry ended, she dropped her face

into her hands. Tears dribbled out through the gaps between her fingers.

'There, there now, don't you go crying.' George bent down to hug her. 'Doc will come, won't he?'

Sophie nodded, exhausted by her pleading.

'You see, how could he refuse someone as lovely as you.'

He had only heard one side, and Sophie took some relief from that. She tipped up the shopping bag to look at the inadequate medical supplies, lemon, honey and paracetamol.

George nudged Sophie, attempting to bolster her with his good humour. 'My mother swore by hot lemon, best thing for a cold. That and her famous chicken soup of course,' he said, nodding towards the bubbling concoction.

'It's so kind of you, George. You shouldn't have gone to all this trouble. How much do I owe for the ingredients?'

'Nothing,' he replied, holding up a hand to stop her speaking, 'I won't hear of payment. By the way what did Kendrick say?'

Sophie's eyes prickled again. 'Oh, George, it's full confinement. He can't leave the house at all for six weeks, no work, no tutoring, no money!'

'Well I gathered there might be a crackdown. The Ministry don't want an epidemic breaking out. Sorry your husband is caught up in it. Unfortunate really.'

George picked up the kettle, filled it and placed it on the stove next to the soup. Sophie couldn't help wondering why this apparently sweet man would want to be an officer. His daily routine the opposite to his nature

'How am I going to tell Finn? He'll go stir crazy.'

'If he feels how he looks, I doubt he'll care for the first week. Bed, sleep and your loving attention is what he'll be needing. Nothing more. I'd wait until he starts to improve.'

With the Christmas holiday looming, they would only

miss out on the three weeks' of term time pay. One thing she was sure of though, time off to care for him was not an option. She needed to earn, and the holiday period was the time she could make extra money. Sophie had no intention of turning to her parents for help, they did enough already, and her mother would only use it as further ammunition against Finn.

George handed her a cup of tea. 'I can always call in to say hi, check all is well while you're on duty, if that helps?'

'Would you? You are our guardian angel, you really are.'

Even with Finn's mumbling keeping her awake, Sophie could not leave the makeshift bed. The guilty weight of fatigue pinned her down. confining her to that instrument of torture worthy of ASSU. Her neck was stiff, and her arm numb from lying on it. His murmurs persisted. She clenched and unclenched her fist trying to get the circulation going, then manoeuvred her legs from under her. They were as numb as her arm, pins and needles running down them to her feet. She grimaced with each cautious step towards the bed, stumbling over a loose floorboard and nearly knocking over the intravenous drip stand. Bottles and pills filled her dressing table. A once pretty room impregnated with the smell of eucalyptus oil and fear. The Foreign Minister had called in favours, he was no stranger to the benefits of bribery. His son-in-law, the sole beneficiary of the Minister's guilt.

He was becoming more unsettled. It was as regular as clockwork. Sophie placed her arm under Finn's back to ease him up off the pillow. 'Finn, sweetheart, it's OK. You're only having a nightmare.' His skin felt hot, but she was sure it was less clammy. 'Come on, wake up darling, you're going to be just fine.'

She put a cup of herbal tea to his lips, irritated by his refusal to even try a sip. She was tired too. He opened his eyes, but with no greeting smile for his wife. Her continued attempts to persuade him to drink at last succeeded, but it was short lived. He moved his head away, stubbornly refusing her entreaties to drink more. Sophie shuddered, listening to Finn's chest rattle with each breath. Anna had said the herbal tea would help loosen the sticky phlegm in his lungs. Unconvinced, Sophie thought it more likely one of Anna's well-intentioned placebos to soothe her own anxieties. She reached across for the thermometer, the long beep signalling a fever, but at least it was coming down. Henry had promised her, he had promised her father, if Finn improved then he could stay with Sophie. Time was running out. Henry would be back later that day to examine Finn. There had been some hopeful signs since her father's visit three days before, but she doubted it was enough. Determined she would not let them take him away to the Treatment Centre, she held the cup to his lips once more, ordering Finn to drink.

Her talking must have woken Anna, who walked into the room a few minutes later carrying a tray with a bowl of steaming water and a small bottle of a herbal oil. Dressed in blue polka dot pyjamas and with her untamed hair, she was doing her best impression of a friendly Medusa. For New Albany records, Anna was a servant, the Foreign Minister's cook, but in Sophie's home she was every inch her godmother. A maternal kiss on Sophie's cheek infused her with hope. 'I'll stay with him, Soph. You need to get some sleep. Aren't you working in the morning?'

Sophie nodded but remained resolutely by Finn's side, watching the rise and fall of his chest, terrified that each rise might be his last. 'I don't know what I'll do if they take him away from me.'

'Darling girl, everything's going to be fine. Henry won't send him away, not now,' she said, taking Sophie's hand into hers. 'Do you really think he would risk making an enemy of your father? That's a battle Henry would unlikely win. No, Finn is staying right here with you.'

She was the woman that had cradled her as a newborn, the woman that watched her grow into the curious girl, the woman that had taught and inspired her. Always there, always her guiding beacon, always her pillar of support. So positive and calm, she alone could prevent her goddaughter from being sucked down into the whirlpool of despair.

'He's definitely improved,' she said, 'and it's only been a few days. He's responding well, he'll be fine, trust me, Finn is far stronger than you think. He wants to live, I'm sure of it. You really do need to get some rest though, I insist.'

Sophie sat back on the makeshift bed, while Anna picked up her long-forgotten stethoscope to listen to Finn's chest. Watching her, Sophie fantasised what it must have been like to work as a doctor, skills ingrained within her godmother, never forgotten. To be a woman not only capable of bringing life into the world, but also to save lives, mend broken bodies, to understand the mystery of human life. What must it have been like to have that ability, then have it snatched away for no other reason than for the misfortune of being born female?

She remembered the small girl drawing in the library while Anna researched the works of Benedictine monks, taking page after page of notes. New Albian ignorance giving her access to the herbalists of the past. When Sophie graduated as a nurse, it was Anna's well-thumbed and underlined, "Causae et Curae" that passed from godmother to goddaughter. Sophie clasped her hands together in prayer, hoping Saint Hildegard of Bingen was listening, that she would guide Anna, and together they would heal Finn.

Weariness had taken control, her eyes disobediently shutting each time she urged them to stay open. Her body ached and she desperately wanted somewhere she could stretch her stiff limbs. 'I might lie on the sofa for a short while.'

Anna turned away from her patient to give her goddaughter another kiss and a hug. 'You'll feel much better, Soph. I assure you. If there is any change to Finn, I promise I'll wake you.'

Sophie left the room knowing that before long both of their nightmares would return.

At the opposite table, a purple nailed lady swiped across her tablet. Little disapproving noises were dripping off her plum coloured lips. Even from where she sat, Sophie could see the article, dominated by a picture of men in surgical masks standing over a cadaver, an arm hanging out from under a white sheet. Deliberately or not, the bangle was clearly visible on the dead man's wrist.

'DIA INFLUENZA, THE INSURGENTS LATEST ATTACK ON NEW ALBANY.'

It was a blatant lie, barely any patriots had suffered from the epidemic. Her workload had not increased beyond the usual winter coughs and colds. The vaccine had done its job, but that narrative was of no use to the propaganda machine. Irritated, she downed the espresso in hope it would charge up flagging enthusiasm for her day off. Exhaustion was consuming her.

'Sorry darling, I had to drive myself, Christopher is with Daddy in AZ One. There was no one to park the car for me. Such a nightmare. And people wonder why we wives get stressed at Christmas.'

Jolted out of her stupor, Sophie rose to embrace her mother. 'Hope the other road users were warned. When was the last time you drove?'

'Oh goodness, donkey's years ago. I was a good driver, Christopher will agree. And, I did get here without incident.' Michelle sat down and picked up the menu. 'Have you ordered?'

'No, I thought I'd wait. I have something for you.' She handed her a small white box, her mother's glee at the unexpected present fading on seeing the contents.

'It's Daddy's watch. What were you doing with that?'

'He left it behind when he dropped by the other week.'

'Daddy didn't say anything to me. Why was he visiting you?'

'He was passing, some business in the area. He knew Finn was ill, probably wanted to check we were OK.'

Michelle placed the box in her handbag. 'I'm surprised he didn't say anything to me. He treasures that watch, Heaven knows why, it's not valuable or anything. A goodwill gesture from some ambassador or Outer World minister, I can't remember exactly who gave it to him now.'

They sat back in their chairs to peruse the menu. Her mother was in an unusually buoyant mood, making Sophie hopeful for pleasant discussions about nothing in particular. She was happy to let the chatter wash over her.

'Oh, and talking of the Capital, it looks just lovely at the moment, what with the Christmas lights and everything. I do love Christmas, don't you?' said Michelle.

'Not really thought about it. Will you be having a pudding?'

'Oh no, need to watch the calories. How can you not love Christmas?'

Sophie hid behind the menu, her answer would not meet the approval of her mother or anyone else listening in.

Michelle pulled it down, saying, 'You look tired. Are you getting enough sleep? Daddy said Anna visited you while I was away.'

'Yes, she stayed for several days keeping me company and helping with Finn. Oh, and by the way your son-in-law is much better now, thanks for asking.'

Michelle ignored her daughter's barbed response. 'Just awful isn't it? How they could do such a thing is beyond me. We let them live and work here and the ungrateful Immis set about making us sick, and right before Christmas too.'

'Please don't call them "Immis", Mum.'

But Michelle had not finished with her tabloid tirade. 'I heard AZ Seven have declared a State of Emergency. Patriots are coming down with it left, right and centre. Disgusting.'

Sophie sighed, pleasant conversation was always going to be a long shot with her mother. She could give her all the facts and figures, the vaccine had worked and for those vaccinated patriots who did get symptoms, it was a very mild version. Though none of that would make any difference to her mother's blind adherence to the accepted opinion of New Albany.

'And I read that flu is just the precursor. If you don't get the antiviral drug within hours of the first symptoms, you will die. That's the reason Immis...um, sorry darling, DIAs, are dying. Not that they should be given it. It's their fault in the first place.'

Sophie leant her elbow on the table, rubbing the indent at the top of her nose. Her mother was hard work and oblivious to her daughter's body language.

'Has Finn had an antiviral?' Michelle continued.

'No, he's feeling much better.' She had no intention of telling her that Finn had been given all sorts of drugs that weren't available for DIAs.

Michelle leant forward, glancing sideways to check the nearby tables and whispered, 'Daddy would get it for you if you want.'

'As I said, he is improving. Just very bored and frustrated.'

'If you say so. Anyway the extra confinement time is a necessity. Stop those insurgents' vicious plan from spreading. Now, where is that waitress?'

'Probably confined and unable to work.'

'I suppose.' Michelle put the menu down and began looking around, waving her hand at a waitress emerging from the kitchen.

'Mum, don't you ever look at Finn, Christopher and Anna, and then read those briefings and think, "This isn't right. This isn't the truth"?'

Michelle quickly stopped trying to catch the woman's attention. Behind a well-positioned hand, she hissed, 'Sophie, if you speak like that in public then you'll get yourself into serious trouble, the sort that kills.'

Sophie understood she was being warned to keep clear of the subject. She struggled to believe that despite all her patriot fervour, her mother could be so cold and uncaring about the people she reputedly loved.

The waitress approached their table. Michelle gave the order, then instantly switched to the safer gossip about friends and the redecoration of the dining room. 'It should be all done by the time you arrive. It looks lovely. I might decorate the tree in silver and blue this year. Emma says it's all the rage. What do you think?'

'Soup for me too, thank you.' Sophie gave the harassed looking waitress a sympathetic smile, before replying to her mother, 'You've forgotten haven't you? I rang you the other week, we're not coming this year.'

'What? No! Why?' she said, loud enough to make the

ladies at the next table tut at the outburst.

'I told you, Finn's confinement. It doesn't end until after the New Year and I doubt even Daddy can get the authorities to overlook it, not when there's talk of a State of Emergency.'

'But I have everything planned. Can't you come on your own?'

It took her a second or two to halt the steady stream of sweary insults that were sitting on the tip of her tongue. When she spoke, it was measured and controlled, 'No. I cannot leave my sick husband to have a Happy Christmas meal with you because otherwise it would mess up your plans.'

'Don't get stroppy with me, Sophia. I don't make the rules.'

The waitress brought their lunch and with the air around the table bristling with anger, they ate quietly, conversation at an end. Sophie spent the time coming up with a compromise. Confrontation was draining and she didn't have the energy for it anymore. 'Look, why don't you pack all the food up, and the decorations if you like, and come and spend Christmas with us in the cottage?'

'What if Finn is still contagious? Should we really take the risk?'

'Given you have been inoculated, even if he were contagious, which he definitely isn't, you still wouldn't get it.'

'I'm not sure. Your house is so small, would we all fit? And then there's Daddy's position to consider. I'll have to discuss it with him and let you know.'

Through an arc cutting across the steamed-up window, Sophie peered at her hibernating garden. Behind her, Michelle wittered on about Auntie Emma's new kitchen. 'She's so organised now, every cupboard filled with labelled plastic boxes.'

Sophie turned back to look at the woman who was increasingly a stranger to her. Anna was handing Michelle another steaming glass of spicy cider.

'Oh, thank you, darling. Are you sure you wouldn't like one too, Sophie?' she asked. Her mother was tipsy, her cheeks full of colour and there was a radiance to her smile that Sophie almost forgot existed. She shook her head in silent response. In her pocket, her fingers gripped the heavy envelope, the letter that needed delivering. The letter that would bring scant joy and immense pain. Just as it did each and every time. 'I ought to go and find Finn. He's been outside for too long.'

'I don't know why he insisted on chopping wood.' Christopher offered. Are you sure he's better? He looks like he'd be blown over by a slight breeze,' said Michelle.

'Fresh air is exactly what he needs right now,' said Anna, taking the seat next to Michelle. 'It's not too cold today and it will help him recover. But Sophie is right, it is probably time to fetch him back in.'

Sophie returned Anna's smile and left the women to their laughter, heading out to the garden where her husband had been chopping wood for the last hour.

He was sitting on an old wooden chair, the axe leaning against his knee. The small pile of chopped wood was barely enough to get through the evening. Sophie knew the real reason he was keen to get out was to escape the claustrophobia of the house. Her cottage was small and with six adults it felt even smaller.

'You should come in. We'll be eating soon,' she called out to him. He turned in response and Sophie saw the brief exertion had left him exhausted. 'When Henry said you needed to keep warm and rest, I am not sure he was thinking you should go out and chop up a forest. This is hardly resting and taking it easy, is it?'

'I like it out here, it's quiet.'

Sophie picked up the axe, it was much heavier than she anticipated. She was forced to use both hands to even lift it. Out of the corner of her eye she caught Finn's grin. 'I'm going to have a go.'

'Do we need matchsticks?' he said, laughing as the axe barely glanced off the log.

'It's just technique, I'll get it, just watch me and see.'

Her second attempt was no better. On the third try, she hit the log, but it got stuck. Finn got up, took the axe off her, lifted it up and bought it down heavily. The log split instantly. 'Next time you're in town see if Bain's have axes especially made for little pixies.'

'It's just practice and technique.'

He put his arm around her waist and brought her in close, kissing the top of her head. She had missed it. Those tender moments had become distinctly rarer.

'What are the others doing?' he asked, sitting back down on the chair.

'Dad and Christopher are hiding in the sitting-room pretending to watch a documentary about cricket, and Anna is trying to prevent Mum from going through all my kitchen cupboards to get me organised.'

'Ah, and you thought you'd escape by coming to find me? It won't work, she'll discover your devious plan and drag you back in to discuss the merits of plastic boxes ad nauseum.'

Sophie didn't want to disturb the happy moment with the letter. Her heartbeat increased as she slipped her hand into her pocket to retrieve it. Like Judas in the Garden of Gethsemane, that letter was the betraying kiss to send him back into the torment of despair. But despite her nervousness, she needed to appear calm and relaxed. 'George popped in with your Christmas letter. I thought you might want to read it out here, alone.'

Finn froze. Sophie pulled her hand out of her pocket and handed him the envelope. His hand trembled as he ran his fingers over the name. It was her mother-in-law's handwriting. At least she was still alive, but the shaky writing gave away her age.

'Dr and Mrs M F Sheehan'

Eloise Sheehan was ignorant of the rules. As far as she was aware her son continued to work as a lecturer at the University. With Sergeant Mason's help, each year Finn would compose his sole letter home without mentioning anything that might require the black censure of a security officer's pen. Finn would never have told her how far his life had altered. And even if he had tried, the censors would have ensured her ignorance. He took the letter, then stretched out the other arm to catch Sophie's wrist. 'Not alone, please stay with me.'

She tried to get as close to him as possible on the cramped garden seat. He prised opened the re-sealed envelope and pulled out the letter. Four pages. The tsunami of pain would be worse than usual.

'Do guards enjoy censoring letters?' he said, his gentle voice distorted by anger and sorrow. 'Does it give them pleasure to redact all semblance of a mother's tenderness?'

Line after line had been blacked out. She imagined the censors, making a game out of the process. Adverbs, any reference to happy events, adjectives beginning with a vowel. Today's objective, reduce a thousand-word letter of love into ten lines of indifference. Evidently, this censor was particularly adept at the task.

'I can't do this.' Finn handed back the letter.

'Shall I read it to you, then?'

He nodded.

She turned over the pages to find the scant words. Squeezing his hand and coughing back the lump in her throat, she began, 'Dear Finn and Sophie,

'We both hope you are well and are ready for Christmas. I expect you will be with Sophie's parents again.' She turned the page. 'Old Arthur has gone, chasing rabbits over a rainbow now. Andy and Nisha send their love. Elliot has been accepted at Carndean.' Another page was flipped over. 'Mrs McManus is in Clare House and doing well for a ninety-five-year-old. Daddy has a new bicycle and still manages to go up to Cairn Top Field every day.' She stopped speaking, rifling through the paper in case she had missed something. 'It ends there, darling. I'm so sorry, that's it.

'Nothing about Evie?'

She shook her head.

Finn rubbed away the tears with the sleeve of his jumper. It was the same agony each time. Twice a year for the last six years, on his birthday and at Christmas. Censorship came early to the lives of New Albians, protection against Outer Worlder radicalisation. Apart from the censored letters all other forms of contact with the Outer World had been banned. Finn had not heard his mother's voice in nearly fourteen years.

'Poor Mrs McManus,' said Sophie.

Finn could only acknowledge her comment with a nod. She looked down at the words, hoping to gleam something that might start a conversation to bring him back from the impending despair. 'Was Old Arthur the man we met when you took me round the farm?'

'No.'

'Oh, who was he then?'

'Dad's dog.'

Sophie remembered the chaos and noise that accompanied the spoilt little puppy. 'But he must be quite young still?'

'It was over sixteen years ago, that is a long time for a dog.'

He took back the letter and brought it up to his face tracing his finger across the inky words and the blackened lines. Lines and words that dissolved with his tears.

'Do you want to come in or shall I leave you a bit longer?'

He didn't respond. Sophie got off the chair, kissing him on the cheek as she stood. 'Don't be too long darling. You'll get cold.'

THE LOCKED DOOR

Tomorrow lives behind a locked door. Today you offer up promises and dreams and tell us they will be ours tomorrow. And today becomes yesterday. Tomorrow is always beyond our reach. Our fingernails wear down to nothing, scratching at that bolted door, and when we look back, we see our dreams rotting on yesterday's detritus.

SOPHIE

They had sat in silence for nearly three hours. Christopher suggested music for the journey, but neither Finn nor Sophie were in the mood for anything other than their own thoughts. She kept going over Tim's instructions, regularly checking her bag for the thick brown envelope. Every cough from Finn sent a tingle of fear down her back. Her head was constantly devising problems she knew didn't exist. She was Sophie Smith, daughter of the foreign minister, problems did not exist for people like her.

Sophie caught a glimpse of their destination in the distance. Occasionally it would disappear behind trees but as they got nearer, so her anxiety increased. It was a grey complex squatting on the outskirts of the city. The road had led them to the concrete perimeter wall, built in haste to keep foreign terrorists out. Or so they said. Sophie strained her neck to see the curls of razor wire connecting each security watchtower, and inside those towers, guards surveilled the patients and staff locked within the walls; a prison cloaked within the facade of a hospital. She flicked a worried glance across to Finn, but his eyes were shut.

Christopher did not slow the car as they passed the entrance. Confused, she leant forward, holding onto the back of the driver's seat, and whispered, 'Christopher, the entrance is back there.'

'Your dad suggested I drop you outside the patriot gatehouse, it would be less conspicuous. Not too many black limos stop outside the DIA entrance.'

If Finn had heard their brief discussion, then he did not

react. That came as no surprise to Sophie. When she made any comment about the flu crisis, he would leave the room, saying he was tired. Such is the exhausting nature of fear.

Christopher stopped the car and, like the dutiful chauffeur he was, held open the door for Sophie. She took in the Albian gatehouse. The watchtowers with its gun-toting guards were replaced with huge planters, each sporting an enormous mahonia, and instead of razor wire, a leafless wisteria wound its way up the wall and along the top. A large sign proudly welcomed Albian patriots to the 'World Class Facility'. Sophie was transfixed by the sign, barely noticing Finn had joined her. He held out his hand. She removed her glove and slid her warm hand into his.

'If you follow the path around the perimeter, you will eventually get to the entrance you need. I'll drive to the shopping village and wait with the other chauffeurs, no one will bat an eyelid. Text my pager when you need me, OK?' said Christopher.

Sophie nodded, afraid to speak out loud.

'Good luck, Dr Sheehan,' he added. Sophie felt Finn's fingers tighten around her hand.

'Thank you, Professor Halmeer,' replied Finn.

The closer they got to the DIA entrance the more prevalent the guards became. About a dozen or so were directing DIAs who had disembarked from the bus, ordering them into queues. Sophie let out a small sigh of relief. Those guards were in the green uniforms of the medical corps, there was no sign of ASSU's ominous black.

Bleep-bleeping of bangles being checked drowned out the scant murmurs in the queue. Ahead of them, guards directed accompanying Albian spouses to the payment and registration centre. Other guards escorted DIAs to an entrance on the left.

While Finn and Sophie waited in line, a luxury coach drove up. It halted by the entrance, its door slowly sliding open, automated steps lowered and two guards stepped on board. The guards were talking, gesticulating to the building. The passengers were nodding their heads, turning to see where they were heading. Unlike the people queueing, no one looked frightened, it was more of a perplexed expression by some and reassured nods from others. They got off and waved them through, watching as the coach disappeared into the vast complex. One of the guards laughed as he returned to the gate. There was a malevolence to it that added to the sinister nature of the place. She brushed it away, blaming her overactive imagination. But, then again why had her dad given her all those instructions?

Finn stifled a cough into his handkerchief. She squeezed his hand, asking him if he felt OK. He nodded. Henry had said it might take months to fully regain his health, and he had certainly improved from five weeks previous, when she feared he would be yet another statistic on the Daily Briefing.

'Bangle!'

Sophie jumped at the command. Finn obeyed the guard and held up his wrist.

'Got an MI, what's the procedure for them?' the young guard shouted.

The other guard didn't even bother to look up, continuing to tap out details on his tablet.

'Same as the others. Gimme the number.'

'568216/2/MI.'

'OK.' He pushed his arm between Finn and Sophie, forcing Finn to step aside. 'Prisoner 568216, stand over there with the others. You Miss, go straight on to Payments and Registration.'

That word, *'prisoner'*, sent an iced shiver through

Sophie. Paralysed to the spot, she watched her husband take his place in the line. It was easy to forget his prisoner status, and that 568216/2/MI was his official prisoner number.

'Move along, got others to check in,' the guard barked at Sophie.

The guard was in his early twenties if that, given the pimples on his face, just carrying out orders. At that moment she felt capable of snatching the tablet off him and slamming it into his face. Ignoring her father's warning to remain polite, she snapped back, 'My husband is of Ministerial Interest, he has special privileges, he's not a prisoner.'

He looked up, ignoring her indignant glower. 'All prisoners are treated equally here. Now move on, Miss.' The visible grasping of his nightstick indicated his next action if she failed to comply.

Defeated, she followed the others into a building opposite the entrance. Sophie collected her number and checked the room for necessary information. Along one wall was a row of about a dozen desks, glass screens separating the clerks from the DIA spouses. Above each desk a red lit number and on the opposite wall, a screen stating which desk the next number should attend. Sophie looked at the piece of paper, 134. The number on the screen said 68.

More people arrived behind her, elbowing their way to a space where they could watch the screen. Each clutching the scrap of paper like a lucky lottery ticket, willing their number to come up. At the desk an elderly man was crying. Clearly hard of hearing, he had failed to understand how to use the headset. The clerk opened a little window in the glass, talking slowly and loud enough for the room to overhear the sad story. The old man couldn't afford the release fee. There was no sympathy from the guard, he just repeated the standard statement from the prepared script.

'If deemed fit to return to society, the prisoner will be kept here for thirty days or until you have the funds for the release fee. If, after thirty days the prisoner is not claimed, then the prisoner will be passed onto Repatriation.'

He might have been talking about a lost dog or a wallet, not an elderly man's wife, his life partner. Sophie turned away.

After nearly two hours of waiting, Sophie's number appeared on the screen. Her back hurt from standing so long in the high heeled court shoes she rarely wore, but sitting was not an option, there were no chairs. The clerk on the other side of the glass indicated to Sophie to put on the headset. She did so and heard him ask for Finn's DIA number.

'568216/2/MI, Mi—'

He interrupted her before she finished, 'I only need the number. Your MI is the first we've had for a while.'

There were unseen taps on a keyboard as he retrieved Finn's file on the computer. His facial expression changed. Unease rose within Sophie, compounded when the clerk left his seat to seek assistance from a guard behind him. Both of the men studied the screen then peered at Sophie. The clerk switched off the intercom to her headset, their deliberations kept secret. A senior guard quickly joined the mime, his flaying arm indicating to the clerk to move. He switched the intercom back on and spoke, 'This prisoner is unmarried according to his file. Or rather there is no mention of a spouse. Who exactly are you?'

'I am his wife. Look, here's my wedding certificate.' Sophie pulled the certificate from her handbag and held it flat against the glass, barely breathing as she waited for a response.

The guard peered at the certificate. 'Miss Smith is it?'

'Yes, yes.' Sophie was also nodding, hoping her physical and verbal affirmations would reassure the guard and speed up the process. On the other side of the glass screen, the suspicious guard seemed less concerned by her urgency.

'We regularly see forgeries of certificates, Miss. It is a well-used method by the insurgents. Find a gullible patriot woman and convince her to be a pretend wife. It seems this particular "husband" has been found out.'

Sophie started to panic; this was not meant to happen. She had to persuade the guard that Finn truly was her husband, rushing out her response, 'Ask the Minister for the Interior, he'll confirm it, he attended our wedding. My own father is Tim Smith, the Foreign Minister. Please, you have to believe me.'

The guard did not reply. Sophie lowered the certificate, unable to judge his face. In truth, she had no idea what her father had ordered, or whether her name had been removed from all files, not just Finn's public file.

'If the prisoner is your husband, as an MI, his details should be held on an Interior Ministry file.' The senior officer's face softened, adding, 'It's not strictly procedure but seeing how your father is Mr Smith, I'll get someone to call and check. It may take a while.'

Sophie smiled back at him. 'Yes, thank you, thank you.' She didn't care how long it took as long as her details were on that file.

'If you've been lying and your name is not registered as his spouse, then he'll be arrested under the Terrorism Act.' The harshness had returned, and he was jabbing a finger at her, tapping the glass with his nail. 'You understand the consequences for you, don't you? Aiding an insurgent is a felony. It's treason. If you confess now and show he's being coercing you, then the authorities can be a little more lenient. Would you like to confess, Miss Smith?'

'I have nothing to confess. Michael Finlay is my husband.'

'Don't say you weren't warned. Take a number and we'll attend to you later.'

The room was just as crowded as when she first walked in. The number on the screen had reached 142. She ripped off a new ticket, 265. There would be plenty of time to call her father, and tip him off about the misunderstanding.

Two hours later she could taste the powerlessness and abandonment that had been her husband's staple for the past six years. Her bottom lip had become sore from nervous chewing. She checked her phone once more, nothing. Sophie's messages and texts to her father had remained unanswered. It was too late, her number flashed on the screen. Sophie hurried to the desk, checking the exits, there were no guards approaching her, but maybe they were on their way, handcuffs prepared and with Finn already standing in front of the firing squad.

Sophie slid on the headset, dreading his voice. It crackled slightly as the senior officer switched on the intercom.

'I thought I'd deal with this case myself. It seems your story has been verified and we can proceed with the registration and payment.'

Relief brought a flurry of emotions. She grabbed hold of the desk to steady her buckling knees. Finn was alive. Behind the screen, she noticed he was turning the monitor to face her.

'Please confirm this prisoner is your DIA?'

Sophie's face reddened and the tears she had been holding back escaped on seeing Finn's picture, complete with his prisoner number below. It was too much. They weren't in a Treatment Centre. It was a dehumanising factory. Her voice barely audible, she replied to the guard, 'Yes, that's my husband.'

'You have to pay one thousand now or the prisoner can be held for thirty days if fit, while you secure further funds.'

'No, I have the money.' She pushed her bank card

through a slot and completed the transaction. His illness had depleted their savings, but there was no choice. At least they did have savings.

She was herded to another waiting room which was equally cramped and told to wait with the others until Finn's number appeared on the screen above. Her eyes were aching from staring at it. The numbers blurred, and she blinked to re-focus, but Finn's number did not appear. She began to gear herself up with the expectation of a guard arriving, telling her there had been a mistake, Finn had been shot for being a terrorist and she was going to be arrested. It didn't happen. After several hours his number lit up on the screen followed by "Interview room 4". Sophie half walked and half ran along the corridor to the room, ignoring the heavy smell of antiseptic as she checked the number on each door along the way. And there were only numbers, no consultant names, no department information, nothing that might suggest what went on behind those dark, glossy green doors. Here there was only secrecy. At the door of Interview Room 4, Sophie knocked and prepared herself for the next ordeal.

Officer Enright was a rotund, balding man, his green uniform far too small for him. The buttons on his jacket were straining to be released from the pressure of holding back his ripples of fat. He reigned over his desk like a toad waiting to flick out his tongue at a passing fly or an unfortunate DIA.

'Miss Sophie Smith?' he said in a voice that was comically high pitched for such a round man. 'So, we've had fun and games with this file, haven't we? Tell me, why the secrecy? Why doesn't your name appear on the prisoner's file?'

The toad liked to get down to business, no *'How do you do?'* or *'Please take a seat.'* Sophie ignored his lack of manners, sat down, placed her bag on the floor and crossed her ankles, smiling politely at Officer Enright before replying, 'It clearly states on his file that my husband is an MI, the removal of my name from the file is for security reasons. If you wish to find out more, you should contact the Minister for Internal Affairs.'

The toad eyed her suspiciously. Sophie genuinely did not know the reason and assumed it was to prevent embarrassment for her father, but she had no intention of using that as an explanation. All these men needed to know was that Finn was legitimately married to her.

Officer Enright huffed and continued to tap on the tablet, the only sound in the room until he cleared his throat for the interview.

'The prisoner has had his blood and other bodily fluids tested and appears to be clear of the virus. We carried out a series of stamina and lung function tests which he passed, but it was borderline. Did your husband develop any complications during his illness, pneumonia for example?'

Sophie shook her head. She knew which lies to perpetuate. 'Can we go home now?' she asked, itching to leave that nightmarish centre.

The officer ignored her question and prodded the tablet with a chipolata finger. Without looking up, he said, 'Given the number of visits by Dr Thatcher and the results from the tests, I am surprised he was not admitted to the centre as per regulations.' Dark eyes stared straight through Sophie daring her to lie. She paused for longer than he expected. 'Well, do you have an answer?'

Get it wrong and it would not only be Henry in trouble. She returned his glare with a wide-eyed innocence. 'Oh well, I suppose we were fortunate that Finn's fever didn't really develop beyond the first twenty-four hours and I was able to control his cough with a herbal remedy.'

'So, why the doctor visits? Do you have money to burn?'

'Oh no, of course not, it just that Henry, Dr Thatcher that is, well, you see he's an old friend of mine and also my employer. He wasn't treating Finn as such, but he did drop by to check on me. He's a very caring man, you see, and he is such a stickler for procedure. So, in accordance with current regulations, he logged all his visits, even though we were just chatting in the kitchen. Most times he didn't even see Finn.'

Officer Enright read the notes again. The medical officer appeared suitably confused but, much to Sophie's satisfaction, he did not question her further. His hand slid across the desk to press a button, leaving a sweaty trail behind on the dark leather. A few minutes later a door to the side opened and a guard entered with Finn, his own clothes were gone, and he was wearing a dark-green, prison uniform. On the top was written "Property of the Albian State Prison Service". It was hard to know if it meant the item of clothing or the man inside. Handcuffed and his ankles shackled, he was led to a wooden bench to the side of the room. Sophie tried to give him a loving smile, but he did not look at her, focusing instead on the buildings outside the window.

A young guard stood by Finn, his vicious smirk leaving Sophie in no doubt that her husband had endured hours of base humiliation. She took him in, from the shoes on his feet to the ginger hair peeking out from under his cap; the young image of her enemy. Sophie was seething.

'Are the handcuffs really necessary? Isn't this just a health check?' she said turning back to the comical amphibian before her.

The toad replied that procedure must be followed at all times. He cleared his throat again, 'I have a question, Miss Smith.'

Sophie had been waiting for this one. Always the same question. Henry had asked her about it the first time he met Finn.

'The injuries to his wrists? There is unusually little

information on his file. It just says he had an accident when he was twenty-five. Can you elaborate?'

The insinuation was obvious, and her practised response was ready. 'If you click on the incident it clearly states my husband was cleaning the greenhouse when some glass broke, injuring his wrists. Our friend, Captain Yossarian was present and gave him first aid. As a fully qualified nurse, I was also able to help. There was no need to take him to hospital and so, there is no medical record of the incident. Captain Yossarian provided a witness statement after the Alien Registration Act came into force.'

He gave her a look of utter disbelief, before tapping on the item and seeing the statement, the stamp of New Albany emblazoned across the middle. Sophie knew he could not doubt the evidence no matter how unbelievable.

Officer Enright continued to delve into the online notes. He stopped swiping, his finger hovering above the screen, then he sat up with satisfied smugness. 'I see you have no children and the prisoner had mumps aged thirty-four. You've not had him undergo a fertility test, have you?'

'No, I don't believe it is obligatory quite yet.'

He pointed out that complimentary testing was available in the centre. An infertile result making an annulment automatic, adding, 'Miss Smith, you are a pretty woman. You'd have no trouble getting yourself a good patriot man. I am currently looking myself.'

The portly officer left his desk, pulling a chair across with him. He sat down next to her, his damp palm rubbing her knee, the heat and moisture seeping through the fabric onto her skin. She would have pushed it off, but that may have antagonised him. The release document needed to be authorised. A rhythmic rattling of shackles informed her that Finn was watching them.

Both her father and Sergeant Mason had warned her about the more irregular aspects of the health check, and she had prepared in advance. Sophie had tied a ribbon in her dark hair and the top buttons on her blouse had been left open. A borrowed pearl necklace highlighted the base of her neck. Her high heels and hideous navy skirt completed the uniform of a dutiful patriot woman. Her father's advice rang in her ears, '*You must show submission at all times.*'

Sophie tipped her head down and looked at the officer through her lashes. 'Oh my, well Officer Enright, if I am ever in a situation where I require a new husband, I shall certainly put you on my list.' Sophie worried the buttons on his uniform would pop off as he puffed out his chest. 'Oh, dear Officer Enright, I wonder if you might help me?' She picked up her handbag and pulled out a thick brown envelope. I understand there is a charity run through the Treatment Centre for the widows and orphans of our brave guardsmen killed fighting the insurgency.'

Officer Enright nodded. His eyes were firmly fixed on the area where her blouse spread open, his brain incapable of simultaneous speech and sexual titillation.

'I have a donation for the fund. If I give it to you, would you be an absolute sweetheart and give it to the appropriate person?' she continued.

He held out his hand for the envelope, clasping it greedily, before slipping it inside his jacket pocket and returning to the desk. To her right a printer whirled into life, spewing out a sheet of paper that came to rest at her feet, 'CONDITIONAL RELEASE' printed in bold red type at the top. Sophie picked up the sheet of paper and looked at the officer. The simpering smile had vanished.

Officer Enright sat back in his chair, elbows on the desk and his multiple chins resting on the back of his hand. 'As the prisoner only just passed the lung function test, he is required to have a repeat health check in six months' time. So, Miss Smith, we will be seeing each other again.' He grinned at her, pulled out a drawer from his desk and wrote down his name and mobile number on a leaflet. 'Here, take this.'

Sophie looked at the leaflet, "Four Easy Steps to Annulment". Her act had gone too far and had provided him with expectations.

'Don't waste time though, you're already damaged goods. Leave it much longer and you'll be of no use to anyone.' He loomed over her with intimidating proximity, his rancid breath sticking to her throat as he spoke, 'We like our women young, healthy and unsullied. Although, in your case, as a former elite, I am prepared to overlook that.'

Ignoring his comment, Sophie stood to leave. 'Where should we go to collect my husband's things?'

The officer indicated to the guard to take Finn away. Sophie assumed the sole reason for his presence was to witness an odious creature lust over her, while she used their savings to buy back his limited freedom.

'They'll take him to the Collection Room.' Officer Enright held out his hand, wiping them on his trousers when Sophie did not motion to take it. 'Hmm, well you must be in a hurry. Goodbye Miss Smith, but I look forward to seeing you again in the Summer if not sooner.'

The Collection Room was empty, save for a sole guard at a desk. She wondered about the other DIAs who had arrived with Finn. Surely some of them were fit enough to return home. Sophie contacted Christopher, who replied he would be waiting for them at the Albian Entrance, then proceeded to stare at the clock on the wall, every passing second increasing her anxiety that something had gone wrong. A buzzer sounded, making her jump. Irritated by the interruption, the guard slammed his paperback on the desk and stomped to the door. Finn was back in his own clothes, although his arms remained handcuffed. She couldn't stop smiling at him and had to be asked twice before even noticing the guard pushing a tablet at her.

'You gotta sign this, Miss.'

Her finger slid across the screen leaving nothing more than a hurried scribble.

They did not speak on the short walk back to Christopher. Her father's chauffeur had spotted them and was holding the car door open. Finn got in first, but when Sophie bent to get in, Christopher grabbed her arm, keeping her back.

'How was it?'

Sophie shook her head, unable to speak. Sliding into the car, Christopher closed the door gently behind her. Through the tinted glass, Sophie saw him standing guard. He understood silence so well. He was ensuring the couple a rare moment of privacy in a public place. She shuffled across the leather seat and held her husband in her arms, kissed him and lied that he'd be fine. He'd get over it. Finn buried his face into her shoulder. It wasn't long before Sophie felt his warm tears seep through her blouse and onto her skin.

FINN

* * *

Tuesday 19ᵗʰ January

He's due back today. It's been six long weeks. I can hardly wait. Funny how you can miss someone, even a DIA.

* * *

Finn settled back into his regular routine of home, work and Miss Fry. He loathed the thought of returning, but they simply could not afford for him to renege on his contract with the Commandant. His illness had been expensive, not just in lost pay, but also the cost of Henry's visits. Added to that expense came the medical check. He didn't even want to think of the bribes paid by his father-in-law. He needed to recoup their lost savings. It was his fault and tutoring Miss Fry was the solution. Undoubtedly, she would use the knowledge about his daughter to her advantage. Stay calm, get on with the lesson. Ignore the games. The past had happened, and he was powerless to change it.

He walked up the stairs to her sitting-room unaccompanied, Mr Johan was nowhere to be seen. Had he gone home, repatriated? Or was he one of the victims, another corpse to be removed. Finn faced the double doors of her sitting-room, contemplating the joy of Mr Johan's escape. He took a deep breath to banish the thought, then rapped his knuckles against the wood.

'568216! I missed you!' Cat hurried to the door as he entered her sitting-room. She wrapped her arms around him trapping him in her hug, then took a step back, holding on to his arm to manoeuvre him this way then that, inspecting every aspect of his physical being. He did not flinch nor try to stop her. He was too tired for that.

'You're so thin. I can almost feel your ribs through your shirt. I shall have to ask for extra cake, fatten you up.' She laughed at her own comment. Finn merely acknowledged her with a slight nod. He just wanted to get on with the lesson, but Catherine would not let him go. 'I am so glad you are back. How will I pass my exam without you?'

'I'm sorry you were inconvenienced.' He turned towards the table, his cheeks flushed. 'We'll need to concentrate if we are to catch up on the missed weeks.' If he emphasised the need for hard work maybe she would stay on topic and they might avoid "Lolita". 'Did you finish reading "Emma", we ought to end that topic, so we can move onto "Sense and Sensibility".'

'I have.' She was still holding his arm. 'Have you noticed how often a heroine marries the older, wiser man in Jane's novels? Perhaps she is trying to say something.'

'Certainly true in "Emma", Mr Knightly is the voice of reason against Emma's meddling.'

Releasing him, Cat followed Finn to the table, took her seat and stretched out to touch his hand. 'And are you my Mr Knightly?'

He had not expected the change in direction, and finding himself floundering, it took him a moment or two to think of a safe response. 'Mr Knightly was a wealthy bachelor, I am a married DIA. I am not Mr Knightly.'

'You're wrong, you are whatever I say you are, 568216.'

How could he contradict her? He was her creature, kept

on a short leash. If he pulled away, she would yank him back until he acquiesced to her whims. Johan was the lucky one. He had escaped the leash.

'Do you know, 568216, I actually prayed for you. Isn't that funny? I'd ignore those interminable sermons, shutting my eyes to think of you.'

Finn pulled his hand away. 'We should move onto "Sense and Sensibility", time is short.' He opened the book ready to start the masquerade of a tutor session.

'Is that it? Aren't you going to thank me?' she leant towards Finn adding in a low voice, tinged with a hint of anger, 'I prostituted my honour to pray for you, I expect your gratitude.'

Finn murmured his thanks while his soul lay crushed beneath her words.

'I want you to read it to me!' she declared, leaving the table to sprawl across her sofa.

He turned to the opening chapter and began reading. Obedience, the sole requirement from his young mistress.

'I can hear your accent. You hide it well most of the time, but when you are nervous it comes out more strongly. Are you nervous? Do I scare you?'

Finn stopped, took another deep breath and continued reading, his slight accent evident in every word.

'Did your wife give you elocution lessons? Were you trying to hide your identity? I can't imagine being her parents, the shock, the disgrace. Were the lessons to soften their horror? If he sounds normal, then they could pretend he is normal. You're not, though are you? You can never be normal.'

He stopped reading again, but his eyes remained fixed on the page. The letters were replaced with images of his past. When he resumed, his accent was crystal clear.

SOPHIE

Exhaustion ruled both of their lives. Finn from nights of insomnia and when he did sleep, nightmares. Sophie had her nights disturbed by Finn tossing and turning, trying to find the sleep that eluded him. Escaping into the grey light of pre-dawn, he'd leave her alone in their bed, cuddling a pillow instead of a husband. Some nights she was too shattered to care. Other nights, riddled with panic, she'd follow him downstairs, finding him cocooned in blankets on the steamer chair outside, his outline visible beneath the bare arms of the apple trees arching over him.

'Another nightmare?' she asked.

He nodded and opened up the blanket, welcoming her onto the chair with him. It was as close as they had been in months. They cuddled in silence, waiting for the robin's song. He obliged, perched on the branch serenading his friendly gardeners.

'I should sleep in the guest room, until I feel better at least. You look so tired. It's my fault,' Finn said, snuggling his wife into him.

Sophie tried to remain calm, dismissing his decision. 'Don't be ridiculous, it's not your fault. You've been ill. Very ill. I nearly lost you. No, I don't want you sleeping away from me. I want to hold you, cherish you, love you.'

'No, it is for the best. I'll sleep in the guest room. It will only be temporary.'

Her blank eyes examined the world beyond the window. Crocuses that once would prick her senses, gently rousing her from winter hibernation, had become no more than corrupted dots and dashes. The code made no sense, rebirth had been hijacked.

It was the missing smile. It was a hand feeling his ribs on the rare occasions he actually allowed her to come close. They existed in the realm of unspoken words and closed doors, living out each day distracted by the concerns of everyday life. Within the formaldehyde atmosphere of the Bridge Tea Room, she closed her eyes, praying that the man she married might one day return to her.

'So much to do, so little time!' Michelle took her seat next to Sophie at the little table, five large bags deposited into the space between them.

'What's the event?' Sophie moved the bags out of the way of a passing waitress.

'Your father's birthday of course, it's just five months away. I want to hold a gathering at the house, get all the right people there. You know, like we used to do when you were younger.'

Sophie had forgotten about her father's seventieth, her mood darkening with thoughts of the coming months interrupted with her mother's complaints. She had no interest in any party.

'Well at least pretend to listen, he is your father after all.'

'Sorry Mum, mind's elsewhere,' Sophie lied. 'I'm due to go on a course in April, I was just thinking about that.'

'More work, and you already look so tired. It's not a course you should be going on, but a holiday. When was the last time you had a break of any sort?' Michelle picked up the menu, delighting at the return of coffee caramel fancies. 'Oh goodie, can't remember the last time these were on the menu. Yes, a holiday would do you good. Tell Henry you need time off, Daddy can insist if you like.'

'No Mum, it's immoral. I can't leave at the drop of a hat

to swan off to the beach just because my father is something in the government.'

'Well, you shouldn't be working. Not someone like you. He is making you old before your time. A skivvy running after him. I'm not sure which of the two of you looked worse at Christmas.'

Sophie was too tired to keep her temper, even in The Bridge Tea Room. 'If you are going to have a go at Finn, I'll leave right now. I just need to know if I can stay at yours during the course or if I need to book a room at the centre.'

Michelle waved her gloved hand acknowledging her defeat. Finn was off limits. 'Is the course at Court Farm?'

Sophie gave the dates while her mother wrote them down in a diary. The authorities held the past as an ideal, or more accurately, elements of the past that suited the current agenda. They all possessed mobiles, but Albian ladies preferred pen and paper for communication. Traditions hand-picked to mirror the government's preferred story, and their patriots followed it with religious zeal. That particular custom held an unintended attraction for ladies who wished to avoid digital snooping; that of paper burning so easily.

'They're weekdays, aren't they? It's not a problem, your room is always ready, but won't Finn be working, it's just after the Easter break.'

Sophie was baffled, assuming it was her lack of sleep that made things confusing. 'Of course, he'll be working. He tutors on those nights and there's no way he'd be going anywhere else. Rumour has it the new Commandant has a fiery temper, and Finn isn't the sort to risk annoyance.'

'I merely wondered who'd be looking after him if you're at home with us. Is he allowed to be left alone, you know, what with all the new rules?'

She burst out laughing. 'Oh Mum, he's forty and perfectly

capable of looking after himself,' she replied, after regaining her composure. 'Quite frankly, he's the better cook, so he'll possibly eat something while I'm away.'

Her laughter belied the fact that she was concerned and had toyed with the idea of asking George to pop in after work, have a glass of wine, play chess, anything to reassure her that her husband was at home, alive and well.

'Funny to think of him as the Commandant.' Sophie's mother pulled off her gloves, flattening them neatly on the table before laying the salmon pink napkin on her lap.

Once Michelle's little theatrics were complete, Sophie asked her mother the question she was expecting, 'Who, Finn?'

'No silly, Commandant Fry. You met him. He was Captain Fry back then. Don't you remember?'

'No, not at all.'

'Oh, you must do, he was seconded to your father's office for six months. He came to the house quite often.'

'Officers came to the house all the time, how am I supposed to remember one random captain?'

Michelle smirked, responding in a low and suggestive voice, 'Well I'm sure he remembers you. Bit of a high-flyer according to Daddy, definitely ambitious. I bet he'll end up in the Government before long. I remember him chatting to you at one of Daddy's summer parties. You were such a jolly teenager back then. All those eligible men lining up to talk to you.'

'That's not how I remember the parties. I remember dull people talking politics and trying to figure out how to climb the greasy pole to the top of the pile. Daddy did well out of those parties.'

Michelle ignored her daughter's barbed comments. 'Well, Captain Fry spoke highly of you, to the point of asking Daddy if he might court you.'

'Court me!' Sophie snorted her tea out with the words. 'What century is that man from? Nobody 'courted' back then, and if he wanted to 'court' me, then presumably, I should have been the one asked. It would have been my decision after all.'

She had learnt long ago to read her mother's mind, and the uncomfortable silence spoke of the disappointment she had become. Sophie, their difficult daughter, stubborn and argumentative and Michelle, the mother berating herself for lack of discipline, unable to compete with the indulgent father. She was their rebel, their independent streak, their only child who opted for the daily danger of being a DIA's wife in preference to the Albian alternative.

Michelle ate one of the tiny cakes laid before her, then, just as she was about to continue sipping, replaced the cup onto the saucer. 'You know, Sophia, some parents were already arranging marriages, even at that time, look at your Auntie Emma's boy, Jack. That marriage was arranged, and it has been a success.'

'In New Albany all marriages are a success, Mum, even when they are not.'

'Given they have six sons we can assume they are contented,' replied Michelle.

'That assumes she consents each time.'

'Don't be ridiculous, Sophie. I won't even entertain that monstrous idea.'

'Why not? It's not illegal. Even says so in the marriage contract that we must obey our husband's will, and honour his name through the procreation of sons.'

Michelle's cheeks flushed, murmuring into her cup, 'If that's what the law says, then who are we to disobey.'

'You didn't have any sons though, did you, Mother?' Spitefulness came easily to Sophie when sleep deprived.

'You were a difficult pregnancy, you know that. I couldn't have any more after you.'

A pause broke the burgeoning row. Sophie's stomach churned as she replayed her last comment. Her mother had always refused to discuss her pregnancy, ending every attempt with the same line. The heat of anxiety filled her, would she be like her mother too? That rising guilt was swotted away with her mother's determination to excuse New Albany's beliefs.

'Jack is a decent man, he would never stoop that low, unlike those Immis. I can only imagine what they'd do if they don't get their own way.'

'Really?'

Sophie pondered the contents of her bag, her infamous *'pharmacy'*. Pills to help the teenage bride relax on honeymoon, even if that meant she lacked any recollection afterwards. Sometimes it was the young and not so young bridegroom requesting some extra help to ensure there would be no doubt about their virility. Pills freely available to patriots only, providing a means for consensual intercourse, even when that consent was a chemical lie.

Michelle would not be swayed. 'It is a proven fact; mixed marriages fail all the time. They are still failing. How many annul their vows, or DIAs abandoning their family for repatriation? No, mixed marriages don't work. Finn is a sweet man, but your marriage will fail one day, it's inevitable.'

Guilt driven heat intensified, scorching Sophie's conscience. Her hat band felt tight, restricting. She wanted to fling it off and push her hands through her hair. Was it really so bad to read those pamphlets in the surgery? She knew she loved him, utterly and completely. There was nothing wrong reading up about the annulment process, given it was her job to advise others. It was her duty to find out about it, surely?

Each thumping beat of her pulsating heart contradicted her apologetic logic. The only way to silence it would be to move on. 'So, tell me, Mum, what happened? Why aren't I hitched to that mighty Adonis, Captain Fry?'

'Oh, you know, Daddy being Daddy again.' Her mother's body relaxed as she waved her hands about with the happy memories. 'You wanted to go away to nursing school, and of course Daddy agreed.

'Oh, you did love dressing up as a doctor so much when you were a little girl. I can see you now, scampering about the garden, wrapping my hand in ribbon bandages and insisting on taking Christopher's temperature. You were such a little poppet. It really did make me laugh when you played Dr Smith.' Michelle picked up another miniature fancy and popped it into her mouth, closing her eyes to savour the rare treat. She swallowed and dabbed her lips. 'I supposed we were all a bit indulgent of your fantasies, but it was mostly Daddy. No one can compete for his affections quite like you. You had him wrapped around your little finger from the first moment he felt you kick me in the womb.'

Sophie waggled her little finger. 'I know. He obviously gave the Captain his marching orders to protect me from death through boredom.'

'Daddy wanted you to finish your studies, that's all. Daft really, he knew once you had children you wouldn't be working. From what your father said, the Captain was furious, made all sorts of threats, baseless of course. I believe he married some other girl just a few months later.'

'Is he still married to her? Finn hasn't mentioned any Mrs Fry.'

'No, she died in childbirth.' Michelle touched Sophie's hand. 'Remarkably, despite his threats, he then asked for your hand again. His poor wife's body was still warm, but you had married Finn by then, so that was that. Shame, he's extremely wealthy according to Auntie Emma, and eligible.'

'I married the man I loved.' Sophie pulled her hand back from her mother. 'Life was far less complicated back then. No restrictions, no curfews, no Internment Agreement. If I could turn the clock back, knowing what our lives have become, then I doubt I would have married him.'

Michelle grabbed her daughter's hand once more, her grip tighter, her voice rapid with excitement, 'You can still annul it, it's your right. I hear the guards are very efficient once papers have been signed.'

Sophie's reply echoed the blame she had been harbouring for the past ten years, 'I wouldn't have married him, not because I don't love him, but precisely because I do. I love him, I love him very much, but I am selfish. I keep him here. Imagine who he'd be now if he had left at the end of his studies as he intended. He married me and is forced to slave away for New Albany. He is a prisoner for goodness sake! I married him out of self-interest, and I regret it.'

Sophie felt the coal black of her mother's eyes boring into her, searching out the truth behind her confession. 'Is Finn unwell again?'

'No, he's fully recovered, fighting fit, just without the fight.'

Her mother's expression made Sophie stop. Michelle would not be sympathetic to Finn's depression. It would be another sign of his failure as a husband.

'I wasn't talking about his physical state, is Finn unwell? Is he having another of his little episodes?'

Her parents had witnessed his bouts of anxiety, collaborating with their daughter by referring to their son-in-law as *'A shy soul'*. The scars on his wrists a testament to his lack of moral fibre, in her mother's opinion at least. Her father stayed silent and hid the truth.

'In all likelihood it's a mild depression following his illness,' she answered. Lying had become second nature to Sophie. Use just enough truth to make the lie plausible. 'Henry says he was very lucky to survive. Many didn't. Maybe it's guilt, who knows, but he is getting better. He'll be fine in no time, he loves the Spring. Don't worry, he'll be as right as rain by the time we come to stay.'

A STUDY IN LYING

TOLBRIDGE UNIVERSITY, AGED EIGHTEEN

I don't need to be a professor to pick out a multitude of inconsistencies in my argument. The letters lift off the screen in a jumbled mess and I pinch the bridge of my nose to halt the pain, but it persists, fanning out behind my eyes, reaching to the back of my head. A wave of nausea crashes over me and I rest on my elbows waiting for the sickness to dissipate.

Marcus spreads across the sofa, engrossed on his phone. His forehead wrinkles in irritation and judging from the frantic typing of his fingers, he is having yet another silent row with Katie. Their stormy relationship baffles me, one minute full on passion the next, sulks and tantrums.

'You could actually talk to her?' I say.

'Nah, she wants to watch a stupid RomCom. I'd rather clean the toilet with a toothbrush than spend two hours of my life watching her fawn over a ridiculous actor.'

'You sound jealous. Besides, a film's bound to be more amusing than babysitting me. I've got a headache, so I'll just head off to bed.'

'Don't you want to eat first, I was going to make a risotto?' offers Marcus, rolling off the battered sofa.

'Sure.'

I don't want to, but if I refuse, it will set Marcus off on another lecture about healthy eating. I've heard his speech that many times, I could probably say it word for word. It's just easier and far quieter to say yes. I'll silently vomit the meal back later. I've got good at that. Sometimes life is simpler when I lie.

Marcus is cheered by his minor victory, already heading to the kitchen, thumbs dancing across the phone screen. He calls back, 'Mushroom OK? Katie loves mushrooms and I'll even let her watch her bloody RomCom if she does the washing-up.'

FINN

'Do you think she was as kind and devoted as the plaque suggests? said Finn, fingering the brass plate.

Carl glanced up from his task of gathering daffodils. 'What's that you're saying, lad?'

'Eloise Philips. Do you think she's in Heaven watching over us, or in Hell, directing the demons of this world, giving them a list of daily humiliations to be performed on me?'

Carl sighed and headed to the bench where Finn was sitting. 'Here, take these to Soph, doubt the dead will mind.'

'Thanks,' he replied, taking the bouquet. He lay the buttery coloured blooms in the small space between them.

'You know what?' said Carl, 'You and I should stop imagining what the dead think and get on with living our own lives.' He picked up the daffodils and shuffled closer to Finn. 'Come on, let's have an evening together, just the two of us. I'll even drink some of that poison purporting to be wine.'

Finn laughed, while Carl hugged him, saying, 'At bloody last. Well they do say laughter is the best medicine.'

He lost his smile and shook his head. 'The only medicine available for people like me is toxic. To be honest when I'm not tutoring, I want to go home and veg. I'm not good company right now.'

Carl squeezed him within his arms. 'Nonsense, lad. You're being defeatist, you're letting them win.'

'Don't you get it, Carl. I lost years ago.'

Finn stood to leave, and as he reached for the daffodils, Carl grabbed his wrist. 'You've got to stop this. You're the lucky one with someone up top who likes you. I bet you'd even get away with murder.'

'Believe me Carl, there are plenty I would happily kill.'

'Hope I'm not on that list.' Carl released his wrist.

Finn shook his head once more. 'No, I could never hurt a daft old fool like you,' he said.

'Not so much of the old, thank you. Guess we ought to head back, they'll be ringing the bell soon.'

'I suppose so. According to that Officer Enright, I am fit enough to work, and that's what I must do.' A shiver ran through Finn and a couple of daffodils slipped from his hand. Instead of picking them up, he sat back down heavily, his hand covering his face as tears escaped, while the comforting weight of Carl's arm rested on his back.

The previous week, he had questioned Finn about the Treatment Centre. Initially, Finn refused to answer his questions, but Carl could be such a persistent bastard at times. Maybe Finn was at a particularly low ebb, or just worn down by his friend's doggedness, but eventually he had opened up, admitting his sense of guilt. That dark shadow of pain which he carried within him every waking moment because he had not been one of the other men. Carl had sat on their bench, unusually lost for words as Finn had recalled the humiliation of the health examinations. The smell of fear surrounding the quaking prisoners. Finn carried the burden of the protected DIA, with a wife who had the right connections, who uttered the right sycophantic words and who handed over the right sized bribe.

'Oh, now, come on Finn, lad. You're just a bit low, once Spring is here and you get a bit of sunshine, you'll see how much better you'll be,' Always trying to inject positivity where none could exist.

Finn emerged from behind his hands with red-rimmed

eyes, and his pale skin marked by digging fingers. Picking up his water bottle, he splashed his face, trying to eliminate the evidence of sadness. 'Sorry about that. Look, you go if you need to,' he said to Carl, who was checking his phone messages. 'I'll be fine, don't worry about me.'

'Nah. It's fine. Someone just wanted me to drop by, later. I'm not going anywhere. Come on, you're OK, now. It really isn't so bad, is it?'

'I'm a number, Carl. I am 568216/2/MI,' he said, accepting his lot. 'The boxes have been ticked and the number can get back to doing the job it has been allocated. I'm so lucky, so fortunate. I have a protector who makes sure the torture of life in this hell continues. You're right, I will be fit and happy just in time to be returned to the holding cell at the Treatment Centre, handcuffed and shackled, with my clothes, my identity all taken away. A prisoner, in prison clothes complete with my prisoner number. I am still in a prison. A comfortable prison, I grant you, but it is still a prison and Sophie has become my prison guard.'

'If you want to know what hell is really like, take a peek inside one of the Labour Camps,' Carl snapped back. 'I'll tell you one thing Michael Finlay, complaining about having a beautiful wife to care for you, having a warm bed to sleep in and food on the table, that's not prison. You'd never survive it.'

He stood up, making Finn regret his admission. 'Don't go, I'm sorry.' He tugged at Carl's sleeve. 'I wasn't thinking. Please stay.'

'I'm sorry too. It's OK to be sad, we all have sad days. Wouldn't be much of a best friend if I abandoned you at the first sign of self-pity, eh?' said Carl, sitting back down. 'You know, these restrictions are just one more over-reaction to an event. Pandemics happen, and governments have to take precautions. Just one of those things. But, you're better now—'

'I want to go home,' Finn blurted out.

'I thought you were teaching after lunch?'

'No, not cottage home, not home to Sophie. Back home, to my family, my parents, my brother, to Evie.' Finn's voice broke with emotion at saying his sister's name out loud.

'Christ Finn, are you talking about repatriation? What about Sophie, she'll be devastated.'

'It's a lie. *'Love conquers all'*, it's a lie. How can love grow and develop here? Every day there is another humiliation to absorb, but that's O.K. because we are in love. We can take it. The truth is we can't, nobody can. How is this a life for Sophie? She works long hours so that we can survive. Constantly insulted, being called a 'Slut', a 'Whore', all because she's married to me. She should be out enjoying her life, bringing up her children, going to the theatre, visiting friends, restriction free. If I stay, I will die, either slowly, driven to take my own life or by the State, one more foreign terrorist hanging from the gallows. Is that what I should do? Ruin the rest of her life? It neither matters whether I leave or die, sooner rather than later, Sophie will be left on her own.'

CAIRN TOP

MELBOROUGH MANOR HOUSE, AGED TWENTY-ONE

The earlier dawn wakes me, and sitting on the sofa in my bedroom, I contemplate Cairn Top. It glows beneath the morning haze, tempting me to venture out. There are no lectures until later this afternoon. Plenty of time for a ride to the top.

A breakfast of cookies and my water bottle filled, I write a quick note for Mrs McManus. I'll get an affectionate telling off and a plate full of sausage and eggs on my return.

I cycle along the private lane to the start of the track. It is stony and steep. Sweat builds upon my forehead. At the field by Lower Sheehan Wood, I stop for some water and watch the ewes with their newborn lambs. The blue of the sky, the green field and the white lambs. I am happy, almost euphoric. Everything is perfect. My tutor thinks I should do a Masters, maybe even a PhD at a foreign university. Dad says it is an interesting idea, one that I ought to consider. I discussed it with Sally, but like most therapists, she just asked, 'But what do you want?'.

Dad says I should speak some more to his friend, Dr Hargreaves. He wants me to go, have a fresh start, anonymity in a foreign land. I don't want to disappoint him again, but New Albany is so far from home.

I keep peddling, beads of moisture rolling down my back, while last night's conversation repeats in my head. Mum said nothing, I know she wants me to stay. Dad argues that it will be good for me, I can do it, I'm so much better now. He talked about me staying with Liam, a sort of halfway house.

I push further up the hill and work through excuses to stay. It's level here and I slow down, taking a breather. There are lambs in Copse Edge Field. I love watching them at this playful stage, but it is so short. They will leave their mothers soon. We must all leave our mothers and face becoming an adult one day.

At the top of the hill I lean my bike up against the oak tree. The field is bordered by a dry-stone wall. A wall I have helped maintain, just as my ancestors had done throughout the history of Sheehans in Melborough. My rural solitude is disturbed only by the breeze blowing against my ears. I can just about make out the engines of an aeroplane far off in the distance. I love it up here, that unique peace and freedom. Even when Dad joins me on the ride, he understands me enough to let me wallow in the silence. Sometimes we lie side by side, cloud watching. At first, he found it difficult, accepting my silence. I'd see him wipe away tears. I hurt him. I hurt them both. Now, it's changed, we have all recovered.

I breathe in the expansive view. Melborough village nestles in the valley, the spire of its church rising above the roofs. On Sundays, I hide behind the other choristers, invisible to the congregation. On the far side of the village is my home. This is my entire world. The prospect of leaving Melborough fills me with terror. I don't need Dr Hargreaves' sales pitch. That university had an amazing reputation, still does according to Liam. He reckons the press exaggerate. Tells me to ignore the reports. It would look good on my C.V and as Dad says, ultimately, I can always come home if it is a disaster. It tempts me, that prospect of stepping outside my Sheehan world. Finally, strong enough to fight back against the monsters that hold me prisoner. An adult, fit and able to follow my own chosen path.

FINN

He was virtually certain he would leave Sophie. It was for the best. He repeated the phrase, his daily mantra, silently chanting it to himself when she dressed for work, again when she kissed him goodbye, and then later once more, when she snuggled up to him on the sofa after a long day. He was doing the right thing, returning home to his parents. That was the only way to free her and give her the opportunity to live a life again. He'd do it before his father-in-law's birthday, that way Sophie could be consoled by all those eligible bachelors and widowers, whose names Michelle loved to drop into any conversation. She'd be happily married to one in no time and he would be but a memory. Leaving Sophie would be a kindness and the only way she could regain any form of happiness. The repatriation process was nothing but a formality; he just needed to request the form, fill it out this time, he would be home for the summer and the peace of Cairn Top Field would be waiting for him.

The only thing that was waiting for him at that particular moment was Catherine Fry. She would be sitting in her comfortable cell, anticipating his arrival. He wondered what ordeal she intended to place before him this time. It had become easier to deal with recently. He accepted her demands with smiles and dutiful obedience. The remaining terms would speed by, it was only four months until the exams and he would be free of her. Once back in Melborough, he would be at liberty to read whatever he liked, listen to whatever he wanted and to freely associate with whomever he pleased. He fantasised about going on holiday to the beach, do a bit of surfing, maybe take a road trip to see all the places he refused to visit when he was younger. It was impossible for his anxiety monsters to be any more terrifying than the living, breathing beasts of New Albany.

* * *

Tuesday 22nd February

I think I am in love. Her name is Connie Reid. I want to be her, live like her, taste the pleasure that lies beyond my grasp. I want her freedom. I want to be held by someone who loves and wants ME, not my name, not the power and position, but ME, just ME.

* * *

It was all about pretence. Finn, the actor with decades of experience. His current role; give life and body to 568216, the happy and relaxed tutor. He would master the part, regardless of the panic raging through him. He'd allowed the character to consume him, softening the edges of the torturous lesson. A portrayal steeped in method, obliterating the restrictions. The general audience were locked out of her sitting-room theatre, and he was alone, on her stage with no one listening, no one watching. A forgotten hour of freedom, three times a week.

The young Lolita had been usurped by the culture and finery of Connie Reid. Lawrence's heroine no more legal than Nabokov's. Finn was past caring and read the lines to make Cat wish she too could be that Lady Chatterley.

'Do you think her life was better than mine, 568216?' she asked him.

'It was a different time and we can't look at the past with

those famous rose-tinted glasses. There is good and bad with every era. Connie was privileged, as are you Miss Fry.'

'Privilege has its own price.' Cat sat up. 'Then again, why should you understand that?'

Finn reddened. He had strayed from the script. Ad lib was not permitted on this stage.

'You're right, Miss Fry, I don't know.'

His pupil nodded and lay back against the sofa arm, her head resting on her fur cushion and her legs stretched out along the full length of the chair. Finn, obedient as ever and back in character, continued reading. He was her comedian, her thespian, her automaton, wound up and made to perform. It was all temporary. His acting days would be over, and he would be free to retire from her stage. There would be no applause and no encore.

'Shall I continue reading?' he asked.

'No, I feel like music.'

Finn listened to his pupil hum along to the playlist she had selected with his toes involuntarily tapping out the beat, and at times, singing along too. The playful lyrics were placing him back into his playroom and his own playlists. Her hand slipped into his and pulled him up. He was not in his playroom and he was not free. His body tensed and his heart pounded to the beat. Catherine's cheek touched his, her voice humming into his ear. He jerked his head away.

'Don't you like my singing, 568216?'

'Um, yes. You have a tuneful voice, it's jus—'

'It's just what?' she interrupted. 'You've changed. I sense it and I can see it in your eyes too. They seem brighter, happier, you won't admit it, will you?'

'Admit what?'

'You enjoy spending your evenings with me.'

Finn did not answer but continued to hold her as they

danced. The act was consuming him. His performance was award winning.

* * *

Tuesday 2ⁿᵈ March

> *I hate my life. Why aren't I allowed to be who I want to be? Who decides my future? Daddy? I doubt it. There is so much unsaid yet understood. Daddy drinking in the club with this army general or that government minister. Am I the glorious prize, or the price to be paid for another man's glory?*

* * *

The weather was improving, but Cat kept the stove burning. The air in that sitting-room was suffocating. Even the iced water failed to refresh Finn. He counted down the minutes of the lesson while Cat ranted about the predictability of Jane's books.

'There is always the rotter,' she said. 'That character who seems delightful but will break at least one of the heroine's hearts. Then there is the mister right, who can't marry for one reason or another. Of course, we always need that one ridiculous person. The clown who doesn't know it.'

'Really? That is not how I see Jane. She wrote about life as she saw it, I always admired her for that. Don't you think she's criticising those people who laugh at superficial differences?' he asked, explaining himself by adding, 'I don't believe she means to make fun of her comical characters, only how circumstance can seem to belittle them.'

Cat snorted at his comments. 'Blaming circumstances is an excuse. They should seize their inner character and rise above other people's perceptions.'

Finn shook his head in disagreement. 'Those in power can make it very hard, if not impossible for others to achieve their full potential, especially when it might threaten the existence of the status quo. Jane did try, she was a middle-class lady. There were expectations, but she tried to break away.'

'Is that what you honestly think?'

Finn nodded. 'In a way, she was a feminist.'

'A feminist?' Cat lay her hand on his face, stroking it gently. 'Dear 568216, you are deluded if you believe that. All she writes about is finding the right marriage for her ladies, one which meets parental and society's approval.' She removed her hand and flicked through the pages of the book while continuing her rejection of his belief. 'The heroine is not allowed to run off with the charmer. It's no wonder her books are on the approved list. The Ministry view her books as a moral code for our young female patriots. You might think you have an independent streak but, in the end, life is all about who you marry. Look at Connie. Do you really think her father would have preferred her to marry Mellors over Clifford? Do you?'

Finn remained silent with images of his own marriage pushed to the fore of his thoughts.

'Your silence is telling, you believe in the status quo, that marriage is more than just a love match, don't you?' Cat persisted.

'No, I believe love is the guiding light within marriage, but there are times when even love struggles. Connie and Clifford could never have a full marriage, and Connie needed more.'

Finn attempted to push away the insidious thought that had burrowed into him, but even as he spoke the words, he realised it was right. He had become Clifford, impotent in every sense. They had married for love but what could he offer her within the Albian ideal? Another time, another place, the union would have been celebrated. By leaving her, he worried she might be forced to change, become another patriot wife and mother. There were moments of doubt, perhaps he shouldn't go, but his doubt was fleeting. He had to free her because he loved her. What happened afterwards would be her decision.

Cat threw her head back, as bored with Lady Chatterley as she was with Jane Austen.

'Why am I even being educated at all?'

'Education is imp—'

'Why, why is it important? So I can discuss the same dreary books with the other society wives? Do you imagine my husband will be interested on my views about Darcy and Caroline Bingley?'

'There's more to education than that.'

'Or am I being given a glimpse of what I won't have? A route to dissatisfaction.'

'No, why would you think that?'

'Because my future is carved into stone, that's why. Will my husband care that I fantasise about meeting my own Oliver Mellors? That I pretend to be Connie, thrilled by my lover instead of that oaf? Chances are he won't have read the book. Not suitable reading for our future officers.'

Finn listened to the frustration and resignation in her voice but could not find it in himself to pity her. Instead, he sympathised for the poor man who would become her husband. It would be unlikely that she would bend to him. The teenager needed a man sufficiently docile to be trained and controlled. Just as she controlled him.

Cat shut the book with a loud clap. 'I've had enough,' she said. 'So what does your wife do all day, given there are no children and she can hardly be accepted at society wives' coffee mornings, now can she?'

'She's a nurse, for a local surgery, mainly looking after the expectant mothers,' he answered, without thinking.

'Did she look after you when you were ill?'

'She did, and I am here to tutor you as a result,' said Finn, proud of his wife.

'Then I shall write her a note of thanks. I was worried about you. I enjoy our sessions, even if we do have to do Austen, but our little extras make the tedium worthwhile.'

DEADLY DECEPTION

Which is the deadliest of weapons? A knife, silently cutting through the veins of life? Or a bullet that shatters flesh and bones? Armaments increase in size, in power and in efficiency. Yet we are all capable of wielding deception with cold dispassion. Those soul wrecking deeds masquerading within acceptable excuses in order to present Machiavelli's gift.

SOPHIE

Sophie watched him while she cooked. He was almost relaxed. His foot was motionless and there was no clicking of his pen. Finn was still using the guest room, but at least he was sleeping. There had been fewer early morning trips to the steamer chairs under the apple trees.

He looked up from his marking, smiling at her. 'Dinner smells good, what are you making?' he asked.

She was surprised. His reluctance to eat properly and her frustrated nagging had led to multiple quarrels. 'It's a roast vegetable risotto.' Whatever the reason for the improved mood and appetite, Sophie was grateful. It certainly made the prospect of going away simpler. She had been wracking her brain as to what to do, even speaking to George. In his usual affable way, he offered his spare room for Finn.

'My wife is a fine cook,' George had said, rubbing his larger than average tummy. 'You won't recognise him by the time you return.'

Although a kind offer it was not going to work. She would have to trust him. Looking at her husband now, her main worry cleared from her mind.

'You remember I'll be away next week,' she said. 'I'm going to stay at Mum and Dad's while I'm on the course. It's only three nights and I'll be back Friday afternoon.'

'Lucky you. Yes, it's in my diary and I'm tutoring on those nights, so there'll be no time to miss you.'

He was fine, she was sure of it, but it did no harm to be extra cautious. 'Would you mind if George pops his head in before he goes off duty? He could text me you're home safe and sound.

You know how much I worry about your journey home.'

He laughed, nodding his head. 'Not a problem, but you'll need to leave plenty of cake.'

Sophie kissed his cheek. She had made the right decision and he was definitely better.

Sophie entered the cavernous reception room, along with all the other delegates on the various training courses. She knew Court Farm well, its grounds, her private playground before the guards occupied its hedgerows. However, the interior of the house remained a mystery to her. She marvelled at the ornate ceiling in the former ballroom, now a bland cafeteria, and imagined the startling colours of elegantly dressed revellers with their flirtatious commentary. All distant echoes lost among the fine details of the plasterwork high above the sullen heads of the uniformed medics.

The orientation desk issued Sophie with her badge and the programme for the two-day course. An elderly officer looked her up and down, then uttered a disapproving huff as he handed her the welcome pack. Sophie returned the man's scowl with a bright 'Thank you' and pinned her name tag on her blouse. Content with her minor rebellion she turned to leave only to find her exit blocked by the arm of a young guardsman. His uniform bore the Rod of Asclepius across his breast pocket, clearly denoting the medical corps. Sophie recoiled with memories of the guards at the Treatment Centre. He looked so similar to the one who had accompanied Finn into Interview Room 4. The same green uniform, the same young face that had smirked at her husband's discomfort and that mop of ginger hair. It couldn't be the same guard, could it? Sophie averted her face and attempted to squeeze past him.

'Well hello Miss Smith,' he said blocking her way.

Shocked at hearing her name, she looked up and saw his eyes were firmly fixed on the breast pocket name badge.

He lifted his face and winked. 'Those badges are a God send, aren't they?'

His behaviour spoke of a boy hoping to be the 'expert lover' of his imagination. Sophie grimaced, pushing against the arm that was blocking her escape. He did not budge.

'Wow, you're the first young female I've come across since Christmas, and the other one was my sister. That's only because no one else will have her.' He chuckled at his own joke.

Sophie avoided eye-contact, noting instead his lapel badge, thinking to beat him at his own game. She read his name, Ryan Cooper, then shuddered at his job title; Medical Officer Trainee. The unwelcome image of Officer Enright filled her head. After a weak smile in polite response to his joke, she asked for directions to room 4C.

'Information like that comes at a price. Coffee?' he said.

'It's OK, I'll ask someone else.' Sophie was in no mood to continue his game.

'Don't be like that, I'm heading that way, I have a seminar in 4F. We're upstairs and along the west wing corridor. Come on, we can talk en route.' He snatched up his bag, putting his arm around Sophie, guiding her towards the staircase. 'So, what you here for?'

Sophie shuffled her shoulders trying to release herself. 'Labour, Birth without Pain.'

Ryan snorted a laugh. 'You don't half hide that baby bump well.' When Sophie failed to respond to his humour, a disappointed Ryan prodded her further, asking, 'Is that possible? I mean, what do they do, hypnotise them?' He chuckled again.

'Drug free birth is preferable for both mother and baby, that way we only use chemical pain relief on those who really need it,' said Sophie, parroting the official health ministry proclamations.

'And we both know who that will be, don't we?' He elbowed Sophie in the ribs. 'Can't have fine society ladies in any pain, can we?'

Once they reached room 4C, Sophie politely thanked him and opened the door with a sense of relief, only to hear his voice calling back to her, 'So, I'll look out for you at lunch then, OK?'

Although Sophie hoped Ryan would be fully engaged with some other, younger nurse, it was pretty unlikely given the dining room was filled with young men and mature women. She was the youngest female in the room by a considerable distance. She wondered what would happen to her profession now fathers were being encouraged to marry off daughters straight from school. Further education for New Albany's girls was not an economic priority, with Government ministers and commentators advocating reallocation of the country's limited resources.

Sophie found a table by an old-fashioned bookcase, its shelves devoid of its previous occupants. Perhaps they were held in a store somewhere, waiting for the day when they might be savoured once more. She sighed, it was more likely they were fuel for stoves in cold winters. Why save books deemed dangerous to civil obedience?

Lost in gourmet dreams, she toyed with the institutional meal of undefined origin, jumping when she felt a sharp tapping on her shoulder. had found her.

'Hello again, I thought it was you hiding in the corner.' Without asking, he plonked himself down onto the chair next to her. 'Whatcha got there, curry? Not me, I'm a burger kind of guy.' He began munching on his burger. 'So, will it work?' he asked, his open mouth of bread and pickle on full display.

Sophie was confused, 'What?'

'Drug free labour, you know, will it work?'

She laughed. 'Yes, but not pain free if I remember correctly.'

Ryan stopped chewing and swallowed. Like an inquisitor caught upon an unexpected detail, his eyes dropped to her left hand and his forehead furrowed with slow thought. There on her fourth finger sat a plain gold band triggering the starting pistol to send his mental cogs whirling. 'You married, then? How come you're here if you're married? That's not allowed.'

Sophie prickled at his words. 'Not that it is any of your business, but we married before The Marriage and Work Regulation came in. It is not retrospective, so I continue in the job I enjoy. I plan to stop once we have children. That hasn't happened yet.'

'Sounds like you are with someone who can't get the job done. Maybe I can help you out, if you're nice to me.' Grinning with opportunity, he offered up another of his mirror-practised winks.

Sophie put down her cutlery and collected her things, intent on sending him a clear message. She had enough to deal with in her everyday life without spending precious free time with adolescent bores.

Ryan ignored Sophie's intentions and caught her wrist, his fingers digging into the flesh. 'Don't leave, we were just getting to know each other, Mrs Smith.'

'My next lecture is due to start. I have to go,' Sophie said, twisting her wrist to release his grip.

'Liar. There are no lectures during the lunch period. Sit down, finish your curry and I promise not to hit on you, deal?'

She stopped squirming and hesitated. Outside, the rain slapped at the window, and in all probability her rejection of him would only cause problems later. Sometimes it was just easier to ignore her anger.

Ryan's toothy grin shone with victory. He released her wrist and held out his hand in apology. 'Let's start again, Ryan Cooper, trainee Medical Officer for Treatment Centre 269, AZ Five.'

Those few words cut through her; the Treatment Centre 269. He was the same guard from that Interview Room 4, she was sure of it. Sophie wondered if he had benefited from the hefty bribe. Doubtful, that was the perk of seniority. Ryan's expectant hand was hovering in the air, waiting for her answer.

She shook his hand and smiled back. 'Sophie, Sophie Smith. How do you do?'

'I know, your badge told me as much.'

She fizzed with questions, all on the tip of her tongue. *What happens to all the DIAs? Where did they go? Why were so few released back to their families?* It didn't make sense. But those questions would have to wait, it was time for friendliness and gaining his trust.

'I hear the Treatment Centres have some of the best facilities in the country. A bit ironic really,' she said, trying to sound nonchalant.

'Why?'

'We all pay for insurance, and those that can't or are DIAs get the best facilities. Doesn't seem fair.'

Ryan nodded. 'Yeah, I hear that all the time. You see there are two sides to the Centre. The Albian one, which is good I'll grant you that. Then there's the DIA side, which is completely separate. I'm training to be promoted so I can work on the wards with the DIAs. It's better pay, you see.

Not too many like working with DIAs. Dirty work, but hey, money is money, right?'

'Well, we'd all like better pay.'

'Too right, love.'

'Why's it difficult?' Sophie asked.

'Say again?'

'Why is it dirty?'

'Ah now, that's the thing,' Ryan leant forward, 'we're not allowed to talk about our work,' adding in a proud whisper, 'It's top secret.'

Nothing impresses more than a secret never to be told. Sophie was well acquainted with the type who'd happily divulge secrets if it furthered their personal path, in this case, the seduction of a youngish nurse. Ryan took another bite of his burger. He was a messy eater. Some sauce had squeezed out of the bun and landed on his shirt. It looked like a splat of blood on his chest. He dunked his napkin in the glass of water and started to wipe the sauce away, while continuing his crude fishing attempt. 'So, Sophie Smith, are you in rooms here? I'm in the Berriswood block.' A damp red stain had spread across his white shirt.

Sophie stifled a silent snigger, lest he saw it as encouraging. 'No, I have family nearby. I'm staying with them.'

'You're staying for the karaoke, though, in the bar? It's tonight.'

'I'm not sure. To be honest, I'm quite tired and it's a long course. I may not.' Sophie noticed an older woman from the morning's seminar was waving at her and with some relief, found her means to end the conversation. 'Sorry, I have to go, I promised to talk to my colleague over there.'

'One drink in the bar, you can't come on these courses and not let your hair down just a bit.'

Sophie listened to the young man's pleas while she

formulated a plan. She knew all the tricks. Years of watching her father courteously extract information from all types of political rivals had instructed her on the benefits of alcohol. Nothing loosened tongues quite like it. 'OK. The bar, six o'clock.'

All bars looked the same to her, dark and miserable. A few people were coming in for a pre-dinner drink and a cigarette. The air was blue and heavy with noxious smoke tickling the back of her throat. She coughed, then scanned the room for the tell-tale green lights of the devices. None were obvious, but she was certain they were there. Every public room in New Albany was monitored. Through teary eyes, smarting from smoke, she saw Ryan enter the bar, confidently strutting towards his theoretical conquest.

'In the corner again, love. Whatcha want?'

'House white, thank you,' she replied.

He returned with their drinks, and before any further greeting, Ryan reached inside his uniform jacket, pulling out a packet of cigarettes and his lighter. He tapped the box on the table and held out the protruding cigarette for Sophie.

'No, thank you. I don't smoke.'

With a slight shrug of the shoulder, Ryan took the cigarette between his lips. He had a satisfied expression and made rhythmic movements with his mouth to produce smoke rings. Three rings rose past her face. Ryan broke them with a crooked middle finger, then, straightening it, gave her nose a patronising tap.

'You should try it. It can make you a bit queasy at first, but you'll get over it, and there's nothing like that first smoke of the morning. You know, it's your duty to support our tobacco industry.'

Sophie responded with her practised insincere smile and

through splutters, explained the annoyance of being allergic to the tobacco plant.

Ryan took the hint, turning his head away to blow away the smoke. His cigarette finished, he picked up his pint of bitter ale and gulped down nearly half before placing it back on the mat. 'Been waiting for that all afternoon. Christ, it's stuffy in those seminar rooms. Our last speaker was so dull, I nearly drowned him out with my snoring. How about yours?'

'They were interesting enough,' she lied. 'It seems we female nurses are too empathetic. If we order them to stop whinging and get on with the job, they'll feel less pain, apparently.'

'Have you been a midwife for long?'

'That's just one aspect, I work in a community surgery. I do all sorts.'

'What about your husband? What does he do?'

'A teacher in a girls' school. School House 87.'

Ryan's eyes widen. 'Wow, my sister was there a couple of years back, which teacher?'

Sophie needed to think quickly. If she told the truth, Ryan might find out that Finn was a DIA. She blurted out her lie without a second thought, 'Mr Pickles.'

She realised her mistake when she saw wrinkles appear on his forehead.

'How come you've not taken your husband's name.'

She had landed herself into a problem that didn't exist moments before. 'Well, would you want to be called Pickles?' She waited for his expected laughter, before explaining that she was Mrs Pickles on official documents as per the law, but given she was Nurse Smith before marriage, for some reason that name had stuck.

'Nurse Pickles sounds like fun.' He gave her an inuendo-laden crooked smile. 'So, what does Mr Pickles teach?'

'Home Studies, cooking, sewing, you know, domestic stuff.'

He choked on his beer, before spluttering, 'You're joking?' He wiped his watering eyes. 'Your husband teaches cookery but can't get a bun in the oven! Wait 'till I tell Margy.'

A rising tide of panic surged within Sophie. 'He only started in that school a year or so ago. She probably never had him.'

'Still a funny story, though.' Ryan picked up his drink and gulped it.

Sophie's panic dissolved away into an idea. Crossing her ankles to the side of the chair, she offered up her most alluring of smiles, used only when absolutely necessary. 'So why did you opt for the Medical Corps? Surely someone like you could get an air force position, maybe even a pilot.'

Ryan lit another cigarette before replying, 'Yeah, thought about it, but fancied medicine more. And, you know, pay and benefits are better in the Medical Corps, especially now. They're desperate for people. Perhaps you should apply too, although dunno if they take women.' He puffed at the cigarette, the lit end glowing. Tapping away the ash he continued, 'There's some sorta problem with the Outer World. Don't do politics to be honest. Long story short, too many DIAs and not enough staff.'

Sophie felt like a burglar after picking open a lock. 'What happens when they come to you?'

He waggled a finger at her. 'Naughty Nurse Pickles. That sorta stuff's classified.'

'Oh, what nothing? How dull!' Sophie pouted her lips and battered her eyelashes in mock disappointment, but Ryan shook his head.

'There's plenty I'd like to tell ya.' He blew a kiss across the table. 'Fancy another drink?'

Sophie's glass was half empty, but not through swallowing

the cheap wine. Each time Ryan turned his head to blow away the smoke from her, or was distracted by a colleague entering the room, she had deposited small amounts into a nearby pot plant. And when she did drink, barely a smidgen of wine made it past her throat.

'Thank you, same again I think.'

They chatted for another hour about family and hobbies. Ryan was on his fourth pint and his conversation was descending into the crude. He quizzed her about Mr Pickles and their failure to produce offspring. 'He does know how to do it doesn't he, I mean you're a nurse. You should be able to show him how to do it?'

Sophie had enough of his insinuating and wanted to move onto the next stage. As she stood, she stumbled and grabbed at Ryan's shoulder. 'Need the loo, back soon,' she slurred. 'Oh, we don't have any drinks left. Let's have a whiskey, my treat.'

'Nope, can't let a lady pay. Doubles or triples?'

He was so predictable. 'Go on, let's make it a triple.'

Ryan was at the bar, glass in hand when she returned. She moved in close, pushing her breast into his chest. 'It's a bit too warm and smoky in here for me. I'm hot. I'm going outside. Fancy coming?'

He didn't need asking twice. They found a bench under an old oak tree where Ryan removed his jacket, laying it across the wooden bars. 'My lady's seat awaits.'

She giggled and tapped the space next to her. He squeezed in as close as possible and put his arm behind Sophie, resting his elbow on the seat back. Judging from his eyes, the alcohol consumed, his lack of dinner and the fresh air, she guessed time was limited for her questions.

Ryan had already finished his whiskey. His head edged closer to her. The smell of his breath intermingling with tobacco smoke made her want to retch, forcing her to turn away from him. 'I can't drink this. I feel a bit dizzy. Do you want it?' she said, handing him her glass. Sophie knew he'd accept. Once drunk, they always kept on going.

'Be a shame to waste it.' His speech was showing the signs of drunkenness. Sophie smiled.

The whiskey downed in one, he dropped the empty glass on the grass, then resumed his position. His left arm had lowered onto her shoulder and his right hand rested on her leg, yellowing fingertips tracing circles on her knee. Sophie followed the fingers while she contemplated her strategy.

'The thing that baffles me is why you say the Treatment Centres are busy,' she said, covering his hand with hers. 'The flu epidemic is over.'

'Did I say that? Oh, well it's politics, isn't it love. It's always politics. Can't send them off.'

'Don't they go home when they are better?'

'Yeah right.' He sneered. 'It's rare to find a fit DIA. More chance of finding hen's teeth. They are poor quality. No, that's usually refused.'

Sophie's stomach flipped as she realised how close she had been to losing Finn. His only salvation, the identity of his father-in-law and the brown envelope stuffed with money.

'Aren't they repatriated?' She hoped he wouldn't notice the change in her voice.

'Nah, just a couple or so, usually courtesy of a hefty bribe. Not many Immis with that sort of cash. Nah, it's all the Outer World's fault. Won't accept them. They've closed the borders to us. Them Outers are a vindictive lot.'

Sophie persisted in her questions, hiding her shock. 'When did that happen? I don't remember anything on the news.'

'You're very curious for one so pretty.' His hand had disappeared under her skirt, his fingers tickling her stockinged knee.

'I find the curious ones are the most adventurous,' Sophie replied, aware of Ryan's intentions.

He interpreted her answer as a signal to move his hand further up her leg. He had reached the top of her thigh and with the tips of his fingers, he was tracing a line between her stocking and bare skin. She tried to convince herself this was to protect Finn. Ryan was far too drunk to pose a risk. 'So, when did they close the border?'

He was kissing her neck, her flesh muffling his words, 'Four years back.'

She felt as though someone had slammed a fist into her stomach. Breathing in, she made some murmuring sounds of pleasure so as not to arouse his suspicions, despite knowing they might arouse him in other ways. She was getting to the truth. 'What about those that register for Repatriation? The healthy ones, I mean. Surely they leave?'

'Nah, sent to the Treatment Centres too. That's why we are so busy. The place is heaving.'

Sophie faked amusement while he described the DIAs arriving at the Treatment Centre. She had conquered him, and his loose talk required satisfaction. He moved to kiss her. With temptation being the greatest of devices, she jerked her head back. He hadn't told her everything. 'Ryan, we shouldn't do this. If we get caught, I'll lose my job, probably get a public punishment and you certainly won't get that promotion.'

'Who's going to see us out here, come on, it's not like we are going to go all the way.' His hand stroked the top of her thigh. 'Go on, don't be a tease. They ain't no guards out here now. That lot are way too lazy.' He stood up to undo his belt, wobbling, then paled. 'I need the bathroom.'

Delighting in her victory, she called after the disappearing youth, 'See ya tomorrow, Ryan.' That lad would unlock more secrets given the right inducement. However, her nagging uncertainty chewed away at her lip. She considered her next move, ignoring the metallic blood seeping into her mouth.

Sophie returned to the bar to collect her things, ordering a chamomile tea to calm her nerves before heading to the bus stop. Her father had offered the car, but a nurse being driven around by a chauffeur might raise one or two eyebrows. If Ryan was to tell her more, it was paramount her background remained concealed.

FINN

* * *

Wednesday 14th April

Why should I choose between these arrogant sneers and chinless smirks? I want the man who'll sees me for whom I should be. Is that wrong? There must be more to life than power and the primo-genitive male line? He's married but she's a mystery. Begs the question why? Who exactly is she? Why hide her name and give him MI status? Secrets and lies, the foundation of all relationships. I see him there, in my sitting-room, anxious to teach me dissatisfaction.

* * *

Wednesday night and the usual routine. Humiliation from the guard who looked no older than a schoolboy, the solemn and wordless Mrs Fran and that stuffy, hot sitting-room.

He waited by the door for Cat to make her entrance. She was late making him uneasy. He shuffled from one foot to another, starting to doubt he had the right time, or even the right day. Squinting at the clock on the mantle didn't help. It hadn't chimed yet, so it must be before a quarter past, but was that a quarter past seven or eight. He reflected on the previous lessons. Had he made her angry? Nothing sprung to mind but that is not to say that he hadn't. Who could tell with Miss Fry? Certainly not Michael Finlay Sheehan. Frustrated by doubt, Finn decided to walk over and check the time.

'Are you contemplating stealing my clock? A little trinket for your wife?'

He jumped. Cat was standing at her doorway. Had she been watching him the whole time? Probably.

'I was… no, sorry. I thought I was late.' Finn was used to Cat's snide comments, but today she wore her coat of anger boldly. There was no point arguing or seeking excuses, there was never any point.

'I didn't give you permission to move, go back to the door and wait for my order.'

Another of her silly control games, except he didn't care anymore. Cat sat on her seat at the table, poured herself some mint tea, and pointed to his seat. 'Come!'

Finn obeyed. She would dictate the course of the next hour, and all the others too.

Cat was sullen throughout the lesson, dismissive of the heroes, contemptuous of the heroines. Every word uttered rippling with her ire. Finn was desperate to leave, but as the clock struck a quarter to nine, he suspected there was more fury to come.

Cat closed her book and peered at Finn. 'What shall we play this evening, 568216? I know, what possessed a patriot girl to marry you?'

Finn took a moment to consider his response. If he answered without too much depth, then she might move onto another game. 'We met at University. She was at the nursing school.'

'That's not what I asked. Why did she get to choose you?'

Again, Finn took a moment before answering, 'We fell in love, nothing unusual, I transferred to the University to study for my PhD, we met, and we fell in love.'

'What's a PhD?' Cat was drumming her nails on the table, increasing Finn's nervousness. Tap, tap, tap, like rain slamming against a student accommodation window. 'Well?'

'Doctor of Philosophy.'

'You're an English teacher, not Philosophy, whatever that is. You're not a doctor either.'

'You're right, I'm not a doctor of anything, anymore.' There was little point dwelling on it. A career denied to him.

'What about your wife? Was she a doctor too?'

'You know it is a prohibited career for Albian women. In a different time, a different place she may well have trained to be a doctor, but not here. Being a nurse is as close as she gets to practising medicine. It is a profession she loves.'

'But, I don't understand why she married you. You'll say love, but that has no purpose other than to make you dependent on someone else.'

'What is the point of a life devoid of love?' he asked. 'We love our family, our friends, our partners and our children. It guides our life.'

'How can you tell who is the more advantageous if your judgement is clouded by sentimentality? No, my husband will serve his purpose. He is not needed to be loved. Position and power, he will be chosen for those reasons alone.'

'Marriage is hard enough with love, without it, it's impossible. You will be sharing a life with that person, and I presume, a be—'

'I will not!' Cat appeared horrified at the mere thought.

Her reaction reminded Finn how long it had been since he had shared a bed with Sophie. His decision had been made. Pretending to be happy was all part of the plan. Bizarrely, he was happier because he would no longer be a prisoner. The need for freedom eroding the strongest of all emotions. Love alone was not enough for New Albany. He would move back on Friday, keep her from getting suspicious. Pretence always worked.

Oblivious to his thoughts, his pupil continued to vent her teenage rant. 'I won't enjoy it and it won't be happening. I've read those books downstairs, remember. He can come to my room, do his business then clear off. Once I'm pregnant, he can stay away until he is needed again. I don't want him in my life.'

'Is that fair, he will be your husband?' He was enjoying her teenage tantrum. But it was an illusion.

'Don't you dare tell me what is or isn't fair. I don't get to choose who crosses the threshold into my bed.' Catherine's cheeks were flushed with her anger, her eyes sparkling, captivating.

Smiles were eliminated by her fury. She caught hold of Finn's chin, forcing him to look at her. 'Why is there no mention of your wife on your file? The name of the spouse should be there. Why does she get to keep you?'

'My wife does not 'keep me', we are together because we love each other.'

'No, that can't be true, there has to be another reason. You didn't answer me, why is her name missing?

All semblance of good humour had gone, Catherine was angry, and Finn's fear bubbled up from within, 'I.. I don't know. A mistake.. just a mistake probably. I can't say, these things happen.'

'What's her name?'

'Sophie Smith.' Finn answered before he was able to think up a suitable lie. He comforted his panic by assuring himself that there must be thousands of Sophie Smiths out there. His 'Sophie' would be safe.

'Were you her first?'

Finn was lost for words. 'I… I… This isn't… no, I don't want to talk about my wife.'

'Was she your first?'

Finn's face reddened.

Cat laughed. 'I bet you weren't hers though. I bet she had plenty of experience. Help guide you along, teaching the teacher, how sweet.' She dragged her fingernail down his cheek, running the tip between his lips. He shuddered.

Finn fought against the impulse to run out of the room, but it was only five to nine. She had discovered a new way to torment him. Use someone else.

'I wonder how many men she practised with before getting around to you. It's strange isn't it? Permitting behaviour like that, indulging it even. Very strange.'

Catherine slipped her hand onto the bare flesh of her waist. She was wearing a double layered flowing silk blouse. Expensive and undoubtedly imported illegally. She lifted the fabric between finger and thumb, delicately, regally, all to expose her stomach to Finn. 'In a few months' time there could be a baby in here, pushing out my flat stomach. Touch my stomach.'

'I...er... no, I don't think I should.' Finn's discomfort was evident.

Cat repeated her order, 'Touch my stomach!'

Eyes closed, he stretched out his cold hand. No illicit excitement, just terror. She still held the power to scare him, even after making his decision.

'Can you imagine a child in here? The genes of a stranger who just happens to be my husband.'

His hand was warmed by the heat of her stomach. Lost in thought, he remembered the joy of Sophie's growing waist, laughing when a tiny foot pushed against his hand.

'568216, can you imagine the child? Are you imagining releasing your genes into me, your child distorting my flat stomach?'

Embarrassed, he snatched his hand away. Cat pushed

back against the chair. Her hand continued to rest on her stomach. He watched her taut skin give under the pressure of her searching hand, seeking that non-existent child.

SOPHIE

Her head drooped off her hand as the bus jolted over another deep pothole. She was tired, physically, but also emotionally. Her interrogation of Ryan had left her with questions, and Sophie needed to formulate a plan to weasel out the answers. Who else could solve them? Her world was populated by the untrustworthy, but at least chance had provided her with the gullible.

She thought of Finn, at home, no doubt playing chess with George. It had become a regular event while he convalesced. Tea and cake in hand, George would disappear upstairs for a game or two, after insisting that Sophie took the opportunity to put her head down for forty winks.

An exhaustion tear escaped her eye. Sophie had replayed Finn's illness multiple times. She had seen flu, dealt with the symptoms of mild to the fatal in her years, but this one felt different, more extreme. The victims had developed secondary bacterial infections, some of those died, not from flu but from pneumonia. And it developed so rapidly. Had that been the fabled pandemic that Anna spoke of when they would chat in the library late into the night? Had the Outer World been affected too? Did they have the vaccine, or enough antibiotics to treat the victims? Were their people safe regardless of birthplace? There was no way for her to know or even find out. That world was a mystery, just like the DIA flu.

So often her nagging memory would force her to relive the stress of his illness. That late-night call to her father, pleading with him to save her husband. She didn't need

Henry's shrugged shoulder to tell her what was painfully obvious. Finn was dying, just like all the others.

She could still hear Henry arguing with Tim. Each determined to have their own way, but Henry lacked that one special advantage, he was not a government minister. It was bravado that had kept his argument going, easily dismissed by someone of Tim's stature.

'With all due respect, Sir, I am the doctor. He has pneumonia. The Health Ministry instructions are clear, I am not allowed to treat him. He has to go.'

'I don't care! Even if you were the Surgeon General, I wouldn't care. If Finn dies, then he dies here with Sophie by his side.'

Sophie had left the bedroom to conceal her tears from Henry, adamant not to let him see her weaken. When she returned to the bedroom, her father had pulled her in close. Tired and paler than usual, Tim's arm had tightened around her as he bent to kiss her chocolate hair.

'Don't worry darling, Finn will be fine, you'll see. I'll do everything I can to keep him safe.'

Henry had shook his head while packing his bag, saying it was tantamount to murder preventing Finn from being transferred. Yet her father had been adamant.

'I'll organise everything. Apart from antibiotics, what else will he need?'

Sophie remembered Henry glancing up towards the chest of drawers and staring at THEO. Positioned on top of the little white box had been the Minister's watch. The light on the box was showing red. Device disabled, device not listening.

Sophie had worked for Henry for years and she knew him well. A devout patriot, but like most, fear of the regime drove most of his decisions. Henry was as capable of defying the regime as any of the others. She had seen him break the rules many times before, yet that night, on hearing her father's demands, he had jutted his chin out in defiance, making him look petulant.

'He's a DIA, he's not eligible, the restrictions are there for a reason. I can't prescribe antibiotics regardless of any money he or you may have.'

'You won't be prescribing anything. Let me worry about that, what else?' Her father would not be swayed.

When Henry had argued about rules only existing for those too weak to fight back, Sophie had almost screamed at his blatant hypocrisy. He always acted the loyal Albian, when she knew the truth. She had kept silent. Accusations were not the answer.

'I won't have anything to do with this,' he had said, *'and my notes will say as much. If I get caught, I could lose everything.'*

The Foreign Minister had tried to reassure him. He had contacts and plenty of experience manipulating the system. But Henry had fired out one last shot. Sitting in that bus, Sophie could feel his grip squeezing her wrist. There had been a fear lurking behind those grey eyes, and even before he spoke, she knew what he was about to say.

'This is a waste of my time, Michael's chances of surviving are remote. Even if I do give you a few days' grace, what's the point? I doubt he'll live that long, to be honest.'

The recollection of that callous off-handedness chilled her. A man's life was of no consequence compared to his career.

'And when he dies? What if you're caught by the authorities, what then? You're willing to risk my future for a DIA.'

It was those final words that cemented her decision. She would risk everything for Finn.

After Henry had left, so did her courage. She had

collapsed into her father's arms, his promises to save Finn of no more comfort than those of an apologetic judge donning the black cap. Even his offer to send for Anna had felt like nothing more than a vain attempt to soothe her pain. Her concern about exposing her godmother to the virus, batted away by Tim.

'She won't be infected.'

Why had he said that, *'She won't be infected'*? Anna was a DIA, unvaccinated and vulnerable. Yet her father was certain. *'She won't be infected.'*

Those words played over in her head, each repetition convincing her further. Her father, the Foreign Minister, a government elite, friend and confidant to New Albany's leadership, a man who had broken multiple laws to save the life of one of the lowliest of New Albany's lowest. That man knew more than he was telling. Saving his son-in-law was necessary to keep a truth hidden.

Her father lounged in his usual seat, feet up on the footstool, glass of homemade rhubarb liqueur in hand, watching an ancient tennis match. He had switched the sound off, no commentary, just silence. Two men dressed in white, a hair band holding back the dark locks of Tim's perennial favourite.

'Deuce, blast it. Come on… oh, hello darling, fancy a drink? It's a good one, even if I say so myself. Mum's at Aunt Emma's cooing over baby pictures.' He didn't give her time to answer, instead fetched a glass and poured the rose-coloured liquid into it. 'I think you might actually like this one.'

Sophie had to concede it was palatable. Sweet and far smoother than his previous efforts. She might even get drunk on it. At that particular moment, the idea of getting drunk on rhubarb liqueur was enticing. Her thoughts on drunken oblivion were ruptured by her mobile pinging for attention.

'Who's that at this ungodly hour?' asked her father, irritated by the interruption to the silent tennis match.

'Just George, Sergeant Mason. He's been playing chess with Finn, lost one game, drew the other.'

Sophie stared at her father, his attention returning to the tennis match. 'Dad?'

'Hmm, oh now that's a good shot.'

'Dad, I need to speak to you.'

'Uh huh, fire away darling. Yes, game, thought that one would never end.'

Sophie briefly glanced across at the screen and a match her father had watched hundreds of times before. The outcome would not change, his favourite would lose in the end.

'Dad, have you got any more of this stuff, it's rather good. I'd like to take a bottle for George, to thank him.'

Tim shot a look back over his shoulder to where Sophie was gripping the handle of the sitting-room door. He paled slightly and gave his innocent response, 'We had best go and look then, hadn't we?'

They made their way through the garden to her father's pride and joy, the 'Booze Den', pretending to be a garden tool shed. Thick concrete walls lined the inside of the wooden structure. Locks protected his experiments, and those same locks protected his secrets from over curious security assistants. He frequently scanned the den to satisfy himself there were no intruding bugs.

Tim switched on the light to reveal a colourful array of liquids stored in rows of bottles and demi-johns. The walls were lined with shelves of books and a repurposed wardrobe stood to one side, its wooden doors hidden with sellotaped notes, recipes and photographs. A younger Sophie looked out from most of the pictures, from baby smiles to teenage sulks. In the corner she recognised two battered armchairs, previously resident in the sitting-room before the second to last redecoration.

'What's the problem? Is it Finn? Mum said he is unwell again,' said her dad while scanning the shelves for the rose liqueur he believed she wanted.

Sophie rolled her eyes. Her mother would never let pass any opportunity to attack Finn. 'No Dad, he's much better, happier. No, it's something else. Dad, what really happens to the DIAs when they request repatriation?'

She decided to get straight to the point, unable to think of any other way to broach the subject. Either Ryan was spinning a yarn to impress her, or New Albany was lying, and that was unthinkable. She watched him stare at the demi-johns, replacing the bottle he had picked up. He pushed his other hand through his thinning grey hair and with that, Sophie's stomach sank. Her father's body language had always been easy for her to read.

'Why don't you sit down and tell me what you know. I'll do my best to answer you,' he said, dropping heavily into one of the chairs.

Sophie shook her head, saying, 'No, I'll stand. Is it true the Outer World has blocked our borders and is no longer taking back its own citizens?'

'Partly true.'

Sophie felt a strange mixture of relief and anger as she heard those words, but her father had not finished speaking.

'It wasn't an Outer World decision. We closed the border.'

'Why, what was the point of that? I thought you wanted the foreigners to leave.'

Her father had begun chewing his bottom lip; like father, like daughter. He looked up and then she noticed the sparkling in his eyes where tears coated his guilt. 'Politics is never black and white, darling. We sway one way, then the other, and what you thought was right, is now declared wrong. Friends become enemies and your enemies, well, they are still your enemies. We are alone. We have no allies out beyond our borders.'

'What the hell has that got to do with repatriation?'

'Sophie, will you please sit down, let me explain.'

'Fine.' She sat in the accompanying chair, smelling its stale history with the pluming dust rising from unloved cushions. Her father had reached over to the rack of bottles and was pulling one out. 'Dad, you are mistaken if you think this is time for one of your experiments.'

He brought out a bottle of illegally imported cognac and wiped off the dirt. 'I need Dutch courage. I never meant for these things to happen.'

Those words chilled her. 'What do you mean, you never meant for this to happen? What things, Dad? What have you done?' She took the glass from his hand, staring at him, daring an answer.

'They accused us of human rights abuses. The DIAs went back home with horror stories of discrimination and onerous restrictions. Some of it true, but not everything, well not at that time it wasn't.' He stopped talking and swirled the cognac before taking a sip. A pause that served to frighten and frustrate Sophie.

'What do you mean, Dad?' she said, reaching across to his glass, preventing him from taking another sip.

He lowered the glass, and his eyes too. 'The DIA programme had been accepted by the populous here. It was working fine, those that stayed could remain with their families, they could work, and those that didn't want that, well, they went back to their homelands. But the complaints persisted. The United Nations passed resolutions, unheard of for them to actually agree on something, but they did. They all agreed we were the baddies and we should be sanctioned.

'They wanted us to abide by other countries' rules. We couldn't do that. We promised our people that we should be sovereign, no foreign country telling us what we could or could not do. Don't you see Sophie, they were interfering?'

'No, Dad, they weren't interfering. They were protecting the rights of everyone. The rights you were destroying under the New Albany First Doctrine. How could you believe they were wrong to interfere?'

'When that interfering becomes sabre rattling. When foreign businessmen eye our mineral deposits, and our fertile land with greedy anticipation, that's when. We didn't have, and still don't have the resources for war, but that's not what you'll hear. Meanwhile we quietly closed the border. Who'll notice? Foreigners aren't welcome. Who even requests a visitor visa these days? Meanwhile, the Outer World hears my beautifully written speeches about DIAs living happily beneath the benevolent New Albian sky. They'd be mad to leave, wouldn't they?' he said with sarcasm slipping off every syllable.

'But DIAs are leaving,' said Sophie. 'Agnes from the shop left, when was it? September, yes definitely last September. I remember now. Agnes told Finn she wanted to be with her father. Her marriage was failing, and Eric wanted to marry an Albian. He said it was job prospects, younger model more like. Anyway, Finn asked her to see his parents. She promised to visit Eloise, tell her everything was fine, not to worry. Agnes left, she did, we said goodbye.'

Tim shook his head at Sophie's assertions. 'She didn't leave, darling. No one has left in four years.'

Sophie shook her head, hair flicking into her eyes. Her father was wrong, she was sure of it. 'No, we gave her money, not much, but just in case she needed a bribe to make things easier.'

Tim had taken her hand and was squeezing it. It felt so cold. 'It wouldn't have been enough. They'd have stolen the bribe and processed her,' he said.

Sophie pulled her hand back, her father's cold fingers almost branding her wrist. 'No, you're wrong. She left, she definitely left. Where would she go if not back to her country?'

Tim had finished the first glass and was re-filling it. He held up the half empty bottle to Sophie.

'No, I don't want any, I just want answers.'

He shrugged and poured more into his glass. Each noiseless sip another punch in the stomach for Sophie. 'Answer me!' she screamed, 'Or I'll...I'll tell everyone. That's what I'll do. I'll tell everyone that the DIA Repatriation Service is a sham. You'll have to answer then, won't you?'

'And what do you think will happen if you tried that? You are the Foreign Minister's daughter. OK they might not shoot you on the spot, but you will be silenced one way or another. You have no proof, I'll deny it. I'll say you are having a delayed breakdown following your miscarriage. No one will believe you.'

'Molly wasn't a miscarriage,' she said, in a quiet voice.

Sophie paced the confined space. Tim was right, she needed solid proof. She wondered how much that blabbermouth idiot, Ryan would tell her.

'Sit down, Sophie. I'll tell you what I can, but please remember the risks, this is treason. If you speak out it's not just your life you'll be risking.'

She returned to the seat as her father drained and refilled his glass yet again.

'Look Sophie, we had to make a choice. We already used labour camps—'

'What? Labour camps, you send them to labour camps?' She leapt out of the chair, disbelief and anger forcing her to move.

'Yes, it made sense. Who wants to pick tea leaves in the burning heat? It solved a problem. New Albany needs cheap labour to survive.'

Sophie held onto the door handle to steady herself, fighting the impulse to hurl the contents of the den at her father. Words crept out of her mouth, 'Free labour, more like it. But they're not, are they? They are not free, they are slaves forced to work, when they had been promised a ticket home. What's it like being a slave owner, Dad?'

She couldn't bear to look at her father, let alone be in the same room. Sophie slammed the door behind her in a repetition of a teenage tantrum. Except this wasn't a tiff over what she was wearing or where she had spent the evening. This was taking innocent people, jailing them for the rest of their lives. It was working them to death.

The damp air soothed her throbbing head. Leaning back against the door, she caught sight of the stars. Glorious spots of celestial beauty, free to all without favour or discrimination. How many eyes were watching the same view? What about those slaves in the camps? Was Agnes still free to wish upon a star? Sophie shut her eyes to make a wish, but her shoulders tipped back as the door behind her opened. Her dad's firm hand preventing her fall.

'Come back in, Soph. We need to talk.'

'I think you've said enough. You are the Party's man, morals not required.'

'Sophie, this is important. Come in.'

Tim poured her another cognac then topped up his own. His hand was shaking as he lifted the glass. Was that his third or fourth drink?

'I never wanted this,' he said. 'I thought we were freeing ourselves of other people's meddling. Nothing works out as you intend, does it?' He smiled. A smile that froze with her icy glare.

'Are you trying to excuse your behaviour? Don't bother, I'm going to a hotel.'

'No Sophie, don't. Please let me explain. No excuses, I promise. All I wanted was to keep you safe. In this country ignorance equals safety. I am the spokesman, the excuse maker. I travel the world spewing the lies that ensure the Outer World stays ignorant. We churn out Government proclamations, making it easier for the guilty to sleep at night. Better to half believe lies rather than scrutinise the evidence that surrounds us. We deal out the propaganda far and wide, and we allocate blame on the most convenient victim.'

How often had she heard it said, *'It's the fault of the DIAs'?'* They were the target who couldn't fight back. Sophie picked up the cognac, its scent swirling around the glass. A wave of nausea crashed over her. She was dizzy with the revelations and the insidious thought that refused to disappear. Once more she escaped the den, this time to vomit into the brambles.

It was a few minutes later before Sophie returned, sufficiently composed to ask her next question. Fear of the answer quivered her voice, 'Dad, was that flu epidemic part of the blame game? It definitely wasn't like any flu I have ever seen.'

Her father avoided eye contact and took another gulp of cognac.

'You fucking bastards? Why Dad, what possessed you?' Tears, snot and vomit choked her as she spoke, 'Why did you infect them? Finn nearly died, others did die, many of them, and here you are telling me it was all part of a government propaganda programme.'

Tim searched his pockets and handed Sophie a tissue. Rejecting it, she wiped her face across the sleeve of her cardigan before demanding a response, 'Don't you dare ignore me, Dad! Why did you infect them?'

'It was a manufactured bacterial infection complete with its own vaccine,' he said.

'I knew it, I knew it wasn't flu.'

Tim shuffled in his seat, draining the last of his cognac. 'No, it wasn't flu, but the lab guys designed it to mimic its symptoms. Once the bacteria infected the lungs there was a reasonable chance of death, especially as they had no access to antibiotics. When the first cases were being reported in AZ Twelve, there was sufficient worry to ensure a high take up of the vaccine.'

'But not for the DIAs.'

'No, they were the target. The authorities expected twenty per cent mortality. Nothing like a bit of panic to keep the masses under control. They sprayed the bacteria in places where DIAs gathered, in the church—'

'Churches? You utter bastards.'

'I'm sorry, I really am.' Tim wiped his face with his hand. He was crying. 'Most of the deaths were at the labour camps. They are overcrowded and with no medical treatment, death rates there were far higher. For the government, it was seen as a cost-effective solution.'

'Cost effective? What on earth were you trying to achieve? You want slaves then you kill them. It makes no sense.'

'Most of those wanting to repatriate are older, maybe partners have died, children with their own lives, who knows? They're not ideal workers. We used the flu to kill off the weakest and leave room for healthier ones.'

'It still doesn't make sense, Dad.'

'It does if you want to free up space for our next healthy victims.'

Sophie sat back in her chair staring at the ceiling. Her world had become a nightmare. 'Who's next?'

'I don't know, but there is always a next in line. Blame must always be allotted.'

How could her father be part of this genocide? How could any sane person be part of this evil conspiracy? He was talking about the people they knew, people they loved, as though they were a mere commodity, their worth as humans valued purely in monetary terms.

Pieces of the puzzle were falling into place and she realised what else he had done. 'Anna was vaccinated, wasn't she?'

Tim nodded. 'And Christopher. I stole two extra doses, fake paperwork. I would have got one for Finn, but my aide is far too nosy, a sudden and recent addition to my staff, probably ASSU.'

'How could you, Dad? You knew all along. And what about Anna and Christopher? What about Mum?'

'They didn't know, none of them. I told them it was vitamins, a boost to help out, nothing more.'

'It doesn't change the fact you knew.' Sophie's accusatory finger jabbed her father in the chest. 'Yet you did nothing.'

'That's not true, and you know it's not.' Tim backed away as Sophie lowered her hand.

'Was that why you got the medicine, to cover up your guilt?' said Sophie.

'Honestly, then yes. I knew we could save him, I had to do it, I had to run that risk, I had to keep Finn with you.'

Sophie flicked her eyes back onto her dad, her brain dominated with images of him arguing with Henry. 'What happens at the Treatment Centre?'

'The Treatment Centre?' He was turning his wedding ring round and round. A habit he could not break. She had seen him doing it while giving speeches, and that time he said he fell in love with her mother the minute he saw her. The same tic, the same tell. 'Nothing, no it's just he would be better off with you, and I was right, wasn't I?'

Her father was lying just as he had been every other time too.

'You liar!' Sophie shouted, frantic to get to the truth, 'You know something, don't you? Stop lying for once and tell me the truth.'

But Tim continued to shake his head and turn the ring. 'There are rumours about me, I've been kept out of meetings, memos. Honestly darling, if anything is going on, then I don't know about it. Please Sophie, please believe me.'

Sophie walked out of the shed, her father's lies ringing in her head and determination flowing through her veins.

Before daylight, Sophie cycled back to Court Farm on Christopher's bike. Stuffed into her knapsack were a couple of blankets and two bottles of rhubarb liqueur, to which she added a few drops of the odourless and colourless drug normally kept for reluctant brides. She found the gap in the wall easily. Away from guards and overgrown, it would prove the ideal location for her trap.

She searched the breakfast crowd in the cafeteria. Ryan was sitting on his own, contemplating the poor excuse for porridge in front of him. Collecting two cups of black coffee, she ignored her tinge of guilt, and took the seat opposite.

'Coffee? Looks like you need one,' she said, thrusting the institutional mug towards him.

'No thanks, I'll stick to water today.' Ryan pushed away the coffee along with the congealed bowl of gloop.

Clearly the boy was unused to alcohol despite the previous

evening's bravado, but she would not let a hangover get in her way. Ryan had to be enticed into her web. 'Oh, Ryan, don't tell me you are a lightweight. I thought we might enjoy each other's company later. Shame, but if you are feeling a little delicate, I suppose I'll have to go home disappointed.'

Ryan's nicotine stained smile told her everything she needed to know. 'Well, Mrs Pickles, that depends on what it is you want from me. A drinking buddy or someone to show you how it's really done.'

'I'm sure we'll come to an arrangement.' Sophie stood to leave. 'My seminar is about to start. I'll catch you later.' She tossed Ryan an air kiss to seal the deal.

Sophie drummed the table with her nail. It was after six, she looked at her watch for the umpteenth time. There was no way he would stand her up, that boy was keen. She almost smelt Ryan before seeing him. The air had filled with the smell of cheap aftershave, drowning out the stale pungency of alcohol and tobacco. Dressed in New Albany civvies, beige chinos, white shirt and burgundy sweater, he handed Sophie her drink. A sweet white was what patriot women drank, so that was what she was given.

'Wine, thank you. I was worried you had stood me up.' Sickly sweet, she ran her tongue around her lips trying to wash off the taste. At least her dad's elderflower wine would have been chilled.

Ryan glugged back half his beer before answering, 'Nah, just wanted to make me all sweet for you.' He added a wink to underline the sledgehammer hint.

'Then I suggest we head outside.' She smiled back, pleased with how her plan was working. 'It's quite dry now and I've found a lovely spot away from the house. We'll be all alone.'

'Then let's get outta here.'

*

She led him through bramble covered paths. At a crumbling wall, Sophie pushed away at the spider infested ivy, revealing a battered door, nature heaving it off its hinges. She squeezed through, the small gap no problem for her miniature frame. Ryan tentatively followed, letting out a hushed 'fuck' when a cascade of spiders landed on his arm. Sophie sniggered. 'Not scared, are you?'

'No,' he replied, a little more indignantly than necessary, 'it's just, I heard about some that can bite, poisonous ones. They were brought in by those Immis. I read about it the other day.'

They surveyed the walled garden in the diminishing light. It appeared abandoned, devoid of cultivated life apart from a couple of elderly apple trees in one corner. Sophie knew it would be the perfect spot.

'I left some stuff here, hang on a sec,' she said, retrieving the hidden bag, then held it aloft like captured treasure for her intended victim to admire. 'Hope you like what I've brought?' Mentally prepared for the risks, she emptied the knapsack of its blankets and tainted liqueur, fairly certain there was only sufficient narcotic to reduce his inhibitions and encourage chat. It was her decision, her choice. It was always her choice.

With one of the blankets on the ground, Sophie lay on her side, her head propped up by her hand waiting for Ryan to mirror her position. The night sky was clear, and a few indistinct stars had appeared to bless Sophie's plan.

'So, are we talking or doing?' Ryan grinned at her, his fingers running down her face.

Sophie intended to test his resolve, tempting him with forbidden pleasure. She was prepared to break the law for the greater good, but was Ryan eager enough to join her?

'Would you like some rhubarb liqueur?' she asked.

'No, I want to stay sober, so I can remember every delicious moment with you.'

She grimaced internally. Undeterred, she poured out two glasses.

'I really don't want any,' insisted Ryan.

Aware that he was leering over her every movement, Sophie dipped her finger into the glass, brought it out, then seductively wiped the sticky liquid across her lips in one smooth, practised act. Ryan's jaw dropped loose with desire, poking regulated morality to the back of his consciousness. Repeating the action, she let the rose liquid slip from the end of her nail. The tip of her finger pressed on his dry lips and she applied the sticky lipstick onto the young man. Then, leaning across, she covered his mouth with hers, his scavenging tongue retrieving rhubarb saliva. Ryan was a boy awake to the possibilities of carnal knowledge.

Sophie pulled back from him. 'Are you sure you wouldn't like some? It's homemade, hardly alcoholic at all.'

Ryan reached forward and picked up the glass, swallowing the drink in one. 'There, does that make you happy?'

'It's much more fun when you savour it,' she said, immediately refilling the tumbler.

He sat up, taking a sip before kissing her cheek. Her innuendo spurring him forward. Ryan nuzzled and licked her neck while Sophie skilfully wound him into her web. Another sip, another kiss. By the time he had slobbered over the base of her neck, he had finished the second glass. She disregarded her revulsion, there were questions that needed asking. Too much drink and he'd be unconscious before she could get any information.

'Shall I tell you a little secret?' she whispered into his ear.

Ryan stopped mid-kiss, perplexed. Sitting up, he stared at her, saying, 'I knew there was something you were hiding.'

Sophie caught a lock of Ryan's hair between her fingers, twisting it into curls, pulling him closer. 'Not hiding exactly, more a fantasy. Yesterday, when you were talking about your work, it sounded so dangerous, so exciting. I'd be so scared, but maybe not if you were beside me.' Beneath her leg, her fingers crossed, hoping Ryan's inexperience would leave him susceptible to her coquettish tripe.

'It's a little warmer than I expected,' she commented, unbuttoning the top of her uniform. 'Oh, your glass is nearly empty. Let me top you up.'

The bottle back on the ground, she placed her free hand between his legs, massaging the inside of his thigh, her fingers moving upwards towards his groin. Ryan moaned with her experienced touch.

Sophie delighted with her choice, he was the easiest of prey. 'And they don't frighten you, all those DIAs in one place? Not even a little bit?'

Ryan slowly shook his head, still mumbling delight at Sophie's caresses. She undid more buttons and with her shoulders back, pushed forward her exposed chest.

Kissing her while fumbling with his belt, it was clear the boy was eager for his prize. He swiped the belt from his trousers and held it high, then swiftly, as though practiced, doubled it over in one hand. The slamming noise as it hit the ground hard made Sophie jump. He stopped, laughing at her shocked faced. 'That's for them, love. They learn to obey me quickly. They're a load of frightened little vermin.'

Sophie fought the temptation to snatch the belt off him and beat him with it, but she needed more answers. Just like the previous night, the more alcohol he drank, the looser he became with the secrets of The Treatment Centre.

'It must be enormous.'

He guffawed. 'Well, it's definitely getting bigger.' He

was kissing her stomach and groping to remove her bra.

Irritated by his ineptitude she unclipped it, letting him lunge hungrily for her nipple. 'I meant The Treatment Centre. You can't possibly fit all those DIAs there, can you?'

'Huh? The Centre? Yeah, no problem. We sort the buggers, you know, a sort of triage.'

Sophie winced when Ryan's nibbling became more aggressive, biting at her breasts. It would be awkward if Finn noticed any bruising, that's if she could convince him to return to their bed. Pushing that thought away, she slid her hand down his loosened trousers. She was getting near the truth.

He lay back to enjoy the pleasuring. The talking had ceased. Sophie needed to reassess her plan. Pulling her hand back out, she sat up.

'Hey, what's up? I was enjoying that.'

She sat astride him, her hands clutching his wrists. 'I think it's time you learnt a lesson off your Nurse Pickles, don't you?'

'And what lesson did you have in mind?'

She leant down, her nipples brushing his lips. 'It's more fun when the woman is satisfied too. You can have that tip for free.'

He lifted his head, to take her left nipple between his teeth, but missed when Sophie arched back.

'Not so fast, Ryan. I want you to impress me with real men's work, while I make sure you know what this woman can do?' She let go of his wrist and unzipped his trousers, reaching down she curled her fingers around his penis.

'Where do you want me to start?' he said.

'Just tell me about your average day and let's see how hot you can get me?' She lay down, one hand working rhythmically inside his chinos, the other unbuttoning his shirt.

'It's quite a responsibility you know, triage. I assess their health then process them.'

'Whatcha mean, process?' She dotted his chest with kisses.

'You're good at this, Nurse Pickles.' He raised his head, pushing his nose into her hair. 'You smell good, too.'

'Remember, it's not my shampoo that gets me excited.' She stopped massaging him.

'No, oh come on. I can tell you stuff to get you sweaty if you like.'

'I do like. You were telling me about processing them.'

'Yeah, well no point keeping the sick ones. I dispatch them to A ward.'

Sophie lowered his trousers slightly, exposing him. Her face buried deep into his stomach flesh.

'Oh God, that's good.' he said, as her tongue tickled the tip of his engorged penis. 'Nurse Pickles deserves a reward I think.'

She nodded.

'Oh God, yeah, um, so yeah, the healthy are shipped to labour camps. Fuck that's good.

Her heart was pounding with his revelations. Part of her wanted him to stop, but another needed to know more, no matter how terrifying.

Ryan rested his hand on her head, gently stroking her. 'Is this doing the trick, love? Is this what you want to hear?'

Sophie worried he was growing suspicious of her questioning. He must not escape her web. She lifted away from him.

'Oh yes, keep talking, all I get at home is cooking and sewing. You make me feel protected. You can feel how hot you are making me if you want.'

His fingers slipped between her legs, rubbing her, pushing aside her pants. Sophie tried to relax, convincing her body to join in with the performance.

'Well, who knew?" he said, his fingers worming around her, pushing inwards. 'Guess I'd best tell you more if that's your reaction.'

She breathed in, then on her outward breath cried, 'Oh God, yes.' She had to protect Finn.

Ryan edged his trousers down further. Whether it was the alcohol and drugs or the sheer sexual desire, any thoughts he may have had about re-education or loss of a stable career, was tossed aside at the prospect of losing his virginity to a married woman. Chemical consent aiding and abetting Sophie's need for information. She bit her lip, only a few more questions.

'Talk to me Ryan. Ward A, yes, oh yes, tell me about ward A?'

He flipped Sophie onto her back. 'I'll tell Nurse Pickles all about Ward A, if that's what makes her happy.' He kissed her, then jerked his finger inside her violently.

Disguising her pain, she replied in a strained voice, 'You're making me very happy.'

'We. Put. Them. Down.' Each word accompanied by his stabbing inside her. She cried out.

'You like that, don't you?' he said, becoming more aggressive.

Sophie nodded through her crying.

'Bet you don't cry for your Mr Pickles, do you?'

She shook her head. It seemed so easy when she formulated her plan the previous night. He'd talk, then fall asleep. It would be easy. Not for the first time, she had been wrong, and it was too late to refuse him.

'Will you scream for me, love?'

She nodded again, whimpering. She lay still and shut her eyes. In the darkness she saw Finn, lined up, shackled, Ryan standing in front of him. Fear and determination made her speak, 'Give me more.'

'Oh, I've got plenty, love.'

He moved his leg over her, tugged her pants down and pushed forward.

'I do this to protect you, Finn. I do this to protect you.' She kissed Ryan, 'Talk at me, and make me scream.'

'Oh God, yes. I need to think,' he said.

'Let me help you.' Sophie poured the remainder of his glass over her face, sensing the viscous liquid roll down, dripping off her chin. Ryan lapped at her like a starved cur.

'Talk, Ryan. Talk. I'm nearly there.'

Through slurping, she heard the words to make her cry out, 'Healthiest…research…drugs test…lab rats.'

'You want more, don't you?'

She nodded.

His face was a contorted mixture of concentration and pleasure. He pushed in harder delighting at her screams. 'Papers written…chaotic… superior humans… purity.'

With that final word 'Purity', Sophie watched his young face convulse with pleasure.

Ryan rolled off in contented post coital and drunken grogginess. He was sleepy. Aware her act was unfinished, Sophie spoke tenderly of his prowess. 'You really know how to make a girl scream, don't you? Don't think I've ever cried like that before.'

He replied with a snore. After ten minutes and certain he was in deep sleep, Sophie dressed him, pulled over the other blanket and pushed him onto his side, just in case he vomited. There would be four to five hours when he'd be unlikely to wake. Enough time to confront her colluding father. He had risked Finn dying at home because going to the Treatment Centre meant certain death.

FINN

'I saw seven magpies today, a secret never to be told.' Cat grinned, pleased with herself.

'In that case, you won't be telling me,' replied Finn.

She slipped off the sofa, accompanied by the music coming from the speakers. A carefree teen dancing her way towards the door where her servant obediently waited her pleasure.

'I suppose there aren't that many Sophie Smiths who are nurses in AZ Five. It didn't take long, a few calls to hospitals, that's all. Sophia Elle Smith, the beautiful only child of our Foreign Minister, married to an Immi. How embarrassing! His fellow ministers must cringe at his misfortune. What price does he pay for your protection, I wonder? Does he tell you?' Her little heels lifted her face level with his, her eyes delving deep into him, searching for his response.

'May I use the bathroom?' he asked as calmly as his racing heart allowed.

Catherine stepped back, disappointed. 'My bathroom? You want to use my bathroom?'

'I meant downstairs, the servants' bathroom.'

'But your hour has started, we might lose fifteen minutes, I have so much I need to ask you and you have so much to tell me.' She flopped onto her sofa. 'OK, if you must, you must, but I intend to keep you here until I've had my full hour.'

'Thank you.'

Cat got up and pressed the bell by the fireplace, seconds later the door clicked unlocking it. The automatic version of Johan. Finn didn't care, he had to escape.

The back staircase was a spiral of nothingness. Steps up and steps down. Finn sat on the top one, looking at the skylight above him. Even the stars were hidden, there was nothing to see in that black void.

How could she know? His pulse throbbed in his head, rapid, chanting out his fear. What will happen now? All thoughts jumbled around in the panic. Questions existed but there were no answers. His breathing steamed along, hitting one question after another, no time to wait for answers. What will happen to us? Had his mistake put Sophie in danger? What will happen?

Finn stared down, another black void that led to the servants' world. A world where a butler is fortunate to die, and a housekeeper is reduced to a silent robot of flesh and blood. What was he, what had Finn become? The bulb above his head reflected in the shine of his shoes. Shoes bought when he was 'somebody', a man who carried a familiar surname. And he was still 'somebody'. Tim ensured his protection. One of only a handful of MIs, married to the Foreign Minister's daughter. Tim was the government, the regime. Tim out ranked the Commandant and there was nobody more important to him than his daughter.

The throbbing had slowed, becoming quieter. His breathing settled and he allowed logic to filter through. Catherine's father was the Area Commandant. He held information on every patriot and DIA in the Area Zone. It was foolish to think otherwise. Catherine might have the information, but it would be useless to her. Sophie, and by association, Finn, were safe from her meddling. The Commandant would not take the risk. All would be fine, just fine.

He knocked on the door and re-entered, waiting for her command.

'You were quite quick. You must have run up all the stairs,

but you are barely out of breath,' Cat said, her manicured finger pointing to his usual seat on the other sofa. 'I thought we might chat first. I do like our chats, don't you? And this is such a surprising revelation, who knew my little DIA was so well connected.'

Finn concentrated on the logic of his argument. They were safe, they were protected. But the wave of panic soon crashed over him again as Catherine flipped over a photograph on the table between them. His heart sped up, adrenaline urging him to flee, while an invisible lead weight held him down, forcing him to acknowledge the image before him. Sophie, aged about fifteen or sixteen, before the days of dress codes, perched on a wall wearing the shortest of shorts, her bare legs dangling in front of her. A dainty green sandal swung off her toes and a tiny halter-neck top exposed her firm, tanned waist. She was so beautiful. Sophie was smiling out of the photograph directly at Finn. But not Finn, he wasn't there, someone else was taking that photograph. Someone else benefited from that smile. Not even the three lads in the picture who were admiring her. Someone else. He recognised the boys' expression. The same one Andy would have whenever Evie brought home a friend from college. It would always end the same way, in the summerhouse, Andy enjoying the guest intimately.

'This is from one of your father-in-law's famous social gatherings for sycophants gorging on his guest list. Daddy took this photo. Were you aware my father knew your wife? He was enchanted by her, even considering marrying her. How funny is that? I might have been your wife's daughter.'

Finn wasn't listening. He held the photo, wanting to screw it up, rip it, throw it into the stove. He imagined the minds of those boys, enthralled by the girl on the wall. One had his arm around Sophie's waist. Why did she let him do that? What right did they have to look at his wife like that?

Cat tugged the photo from his hand, making him look up at her, 'Did you hear me 568216? My father was going to marry your Sophia Elle. Isn't that hilarious!'

Finn was shocked, he had no idea about Sophie's life before they met. He assumed he was the only boyfriend she had ever had. 'When?'

She was young in the picture, probably too young to marry. Sophie was the giggling nineteen-year-old when they met, in her first year of nursing school.

'Daddy wanted to marry her straight away, but your father-in-law asked him to wait until she was older. Such a disappointment for my father.'

'Why? He refused your father because he believed Sophie was too young.' Finn struggled to stay logical, when his brain wanted to scream abuse.

'A father just doing what's best for his little girl. Well you should know,' she said, laughing as her tutor turned away, his cheeks flushed. Cat had found his open wound and delighted in poking it with a dirty stick.

'In reality, it was a lucky escape.' She hadn't finished inflicting damage on him, continuing, 'You see those boys. Daddy had it on good authority that she screwed each and every one. It was such a difficult time. On one hand you had those like Daddy, patriotic and moral, then you had the likes of Sophia Elle, happy to throw open her legs to anyone who fancied a go. How do you know she's not enjoying herself right now? Bewitching a patriot for her own gratification. Do you really believe a woman like that would tell you everything?'

Finn followed her lips as she spoke, none of the words entering his closed off brain. It was all lies. He trusted Sophie implicitly, she wouldn't do that. That's not her.

'Are you worried about the lesson, 568216? Let's go to

the table and we can discuss Elinor and Marianne's views on morality.'

* * *

Thursday 15th April

> *I have him, I have his secret. So, he's a jealous little mouse. I saw his face, colour rising in those cheeks. He doesn't know about his precious Sophie. I am his magpie, the teller of secrets. What else shall I tell him? He'll thank me, he must. Truth will always reveal itself.*

* * *

SOPHIE

It was late by the time she got home. Sophie waved to the security guard, stopping to chat with the corporal. Beaming smiles and laughter masking her turmoil. They engaged in the usual set exchange, Sophie asking about his wife and sons, and then listening attentively about his boys' academic successes.

'You must be so proud, of your boys. Well, I ought to let you work, Mrs Anna is bound to have cooked me something delicious and I really should head in and do it justice. Hope I can stay awake long enough.'

She didn't wait for the corporal's reply and headed straight for the house. The light in her father's study was on. A shadow passed before the slight gap in the curtains. The sight of him roused her anger to an unknown level. For a moment she contemplated her place in the darkness of the garden. Could she go back to the corporal, steal his gun? Patricide would not provide the reason why New Albany had declared war on DIAs, and her inevitable execution would not protect Finn, more likely hasten his own death. As much as she wanted to do it, murder would not solve a thing.

'Is Mum in?' asked Sophie, strolling into Tim's study.

He looked up, surprised, smiled and then said, 'I thought, well, never mind. Yes, Mum's upstairs having a soak.'

'That sounds nice. I might run one myself.' Sophie wandered around the ample room, looking, but not looking. She wondered if the books lining his shelves discussed the cost effectiveness of genocide. Sophie intended to have nothing more to do with him after the previous night. Doubtless he would argue he hadn't meant for any of this to happen. Her love had been replaced with loathing. She had discovered the truth, now she needed the facts. Stopping by his desk, she wrote, 'I know what you do!' across the file he had been reviewing.

Tim's head nodded in acceptance. He placed his pen carefully on the desk and removed the graffitied paper, burning it on the fire. Only then did he return his daughter's disdainful scowl with his shame filled eyes. 'Fancy a drink, darling?'

The Booze Den was a mess. A demi-john was lying on its side, a crack radiating down from its mouth. The floor was stained red from the blackberry wine, its cloying alcoholic smell sticking to her lungs as she breathed in. 'What happened?' said Sophie, raising her hand to protect her nostrils.

Her father shrugged his shoulders and flopped into the armchair. 'I was sorting something out after you left.'

Before Sophie could question him any further, Tim had opened the cognac and was pouring a generous measure into last night's glass. He held up the bottle, peaking her barely controlled fury.

'Really? You want me to sit down and drink with you?' Sophie was physically shaking, while her father downed the cognac, unable to meet her eyes.

'Look at me! You are murdering them and all you do is play with alcohol.'

Tim was absorbed by his drink, adding fuel to her burning temper. An invisible creature took control of her body, grabbing her arm and swung it towards her father. The crystal snifter flew out of his hand, smashing among the discarded bottles on the floor.

'LOOK AT ME!'

Culpable eyes looked up and previously unseen greyness

descended into the lines crossing his face. Tim showed all the fragility of age, her jovial friend consumed by the evil of murder.

'I hate you. I want the truth and then I never want you in my life again. Do you hear me? Never!'

'Sophia! Please, let me explain,' said her father, finally jolted into a response.

'Why? How do you explain mass murder? For God's sake, you don't even consider them human.' Sophie was gasping between words, her face fierce with heat and tears.

'Sit down. I'm not going to excuse what has...is happening. There can never be an excuse, but please, my darling, let me speak, let me explain. I never wanted anything like this to happen. Truly, I couldn't stop it. There was nothing I could do. Please, Sophia, my darling, please let me explain.'

Sophie stared back at the stranger who had once been her father. His face was tear-stained and his whole body was shaking with guttural sobs.

'I'm listening.' Her arms folded in defiance. Their roles had been reversed. A penitent Tim quivering beneath the serious glare of a furious child.

'How can you even think that of me? I'm your father, you know me. You know me better than anyone.'

'I thought I did, I was wrong.'

'You're not wrong. Why do you think I did what I did to stop Henry sending Finn to the Treatment Centre? I'd do everything in my power to protect the two of you. I love you. I love you both. Finn is the gentlest, sweetest man in this godforsaken country.'

'Protecting one DIA does not exonerate you from murdering hundreds, or is that thousands? Does your secretary hand you a daily spreadsheet, deaths achieved, and bodies disposed?'

'Things got out of hand. I was in too deep. Speak out, and it is high treason. Are you even aware how New Albany deals with high treason?'

'Hanging, which is what you deserve!' Sophie spat back.

'I do, maybe you are right. But what about your mother, what about you? What about any children you may have? Do you all deserve the gallows for my actions?'

It took a moment for the horrific revelation to make any sense, but when it did, her hand shot up to her mouth. An indistinct 'Oh, my God,' slipped out from between her fingers.

'I was their perfect fool. Don't you see, Sophie? I was ambitious, a devoted family man, a party loyalist, everything they needed. They flattered me, they promoted me, they gave me power and prestige. The bill comes later. It always comes later, and you don't get to know the price in advance.'

Sophie sat in the seat next to her father, her legs no longer capable of withstanding the strength of those words.

'You could have spoken out, challenged the Party, reported what was happening. I never thought you a coward.'

'Do you remember Jonny Keeler?' asked Tim.

'Millie's dad?' she replied. Confusion mingled with a creeping dread as she remembered shared confidences and sleepover giggles of childhood friendship. Memories forever blighted by Millie's murder.

Newly married, Sophie had endured whispered condolences, with wary glances towards her Outer husband revealing her colleagues true concerns. She loathed them, but when evening came and she was alone with Finn, she did wonder what must go through the minds of people like him. What would lead them to commit such a heinous atrocity?

Her father was crying, his trembling hand reaching out to hold hers. She drew it back. 'No, Dad, you told me it was the Outer terrorists who killed them, it was their fault, you said so. They killed Millie and the others. Their deaths had nothing to do with the crimes you are committing now.'

He was shaking his head. 'Don't you see, darling, he saw it coming and wanted to go public. He was going tell the truth, they couldn't allow it'

'Who? Who killed them?'

'I still see their bodies you know, every time I close my eyes. Deborah and the girls, I see them hanging from that oak tree.'

'Who, Dad? Tell me who?' Sophie was becoming desperate, that dread she earlier felt swelling up inside her, consuming her. 'Who killed them?'

Tim's grabbed her wrist, lifting his face up. 'We did.' Under the dim lights of the hut and with his skin drained of blood, he resembled a macabre version of himself, a ghost to relay the petrifying truth. 'We sent our own patriotic terrorists, complete with their own film crew, to ensure silence. You see, that is how you control rebel ministers. You give them a glimpse of their future. We all watched the recording.'

The room swirl around Sophie, her head light with her father's words. She bent forward, retching.

'Here, use this.' Her father placed a plastic waste bin next to her. The weight of his arm on her both comforted and repelled her. She wanted to leave the hut, but her body had other ideas.

'It's not the first time I've seen this reaction,' he continued. 'You are in good company with some of New Albany's highest ministers. You see, they put us in the St Stephen boardroom to watch the footage. They compelled us to watch the whole attack. Even now, all these year later, I smell that vomit if I have to go in there. It's as though it came out of us and became impregnated into those oak panels.

Sophie carefully sat back up. 'What do you mean, you

watched footage. Wasn't it enough to order their deaths?'

'No, I had nothing to do with that, none of us did. Watching the executions was a means to silence us. Don't you get it? Assassinating Jonny might have stopped the truth getting out, but for how long? They had to guarantee our silence too. Witnessing the children having their throats slit...' he paused, shrivelling back into his chair. 'Oh God, Sophie, Jamie was barely a month old, an innocent. Both of the boys, how could they do that? Tears were rolling across his face, glinting in the weak light. He shook his head as though to compose himself. 'Then what they did to Deborah and the girls. How can I ever speak out? I see them but it's your face on the corpses, it's your mother's jerking body hanging from the tree. They kept Jonny until last. He had seen it all. That bullet to his head must have come as a relief after the torment they put him through.'

'And our government did that, murdered eight people, just to ensure others wouldn't reveal their grotesque policies? Somebody would have said something surely. They can't all be as spineless as you, Dad.'

Tim shrank further into the chair with her insult. 'Speak out and rain untold horrors on those we love? That takes rare bravery, my darling. Would you be brave enough?'

Sophie was immobile, stupefied by his confession.

'What price would you pay to protect the ones you love?' he said, brushing away a lock of hair that had stuck to her cheek.

She gave no answer, but in her head she was reliving what she had done and planning what else she'd do in order to protect the man she loved.

'Can you forgive me?'

She waited before answering. Her father's entire body imploring her to grant absolution. 'I don't know, I can't think about that right now,' she replied, shying away from him, as though his presence alone might infect her with cowardice. 'What happens next, Dad? Are you just going to let it continue, silently ignoring the deaths of others?'

'No, not this time.' He picked up his tumbler and resumed drinking the whiskey. The glass drained of the last drop, he continued, 'After I spoke to you last night, I contacted a friend from the Outer World. New Albany's executioner is hungry again and I can't let anything happen to you. You mean everything to me, everything.'

'Outer World contact? What are you talking about and what if the Surveillance Unit finds out? I don't understand,' said Sophie, taken aback by his revelation.

'Oh come on, you must have realised by now that this hut is nothing more than an elaborate hoax. There's small bunker under the floors. Why do you think I am so obsessive about keeping it clear of any listening devices? Not so I can play with wines and spirits, but so I can communicate with the Outer World. That's why it is such a mess. I was in a hurry.'

'You're a spy?'

'I'm not sure spy is the right word, more a helpful informant. When I do my tours, my apologising rounds of talks, I never know which of their people will make contact, but one always appears. A cricket match, a fashion show, a classical piano concerto, one always appears. I tell them the truth about what is going on, it's only ever conversations.'

I even saw Finn's mother once, outside one event, she was protesting.'

'Dad, if you are spying for them, then they must know how bad it is here. They could attack, save us!'

Tim made the same amused chuckle that he did when she was a child, asking about the fairies in the wood. 'My darling, would that politics were that simple. I sometimes think that we are the focus of all their available anger. No one has the time nor energy to turn their mistrust on other countries, so those governments get to live peacefully creating their own versions of chaos and disorder while their nation's public eyes and guns face us.'

Silence hung between then, Tim waited for a response, but Sophie had picked on one of his sentences, twirling it around, more confused than ever.

'Dad, how did you know it was Eloise? You've never met. What are you not telling me? Are you in contact with them? Finn needs to know if you are, it's only fair. He misses them, he misses them so much.'

'No, I'm not in contact. Maybe you were always destined to marry Finn, who knows; your blasted fairies playing tricks on me. I met Finn's mother many years ago, she hasn't changed much'

'You met Eloise?'

'It was before Finn was born. She might have been pregnant with him, can't remember. Look, Eloise still ran Finlay Communications with her father back then. Her father, Michael Finlay became the focus of my hatred. Everything he and FinCom stood for was the polar opposite of what we believed New Albany should be. I was a blind fool. I let dogma dictate. While I focused on my hatred of Finn's grandfather, the power behind me prepared the ground for their own victory. I was just a puppet.'

'Maybe you could get a message to Eloise, through your friend, somehow.' Sophie's desperation clinging to the barest of hope.

'No, darling. It's too dangerous. Do you think ASSU are unaware of the connection? If I talk to her, it would put all of us in danger and, knowing that lot, all of Finn's family too. I have something else in mind.'

'What?'

'You and Finn are going to escape. I have to let you go, if we can get out later then we'll try.'

'Will it be safe? What if it is a trap, those smugglers are bastards.'

'We won't be using smugglers. I know of sixteen who have tried to defect in the last ten years, only five have succeeded. It will be very dangerous indeed, but we have to try. I can't protect you and Finn any longer.'

'I don't know if I am terrified or thrilled. Finn will be—'

'No! You mustn't tell Finn.'

Sophie sat bolt upright, 'Why not? He has a right to know.'

'No, it's too dangerous. The more people who know, the higher the risk of failure. What if I can't get you out, you think he could survive that disappointment, on top of everything else?'

Sophie said nothing. Her father was right, Finn needed to stay ignorant for his own safety.

His face was ice cold, but he was breathing. She had returned unseen. As far as security were concerned, Sophie Smith had left the premises at nine thirty-eight. There was work to be done. She emptied the remaining liqueur on the ground, spilling some on the blanket, before tossing some of his clothes aside. She undressed and scattered her clothes in random directions. One stocking got stuck in a tree. It looked so ridiculous she let out a little giggle. Naked, she laid down next to him, cuddling him tightly to warm him up. Sophie pulled the second blanket over them and gently rubbed his limbs. The moonlight silvered the apple tree branches giving the impression it was a metal cage above them, but the breaking dawn would bring colour and life back to that monotone garden. She had to work fast.

Sophie whispered in his ear, 'Ryan, it's time to wake up, come on sweetie, time to wake now.'

He groaned, eventually opening an eye, clearly struggling with recollection, questioning her, 'Who are you? Where are we? What's happened?' He peeked down at his body, then at her, making the correct assumption. 'Oh God, fuck. I'm fucked. Fucking, fucking fucked. What the fuck have we done?'

'Well, fucking fucked sounds about right. It was fun, didn't you have fun? Shall we play again?' Sophie pushed the terrified boy onto his back and sat astride him. 'I thought I heard a guard, but he went on past. We have about forty minutes until dawn, if we are as quiet as mice? No screaming this time.'

Ryan pushed her off him, petrified. All memory of sexual pleasure obliterated by the prospect of public humiliation and censure. Sophie had been right to pick him.

'No fucking way. Get off me you whore. You slut, you fucking slut. If I get caught my life will be destroyed. You fucking, whoring slut. What if you're pregnant? Oh God, they'll put me in jail.' He shoved her away, scrambling for his clothes, collecting what he could, a jumper, his trousers and shoes.

Sophie hugged her knees, watching his little drama with some amusement. 'Relax Ryan, if I am pregnant then you'll have done me a favour. You don't look that dissimilar to my husband, only younger and, well there's more of you to get a girl excited. I'll sleep with Mr Pickles tonight and he'll be delighted. If there's a child in nine months, well then, he'll be overjoyed.'

'You're a class A whore, you know that, don't you? You disgust me!'

Chilled by the pre-dawn air, Sophie snatched up the

blanket while Ryan darted to and fro collecting some more clothes before escaping the scene of his crime. She hoped he'd spend the remainder of the day in a state of extreme nausea and worry. There would be no baby, she knew that for sure.

Once he had run off, she gave the garden a quick check to ensure there was no evidence of her presence. An hour later, Sophie had returned to her parents' house unseen by the security. By eight o'clock she was showered, in a fresh uniform and waving goodbye to the guard on the gate.

If Sophie thought she would sleep on the bus back to her cottage, she was wrong. Terrified and excited in equal measure, she fantasied about their freedom, but at what cost? Her home, her parents? Her father was going to risk his and her mother's life to set them free. The odds weren't on their side, but there was no going back, it had to be tried. Tim was right, as much as Sophie wanted to share the news with Finn, and despite his improved health, it would be too dangerous.

Finn barely acknowledged her return. A peck on the cheek and a meal on the table. He showed little interest in what she had learnt, made a polite enquiry about her parents' health and then, silence. The miniature portion of lasagne travelled around his plate in a mealtime dance before the tragic climax, disposal in the waste. He mumbled about being tired and headed off to bed in the guest room.

Alone in the kitchen, Sophie drank her herbal tea. He had been improving. George had sent a text the previous night as agreed. All was well, they played chess, Finn had won. There had been no new restrictions. Something else must have triggered it. In the past, when he feared anxiety getting the better of him, he would share his thoughts with Sophie, but this silence was different. Expert in guiding him through his black days, Sophie knew to tread carefully. Sometimes it took longer than others, but Finn always recovered, his mood improving and his anxiety dissipating.

Henry had called her that morning, there was no way he would give her time off to spend the day with Finn. Retrieving her mobile from her bag, she sent a quick text to George. Moments later it pinged. He was going to be off duty, so he'd pop by in the morning. A walk sounded like a great idea.

It was later than she had hoped by the time she reached the cottage. Finn's muddy walking shoes were outside the kitchen door. A good sign. George had texted saying his wife had prepared a picnic for them and they did a lovely ten-mile circular walk towards the south of the town. Finn had been quiet but no more than usual.

Sophie stepped into the kitchen and found her husband marking a child's essay. He did not look up in greeting, he did not smile.

'Your dinner's in the oven, I've already eaten.'

'I see from your shoes you went for a walk, anywhere nice?'

'Seeing as George probably reported it all to you, I'm sure you know that we walked to Hanbury Common. I was suitably chaperoned.'

Finn put the essay down and left the room while Sophie's ears burnt with the chastisement. It was for his own good, he would understand that eventually. Upstairs, the guest room door slammed shut and she forced herself to remember other bad days.

Back in the kitchen, she ate her dinner alone. Only once

she put her plate in the dishwasher did she noticed the absence of other dinner plates. Finn had not eaten again.

The weather report said it would be warm, an ideal day to spend in the garden with Finn. She prepared porridge for breakfast and a cup of chamomile tea with an added teaspoon of one of Anna's herbal remedies. Sophie had stocked her garden with a multitude of useful plants. Anna had suggested the tincture of St John's Wort several years earlier and it seemed to help when he was a little down. It was a relief to see him eat most of the porridge, however the chamomile tea was more problematic.

'You'll get dehydrated if you don't drink anything,' she said, pushing the cup towards him.

'What's wrong with ordinary tea, or water for that matter?'

Finn's mood had not improved, in fact it appeared to have worsened since her return from Court Farm. Sophie was confused and uncertain how to help him, entering into a row over chamomile tea would not be a good start to the day.

'Nothing wrong with water, it's just that chamomile, well it can have a calming effect. You've been tense recently, busy with school and tutoring. I don't know, perhaps I thought I was being helpful.' She got up and opened the cupboard. 'Shall I make you a different tea. Let me see what we've got...' Behind the boxes of chamomile she saw a distinctive green box. 'We have mint. Would you prefer mint?'

The awkward atmosphere in the garden was accompanied by the noise of tools turning the earth and the occasional bird song.

'Finn, pass me the trowel, would you?' Her excited voice sounded too loud to her and she lowered it, gently adding,

'I've found a free plant. Self-seeded by the looks of it.' Sophie pulled out the weeds surrounding the little plant, then plucking a leaf from the stem, she held it up. 'Look, can you see the little dots.'

Finn bent down and squinted, his eyesight seemingly worse. 'Not really, what is it?'

'Hypericum perforatum, St John's Wort. A very useful plant. The leaves and flowers are edible, something different to add to a summer salad.'

'If you say so.'

Under his uncomfortable glare, she removed the plant, replanting it near the bench.

'Why haven't you annulled our marriage?

Sophie fell forward, stunned by his question. Her hand landed on the recently planted seedling, squishing it under her palm.

'You have plenty of reasons to, you don't have to put up with me, with *"my episodes"* as your mother calls it. She'd be absolutely thrilled,' he continued.

Sophie wiped the mud off her hands and breathed in. It was going to be one of those days when her patience would be tested, but she had been there before, and all her coping skills were ready and waiting.

'Finn, you are low, that's all.' She stood up and faced her husband. He looked so pale. 'I'm just trying to help. Anna told me this sometimes happens after a serious illness. It's not your fault. It's never your fault. I won't annul our marriage because I love you. You are my everything.' Tugging him by the arm she manoeuvred him to the ground. 'Come on, tell me what's up and let's work through it. You'll improve eventually. I'll take care of you as best as I can until you do. My love for you doesn't change just because you have black days.' She leant in to hug him, but he shied away. He had never done that before.

'Why didn't you let me meet your parents before our wedding? They must have been curious and yet the first time I met them was after the signing ceremony. Why did you hide me from them?' He couldn't even look at her when he spoke.

'Because you might not marry me if you met them first!' She gave him a jokey punch, but Finn neither smiled nor laughed. Sophie shrugged. 'Look Finn, I wanted to, but they objected to me marrying you. Well, mainly that was Mum, Dad just worried. He anticipated difficulties for us. He did ask me to reconsider though. He likes you. I'm sure he does. He loves you. You must realise that by now.'

The obstinate silence that followed was punctuated by a blue tit calling from the apple tree. Neither turned towards its song. Finally he spoke, 'What about the Commandant? How long have you known him?'

'What about him?' Sophie was mystified by his behaviour.

'How long have you known him?' he repeated.

She sighed with his persistence. 'I don't know him.'

'That's not true, is it? You met him. You were going to marry him. Or maybe I shouldn't have found out about that?' Finn had found a small stick and was scraping out the moss from a crack between the edging bricks. That crack had become his focal point, vigorously scratching it, deepening the brick's wound. Sophie wondered what was going on in her husband's head. During his black days of the past he sought refuge in his music. Earphones permanently on his ears, withdrawing himself until Sophie could coax him back. That unheard music continually playing in his brain, a melancholy lament or an explosion of percussion driving his uncharacteristic behaviour. She knelt beside him, placing her hand firmly on Finn's, halting the stick's movements. His fringe was getting long, and some hair had flopped in front of his glasses. With her other hand, she gently pushed it back, dark grey shadowed eyes staring back at her. 'You didn't sleep last night, did you?'

Finn snapped his hand away from hers, folding his arms, 'Don't change the subject, did you marry me on the rebound? Did he find out about your boyfriends? Was I your naïve foreigner? One way of avoiding an arranged marriage I suppose.'

It would have been so easy for her to lose her temper. He was goading her, being irrational and not fully in control of what he was saying. He needed to rest and then she would talk to him, explain things clearly.

'I'm not going to answer anything until after lunch. If you want to ask me then, you can, but only after you have eaten and had some sleep.' She stood up, towering over his hunched body. 'Lunch is already made, I only have to heat it up. It'll be ready in ten minutes.'

Much to her relief he followed her, ate his soup and even drank some chamomile tea. They did not talk. While Finn loaded the dishwasher, Sophie retreated to the sitting-room, curled onto her favourite chair by the window, and examined the progress of her embroidery She was surprised, but did not halt her sewing, when Finn joined her. On the coffee table lay another pile of essays, grabbing the top one, he slumped into his usual corner of the sofa.

THEO's light shone red with the absence of communication, the occasional snip of scissors, or the clicking of a pen, failing to register within its memory programmed noises. There was only so much sulking that she could bear, at least music would be a distraction from his obstinance. 'THEO, play Mozart, Symphony No.38 in D major, "Prague".'

Its light turned green and the sitting-room filled with the orchestral crescendos and diminuendos of Finn's favourite piece of music. She didn't understand its significance to him, only that it was the piece he played most when the reality of their world became intolerable. Sophie kept sewing. His furious stare made her ears burn red, but she would not respond. The clicking stopped. She didn't look up. Then the clicking restarted, stopping once more as he shifted position to lie across the sofa. By the time the 'Andante' had finished, his pen had dropped out of his hand. Finn was asleep. Sophie put the needlework away and draped a blanket on his recumbent body.

The planting was almost complete, and the garden would look stunning by mid-summer with all its colour and wonderful scents. Anticipation as much a part of this piece of art as the eventual show. She would be checking her little plants daily for evil slugs and snails. Sophie, a ruthless murderer when it came to those vile stealing gastropods. An avenging angel, she smiled at the thought of her beloved plants protected by her nematodes, busy using their hosts to wreak havoc within those slimy, thieving molluscs.

The kitchen door's handle announced Finn's arrival. Normality had resumed, because there he was, holding two cups of 'builders', offering one to Sophie. She accepted his liquid apology. He must have searched the cupboards. The box had been hidden behind a pack of washing powder. Although she tried to reduce his caffeine over the years, Finn had proved to be annoyingly stubborn. He liked his ordinary builders tea and no amount of *'poisonous'* herbal tea was going to change his mind.

Since the import ban, Camellia Sinensis had been cultivated in AZ Eight. The Area's micro-climate was perfect for home grown tea and the Albian elite. Her own family spent most summer holidays there, sailing with her father in the coves around the coastline. A place of happy memories for her. A place to strike fear in unfortunate detainees arrested for sabotage, or as she now knew, a DIA hoping to be repatriated only to be sent to the labour camps nestling among the hills. Those unhappy captives compelled to pick tea leaves for Finn's daily addiction.

'You're like a sniffer dog when it comes to finding tea.' She clutched the cup staring at the liquid and all the misery it contained, before placing it on the ground.

'Thanks. Did you have a good sleep?'

'Yes, thank you. Loads of marking left, though.'

Sophie joined her husband on the bench, if he wanted to talk, it was up to him to start the conversation.

'Have you finished?' he asked after what seemed like an eternity.

'Just a few more, I'll do those later. I got some pork chops for dinner. Is that OK?' she said, smiling back, hopeful for more conversation.

'Yes.'

He looked away from her again as though it were her face giving cause for pain. If she could take away that hurt, she would, but the 'Why?' was a mystery to her. A robin caught his attention. It flew down onto her garden fork, its tiny head jerking from side to side observing its two gardeners.

'Were you really engaged to Commandant Fry?' he asked.

Sophie had no idea where he had got his information, and thinking it was the cause of the problem, she smiled at him and shook her head. 'No, my love. Goodness, why would you think that?'

'I...I...someone told me.'

'Finn, if I were engaged to Commandant Fry, then it's news to me. I don't know the man. I hear there are arranged marriages where the bride and groom meet for the first time at the signing ceremony, but do you really think my parents would consent to that? Well, let's not talk about Mum, but Dad? You honestly believe he'd ever do that to me? You know it is completely preposterous. Anyway, I only found out recently that I'd even met the man. Not so much me meeting him, more a case of he met me, I've no recollection of him at all. Mum told me before I went on the training course, I think.'

'And you didn't think to tell me?'

'Tell you what?'

'About the Commandant, of course.'

'Oh, good grief, Finn, it was a bit of trivial gossip that meant nothing.' Sophie was irritated why something so innocent and banal was causing him so much angst.

'It's not trivial to find out your wife had been someone else's first.'

Finn's remark sparked an angry response from Sophie. She wanted to yell at him but instead resorted to biting her bottom lip, before answering in her measured and calm way, 'I wasn't anybody else's, firstly I am Sophie Smith, I belong to no one, I choose to be with you. Secondly, I had no idea he had asked my father to marry me. I presume Dad refused permission, wanting the Captain to wait until I was older. By the time the Captain came back to my father, I was already at nursing school with the love of my life. Captain Fry wouldn't have stood a chance, even if I had known about him.'

'And what about others?'

'Others, what others?' He was getting ridiculous. Sophie had never known him to be so jealous.

'Other boyfriends, sexual partners, you know what I mean.'

'Friends who were boys, yes they existed. I wasn't kept separate from the opposite sex like today's girls. I met, I chatted and like any other normal girl, I fancied. The first man to make passionate love to me was the man who was, and still is, my husband.'

Sophie stared defiantly into Finn's face, he had to believe she wasn't lying. What was the point of telling Finn about him? He had been a mistake. It wasn't as though it was a total lie, she only felt passion when she was with Finn. Pretence must prevail. 'That's the truth, the whole truth and nothing but the truth, so help me God.'

As the days passed, Finn appeared to improve. Sophie was unsure if it was telling him about the Commandant or the St John's Wort. The weekends were generally better than the weekdays with Monday evenings being the most tense. She believed Commandant Fry was the cause. After all, Finn was teaching his daughter. He never mentioned if he had met the Commandant, but it must have been him telling Finn about his 'engagement' to her. Who else could it have been? Her mother? Sophie doubted her mother could be so callous as to knowingly lie purely to cause hurt, but the more she thought about it, the more plausible it became.

Sophie put away the ironing board and went in search of Finn, finding him in the sitting-room, planning lessons.

'It's a lovely afternoon, do you want to go for a walk by the river, we'll take a picnic?'

They had been working all morning and needed to get out. A walk together would do them both good.

Finn stopped writing, his jaw lowered as though about to speak, but God had pressed the pause button. She realised her mistake and should have never have mentioned the river. No amount of cajoling would alter his well-founded aversion to the place. 'Do you mind if we go another time?' he said, picking up his pen once more.

Sophie wasn't about to force him, that was usually counterproductive. 'Well what about tea in the garden, proper tea? Not my disgusting herbal stuff.'

Finn stood up, his hand on her arm to stop her leaving. 'I'll make it then, can't trust you, you might accidentally on purpose make mine out of some disgusting garden leaf.' He winked at her.

As he left the room, Sophie felt the weight of the previous days lift. He was recovering.

They sat in the garden surveying their hard work. She adored her garden so much and hated the prospect of leaving it, but she would. Leaving behind the life she knew would mean her husband might be free at last to live a life. There was no competition. The escape plan was nothing more than a vague theory. Until her father returned from his latest goodwill trip, it would remain that way, an unanswered message.

Finn basked beneath the sun's warmth. The recent sunshine had tanned his face and childhood freckles dotted across his cheeks and nose. He looked so relaxed and content, almost lost in his daydream world. A world far away from life in New Albany. Ignoring a slight moment of guilt, Sophie interrupted his peaceful dream, 'If you were allowed to have only one plant in the garden, which would it be?'

He responded without hesitation, 'The rose by the kitchen door. I love its simplicity, the scent as you brush by, the way it starts off one colour but fades to another. What's it called?'

'I think it's "For your Eyes Only",' she replied.

'And are you for my eyes only?' asked Finn, his eyes flicking open and shooting a look at her.

'Yes, my darling, forever.'

His hug was a simple expression of love, but it meant so much more to her.

'Have you got a busy week ahead?' said Sophie as she snuggled in, relishing the closeness.

Finn removed his arm and picked up his cup. 'Mock exam preparations. Pointless exams for girls who don't care.'

THE GOVERNOR OF LIFE

Passion. Jealousy. Ambition. We each carry one within the veins of our character. Venom that desires nothing more than to poison our world. A viscous fluid that seeks the cracks and weeps out of its porous human container.

FINN

The lengthening days of spring meant it was still daylight as he crossed town to get to the mansion. Ahead, on the green, he saw a gathering crowd of mostly patriots, standing in an arc around the north side, their phones primed to take pictures. The low rumble of whispered voices made his innards constrict. Distracted, his front wheel hit a pothole swerving him into the path of a guard.

'Oi! Watch where you're going.'

Finn got off his bike to apologise, but before he could utter a word the guard was grabbing his sleeve. 'If you head over to your left, you'll get a decent view. It's Corporal Ross today and he's got a stonking left hook.'

Finn did not need to ask what was about to happen. State sponsored cruelty. The guard had moved on and unseen by anyone around him, he surreptitiously pushed the bangle as far up his arm as possible and headed to the edge of the crowd. If he tried to leave, there might be questions from the guards on the other side of the green. He needed to stay inconspicuous. With no physical difference to distinguish him except for his slight accent and the ominous bangle, he might have even been taken for a patriot. He knew to stay silent throughout, these events had been known to get vicious. At least at the back, he might miss seeing as much as possible, even if the sound of battered flesh and bone would drive into his skull, ready to replay whenever he thought himself happy.

The man was dragged to the centre of the green. There were three guards, always three guards. Two to hold the DIA and one to read the charge.

Everything about the guard reminded Finn of a fairy book town crier. Legs slightly apart, chest puffed up, the tablet held high, and finally his voice, clear and sonorous, echoing off the building opposite.

'Prisoner 432890/7, you are charged with showing disrespect and breach of contract as determined by the terms of your employment. You are sentenced to six minutes of punishment.'

The bangle was read and the DIA acknowledged guilt by signing the guard's tablet, his shaking hand visible to all. Only those DIAs looking for a permanent release from captivity would dare refuse to sign.

Procedure complete, the tablet was placed in a bag and the guard's gun swung around from his back. While the other two held the poor man's arms, the butt of the gun was repeatedly thrust into his stomach. Two minutes of brutality, while the next guard limbered up for his turn. Finally, the third one took over. There was no formula, each soldier was free to employ whatever cruelty he could conceive provided he didn't kill him. That right was the domain of others. Some of the patriots in the crowd cheered on their favourite guard as if they were boxers in a ring. Finn wondered briefly which one was Corporal Ross. All three seemed proficient in left hooks as far as he could tell. To the left of him he overheard a few spectators laying bets on how long it would be before the DIA would be rendered unconscious. Attitudes had changed in the nineteen years since he first arrived as a twenty-one-year-old student. Tolerance, forgiveness and kindness, had become alien values to devotees of New Albany. Those who would speak out, silenced years ago.

Punishment completed, the man was left abandoned on the green, bloodied, but conscious. The gamblers sulked away from the gathering, aggrieved to have lost money to the bookie. That same bookmaker ambled over to the guards, shaking their swollen fists while passing them a few notes. Youngsters took pictures with the punished man. The crowd dispersed happily commenting on the spectacle while the injured man struggled to his feet. Finn wanted to help him up, but that would leave him vulnerable to attack. He heard the braying voices of the youths, play fighting behind him, eager to find a DIA punch bag. An old lady walked over to the DIA prisoner. He was bent double, spitting blood onto the grass. With her arm around him, she guided him back to her house. A patriot, and like his wife, someone who remembered those years when tolerance, forgiveness and kindness were virtues to be honoured.

* * *

Tuesday 18th May

Nothing fits anymore, I need new dresses. I shall tell Daddy to take me to Area Zone One. I suppose I could wear the burgundy dress. It's too short now. He'd see my knees. I wonder if that's his 'thing', legs? Or maybe he'd prefer another part of me. That sop Daddy invited for Sunday lunch couldn't take his eyes off my breasts the whole time. They are rather fine, though. It seems a shame to hide them behind all these layers. No one will know.

* * *

There was no time to dwell on the man on the green, he was in danger of arriving late. Eight o'clock on the dot he entered the sitting-room just as Cat was stepping out of her bedroom, her hair wet and already dressed in her night clothes. A pale blue silk gown covering a matching silk night dress. His evening had just got worse. Embarrassed, Finn blushed and inclined his head, so he wasn't looking at her. 'Would you prefer me to leave the room while you dress, Miss Fry?'

'No. I want an early night. It's more convenient for me to get ready before our lesson. You may sit.'

Yet another game, goodness knows who she was pretending to be this evening. He sat down facing the setting sun. With an elbow on the table, he used his hand to shield his eyes.

'You seem agitated tonight, has something upset my 568216?'

'I'm fine, the sun's in my eyes, that's all. I have a past paper for you. Not long until the exams now.'

'What do you think?' she swirled around, opening the gown for effect.

'I...I...' he had to reply, that much was certain, but what could he say to a teenager, dancing about in a silk nightdress. 'I like the colour.'

She stopped, and pulled out her chair, her cheeks flushed by activity. 'Or is it the flesh that lies beneath that interests you?' Catherine reached out for her book, opening it at a dog-eared page, doodles of naked women snaking up the side where notes should be. 'We should get on, I suppose. Your fantasies will have to wait a little while longer.'

Finn lowered his hand to pick up his pen, the sun briefly burning into his retina. He thought to let the sun do its damage, blind him, release him from his agonising commitment.

'Austen is insufferable,' she said, snapping shut her book. 'There is so much more out there.'

Finn pushed the exam paper towards her. 'Well it's only for a few more weeks and then you'll be free of me.'

'Not sure I like that.' Her perfectly shaped smile belied

the menace that sent a shiver through Finn. She pushed the paper back across the table. 'I'm reading Tess of the D'Urbervilles at the moment. Tell me, 568216, who do you prefer, Alec or Angel?'

Finn tried to avoid her games. 'You need to concentrate on the exam work if you want to pass. I suspect your father will not be happy with me if you fail.'

'I won't fail because you are going to read the paper first and tell me what to write. It will be a top grade.'

'No...um...no, I can't. I... er...no... I don't have access to the paper.'

'You will this time. The paper will be here for you a week before the exam. I expect you to write perfect answers for me.'

Finn knew better than to ask 'how?' or 'why?' That was what was going to happen and that is what he will be ordered to do. It crossed his mind to give her false answers. He was leaving after the exams after all. Only a few more weeks of her manipulating, then he would be back home with his family and with Evie.

'Why is a top grade so important?' Finn watched her fingers flicking nail varnish into the air. The tiny pale pink confetti tip-tapping as it hit the ignored exam paper. He had given hours of torturous lessons to a girl who would stop learning the minute a gold band was placed on her finger.

'It's all part of the sale process, I suppose,' she replied. 'Only child of an influential man, not dissimilar to your Sophia Elle. But as a high value bride, and vessel for a powerful man's sons, I will marry well.'

He ignored her insult. New Albany had declared their marriage tainted, not them. They had been happy. 'And does your father have a candidate in mind?' he added.

'My father is considering offers. He'll make a good deal. The best candidates want a wife who can charm, sparkle at dinners, understand the machinations of political power. If I were just beautiful, I'd complete my role as a womb for his sons, but I'd fail in other important roles. Does that make sense to you?'

Nothing made any sense to Finn these days. Why should he be surprised that her views on marriage were akin to a business transaction? That is what it would be. The sale of a daughter to a man whose long-term prospects would further her father's ambitions.

'Why did your father never remarry?' He immediately regretted his question, as Catherine's cheeks rose in mirth, her head thrown back in laughter.

'You silly man! My father never loved my mother. She was convenient and very, very wealthy.' She waved her arms around the room, indicating where their riches had originated. 'Do you remember when we discussed "Pride and Prejudice"?'

'Of course.'

'My mother was the Anne De Bourgh of New Albany. Incredibly rich, and incredibly weak. Mentally and physically. The perfect match for my father. She was never the sort to take to pregnancy well. My father ensured she suffered. As long as there was a live birth, he really didn't care how she was treated. She was fifteen when she had me. I resemble my father in size and stature, she was small. My mother survived but he had her sent away to rest. You'll not hear this from anyone else, but that weakling took her own life. The official story is she slipped and fell into the river that runs through the hospital grounds.'

Finn was disgusted to hear the way the Commandant had treated his wife. It explained the strangeness of Cat. How could she possibly be balanced when her world view was so deranged? A niggling thought made him question her again.

'That doesn't explain why he didn't marry again.'

She poked him with her finger. 'Oh, my creature is very bold with his questions tonight.' Her long fingers stretched over his, caging his hand onto the table. He was about to apologise, when she lifted her hand and placed a finger to his lips. It was soft from her grapefruit moisturiser. He could almost taste the fruit. 'Shush' she whispered, 'I don't mind, 568216, I find your curiosity endearing. His first love is the pursuit of power. Money is a useful tool but not the ultimate goal. Unfortunately, his chosen route was barred. The one he needed was married, but he is a patient man. She'll be free one day and then he will possess her again.'

That persistent worry lurking at the back of his mind was correct. The Commandant still coveted Sophie but warning her would mean revealing Finn's plan to repatriate.

'Don't worry,' she said.

Brief surprise was replaced with anger as she continued talking, 'Daddy gets plenty of practice at the club. He doesn't miss out on female company. These clubs are well stocked with girls who fail to have the social standing to acquire a husband. Most are the offspring of DIAs; nobody wants to marry a mongrel.' Catherine's dirty stick of insults pressed into his forever opened wound.

'Extra marital relations are forbidden, even for officers and officials,' said Finn, hoping his moralistic stance would curtail her attack.

'You are the most naïve man I have ever met,' she replied. 'Rules are flexible, they exist to be bent and broken by those powerful enough to do so.'

THE BIRTHDAY PARTY

MELBOROUGH MANOR HOUSE, AGED EIGHT

I can hear laughter and music winding its way up the stairs to my sanctuary. Mummy is too busy stressing about guests to notice my disappearance. Here, I am free to play with my other, more silent friends.

Evie watches me play. I point to toys and she hands them to me. Every now and again she touches her hair. I wonder if she misses her long ponytail. She cut it off this morning, especially for the party. I liked her long hair, but this is better.

'Darling, don't you think it's time to go downstairs, meet everyone. Uncle Pete is here too. He wants to say hi.'

I shake my head. Parties aren't for me. Silly games and strange adults talking at me and asking Mum if I have learnt to talk again. I take Kitty from Evie's hand and go to my piano. Headphones on, I block out the world.

Evie follows me, making room for herself on the stool by bashing her hips against mine. 'Shove up!'

I can't be cross with her. I let her remove the headphones and we play. Janie, my most recent piano teacher gave me a book of duets, but we don't need the music anymore, we just play. Sometimes Evie improvises, and I follow her lead. I have forgotten all about the party downstairs. I grin at Evie and she grins back. 'You'll be teaching me, soon,' she says.

I snuggle up to her and smell her perfume. It's different not her usual one. Her phone lights up, Maya is texting, and I read the message too.

'Are you coming, or should I go upstairs? Mxxx'

Evie texts back, 'Be right there, Exxx'

She turns to me. 'Finn, I have to go downstairs now. Why don't you come with me? You could meet Maya. She'd love to say hello.'

No. I don't want to hear that. I have no interest in sharing Evie with a stranger. It's bad enough she's away at college all the time. I listen to Evie telling me all about this friend, how kind she is, how lovely she is. I don't want to hear it. This stranger will take Evie away from me forever. I'm sure of it.

I didn't ask for a party. They thought it would cheer me up. I want to be the spoilt birthday boy, demanding attention. But only if it comes from Evie. Why should I meet her friend? I want to say no, but that behaviour is wrong, hurtful. I can never hurt her. I summon up every ounce of courage I possess, but, unable to voice the words she longs to hear, I nod my head instead. With Kitty tight in my hand, I follow her downstairs to the party.

FINN

* * *

Saturday 22 May

I saw him, walking bold as brass into the optician. She was with him. Well I suppose he can't go in on his own. I wanted to stop the car. I wanted to walk up to them, let her see me. He was smiling. I could see that much. An audacious smile. A smile that belongs to me.

* * *

The optician stood back, 'How's that?'

Finn was amazed, for the first time in two years he saw things clearly again.

'Hang the expense!' she had said, assuring him they had enough in her account, and he really ought to have glasses that corrected his vision instead of making it worse. He rarely asked about the finances, his own account closed by the authorities several years previously, and access to all his offshore accounts blocked. Regardless of how much they tried to save, there would never be enough. Whatever they put away, there was always another expense to deplete it. The glasses, Henry's visits when he was ill or random bribes; normal life for a mixed marriage consisted of a series of expensive bills.

'They look good on you, Finn. Happy Birthday,' said Sophie landing a sly kiss on his cheek while no one was looking. The optician had left the room to find the tablet and microchip reader. All details had to be recorded, no matter how trivial.

'I should hope so, given how much they cost, but there is a small problem with these new glasses,' he replied, pulling away from her as he heard footsteps behind him. Seeing Sophie bite her bottom lip and assured the optician was still in the back room, he leant back in and gently added, 'I see you clearly now and have absolutely no idea why such a beautiful creature chooses to be with a man like me.'

'Because my darling Finlay, there is not a single soul on this planet who can compare to you.'

* * *

Tuesday 25ᵗʰ May

I have told Mrs Fran to prepare a party for Thursday. I'll impress him, let him see how much I value him. I want his present to be special, symbolic. After all, he's not just any tutor. A jumper or a pen would be impersonal, tame even. I want bold, imaginative and exciting. I want to see that smile, the one reserved for me.

* * *

'Your file says it is your birthday on Thursday. Congratulations.'

Finn thanked Cat and took his seat.

'Are those new glasses?' She peered closely just centimetres from his nose. Her perfume wafted up from her neck, a heavy musk, not the light flowery scent of a girl. The heavy black satin of her nightdress brushed against his hand. It gave him goose bumps that ran down his back. He moved his hand away.

Cat picked off his glasses from his face and sat them

on her nose. 'You are truly blind. I can't see a thing!' She laughed as she returned them onto Finn's face, pushing the gold bridge upwards. 'How long have you needed specs?'

'Quite young, five or six, maybe younger, I can't remember to be honest.'

The lesson began normally, and Finn went through past questions with her. For a change, Cat played the attentive pupil. As though absent-mindedly, her hand dropped off the table and touched his knee while she discussed the choices that kept Edward Ferrars and Elinor apart. As he listened to her answers, he watched her fingers tracing circles on his thigh. He daren't interrupt her in case it gave her the opening to change topic. Better to endure her unwanted touch than be subject to her intrusiveness.

'I've had enough for today.' Without warning, Cat stood up and returned to the comfort of her sofa. 'I want a drink. Pour me a drink!'

Finn glanced at the clock, it was not even twenty-five minutes past eight, her lessons were getting shorter, the period of taunting increasing. He dreaded it. He placed the glass of caramel flavoured vodka on the table before making his way to his sofa.

'You didn't accept the last gift I gave you. I will need to be more inventive this time. What does my funny little creature want from his mistress?' She stretched across the coffee table and handed him "Tess". 'We are on Chapter XI. You may begin.'

Finn read and she feigned sleep. Her gown fell open, the fabric hinting at the contours of her body. When the clock struck the hour, Finn closed the book relieved and left the sofa to fetch his things from the table.

'Did I dismiss you?' She hadn't moved and her eyelids were shut.

'I'm sorry, it's nine o'clock. I thought you were asleep.'

'Alec took advantage of Tess while she slept, is that your intention too?' Cat opened her eyes staring back at him, accusingly. A face both beautiful and terrifying. There was no youthful charm, just a controlling old woman in the body of a young girl. Her alluring disguise uncovered, revealing the hideous gorgon that lay on the sofa in her silken gown. 'Sneaking away before I dismiss you. There I was thinking my creature was fully trained. Seems I was wrong.'

'Sorry, Miss Fry.' One thing he had learnt, arguing with her was a waste of energy and the only person who would feel angst would be him. Easier to just allow her to believe she was the mistress of his fate.

'I will deal with you tomorrow. I'm tired. You may go.'

STOP

TOLBRIDGE UNIVERSITY, AGED EIGHTEEN

The pill in front of me is supposed to make me feel better, happier. I'll see life in a new light, back to my normal self, they say. But I have never been normal, have I? Who am I, the silent child, the fearful teen or the terrified student? I am confused, life is confusing, I want to make sense of the chaos around me. I want the fog that engulfs my brain to clear. Above all, I want the headaches to stop. The constant throbbing. All day, every day, throb, throb, throb. What's the point of sleeping if it just means waking to more pain, another day with a splitting headache dictating my actions? I crave release from this agony and the answer is not the little pill next to my glass of water.

I tried calling her, but there was no answer. I expect she is at work. She normally answers when I ring, though. Evie never ignores me. There must be a plausible explanation. She forgot her phone, she's in the bath, she's in the middle of a complicated procedure. No, not that. Evie leaves the phone with the receptionist, just in case. Something is wrong. She always answers. Maybe I ask too much of her. I'll try again.

Voicemail. My headache is back. The pain is back.

Today is Wednesday. Definitely Wednesday. Was yesterday Tuesday? No. Yes, it was Tuesday, I'm sure of it. Then today must be Wednesday. Marcus always plays rugby on a Wednesday and after, goes to Katie's. He won't be back until tomorrow afternoon.

I push the capsule around the table with my middle finger, rolling it back and forth, watching it give under the pressure. Will it burst open? That powder spreading out across the table. Is that what is happening to my head? An unseen pressure pushing down on me, in control of my thoughts and actions? How much more pressure do I have to exert to burst open my head, to let out my imperfect brain loose on the table. The pain would stop. Everything would stop.

FINN

The graveyards possessed a serenity few people saw, but for Finn it was somewhere that bloomed through its symbiotic relationship with death. Carl would tease him that he was searching for ghosts, and perhaps he was.

That History teacher's approach through the gate was less than serene. The prospect of the forthcoming holiday putting a rare spring in his step as he hummed his way towards Finn.

'Ready for the holidays? I can't wait,' said Carl, sounded giddy with anticipation.

'Hello Carl. Have you come to disturb the peace again?' Finn was lying on the ground with no intention of moving.

'I come to spread happiness and good fortune to all who meet me on this glorious May afternoon!'

'Ah, no lessons after lunch, then?'

'No, none whatsoever. I am savouring the joy of a redundant teacher. And, seeing as you are never going to eat in the staff room, I must come in search of you.'

'I've finished my lunch I'm afraid. Nothing for you to scrounge. You missed a good one. Sophie packed my lunch. Pasta salad, fruit and a homemade cookie.'

'Dammit, it's Wednesday. I always forget she makes your lunch on a Wednesday.'

'There's some poison over in the flask. You are welcome to that.'

'No thanks.'

Finn chuckled as he listened to his friend's chatter. Above him, a blue tit darted between an ancient wisteria and its nest in the cherry blossom tree. 'Birds are so lucky,' he announced, interrupting Carl's gossip about the Head's latest affair. 'I mean, just look at that blue tit. Free to fly away the minute it feels threatened. Don't you envy those birds?'

'You know what, Finn? You can be quite strange sometimes.'

'I've had a lifetime of that,' he replied. 'What's wrong with being different, seeing the world differently?'

'We both hope for a different world,' said Carl.

'My mother used to say I was different. Sometimes I'd ask her if I was a disappointment. Not a proper Sheehan, not like my brother and cousins. She never really answered me. Just said I was her blue-eyed late surprise.'

'But you seem happy today. Good news?' Carl nudged him with his foot.

Finn shook his head, but he did feel strangely happier, maybe it was from watching the birds or maybe it was Sophie's poisonous tea. He folded his arms behind his head enjoying the mid-afternoon sunshine. It was warmer than he expected, and he'd rolled up his sleeves. His bangle dangled freely in the crook of his arm, with the pale insides of his wrists clear to view. With his eyes closed he didn't notice Carl staring at his jagged scars.

'Why did you come here, Finn?'

'To eat my lunch. I always come here. You should know that,' he said, misunderstanding Carl's question.

'I don't mean the graveyard. I mean to New Albany. Why did you leave your home, why that University? Were you mad, why would anyone willingly come here?'

Finn sat up, his happiness draining away as he understood what Carl was really asking. 'It was different then, some strange rules, but foreigners could come and go with relative ease. A close family friend worked as a professor at the university here. He suggested to my parents that it might be

281

good for me to study abroad. Good for my career that is.'

'Is that the truth?' asked Carl. He got off the bench and sat on the ground by Finn,

'Yes, why? I'm not lying to you.' He tensed with the uncomfortable thought of telling the truth. He wouldn't do it. He couldn't do it.

'Perhaps it has to do with the scars on your wrists.'

Finn was already tugging down his sleeves, irritated by his foolishness. 'That's none of your business.'

'Did it happen here? No one would blame you. I've considered it many times. End this misery.'

Finn spun round, uncharacteristically angry at his best friend. 'I want to end the misery of being here, free to live, to enjoy life again, instead I am the canary locked inside this cage. I need to be that blue tit, free to fly back home.'

He left the graveyard, his mind full of anger. Carl's nosy chatter had gone too far, touching the rawest of nerves and hurtling Finn back to the nightmares that constantly shadowed him.

* * *

Wednesday 26th May

Well, Fuck them! That's it, a done deal. Brandies sipped from crystal goblets and cigar smoke choking the room. I am presented with the result, everything I despise.

* * *

Cat was waiting on her sofa, her hand beckoning him into the room. 'Come, sit by me.'

Finn took his usual seat on the opposite sofa.

'No, today I want you next to me. I've had some news. I

don't feel like Austen today. I want to talk.' Sliding her legs off the sofa, she patted the space next to her. Dark warnings engulfed Finn, but despite it, he obeyed.

'Have you decided what you would like me to get you for your birthday?' she asked, her hand pushing down on his knee.

Her perfume filled him, catching the back of his throat. He coughed. 'No, there is nothing I want.' He would have added, 'from you', but once antagonised she had a spiteful tendency to strike back.

Catherine didn't say anything, distracted by a loose thread on her dressing gown. She tugged at it, but it refused to snap. After a couple attempts, she pushed that part of the gown away, irritated by its mere existence. 'I'm getting married.'

Finn was puzzled. 'Isn't that what you are preparing for, to be the dutiful Albian wife.'

'Of course, but theory is now reality. It's going to be Captain Michael Harper. My buyer has a face and the correct pedigree. The deal my father hoped for.'

Did she want sympathy from Finn? Did she want him to say, it will be a marriage of equals? There would be no equality in that marriage. He possessed all the legal rights, she had none. Her father had found a buyer he could manipulate, he had sold his only child in his pursuit of power and wealth. It was dawning on her that the seventeen-year fantasy had reached its conclusion.

'I am sure he considered the options carefully,' he said diplomatically. 'As you say, a father's skill is in making the most advantageous choice.'

'Will you continue reading to me?'

Her meaning was unclear, now in the lesson, or did she mean into the future. A tethered pet entailed to her for all eternity.

'We should continue with exam preparation, it's only a

few weeks away,' said Finn, inching away from her.

She grabbed his arm and pulled him back. 'I want preparation, but not for a silly exam.' Her grip was tight and Finn could feel her nails digging through his shirt and into his flesh. 'Tell me what will happen to me after the contract is signed,' she continued. 'Tell me who I'll be once I cease to be Catherine Fry.'

Finn was sure he saw a tear develop in her eyes as she turned to pour her tea. Stopping halfway, she replaced the pot onto the table and said, 'Fetch the vodka!'

Cat was on her second glass. Finn had managed to escape her and sat in silence on his sofa. The only sounds, a tumbler being placed on the polished coffee table and Finn's tapping shoe.

After twenty minutes, she got up, handed "Tess" to him and lay her head on his lap, her body stretched out over the rest of the sofa. Most of the time she kept her eyes shut, listening to the tribulations of the drama, occasionally opening her eyes and staring at her tutor, unnerving him, smiling at his stumbled words. He kept his eyes firmly on the page, refusing even to glance down at her young face or that exposed chest beneath the silk night dress, loose and deep cut. All part of her plan, a plan in which he would not participate. The clock sounded his release, but Cat did not move. She would not release him.

'How many people have you had sex with?' The glint from her green irises expected a reply.

'Why do you want to know? Extramarital relations are forbidden and I've no interest in breaking the law.'

'That rule didn't exist when you first arrived, it was just another expectation. I doubt it even exists at all outside our country, and we both know about Sophia Elle's attitude to sexual relations.' Finn squirmed beneath the weight of her head.

'How many women have you slept with?' she repeated. 'Answer me, 568216.'

'I was a visitor to your country, I wanted to be a good guest, your home, your rules.'

'You haven't answered me. You were in your twenties. Are you telling me you never had sex before you arrived here?'

How could he answer her? She wanted him to divulge the most private aspect of his life to a girl who desired the information purely to torment him.

'It must be strange to think that when you die, there will not even be an accidental "Little 568216" out there with those blue eyes and delicate features.' She lay her hand on his cheek, a finger running down his nose.

Finn shut his eyes. He could not answer. He would not answer.

'Do you mind the fact your child died and now you can't have anymore? Does it make you sad? Or are you another Mr Farnborough? Your marriage a convenient deception to hide your true perversion. Perhaps I should ask how many people you have had sex with?'

He had to stop her, lying to break the silence, 'Apart from my first undergraduate year, I lived at home. I had plenty of friends who were girls.'

'And did any of these *"friends who were girls"* put their heads on your lap? Did you read to them, too? She propped herself up on her arm, her hand sliding under his shirt, tickling his chest. 'Did they touch you like this? Did they kiss you?'

Finn snaked his fingers around her wrist, encircling her slender joint, dragging her hand down. She didn't resist or appear angry. The opposite, her face filled with a victorious grin.

'No, they did not,' he said. 'I hadn't met the girl with whom I wanted to share my life. They respected my decisions. I needed love and I didn't love them. I liked them but that wasn't enough. There is only one woman who I have loved enough; my wife.'

She laughed at him. 'A virgin groom, how patriotic. If it wasn't for the fact you were born an Immi, you'd make the perfect poster boy. Virtuous, moral, dutiful and obedient. And you are my obedient little creature, aren't you?'

To his surprise, she stood up, closed her gown and pressed the bell to unlock the door.

'Make sure you are on time tomorrow. Do you like chocolate? We shall have chocolates, chocolate cake and champagne, then you can open your present. I am looking forward to tomorrow.'

BROTHERLY LOVE

MELBOROUGH MANOR HOUSE, AGED TWENTY-FOUR

We each laze on a conservatory couch gazing up at the February night sky, armed only with a glass of whiskey, the bottle and a jug of ice to keep us going. We were never close, but now Andy is making the effort to spend time with me. I imagine it is his guilt that drives him. A desire for forgiveness. I only want his love, that's all I've ever wanted.

'Nisha seems nice, is she the one?' I say, more to break the silence than for any other reason.

Andy chuckled, 'If you mean, are we living together and about to buy a house? Then yeah, she's the one. But don't let on to Mum, she'll be buying a hat before you even say engagement.'

I am happy for him, years of searching, of breaking girls' hearts, cheating and lying. Now he finds love still waits for him.

'Congratulations, bet there were times Mum despaired that any of us would marry.'

'Hang on a minute, we'll be living together, no talk of marriage, way too early for that kind of stress.'

I have been living under The New Albian rule too long. Loving someone means marrying them. There are no other options. Andy's response baffles me, maybe because I love Sophie and want to be with her. I desire her so very much.

'You really don't have to marry Sophie, you know,' my brother says. 'Come back home, bring her with you. Live together awhile, find out about each other. I mean how old is she? Eighteen? Nineteen?'

'She's twenty.' I gaze up at the stars. It would be a dream come true, but dreams are fiction and cannot overturn reality. 'Besides, New Albians aren't allowed residency visas, we checked. It's to do with the sanctions.'

'Come off it, Finn, you're a bloody Sheehan, of course they'll bend the rules.'

'Maybe, but if she defects it might have serious consequences for her family. It's not a risk she'll take at the moment.' I don't tell Andy my hopes of moving back to Melborough together with Sophie and any children we may have. 'What's the point in waiting?' I say, 'I've nearly finished my PhD, have a good job offer and we want to be together. I love her. I want to be with her, so I should marry her.'

Andy sat up on the lounger, staring at me. I understand his body language so well. I have irritated him, just as I did each day as a child. There will be no reconciliation tonight. 'For fucks sake Finn, you're still a kid yourself, I mean, have you actually slept with any other women? You can't just say you love her and want to marry her because she's the first to let you into her pants.'

He knows my Achilles heel. Talking about relationships is hard for me at the best of times, talking about my own sexual history with him is impossible. Even if Andy notices my discomfort, he will ignore it, as long as he wins his point. I bring my legs up to my chest hugging them tightly. The onslaught will soon begin.

'You have slept with her haven't you, please don't tell me you have gone all Albian on us?'

I employ my usual tactic. Silence.

'Fucking hell, Finn are you mad? She's sweet, attractive but that's no reason to marry her. You'll be trapped there.'

He waits for a response but there is nothing forthcoming. There is nothing to say.

'I know what you are thinking. You've got to follow the rules, he continues. 'We've all heard about their peculiar ways. It's bollocks. These places are all the same, one rule for the little people another for the ruler. You think they are not all fucking each other behind closed doors.' He waves his hands about, the whiskey in his glass slopping over the side, running down his hand. He doesn't care. 'And what about when you get the girl pregnant. Two kids with a kid. Sorry Finn, the only thing you should be doing is finding a job here and escaping her and her nutty country.'

I want to leave, go back to my room. Instead I sit there, my brother swearing at me, telling me what a fool I am. That there are more fish in the sea. I'll enjoy the chase. He'll sort some sweet girls out for me if necessary, quiet girls, like me. He doesn't understand, I have met the only girl I want to be with, without her, I will be lost once again. She is my missing piece. She is the glue that holds me together.

'Look, I'm sorry Finn, I truly am. I haven't been the best big brother, I think everyone can agree on that, but I don't want you to go back. It's repressive, dangerous. It is not the right place for you. It's not healthy for you. How will you cope if you become ill again?'

I can't stand hearing his words, and I hurl an explosion of excuses back at him. 'I love her, Andy. If I don't go back, I won't cope being here, she is everything to me. I am happy when I'm with her. She keeps me sane. Don't you see? It's just as dangerous for me to be without her.'

FINN

Sophie was in the sitting-room when he got home. She had been watching a film but had fallen asleep, her sewing tipping out of her hand. He looked at the same beautiful girl that had won his student heart. The first girl to make him throw caution to the wind. The first girl to make him want to abandon everything just so he might hold her in his arms. The first girl with whom he believed anything was possible. The first girl to make him feel desire. He wanted to wake her. Take her upstairs. Make love to her. He couldn't do it. If he did, he knew it would be impossible to leave her in the summer. He would be condemning her to more years of misery and he loved her too much for that. Silently closing the door behind him, Finn made his way upstairs to the guest room.

STANDING IN FEAR'S SHADOW

A weakened sun casts long shadows, bathing us in the cold darkness of inevitability. We wait, chilled, momentarily incapable, captured by its encompassing hold. A monochromatic world, and in it, our hearts drum out the seconds, a weak but rhythmic beat encouraging each faltering step towards the colour that lies beyond.

SOPHIE

With the click of the gate, so began the annual ritual. Sophie bustled George and Carl out of the kitchen, shooing them with a 'That must be him, quick let's get out of here.'

'Hello, Sophie. Where are you?' called Finn, content to play the role of surprised husband.

'In the sitting-room,' she replied, elbowing Carl and shushing George's incessant chatter.

And there he was, standing in the middle of their sitting-room, acknowledging the birthday wishes from his wife and friends.

'I baked you a cake,' she said.

'Of course you did. Victoria Sponge?'

'With apple and bramble jelly, no seeds. Come on, Finn, time to blow out the candle and make a wish.'

The cake was on the coffee table. A simple offering with icing sugar barely dusting the top. In the middle was a short stubby pink candle used for her birthday nine months before. It had graced their birthday cakes for eight years. Sophie only lit it when Finn was in position to blow it out.

'Make a wish,' she said, violently shaking her hand to extinguish the match.

His eyes screwed up shut giving him the appearance of a child, innocently waiting for his surprise. It had been that innocence that first attracted Sophie. She marvelled at his ability to see the world through those childlike eyes, it was only later she figured out it was a coping technique to keep the harshness of real life at bay. Sophie shut her eyes and made a wish too. A wish to escape, a wish to start a new and totally free life. She sealed her bargain with the birthday cake gods by giving Finn a chaste kiss on his cheek.

'So, what did you wish for?' asked George.

'He can't tell you, otherwise it won't come true,' said Sophie, before Finn had a chance to answer. 'Tea?'

'How did you guess?' Finn laughed and sat down.

'Because I know you inside out and upside down. You always wish for tea.'

The party was short, predictable, wallowing in its own sense of normality. Sophie handed out cake, poured tea and wondered where they would celebrate his birthday next year. Who would pour the tea? Would there even be tea? Yes, yes, she had to believe there would be tea and cake again, and next time there would also be the sweet taste of liberty. It put her in a good mood and with that, she made up her mind. They had been apart too long, it was time to seduce her husband back into their marital bed.

FINN

* * *

Thursday 27th May

I'm so excited, the food looks wonderful. I can't wait to see his face when he arrives. I went to so much trouble. My surprise is inspired. I told Daddy I wanted chocolates and champagne for being such a good girl. He's so happy at the moment that he'd give me anything.

* * *

'I promised you a party. Do you like it? Mrs Fran has been so busy.' She was standing by the table, her arm indicating towards the feast laid on a pristine white linen cloth. Starched and intricately folded napkins stood to attention inside fine crystal flutes. To Finn they resembled a pair of daggers pointing up to the ceiling.

On the table were plates of miniature sandwiches and tarts, together with bowls of chocolate bonbons. An ice bucket contained a bottle of champagne, and in the middle, a chocolate cake, elevated above all the other delicacies. It was the star of the party, a work of art. Mirror-like icing reflecting the flames from the tall white candles that circled the edge. In its centre, skilfully written in white icing, was 'Happy Birthday, 568216'. Six numbers that held him transfixed. Six numbers rendering him a prisoner within her gilded cage. No amount of cursive calligraphy could swirl away that fact. Behind him, Catherine had her hand on his back, guiding him to the table.

'Blow out the candles and make a wish,' she said. Even if she meant it kindly, it came out as an order.

They called him 'alien' but how could that be? He was human with feelings yet here was this girl who was totally blind to humanity. The only explanation that made any sense to him was that she was an extra-terrestrial, play-acting at being human only to be unmasked by the errors normal people avoided.

'Hurry up, else your wish might disappear.'

Finn bent to blow out the candles. For the second time that day he made a wish for the torment to end.

'Open wide, 568216.' Cat picked up the bowl of chocolate truffles and held one out to him.

Finn kept his mouth shut.

Her smile faded along with joviality in her voice. 'I said, 'Open wide'. You still have to do what you are told, even at your birthday party.'

Finn lowered his jaw to accommodate the chocolate. It could have been a cyanide tablet for all he cared. He bit hard on the chocolate, releasing a liquid centre. Finn thought it might be cherry, but he didn't really care, he just swallowed.

'You should savour it. They were smuggled in over the border in AZ Twelve. Cost my father a small fortune. Can you taste your home?'

There had been no sweetness. The chocolate was dark and bitter, and the liquid was sour. A fitting bonbon to mark another year of imprisonment.

Every one of her actions added to the dread building up inside him. The champagne cork popped and with it brought back painful memories. Memories he tried to suppress. Memories he wanted to obliterate of an anniversary destroyed by a kiss.

His pupil insisted he sat down while she gathered some

of the tiny sandwiches on a plate. 'Today I am your servant. Isn't that funny?' she said as she handed him a champagne flute. 'You're not going to refuse tonight, are you? Not on your birthday?' Cat offered up the plate, 'Mrs Fran will be disappointed if you don't eat her hard work. If you lose much more weight, you'll disappear and that would never do. I'd miss you terribly.'

He plucked a sandwich from the plate, smoked salmon and cream cheese, Evie's favourite. Mrs McManus's voice rang through his mind.

'Such a spoilt princess, but we love her, don't we, my Little One?'

Cat was sprawled across her sofa, her head barely lifted from the horizontal. Champagne dribbled across her lips, the glass marked by her dusky-rose lipstick. She was languid. Her life was indolence, and that brief foray into servitude had left her fatigued. Her arm dangled off the sofa, brushing tracks into the velvet pile of the rug. She stopped and rolled to her side, reaching for something under the seat. Her loose hair cascaded down, shielding her face, and when she sat back up, she appeared flushed. Puffing, she flicked her hair away. There was an innocence to her he had not seen before. Her high cheekbones glowed with youthful health. And those eyes, they had become emeralds sparkling bright with excitement. To Finn, Cat's face had become almost illuminated, and dominating it all was the wide and open smile. Pearl white teeth, perfect in shape and form, surrounded by her plump, rose lips.

She put the box on her stomach, her fingers tracing over the raised flock of the pattern, swirls and florets in a deeper shade. Around it was a gold chiffon ribbon, tied into an elaborate bow, its ends long and trailing across the shallow box. No matter how beautiful it appeared, Finn couldn't help thinking that its beauty masked a sinister content. She leant forward, presenting it to him. He could see it was heavy from the way her stretched out arm trembled. And it rattled.

'I had it made especially for you. I think it is very appropriate, now you know how to be obedient.'

He took it in his hands and lay it on his lap. It weighed him down. A damper to his voice as he offered his whispered thanks. The gold chiffon was soft, sliding through his fingers like baby's hair. A gentle tug was all that was needed to make the bow fall open. A white box lay inside the wrapping. Finn lifted it out of the paper. There was raised gold lettering, "Coulter and Co, Purveyors of the Finest Pet Accessories", hinting at the luxurious nature of the gift. Layers of pale gold tissue paper concealed the rattling item. Snake-like, it slid about as he unfolded the tissue. And it did look like a snake, all curled up in the paper, with the scaly skin of green plaited leather. Faceted, jewelled beads were entwined within the straps, reflecting the light. It was of the highest quality and undeniably carefully constructed, but the quality only served to deepen the pain it was inflicting on him. A dog leash, she had bought him a gold choke chain and dog leash.

'You must look at the tag.' She was leaning across, pointing at the grip. Below it was attached a gold dog-tag with both sides engraved. On one side, 'If found please return to owner, Miss C Fry', a telephone number beneath. He turned it over. '568216/2/MI'.

'Do you like it? I thought it symbolises our relationship. English teachers always go on about symbolism.'

He could hear her laughter, although it felt distant. The whole event must be imaginary. How could it be real? How could he be sitting in a girl's sitting-room staring at a dog leash that was meant for him? It was a nightmare and no doubt the laughter would soon stop and be replaced with Evie calling him down for breakfast. This wasn't happening. It couldn't be happening. He felt a warm hand on his, but they had slender fingers, the nails manicured and glossy. Evie's were always bitten short and painted dark blue.

'Don't you just love it? I think it's inspired.'

He put the leash back in the box along with the choke chain and placed it on the table. He was visibly shaking with anger. 'Is that how you see this, as a relationship? I am paid by your father to teach you. It was you that decided to use these sessions to humiliate and abuse me. How does that constitute a relationship? If you want a pet, then I suggest you ask your father to buy you a puppy. I have no intention of being your cowed creature anymore.'

'Is that your thanks? He pays for you to be mine. Mine to use how I want three times a week. You have no say in what I do, you are here to obey.' She picked up the choke chain and held it in front of him. 'If I want to use this, then who's going to stop me? You?'

Before he could think of a reply, Cat was on his lap, her knees either side of him, wrapping the chain around his neck. He could have pushed her off. He could have tried to escape, but it would all have been futile. Cat was the one in control and whatever he did would have led to the same outcome, a teacher struggling to breathe. Instead of a fancy gold choke chain, it would be a hangman's noose around his neck.

Cat clipped on the leash and started to pull, smiling as she tugged it tighter. 'I want you to remember this next week. You may think yourself free of me, but school holidays cannot liberate you. It doesn't matter where you are, it cannot change who your mistress is, who you belong to. If you try to forget, there's always your tag to remind you.'

* * *

Thursday 27th May, 11:49pm

I hate him. Who does he think he is? Crawling back to her when he should be here. I'll make him pay. He'll pay for his treachery. He's mine, not hers. He'll never be hers, it's an act. She doesn't love him. Why can't he see what is so obvious? I will make him see.

* * *

SOPHIE

The remnants of the birthday cake lay before her on the kitchen table. Out in the hallway, the deep atonal clang from her grandmother's clock echoed the hour. It was midnight. She would be on duty again in a few short hours. A damp handkerchief, hot from her fury, lay screwed up inside her hand, ready to mop away her tears. Finn was in his room, the door shut to her. She no longer understood him nor how to fathom what on earth was going on in his head.

FINN

'It was you who wanted to talk, remember?' said Carl. 'I prefer actual speech to telepathy.' Receiving no response, he dropped on the bench with an exhausted sigh. 'Fine. Telepathy it is then.'

Finn briefly glanced up from the tombstones when his friend commenced his ritualistic scavenger hunt. After a few minutes of hearing his lunch being swallowed, Finn stopped pacing and sat down next to him. 'I'm not going back.'

'Head won't be pleased,' he said, his words muffled by a mouth brimming with left over Victoria Sponge. 'And don't you think I'm going to cover. You've got class eight, bunch of bloody psychopaths.'

'I'm not going back to her, yesterday was the last time. I'm not doing it anymore.'

'Sacked!' Carl spat out the cake in choking response. 'What the fuck did you do?'

'Not sacked, resigned. I told the headmaster first thing.'

'Shit, Finn, why would you do that?

'This is an extra employment contract and I have the right to refuse it. I'm not obliged to take their money and I'm not a slave at her beck and call, no matter what she thinks.'

Carl returned to his search through the lunch box. 'We're always at someone's beck and call. We don't get to choose, my boy. You should know that by now.'

'He can't compel me to teach her.' He shook his head, emphasising his disagreement. 'No, if he asks, I'll say she is far too intelligent to need my help. It would be wrong to take his money. There, nothing rebellious about that.'

'You're deluded if you think the Commandant will accept that excuse, it'll be considered a slight against him. I doubt he is the forgiving or understanding type.'

'No one can force me to take extra employment. I don't have to do this anymore. I can't be forced.' Desperation in Finn's voice betrayed the man he had become, a condemned prisoner pleading his innocence.

'I think you'll find they can,' replied Carl.

The last lesson of the day and before him sat a class of drowsy teenage girls not in the least bit interested in the interaction between Marianne and Elinor. Only another hour, and then he would be heading home to pack for a weekend of freedom.

He caught sight of them first as they stood by the glass panel of the classroom door. Three guards talking to the headmaster. Attempting to ignore them, he focused on the lesson.

'Miss Anderson, was Marianne foolish or passionate?' His accent was more prominent with a slight quiver in his voice. The imminence of fear wrapping its fingers around his throat, tightening with the continued presence of the guards.

The scraping of the door opening was the signal for the girls to immediately get to their feet as the head walked in, with those three guards in step behind him. Finn's face reddened and a knot of anxiety twisted within his stomach.

The head's shoulders were slumped carrying the body language that confirmed Finn's terror.

'Sit down,' he said to the waiting girls. And they did, instantly without a murmur. They knew too. 'So, um, Mr Michael…' his attempted smile was joined with downcast eyes and a shaking hand on Finn's arm, 'would you mind accompanying the guards outside? I'll take your lesson.

What are we doing?'

Finn realised it would be pointless to object, he had been trialled and found guilty. 'Sense and Sensibility. We are discussing Willoughby's arrival at Cleveland'

'OK, yes, very good, yes. Cleveland, yes, good.'

Finn knew the procedure. Carefully removing his new glasses, he stepped out of the room, a guard behind him, the other two each holding an arm.

From the school lawn, Finn glanced up towards his classroom, wondering how many of his pupils would be watching the unfolding event. Undoubtedly, they too had seen this sort of thing before. Their phones primed, ready to share photos with friends.

Finn faced the guard as ordered. He was one of George's regulars from the guardhouse. A pleasant lad who had chatted to Finn about his love of ghost stories just a few weeks before. And like the ghostly apparitions of his imagination, his lips moved, but with indistinct words. Finn didn't need to hear them, they were resonating within him from that day on the green when a different trembling man stood awaiting the fulfilment of his sentence.

Another guard, older, burlier, pushed up Finn's jumper sleeve, revealing his DIA bangle. He aimed the reader at it and scanned the microchip. Finn scribbled what should have been his signature on the tablet, but his arm appeared to have lost the ability to write letters. It didn't matter as far as the guards were concerned, the consent form was signed, and they had the right prisoner.

No matter how much Finn wanted to look away, he couldn't. He watched the guard's every movement. He was a man carrying out his duty, just doing his job. There was a sense of fascination for Finn. Maybe these guards had sat an exam, 'Paper 101, Punishment Beating, Procedures and Execution'.

'Ready?' asked the young man, his preparation complete and all set to start.

Finn nodded. A pain radiated from his neck, every muscle tense, much like the rest of him, anticipating the moment when the guard would remove the rifle from his shoulder. What he was not expecting was the pistol-whip to the back of his head.

* * *

The child stands in a crystal-clear brook. Rocks lie beneath his feet, sharp points cutting into his young flesh. His weakened body collapses. The pain from the blow to his head shoots through him as he disappears below the surface. Icy water catching him, surrounding him in its malevolent embrace, its cold tentacles crawling into his ears, pushing up through his nose, prising open his mouth and chilling his body, seeking out its ultimate goal, a watery revenge.

* * *

Finn tipped his head skywards and pinched the top of his nose, stemming the flow of blood. His head was throbbing from the pain.

Giggling girls were taking pictures. One of his younger pupils, Miss Henshaw, approached him, genuine concern expressed in her innocent eyes. 'Would you like me to find Matron, Mr Michael?'

'No, I'll be OK, thank you.' He shut his eyes to the inevitability of the situation. This is just what happens to DIAs who express free will in New Albany. It wasn't the first time he had been on the receiving end of a guard's fist. And probably not the last either.

'Here, put this on your face.' Carl handed Finn an ice pack. 'I assume Sophie is a dab hand at knowing how to get rid of bloodstains?'

Finn winced with Carl's black humour. 'Yeah, she's an expert.' He lay back on the grass, too dizzy to sit up. 'Guess I know why they train them for punishment beatings now, fewer blows but greater efficiency,' he added from beneath the freezing pad of gel.

'Apparently Harrison lost a packet on you — thought you wouldn't last the full six minutes.'

'Well, that's something I suppose.' Finn managed a crooked smile, knowing if the beating hadn't been fixed then Mr Harrison would have been celebrating his win. 'I was lucky, Carl. I was barely conscious for most of it. Inflict just enough damage to hurt but not cause serious injury. At least, not to my body.'

'Where does it hurt the most?'

He pointed to his side. Carl slipped his cold hand under Finn's shirt, and he welcomed that chill touch against the hot swelling developing around his ribs.

'Cracked, possibly broken. Did they use a baton?' said Carl.

'No, a boot or the butt of the gun. I didn't ask. Weren't you watching like everyone else?'

'Don't you know me better than that? Here, can you stand?' Carl put his arms around Finn. 'After three. One, two, three!' He tightened his grip, heaving him up from the grass. 'Good lad. Up you get.'

Intense pain coursed through Finn and he turned away. Even through his dizziness, he was aware of the tears glazing his eyes.

Carl reached out as Finn stumbled, catching him before he tumbled back down. 'You won't make it home by yourself. I'll drive you. Is there anything you need from the classroom?'

'Just my glasses, at least I had the good sense to remove them first.'

* * *

Friday 28th May, 3:45pm

They'll have done it by now. All that effort and expense, and yet he believes he has the right to snub me. His status is meaningless, he is a DIA, no better than any other. He has forgotten what he is. He thinks he is just like me, but he's not. He can never be like me.

* * *

As soon as they entered the garden, Finn made his way towards the apple trees.

'Shouldn't you go inside, lie down or something?' asked Carl.

'No, I'd rather stay out here,' said Finn, lowering himself gingerly onto the steamer chair.

'At least let me get you something for your head, where does Sophie keep the painkillers?'

'In her handbag. I think there might be some antiseptic in the first aid box in the bathroom cabinet.'

Carl returned five minutes later with the ointment, a glass of water and the blanket from the guest room bed.

'What did you mean by "gentle beating this time", you've never had a punishment beating before, have you?' he asked while dabbing the cuts on Finn's face, his right eye already closing up. Finn lay back on the chair as Carl probed him, tensing as he remembered the humiliation. How many more humiliations had he suffered since that day? It was almost trivial compared to the previous night's degradation.

'It doesn't have to be an official punishment beating for a DIA to be punched and kicked. You just have to annoy the wrong person,' said Finn, hoping it would stop the questions, but knowing it wouldn't.

'When did it happen?'

'Just after the programme was introduced. Sophie and I were celebrating our tenth anniversary by the river. Tim gave us a bottle of champagne and we thought we would have a picnic. I hadn't learnt to keep my bangle hidden, I kissed her. She is my wife, Carl. I should be allowed to kiss my wife whenever, wherever. Dr Sheehan kissing Mrs Sheehan, but the programme does not allow for such luxury.'

Finn had relived the memory so often that it had become ingrained in his consciousness. The sound of the flowing river, the smell of the recently cut grass, the chatter coming from the pub at the top of the slope. The electric blue mascara that Sophie once favoured. The intoxicating scent of summer flowers and the musky perfume coming from Sophie's neck.

'A former pupil saw us. Her fiancé, a guardsman, saw us too. He didn't take too kindly to a filthy DIA seducing a patriot woman in plain daylight, making his views patently clear. The next day, along with a group of his friends, they used their fists to instruct me on what happens to aliens that dare to fall in love with an Albian.'

'Gits! Was Sophie there?'

'No, thank God. I don't know how far they would have gone, Sergeant Mason interrupted them.'

'That sergeant is one of the only decent guys in that guardhouse. Were you OK?'

'Concussion and bruising mainly. My glasses were smashed so it didn't matter I couldn't see out of my left eye.'

Finn made light of the injuries but the one that endured was the ominous threat made by the guard.

'We know who she is, that whore of a wife, we'll make sure she knows what it's like to be with real men. We'll take turns. Bet she'd love it, scream for more.'

The innocent belief that privilege was enough to protect them from the arbitrary rules and regulations of the regime, was blown apart by a loving kiss. That young officer had stalked his sleep, stood at his shoulder, waited for him in the shadows. Michelle was right, Sophie would always be in danger while she was married to her alien husband.

SOPHIE

The collection of bottles clattered against each other as the bag landed at her feet, but exhausted from her extra shift, she left it on the floor. There was no sign of cooking in the kitchen. Scanning the room for a note, she caught sight of him in the garden, lazing on the steamer chair. Irked, she was about to give him a piece of her mind, irritation propelling each footstep. The closer she got, the slower her steps became. Why was there a blanket over him? And the one her grandmother made too. It made no sense. The evening was warm. Why hadn't he awoken? She wasn't being particularly quiet. Dread crept into her thoughts, batted away with her upbeat greeting, 'Hello darling, what a day I've had. Hope you've packed the suitcase before lazing.'

Finn stirred, and her most feared scenario disappeared with relief, he was alive. He moved slowly, carefully. He was in pain.

'What happened?' She crouched down to take a closer look at the angry bruising on Finn's face.

'Came off my bike, walked into a wall, fell down some stairs. You choose.'

'Let me take a look.' Gently moving up the swollen eyebrow, she examined the damage to his eye. 'That's going to be beautiful in the morning.'

Finn lay back in the chair while Sophie grabbed the other one and dragged it close. Adopting her caring nurse persona, she held his hand, waiting for an explanation. Thwarted by his silence she resorted to speaking first. 'The guards? Did they do this to you?'

He nodded. 'And in full view of the girls. They'll have plenty of pictures to show their parents.'

'A punishment beating? Why? Did George do this?'

'I'm sure George knows all about it. Procedure was correctly followed this time, and the right guards sent to carry out the order. Corporal Foster kindly knocked me out, so at least I didn't know what was happening for most of it. Still hurts though. The complaint will be on file for all Patriots to see. 568216/2/MI, alias Michael Finlay, guilty of showing disrespect and a failure to carry out his contracted duty. Sentence: Punishment Beating.'

A shiver ran through Sophie as she recalled her father's warning. He now had an offence on his record. With that misdemeanour on file, Finn was one step closer to execution. Inhaling deeply, she covered her anxiety with her customary calmness. 'But what did you do?'

'I gave in my resignation.'

She dropped his hand in surprise, then quickly scrabbled to retrieve it, lest he thought she was angry with him.

He turned away from her. 'I wanted to resign, that's all, but the Commandant was determined I continued to teach his daughter. All I did was try to resign and even that right has been stolen from me. I don't want to teach her, I want to be with you.'

Anger against the Commandant fired up inside her, but with his final sentence, she realised the Commandant was only one part of the problem. Seeing his anguish, she knew delving deeper into the reason for resigning would not help. Offering up a comforting smile, she replied, 'And I want to be with you too. Now, come on inside, let me check out those bruises.'

*

Grumpy with pain, and at the prospect of spending a weekend with her mother, Finn's behaviour was more stubborn than usual. Every time Sophie tried to help him, he snapped back that he was perfectly capable of getting himself ready.

'Oh, for goodness sake Finn,' she said, slumping onto the chair. 'If you're going to be like this then we should cancel.'

She saw him wince with pain as he tried to put on his shirt. He stopped with one hand half-way up a sleeve, his head lowering in acceptance of defeat. 'I'm sorry Soph, I don't mean to take it out on you. I love you. I really do. Even when you're angry.'

'Then let me help you, you imbecile, and we might just about be ready before Christopher arrives.' She returned to his side and pulled the shirt up, guiding the other arm into the sleeve. He yelped, then kissed her.

Outside a car drew up. 'Christopher's early,' she said, peering out from behind the curtain. 'I'll be back in a sec. I'll just let him in and then I'll sort you out. Don't try putting anything else on, do you hear me, Michael Finlay. I don't need you breaking a leg too.'

She raced down the stairs, jumping from the second to last step, and flung open the front door. But Christopher wasn't there, instead he was holding open the rear passenger door and her father was getting out with all the stateman's demeanour of an Albian Minister. They both knew to act out their roles if there was even the slightest chance of a pair of spying eyes.

'Dad, how come you're here too?' she said, once he reached her.

He hugged his daughter, kissing her on her cheek. 'News travels fast. Thought I might be of some help with Finn. How is he?'

'Not great to be honest, his ribs are cracked. Somehow I

don't think he'll be the life and soul of the party this weekend.'

'Has he ever been?' He ran his hand through his hair, uncertainty casting a shadow of guilt in his expression. 'I tried, I really did. George had to make it look real. The lads did the best they could in the circumstances.'

Sophie responded with a childlike bear hug. 'I know.'

They couldn't blame George. He had no choice.

OMNIA VINCIT AMOR

MELBOROUGH MANOR HOUSE, AGED TWENTY-FOUR

Sophie's eyes flick from Mum to Maya, as though they are the mysteries she most wants to decipher. She doesn't laugh like the rest of us when Mum snatches away Andy's plate, all because he's texting at the table. Sophie expects harsh punishment, instead she witnesses a diva performing on the stage of her dining room.

'Soph, you know my mum doesn't mean it when she said Andy should sleep in the barn, it was a joke,' I tell her later.

'I know, it made me sad in a way. Mum used to joke all the time, but now it's all about appearance. She would say that and mean it.'

I try to make her laugh by saying that maybe she should marry Andy and let her mother loose on him, but her reply sends a brief chill through me.

'No, I couldn't do that to him.'

Her giggle relieves that momentary doubt.

'Shouldn't I meet her, well both of them? I will be their son-in law after all.'

Sophie shakes her head. 'No, darling. We'll be married soon, and Daddy is so busy, there's no point. He's consented to the contract and that's all that needs to be done. Mummy would probably fret about the service and whatnot. No, best to meet them at the signing.'

I'm disappointed by her response, worried she is slightly ashamed of me. She snuggles up and the perfume in her hair rises up, eliminating all doubting thoughts. I love her, and she loves me, that's all.

'Finn?'

'Hmm.'

'Is Evie, you know, one of them?'

'Is Evie in a relationship with Maya? Was that what you were going to ask?' I knew this question would come from the moment I saw Sophie's expression when Evie introduced Maya to her. I should have warned her, explained. How do you explain something that is so normal in one world and totally alien, forbidden in another? I had chickened out, but now I must confront her question. 'Would it make a difference if I said they were? They have been together since college, they love each other deeply, just like you and me. It's not illegal here.'

Sophie's prolonged silence frightens me. Have I misjudged her?

'No, I don't think it does make a difference, not to me. It's just, well I'm not really sure to be honest.'

Her answer pushes a pin into my balloon of fear, but not enough to puncture it. 'Not sure about us, or about Evie and Maya?' I ask, worried she has handed me an impossible choice.

'I am very sure about us, you don't need to worry.' She kisses my hand. 'Don't mind me, I'm just tired. It is so different here to what I imagined.'

The balloon of fear is punctured. 'And what did you imagine?' I pull a funny face and stick my tongue out. 'Monsters out to eat you up?' I grab her sides, tickling her, and her eyes shine with laughter's tears. I brush them away, my hand warmed by the heat from her cheek. 'I promise you, Sophie, I will never be a monster to my woodland pixie.'

'And would you love me, even if it were illegal?'

I take her beautiful round face into my hands. 'Laws can't dictate who we may or may not love. That is a power far beyond

315

the capabilities of politicians. Love always finds a way.'
  'Omnia vincit amor,' she says.
  'It does indeed, my love. It does indeed.'

FINN

No Smith family meal was complete until all had gathered in the cosiness of the library. Although the evening was not particularly cold, Tim insisted on lighting the fire.

'I love the sight of flames. And that smell, it speaks to my inner prehistoric man,' he said, stabbing it with an ancient poker.

'Speaks to your inner arsonist, more like,' said Christopher. 'I lived with you, remember. You were a nightmare with dinner party candles.'

Funny how a small comment could set off a raft of conversations. Tim and Christopher talking of school and college days, Michelle and Anna trying to out-embarrass the other with their worst fashion mistakes, while Finn and Sophie curled up on the oversized armchair enjoying the reminiscing. It didn't matter that they had heard the stories one hundred times before, in that room they were a family. They were best friends. They were equal. No one mentioned politics, restrictions, shortages nor curfews. No one spoke about punishment beatings. New Albany would make its demands and they would each perform their roles, but not in that library.

The warmth and pleasant, safe chatter had lulled Finn, the painkillers Sophie had given him were working and he felt relaxed and comfortable enough to rest his head on her shoulder, closing his eyes.

'What about you Finn? Do you remember the first time we met, on the Medical School Campus?' said Sophie.

'Hmm?' He really didn't feel like answering.

'What did you say, Sophie?' said her mother, reaching for the bottle of bramble liqueur.

'Oh, I was just asking Finn if he remembered when we first met. You were lost, remember?' She twisted, jogging Finn's head off her shoulder. 'I think you must have been on your way to see Dr Hargreaves?'

'Don't remember.'

'You must do, he came to our wedding. You remember him, don't you Mum?'

'Vaguely. There were so many there. Wasn't he the professor you lodged with, Finn?'

'Maybe, I only lodged for a short while. I can't remember to be honest.' Finn remembered perfectly well. The mere mention of the name made him feel queasy. The man who had persuaded him to leave the safety of home and study in New Albany. Secrets and fears revealed in Liam's office. His nodding head and scribbling pen, taking page after page of notes on how Finn felt, the side effects of the latest antidepressant, checking on what he was eating. Every mealtime an opportunity to analyse Finn. After a year of living in the Hargreaves household, he had managed to convince his parents he was fine, and he ought to move back into a student dorm. They celebrated his achievement but insisted the consultations should continue. Finn had remonstrated with himself after that. He always gave a better performance live. He should have gone home to tell them instead of over the phone.

Liam was the first to escape when cultural assimilation advice became restrictions and fines. And it was Finn's confidential treatment file that lay open on the Dean's desk the day he requested Finn's resignation.

'Finn's face was a picture.'

Finn looked across to his wife, worried that in her tipsy state she would reveal things he wanted forgotten. She smiled back at him before continuing her story. 'Honestly, he was so sweet. I said directions would cost him and he genuinely thought he had to pay me, started patting down his pockets for his wallet.' Sophie was tapping his arm, 'Oh darling, you looked so baffled when I said payment would be a drink in the student bar, six o'clock sharp. I was quite surprised when you turned up ready to pay your dues.'

Relieved, Finn edged towards his wife, the softest of kisses brushing the down of her cheeks and whispered, 'I was brought up to pay my bills promptly.'

'I've been thinking Finn, why don't you stay on after Sunday.' Tim was slouched back in his chair, swirling the deep red liquid around the glass as though ignorant of the surprise with which his comment was received.

'Thank you, but I —'

'I insist, Michelle and I were talking earlier, it will do you good.'

'Do you mean that, Mum?' Sophie was staring at Michelle.

Her mother lifted her head and replied, quietly, 'Yes, of course. Don't worry I won't eat him, and given all the weight he has lost, he'd make a poor meal.'

Sophie left Finn's side to give her mother a hug. 'Thank you, Mum.'

He couldn't remember the last time he had seen Sophie embrace Michelle. And she must have realised that too, holding onto her daughter's hand long after Sophie had released the hug. She kissed Sophie's knuckles before standing up and heading towards the piano.

'I think we should have some music.' She raised the piano lid and tapped the nearest keys. 'I wish I could play this instrument. Come on Finn, why don't you play for us? Payment for the extra board and lodging.' She laughed. 'Something tuneful and jolly though.'

'No Mum, Finn's not up to playing tonight, leave him be,' said Sophie, but Finn was already heaving himself out of the chair.

'I don't mind.'

His fingers hovered over the ivory and black coloured keys, practising invisible scales while he wracked his brain for the music that had been filed away. A succession of music teachers jostled for priority in his memory. The ones who shouted at him, they never lasted long. Then the ones that sat quietly, occasionally dozing as he laboured through a dirge of exam pieces. Finally, he settled with Janie, and the stories she made up as they played. Always smiling, always comforting.

'What will you play?' said Anna, interrupting his time travelling to return him back into exile.

'I'm not sure, but something will come to me.' Finn scanned his audience hoping for inspiration. Anna was curled up on Christopher's lap. They seemed so content to him, unconcerned about the restrictions that ruled their life and made Finn's the shadow of his previous dreams. Michelle had returned to Tim's side. She was twisted in the seat, her back to Tim, leaning over the armchair towards Anna, chatting and chuckling like the outside world did not exist for them. And in a way it didn't, Tim made sure of that. He envied them. How he wanted to be back seated next to Janie, playing Bach's minuet. The first piece she taught him. His fingers were already dancing out the melody, light and spirited before he even realised he was playing. A scented candle burnt on the windowsill, its cologne recapturing the exotic fragrance of his piano teacher, bringing her back to him, beating out the pulse inside his head.

It ended too soon, and he didn't want to stop. To stop would be to banish Janie, and that normality of childhood was too precious to abandon. He listened to the soft voice telling him about Beethoven as he practised the 'Moonlight' sonata. A man deaf to the world outside, but music remained alive within him. He progressed through the movements, enticing him further and further away from the Smith's library and directing him back to freedom. The aching lament of the adagio became an escape. Each note a memory of home, of Melborough, his parents, Andy, and Evie. Always Evie. He felt her hand resting on his back as she turned the music, encouraging, laughing as she popped chocolates into his mouth. But Finn's mind was always finding ways to challenge his happy thoughts, and he tasted the bitterness of dark chocolate and sour cherry. His heartbeat chasing the presto agito, its rolling bass notes reminding him of the relentless wretchedness of his life. A guilty man playing with all the depth and feeling that comes with betrayal and desertion. He wanted to slam his hands down, stop the deceit but, despite his breaking heart, Finn persisted. His show must go on and Sophie would one day see his desertion as an act of love. His heartbreak would be the price payable for that devotion, and his betrayal the price to give her freedom. Some things are worth their high cost. He played the final notes, then drooped, exhausted by the emotion, deaf to the applause around him.

'That was my mother's favourite piece.' There was a hard edge to Michelle's voice, as though he had displeased her. 'It always makes me think how unlucky Beethoven was.'

'Why?' said Anna.

'Because he never found lasting love. Take that sonata, he dedicated it to Guilietta Guicciardi, a countess. She would never have married someone like Beethoven, and he ended up childless and alone.'

Finn felt her dig slide through him, he wanted to retaliate, if not in words then in action. He returned to Sophie, her arms wide open to welcome him back onto her chair.

'But Beethoven did know love,' continued Anna. 'He had his Immortal Beloved. Happy the person that gets to say they had a love so profound it becomes immortal.'

Michelle smiled. 'Maybe you're right, and with that happy thought I am going to bed. Good night.'

It wasn't long before Anna and Christopher returned to their flat over the garage, and with the anaesthesia of drugs and music wearing off, Finn began to shift uncomfortably in the seat, pain searing through his battered body. With his wife's arm to support him and the promise of more drug relief, Finn called it a night and headed to his room.

SOPHIE

Sophie returned to the library where Tim sat in the dark contemplating the flames in the fire. She cuddled up next to her father, automatically reverting to a childhood posture.

'Did you and Mum mean that?

'Mean what?'

'Finn staying. He'd be quite happy to stay at home you know, and I'm not convinced Mum is that keen. Finn really isn't up to dealing with her tantrums.'

'I invited him and that's the end of it. Your mother will not say anything impolite to Finn. I promise she'll be on her best behaviour.'

Her face rested on his jumper, rising and falling with his breaths. Childish comfort was flung aside with adult reality. The man inside that jumper was a murderer, and a prisoner. A man who permitted the deaths of others to protect his own. She was about to move when her father placed his arm around her, bringing her in close to him. His lips brushing her forehead. She was trapped by his love. Unable to forgive his decisions, she could at least understand them. She too was trapped by a love, and without the desire to escape it. The sofa, fire and Dad were a far preferable way to finish the evening.

'Would you like to try my new gooseberry wine?'

Sophie gawked opened mouthed at him, uncertain whether it was excitement or fear that made her heart leap into her mouth.

'It's all set for the first week of the summer holidays.'

Sophie collapsed into the battered chair by the tea chest, stunned by her father's revelation. It was too soon. 'That's just four weeks away!'

'It's the only possible window. We have to try it. This might be our one and only chance. I need to get you both out, there are rumours. The Government is happy with the results of the manufactured flu epidemic, and now they want to speed up the process of national purification.'

Those words sent shivers through her. 'What are they going to do?'

'Further restrictions, more beatings, more anti DIA propaganda, I'm not sure for certain, but Finn is high risk. I doubt he is well enough; the illness has taken a hefty toll on his health and this beating won't have helped. They'll want to send DIAs to the Treatment Centre for the slightest thing. I expect Henry has already received the long list of ailments that now require a one-way trip to the centre.'

Sophie remembered Finn's appointment with Officer Enright scheduled for early July. There would be no release for him this time, no matter the size of the bribe.

'Isn't that the week of the big birthday party? Is that the cover?'

'It's been postponed. I managed to convince your mother that the garden is at its best in September. Given I am only going to be seventy once, I want to choose my present. We are going on holiday to AZ Eight, just like we did when you were a little girl. I'll take you sailing in the coves and your mother will sunbathe.'

'And Finn?'

'You are going to teach him to sail.'

Horrified, a well of panic swirled inside Sophie. 'Dad, he's terrified of water. I don't think he can even swim. Are you mad? I can't see this working.'

'We are going to have to make it work, it's our only option.'

'Have you told Mum?'

'No, she mustn't know, she'll be distraught to lose you. I doubt she would inform the authorities, but I can't be one hundred percent certain. No, your mother must be kept in the dark.'

Sophie nodded in agreement. Doubts about her mother's trustworthiness had plagued her thoughts for a while. 'When do I tell Finn?'

'Not yet. I'll let you know when, probably once we arrive at the house. The less he knows the better. He needs to stay well. Do you understand? He cannot come to the attention of the authorities, especially now he has a misdemeanour. I may not be able to save him if anything else goes on his file.'

By the time Sophie returned to her parents' house on the Thursday night, Finn appeared notably better. His face was a myriad of colours, but he was able to move around a bit more. That night, after he had gone up to bed, she made her decision. They had been apart too long.

He was reading a book from Tim's library when she entered his room. Neither needed to say anything, it was just understood.

'Shove up. I was cold, so I thought I'd join you.'

Finn put the book down and gingerly inched to one side, giving her space in the bed. She snuggled into him, landing her cold feet on his, and kissed his shoulder. 'I love you Dr Sheehan.'

He curled his arm around her, lowering his face into her hair. The delicate touch of his lips and his breath tickled her scalp. 'And I love you too, Mrs Sheehan.'

*

The early morning was her favourite part of the day. While the household slept, Sophie made herself a herbal tea and headed out into the garden. The dawn chorus lifted her spirits, it was going to be a beautiful spring morning. Sophie had come to realise that this would likely be the last time she would enjoy her parents' garden. There were a mere twenty-four hours left to absorb as much as she could and to take it away as a precious memory. Leaving her life behind would not be a simple act. It would also mean leaving her parents. Abandoning everything and everyone she knew and loved, everyone except him. Finn would be with her.

Sophie had forgotten how much simply lying next to him could relax her. The soothing lullaby of his breathing and those brief touches as they turned in the night. After a good sleep, the early sunrise had woken her, and she lay in the bed content to daydream about their future. Where would they settle? Near his family probably. His parents must be quite old. It would be good to spend some time with them. Perhaps they'd go to Evie's? Last they had heard she ran a veterinary practice on the other side of the world. What about Andy, he had three children of his own. She imagined her own unborn children, playing with their cousins. Once they escaped, she would be free to have children. The circumstances would be right at last. There would be no more lies.

Every minute of that day was a minute to treasure. In the late afternoon sunshine, her father and Christopher played tennis, while on the croquet lawn, Finn lost gallantly to Michelle and Anna. He always lost to them.

She left them playing and continued her journey of memory gathering. At the far end of the garden, close to the perimeter was a copse of beech trees, home to her fairies. Christopher and Tim had built her a fairy castle high up in the branches. It wasn't hard to find, although it didn't seem quite so high up these days. She took off her sandals and held onto the rope and placed a foot on the tree, letting the rope take her weight. It held. Hand over hand, her bare feet walked up the trunk. An eight-year-old girl once more, she entered through a hole and scrambled into her secret castle. It was exactly as she left it. Filthy, full of leaves and spiders, but otherwise unchanged. To one side was a small pink seat and a plastic table. The squirrels had knocked off the toy tea set, and the miniature cups and saucers were scattered around. She picked up the teacup and saucer and placed it next to the faded pink teapot. Crossed-legged on the treehouse floor, she lifted the pot. 'May I offer you some tea, my dear Oberon? It is such an honour to have you visit my castle,' she said to her invisible guest.

'Is your old Dad allowed to join the party?'

Sophie jumped at the sight of her dad's head appearing through the hole. 'Christ Dad, you gave me a fright. What on earth are you doing climbing up here? The rope must be ancient, you could fall.'

'Hasn't broken any of the other times I come up here. I replaced it a while back, just in case.'

A little tin box slipped out of his hand and clattered on the wood. Sophie leant forward and grabbed her father's wrist, pulling in unison with his efforts to heave himself into the hideaway.

'Dinner won't be long,' he said once he had brushed away enough dust to sit down, 'and this might be the last chance I get to spend time alone with my little girl in her fairy castle.' His voice caught, he coughed to disguise it, but she had heard it and it made him seem fragile. He had become an old man, and one she would be consigning to the cruelty that reigned over their lives. She wept.

'I don't want to go, Daddy. Isn't there another way we could all escape? It would be bearable if we could all leave together.'

He shook his head, saying words of little comfort, 'No, my darling. We've left it too late. This is your only chance and you must take it.' He drew her in close with his own tears dripping into her dark brown hair. After a few minutes he reached for the tin, it's content rattling when he handed it to her. 'I have something for you.'

Sophie wiped her face, smearing her cheeks with grubby hands. Her confusion faded once the little lid was pushed off. Sleeping pills were easily recognisable to Albian nurses. 'Why are you giving me these?' she asked.

'You can't risk needing to get a prescription for Finn. I had these already, getting anymore may become tricky with my ASSU secretary investigating every memo and request. It's going to get much harder to protect him, and you mustn't go to Henry. He can't be trusted, no one can.'

'No Dad, I can't take these. A DIA with unprescribed narcotics can be arrested for drugs offences, you know that. His injuries are much improved, and Anna's poultice really helped.

'Your bag's secret compartments will keep him out of danger then. And you must be realistic, Sophie, he's not been well since Christmas, has he? I don't blame him, I'm not sure I'd have coped as well. I have some antidepressants too. I got them a while back, on one of my trips. They're here if you need them.'

'No, he won't take them. Antidepressants used to make him feel worse, headaches and stuff. He came off them before we married and swore never to take them again. We've managed without them, we always manage.'

'Darling, this isn't a game. Any hint of a mental crisis

will be his death warrant. Do you understand me? He must stay well, if it means he has a few headaches, then so be it. A bad head is a small price to pay compared to the alternative.'

Sophie crumbled into her father. 'Oh, God, this is such a mess, why have our lives been allowed to disintegrate like this.' She lifted her face, the agony of stolen years searing through her. 'This is not how I imagined my life. I wanted to be a doctor. I wanted to travel. I thought I was free. How could you be part of this nightmare?'

'It became too dangerous to pull away, you know that,' he said. 'I believed we were creating a utopia, but it turned into a mechanism to enrich the chosen few. I was blind, I thought I was part of the elite, but like everyone else, I was being used. I had no idea until it was too late that things would go so wrong.'

'Wrong? Wrong is not the word I'd use. Fucking disaster is a better description!'

Tim smirked. 'You may well be right! I've fucked the country I loved.'

'What do you think will happen next, Dad?'

'God knows. They've barely scratched the surface of their depravity. We smashed Pandora's Box long before you were born, and consequences multiply with each passing year. I once clung onto the belief that Hope always exists, but now I even doubt that.'

The journey back left Finn tired and in pain. Christopher put the suitcase down in the hallway. 'Shall I help you upstairs?' he said and like a caring medic, placed his arm around his waist. 'Looks like you could do with a rest.'

Finn didn't answer, nor did he resist the help. He clutched the bannister for the slow walk upstairs. 'I'll be OK from here,' he said, wriggling out of Christopher's embrace.

Sophie shrugged at her husband's stubbornness, picked up the bag and followed him. Before disappearing onto the landing, she called back down to Christopher, 'You know where everything is, why don't you make some tea. The proper stuff is in a tin which says dishwasher.'

To her relief, Finn continued past the guest room and back into their own bedroom.

Christopher was already pouring out the tea when Sophie entered the kitchen. 'Does Finn want one too?'

'No, he just wants to sleep. I'll make him some supper when he wakes. Would you like something to eat? I make a mean omelette.'

'Thank you, I hate stopping on journeys when I'm on my own.'

It took her no time to whip up a couple of cheese omelettes, and soon they were sitting at the table enjoying the early dinner. Sophie wondered about her godfather, a man who had been part of her entire life, yet he remained an enigma. He never spoke of his life before the regime, other than his friendship with Anna and her parents.

'Come into the garden, we can drink out there,' she said once they had finished the meal. 'It's looking good at the moment. '

She snipped some Sweet Peas and gathered them together into a little bouquet before handing it to him. 'Here you go, a thank you from me.'

He buried his nose in the flowers inhaling their sweetness.

'Why did you stay?' she asked him as he lifted his face.

'Thank you, Sophie. They're gorgeous and will make the flat smell delicious.'

She was going to be deterred by his side-stepping her question. 'Why didn't you and Anna leave like the others?'

He sniffed the flowers again, then placed then next to him. 'We were both very young when we moved here with our parents, we virtually grew up together. We loved our life.'

She sat beside him, smelling the leather and security that surrounded him. 'But you must have realised things were getting bad when they introduced the DIA programme. Finn stayed because of me, but you and Anna could have been free.'

'And go where? This is our home.' He smiled, his face wrinkled by the laughter lines of an optimist. 'Neither of us ever wanted to be parents and to be honest, life was perfect. When things began to change, your father advised us to go, start a new life, but where? Both of our parents had died, and we had no other relatives. You and your parents are our only family.' He hugged her. 'Don't worry about us, Sophie, we've been the lucky ones. Your father devised the plan where I would be his driver-cum-gardener and Anna the housekeeper. A flat over the garages. A property that is protected and not monitored. He kept us safe, isolated from everything. Inside the perimeter wall we are Anna and Christopher Halmeer, your parents' friends, not their employees.'

'But you did take on those roles, why?'

'You've got to do something. Your dad didn't need a theoretical physicist and a former cardiothoracic surgeon. So, driver and cook we became, to keep us sane.'

'But, what if it gets worse, I couldn't bear anything happening to you.'

Christopher chuckled in the same way he had done a thousand times before. Nothing seemed to unnerve his calm character. 'Don't worry, we'll be just fine.'

The clock had just struck seven when Finn finally made it

home from School House 87. Despite the bruising on his face, he looked as white as a sheet.

'Christ Finn, what happened?' Sophie said, helping him into a chair. 'I've been so worried.' She didn't tell him that during the anxious hours of waiting, her head had been full of images of execution squads.

Finn pressed the pads of his thumbs into his temples, as though he might squeeze out the pain. 'It turns out it is a lot harder to cycle when you have cracked ribs. I had to walk into school and then walk home again. I'm shattered. I can't do this all week.'

Sophie stood in silence, then erupted into laughter.

'Glad you find it so funny,' said Finn.

Noting he was miffed, she stroked his arm, giving him a peck on the cheek to amend for her insult. 'Oh believe me, given the thoughts I've had for the past two hours, suffering a long walk is a blessed relief.'

'A long walk and then a horrible day,' he added.

'Let's have dinner and you can tell me all about it.'

Although she made light of it, she didn't know for whose benefit. Finn told her about the comments from the girls, every lesson beginning with a barrage of questions asking him what he had done, and how embarrassing it must be to be beaten in front of everyone. Mr Harrison had called out as Finn passed by, 'Not an MI anymore? No more special privileges for Mr Michael.' Even the head questioned him as to why he had been punished. Then to end a bad day, a two hour walk home to be greeted by a laughing wife.

'You should take the bus for a while, give your ribs a chance to fully heal,' she said.

'It's humiliating and slow,' Finn said as he left the table to load the dishes into the washer. 'People crammed into the back, while the patriot seats remain empty. It's all so illogical apart from everything else.'

'It might be that, but you don't have an alternative. I'll pack you something extra to eat before you get the bus, there won't be time for you to eat at home first, and it will be tight getting back before your curfew starts.' She reached for her bag, rummaging through it until she found her phone. 'I'll ask George if he could add an extension to your curfew pass.'

Finn didn't respond. While Sophie chatted to George she watched him, plate in hand but staring at the blank wall, all the while his other hand roughly rubbed at his neck, as if to soothe an unseen injury.

OBEDIENCE ABOVE ALL

To whom do we owe obedience? Our parents? Our partners? Our betters or to our own desires? We deny the rebel, wishing for a peaceful life. Obedience is the cosy home. And rebellion? That is the wilderness. Yet we hear it tapping on the window of our conscience. It pricks us with guilt, holding open the door to the adventure that exists beyond the claustrophobia of duty.

FINN

'You're late, 568216!'

Finn dropped his bag on the table. He ignored her and removed his books and pens from his bag, neatly setting them out. He said nothing. Cat scrutinised him, watching from her usual position, lounging across the sofa. Her head was propped up by the large fur cushion while she dangled her legs off the end.

Finn was sure her legs had not been so long back in the Autumn, or maybe everything else had shrunk, including him.

'You're late, and you must answer me,' she repeated, her tone filled with the certainty of position.

'It was a statement not a question, therefore did not require answering. However, I will apologise for arriving a few minutes late,' replied Finn. He daren't look at her for fear his temper would burst out.

'You really are starting to show a bold side to your character. Not sure whether it's endearing or not anymore.'

Finn sat down on the chair, pain adding to his straining temper. 'I walked here. It took slightly longer than I had anticipated.'

Cat swung her legs off the sofa and approached the table. Pressing her hand down on his shoulder, she took a closer look at Finn's damaged face. 'It's amazing, a true kaleidoscope of colours.' There was a large green and purple bruise high on his cheek bone. She poked it. 'Does that hurt?'

Finn breathed in to avoid flinching.

'It seems so. Did you learn your lesson?' She grinned and pressed harder.

'That depends, I certainly learnt a lesson.'

Cat sat down, pushing her book to one side. 'And that is the most important lesson. Where would we be without obedience?'

* * *

Tuesday 8th June

> *I thought his bruises would cheer me, appease my frustration, but they did nothing except remind me of his defiance. I loathe this temper that keeps rising, simmering beneath my breast. I want to lash out at him, bring him to heel. I don't want to hurt him, but I must. What right does he have to be so defiant but not me, a Commandant's daughter? Why can't I be ME?*

* * *

It was Friday before he got the message from George that his birthday letter had finally been released from the censors. Finn waited in line at the guardhouse desk for the young officer to attend him. Hands hidden in pockets and a mask of calm indifference to conceal his terrified soul. Passing guards greeted him like an old friend, but Finn remained in no doubt, he was their prisoner, a number.

'568216/2/MI, you have a letter for me,' he said to the guard who cheerfully waited to attend him.

'Sure thing, Mr Michael, let me take a look.' The guard turned his back on Finn to rummage through a filing cabinet. 'So, how's Miss Sophie? Lovely weather we're having at the moment, aren't we?'

'Hmm, lovely, yes.'

'Bet her garden is a picture. Sergeant Mason says there

isn't a garden in the whole of AZ Five that can match hers.'

'Yes, it's beautiful.'

'Ah, here it is.' He returned back to the desk. 'If I could, you know, your bangle please, Mr Michael?'

Finn lifted his arm onto the desk and unbuttoned his cuff, letting the bangle slip out from under his sleeve.

'Oh, um, you should really have it on show the whole time.' The guard aimed the microchip reader and they both waited for the bleep. It came, followed by taps on a keyboard. He picked up the envelope and handed it to Finn. 'Look, I won't say anything about your bangle, seeing as it's you, but do watch out in other guardhouse areas. Let's just say, some guards enjoy their power a bit too much and love to make things difficult for any DIA crossing their path.'

'Yes, you're probably right. Thank you, Corporal Phillips.'

The letter safely tucked away in his pocket, Finn turned to leave. He was not one to prolong his visits to the guardhouse with any more pleasantries than the bare minimum. At the exit, he stopped to look at the poster. It had been there forever, a fresh-faced man smiling down at him. But there was nothing reassuring about his black uniform, with its silver buttons shining on the cuffs. The darkness of the uniform contrasting with the flash of white collar. The bottom of the poster was worn, the corners ripped and curling up. George was supposed to replace it with an updated version each season, but he never bothered given the content never changed.

'Our repatriation team will see you back home to your loved ones with care and efficiency. Apply here today.'

Although he had intended to apply, he hadn't actually filled out the form necessary for the process to begin.

'Something wrong, Mr Michael?' said Corporal Phillips,

disturbing Finn's thoughts.

He sensed that the corporal had been watching him stare at the poster. He shook his head and put his hand in his pocket feeling the letter. Even without opening it he knew there would be more black lines hiding Evie from him. His decision confirmed, he returned to the desk. 'No, nothing wrong, but would you mind telling me what's needed to request repatriation?'

SOPHIE

Saturdays were the worst day of the week. Ailments, all saved up to be dealt with on the patients' one free day. Life was hard for ordinary patriots too, playing their allocated role in the game devised by the Albian elite. Those distant deities, the only ones who were at liberty to enjoy their lives. Yet were they as free as she once believed? Maybe everyone lived within different levels of misery. Occupied with a head full of rebellion and bureaucracy, she didn't see him arrive and jumped when he coughed.

'Oh, Sergeant Mason, what a pleasure to see you, nothing wrong I hope.'

'Miss Sophie, we agreed, George.'

'Sorry, I thought that was for home only. Is there a problem with the extension to the late pass? Finn still can't cycle long distances. He'll probably need at least another week.'

'No, not the extension, that's fine. I thought you ought to know. He's signed a repatriation request form.'

The first thing she did was ring her father. George had already informed him about Finn, that was the agreement. Tim made an excuse to visit her and be with her for lunch the following day. Sophie implicitly understood not to say anything to Finn. Her day carried on as normal. They enjoyed dinner beneath the shade of the apple tree, relishing the sultry heat after the sunny day. Later, curled up in bed next to Finn, she kissed him goodnight and felt his arms become heavy on her as he fell asleep. Throughout it all, she desperately tried not to scream at him, the man she loved, the man for whom she gave up safety. That man intended to desert her.

Memories of the last time flooded her mind. She recoiled at the deceit. Decisions taken to ensure her own protection. How could she possibly know the disaster that would follow? It had been devastating for him. And for her too. But Sophie's pain had been filed away in her own private, little box. There was no time to risk it again. George said Finn had indicated to the corporal that he would stay until the last day of term, the day they were due to go on holiday. It might take six weeks to be certain, and there was no guarantee she would get pregnant first time. Her only option was to convince him to stay. If she failed and he repatriated, then wouldn't she be as guilty of his murder as Ryan?

'Slow down, will you, I can't keep up,' called Finn.

Sophie had not waited to greet Henry after church, purpose and anger speeding her along the track home, propelling her several paces ahead of her husband. 'Sorry, I forgot. I want to get lunch on early, before Dad arrives.'

'It's only just nine o'clock, we've been up since six. Can't we have a gentle stroll back?' He caught up, holding his hand out for hers before remembering where they were. Shoving his hand back into his trouser pocket, he added petulantly, 'You don't need four hours to cook a chicken. And remind me, why is your father here?'

Her lies were well practiced. 'Dad has a surprise, about his party. I'm sure that's why he's visiting. I'm doing stuff with Mum and he needs to know some details without her finding out. Do you see?'

'No, not really. Remind me never to have a seventieth. It sounds far too complicated.'

Sophie walked beside him in silence. Life was complicated, and survival harder.

Christopher suggested to Finn that it was a pleasant day for a walk up to Hanbury Common. They wouldn't go too far, and they'd be back within an hour. Once they had left, Tim led Sophie into the garden.

'A repatriation request form is not the same as signing the actual consent. It merely states what they can expect from the procedure.'

'It's a pack of lies, Dad. None of what it states will happen. It might as well say they are going to live in a golden palace with caviar and champagne every day. It isn't going to happen.'

'Desperate people will believe any lie and act accordingly. When they find out they have been tricked, it's too late to do anything about it. Before they discover the truth, they will believe those lies against all evidence because it is an answer to their woes. Do you understand me?'

Sophie nodded.

'New Albany was not conceived and born through violence,' he continued. 'They didn't need to coerce the people to accept them. They understood the lies the people wanted to hear, and the public rewarded those liars with influence. A malevolent power, diminishing their rights and freedom, but that is not what they see. It is all smoke and mirrors, conjurers on the stage leaving their audience wowed by their trickery. And all the time the slogans and rallies continue, *'New Albany will save you'*, just not today.'

Sophie held her father's hand as they sat in silence. They had both ignored the deception, always believing that it couldn't interfere with their life too much, they were the protected ones. They were the elite. An immature apple dropped from the tree and landed at her feet. She picked it up and held it in her hand. Gravity exists, earth is a globe and New Albany is not Utopia. In the end fundamental truths must be revealed.

'Unless Finn signs that consent form, nothing will happen. Not unless there is any other reason to take him. Is there another reason, Sophie?'

'No, not at the moment. He's quiet and tired but that might be the hours he's working. We hardly get to say three words to each other. Getting a letter from his mother always causes some upset, but this time he seems to be dealing with it better than usual.'

'I should think that is because he too believes the lie that he will be seeing her again soon.'

Sophie had nothing to say. She had both believed and ignored their lies. A woman as guilty as the two-faced politicians. It had gone on for too long. 'I have to tell him the truth, Dad. I have to stop him!'

'No, you mustn't.' Tim stood, kicking the little apples at his feet. 'Lying is our national pastime. We are world champions at deception, but Finn is not a man who understands this game.' He sat down again and bit his lip. Sophie could tell he was devising yet more lies. Finally Tim spoke, 'I suspect you'll need to tell him you found out about the request form. He will probably guess that is why I am here. Say that I told you. My sources informed me, and I thought you should know. Tell him you understand why he feels he needs to go. Convince him to stay until after the holiday. What you must not do is tell him about the Treatment Centre, nor that the holiday is the escape route. Do you understand? He mustn't find out. He is too innocent to bear the truth. It would destroy him.'

WHERE'S MR STEINER?

CARNDEAN PREPARATORY SCHOOL, AGED SEVEN

*I want to hurry. I really do but I must find my glasses. I
search under the bench once more. Nothing. They must be
in my bag.*

*'Come on, Finn, we'll be late for History,' Tom calls back
to me from the door.*

*The others are already waiting in line. I see her, standing
at the doorway, her eyes narrowing as she examines this
messy line of boys, red fingernails drumming her upper arm.
I want to run away, my stomach squeezing tight at the sight
of her. It flips with her opening mouth.*

'Hurry up, I am not paid to stand here!'

*Where's Mr Steiner? I like Mr Steiner, he's funny, he
makes me smile. I don't know who this lady is, why is she
walking towards me? What have I done?*

*She yells at us to tuck in shirts, tidy our ties and do up
our shoelaces. My shirt is tucked in and my shoes are clean,
I polished them. I did it this morning. I have definitely tied
my laces. Why does she still come nearer? What have I done
wrong? I face the oak-panelled wall, hoping she'll go away.*

*My heart beats faster when I spot the graffiti carved into
the wood. I am next to it. I recognise his scrawl, 'AS'. He told
me I was to write my initials next to his. I trace my fingers
over the letters, I want him to like me. I had lied, told him I
had done it. He'll never know. Why would he? He hates this
place and will never return. He said so. He laughed at me.*

'You'll be so miserable, I mean, look at you, you're a

343

weirdo.' he said before I left.

He's right, I hate it. I want to go home. Why couldn't I stay at my old school in the village? Jack didn't leave, nor any of the others. Why me? I want Mrs McManus to be waiting for me at the school gate. I want her bear hug and that smell of the kitchen. Why does that bony teacher glare down at me? What have I done?

'Hurry up boy, we haven't got all day. You can stare at walls in your own time.'

She finds my face among the other eighteen boys' pictures on the paper held in her hand. Seventeen smiling faces and me.

'Is this you?' she says, pointing to my picture. There's writing underneath, but without my glasses it is just a yellow blur.

I nod and hurry after Tom.

I watch the changing grey scribbles on the interactive board, squinting to try and make them form letters. I search through my blazer pockets again hoping they'll materialise like a clever magic trick.

Tom leans over, whispering to me, 'Where are your glasses?'

I shrug.

'Are your spare ones in the dorm? Shall I ask to go and find them?'

I nod, and Tom immediately throws up his arm calling out to 'Miss'.

The fake teacher checks the list, her red fingernail tracing across the images until she finds Tom's happy face. 'Pereira, you had plenty of time to use the toilets before the lesson.'

Tom lowers his arm and makes a face at me. He knows when not to argue. He picks up his pencil case and searches for his special pen, the blue dolphin one. He wants to get on with the lesson, while I just want to go home.

FINN

Finn's bike was hanging up next to the garden gate. He had fashioned a little roof out of old bits of wood to protect it from the worst of the weather. For some unknown reason he stopped and stood beside it, examining its timeless engineering. He spun the front wheel backwards and the spokes disappeared into a blur. Lost in his imagination, he pretended that wheel was some illusory time machine, able to return him to days of freedom. A decent bike, Tim bought it for him as a gift when the driving restrictions came into force. On his bike he was anonymous.

Once his bangle was hidden from view, he would let his mind wander. Dr Sheehan once more, off to give a lecture to the students at the University. That wretched bus journey was long and a constant reminder of his prisoner status. The bicycle was tempting him towards defiance. He refused to allow the beating to deny him anymore moments of scant liberty. It was a beautiful morning for a rebellion, and he was going to be the willing rebel. Placing his bag carefully on the floor, he lifted his arms up to grab the frame. It took him several minutes to compose himself from the sudden burst of agony. One foot on the pedal, he scooted off down the lane, cycling on the flats and downhills and walking up the hills. It had to be better than the bus. What's a little pain compared to the ritual humiliation of a New Albany bus journey?

SOPHIE

Sophie had rehearsed the conversation in her head a thousand times, searching for the elusive right words to save Finn from repatriation. Even finding a suitable excuse to bring up the topic eluded her. The arguments, the excuses, they were all drowned out by the screaming voice in her head. Words that never changed, becoming louder, ever more insistent. The neediness of her selfishness. *'You want to leave me!'*

Finn's was bike propped up against the wall when she arrived home. She stared at it, certain it had been hanging up when she left early that morning. In the kitchen, Finn's bag was lying in the middle on the floor, its contents spilling out. Her pace quickened as she headed to the sitting-room, to find him sprawling across the sofa, clutching his side.

'I need some painkillers.'

'Hello, darling, have you had a good day? Oh, and by the way I'm a complete idiot, do you have any painkillers to dull this self-inflicted pain. Was that what you meant to say?'

'Let's have that conversation after pain relief.'

'Serves you right for not getting the bus.'

'I am never getting on a bus again. Never!'

Sophie returned to the kitchen, chuckling to herself as she rifled through her medicine cabinet of a bag, but stopped when she saw a little flask of liquid hiding underneath some pamphlets. Just something to make him less inhibited, chattier, truthful. She remembered Ryan's laughing face as he talked about the buses to the Treatment Centre.

346

'The best bit, they get on the bus at the Repatriation Centres, thinking they are going to the airport. They are allowed to sit anywhere, such a novelty for them. Comfy seats, air conditioning. All that luxury just to freight them to the Treatment Centre.'

She recalled those coach passengers arriving at the Centre, politely listening to a guard unaware their journey home had already ended. The time had come to tell him. He would not be getting on any more buses.

'Mum's just rung. Dad's cancelled the birthday party. I know you were dreading it,' said Sophie. She was carrying a supper tray down to the garden table. The evening was clear and warm, ideal for an al fresco supper of salad and truth.

'I wasn't dreading it because I wasn't going to go.'

Sophie ignored him, she had battled through enough arguments over the party and it was no longer an issue. With her most convincing face concealing her nerves, she explained the plans for a family holiday, just the four of them. Sun, sea and sailing.

'Sailing? You are kidding, aren't you? You want to get me enthused to go on a holiday that I don't want, with the inducement of sailing? Are you the crazy one? And here I was thinking that was me.'

'You are not crazy and yes, I want to take you sailing. You'll be perfectly safe. I know the area well. It will be good for you.'

'Why do people always say that? *'It will be good for you.'* My parents said that before sending me away to Carndean. Then senior school insisted Tolbridge was the only place to study. That charlatan of a doctor persuading me to come to this hell hole, and now you. I can only wonder at the misery that will befall me. It won't be good for me. It will be horrible.'

Sophie's well-planned argument crumbled with each sentence, exasperated by persistent stubbornness. 'Oh, for God's sake Finn, you can lie on the beach and drink cocktails, or bird watch for all I care, as long as we just relax for a week.'

'I can relax in our garden too.'

She was being thwarted. In her head, Finn would listen to the plan calmly and accept it wholeheartedly. He would tear up the repatriation form, convinced by her argument. They would enjoy a fabulous holiday and escape to freedom. In her anger and frustration, the words did not form as she intended. 'Why do you want to leave me?'

'I see. I suppose I should have gone to the guardhouse near the school, I forgot about Tim's tame spy.'

'You like George, don't deny it, anyway he would have found out regardless of where you went. You didn't answer my question, why are you going to abandon me?' Sophie's eyes brimmed with tears, saying those words out loud to his face dragged up all her fears from her past.

'I am leaving you because I love you.'

'That doesn't make sense, you want to break my heart, leave me distraught, bereft, all because you love me?'

'Yes, I do love you. I love you very much, so much so that I would give my life to protect you.' He took her hand and squeezed it, his wedding ring hard against her skin. 'You deserve to have a life, a wonderful free life. How can you when you are shackled to me? You're reduced to the role of prison warder. Don't you see, you are as much a prisoner of this programme as I am.'

'No, Finn I don't. We are together for better or for worse. I am not your jailer. I am your wife who chooses this life because I love you.'

'But we don't have a life, do we? I can't take you out to the theatre, a restaurant, not even a shopping trip without prior permission. I can't kiss you in public nor hold your hand. Because I am prevented from doing these things so are you. It's time you were with someone who loves you as much as I do. Someone who can take you out to wonderful places. A husband who can kiss and love you as much as I've wanted to. You deserve to have children.'

'Is this what it's really about, children? Darling, it will happen for us, I'm sure.' She slipped her hand out from under his and grabbed his arm. 'It will happen, you need to believe it too.'

'No Sophie, as much as I want to believe you, I have to accept the situation as it is. It's better for you if I go now and give you the space to find someone who can definitely give you children. Don't worry, I'll be fine, I'm sure. I'll be back with Mum and Dad. I'll have Evie with me again, so you don't need to worry about me. Just get on with having the life that's denied to you at the moment.'

'You still don't get it, do you? I love you.' Her voice was distorted as she battled to make him understand. 'I don't want theatres, restaurants or shops. I don't need your kisses in public to feel the warmth of your lips on mine each time I look at you. You are with me every moment of the day. Children will be part of our future, but we can love and live without them too. We are who we are because of our love. Without you I cease to be.'

Finn unpicked his wife's fingers from around his arm and let his face drop into the palms of his hands.

'Talk to me, Finn. Please, talk to me.'

His justification was muffled but clear enough for Sophie's heart to almost stop with grief.

'This is killing me, Sophie. I must go.' He sat up, looking

her in the eye. 'I'm dying here, and I will die here, either because of this abominable regime or by my own hands. It is not a question of if, it is when, and it will be sooner rather than later. Wouldn't it have been better for me to die at Christmas?'

'No, no one will hurt you again. I promise, please Finn, believe me. I'll keep you safe.'

'You don't understand, it's already too late to save me. At the mansion there was a DIA, Johan, I was jealous when I heard he had died. He was free from this daily torment. Darling, I love you so much and I do want to live. I don't want to die, but it's a daily battle, staying here is killing me. It is killing all of us.'

Sophie raised her hand and caressed the face of her husband, broken by years of imprisonment. Her love and special privileges insufficient to shield him from an Albian slow death. 'OK.'

Finn looked up, startled.

'But there is a caveat,' Sophie continued. 'You do not sign the consent form until we return from AZ Eight. Go on holiday, learn to sail and when we return, I will go with you to the guardhouse. I won't stop you. First let me enjoy a week of make-believing we are a happy ordinary couple on a beach holiday.'

His silence worried Sophie. She had taken a risk letting him believe he could repatriate. There were so many what ifs running through her brain that she barely noticed him take her hand and kiss it. 'OK, I promise to wait.'

SLAVES AND MASTERS

CARNDEAN PREPARATORY SCHOOL, AGED SEVEN

Mr Steiner makes lessons fun. He lets us play, pretending to be the Roman slaves and masters. He laughs with us. Not this teacher, she gives us worksheets. Tom whispers the answers to write down. I need to find my glasses. I'll get into trouble if I have lost yet another pair.

My fingers blindly pick their way through the screwed-up bits of paper, mouldy sweets and lost pen tops that live at the bottom of my bag. Is that them? I freeze, a moment of panic as I hear my name.

'Sheehan, which picture goes with the description of the slave?'

How can I answer her, there is nothing for me to see? I lower my eyes and pretend to read my worksheet. Tom, like half the class, has his hand up ready to shout out the answer. If I focus on the desk, she'll ask someone else. They always do.

She's getting closer. Go away! Go away! The click clacks of her shoes on the floor keep time with my heartbeat thumping in my chest. Go away! Go away!

Tom's speaking. He is stammering out an excuse, telling her about my lost glasses, but her angry reply silences him.

'Sheehan, answer the question, I am waiting.'

Tom wants to help. He understands.

'Pereira, I've already told you to be quiet. He will obey me. I will not tolerate his stubborn behaviour.'

Her hand grips my arm, dragging me away from the desk, past the other boys. Seventeen horrified little faces and me, sobbing. She stands me in front of the board and points up. 'There, can you see the board now? Which description matches the picture of the slave?'

Tom's voice calls out again, 'Miss, you're frightening him. He can't speak when he's scared. I am getting matron. She helps him.'

'Don't you dare leave your seat. I know his sort. He's just another spoilt, little rich boy who doesn't want to work. He needs to learn there are consequences.'

The bell for break rings loudly, but no one moves. The room is silent except for my rhythmic sobs.

'Sheehan, you will learn. You're just a stubborn and selfish boy. Answer the question, or I'll punish the rest of the class. What's it going to be?'

FINN

It was the following week before Cat found out about the repatriation request form. Finn knew she regularly checked his file to see if there was anything new with which to torment him, and it was inevitable that she would find out about the request. He did not even duck as the teacup came hurtling through the air, smashing against the wall next to his face.

'How dare you!' Cat screamed at him, beating about his body with her fur cushion. Finn protected himself from the assault, shielding his face with his arm. Exhausted by her fury, the pupil dropped the cushion and stood in front of him. 'Do you really think you can just go? You will never leave me. I won't allow it. Do you understand? I won't allow it!'

'Don't worry, Miss Fry. I've no intention of leaving you in the lurch. I'll go after my contract is finished at the end of term.'

She turned slightly, but only to get the momentum to hit his face hard with the back of her hand. Finn felt a trickle of blood seeping out from his cheek where her engagement ring scratched it.

'Your contract with my father might end there but I'm not letting you go. You are mine, and mine to do with as I please. I will keep you. I am not going to that fop of a husband without you. Do you understand? I own you.'

'Yes, I do,' Finn said, 'but, slavery does not form part of the DIA programme just yet. I cannot be obliged. If I choose, I can be repatriated, and I choose that, not you. You will have to find another pet to abuse.'

Finn waited for the response, knowing it would be both nasty and vindictive. Cat couldn't stop the repatriation once he had signed the consent form. It would be over, and he would be gone.

Her anger spent, the barrage of insults suddenly ceased as she flopped back onto her sofa. 'I don't want a lesson today.'

'Shall I leave?'

'No, you are going to stay right here.'

With each passing minute, his initial anger fell further into the dread of foreboding. She watched him with a stare that skewered Finn to his seat. Finally, at five to nine, she reached under the sofa and pulled out a box. Finn's heart sank as he recognised it. "Coulter and Co." The slender white box rested on her stomach, her fingers running over the gold lettering before she slowly lifted the lid. Out came the green leash with its gold tag. Out came the choke chain.

'Come!' Cat pointed to the rug next to her, but Finn, the rebel, did not move. 'I said "Come!" Remember, I can fix it so that someone you care about receives a suitable punishment if you disobey me.'

Finn maintained his impassive stance with her threat. He would not be her tamed and cowed creature anymore. He almost felt pride at his defiance. He was strong enough. He would survive her. He would be free.

She slid the leash and chain through her fingers. It's metallic rattling competing with the high pitch tick of the mantle clock. It chimed the hour and she let the leash slip out of her hands and fall, curled up on the floor.

Finn stooped to pick up his bag.

'I didn't say you could leave, did I?'

'Are you going to keep me here all night?'

She laughed. 'Well that would be interesting, but no, not tonight. You're friendly with Mr Farnborough, aren't you?'

'Finn nodded, a little lost by her direction.

'His brother is a saboteur. I bet there are many reasons to investigate Mr Farnborough.'

The implication was made clear. His earlier courage slipped from him, just like the leash slipping from Cat's hand. Obey or watch someone else get hurt. He was certain Carl had many secrets that could send him to a labour camp or worse. Finn's choice, humiliation before a seventeen-year-old or risk her angry attack on a friend. He was in no doubt she would carry it out. His own bruises testament to her sadistic nature. The rebel was banished, and Finn knelt on the rug beside his mistress. The choke chain weighed heavily around his neck as the leash pulled, tightening her control. He clawed at the chain, desperate to breathe, yet still she tugged harder. The last thing he saw and heard before losing consciousness was her monstrous face and her red lipped mouth screaming out her curse. 'I own you.'

* * *

Wednesday 16th June

You think yourself better than me. You think you can be free. You want to escape me. You're not, you can't, it will never happen. You are tied to me and I will not let go. Freedom will only be achieved inside my world. You can only be free when I am free.

* * *

He waited until he was on the lane to the cottage before dismounting the bike. His shirt was damp where Catherine had thrown the jug of water on him. Dazed, he had almost fallen down the stairs once she deigned to dismiss him. The ride to the lane had happened in a blur, his mind whirling from that night's terror.

Seated on the ground, his knees up against his chest, Finn tried to focus. All those sessions. All those memories. All those hours talking. He refused to let the panic overtake him again. Did she know about his past? How could she? Tim had removed all reference to his earlier illnesses from his medical record. He didn't want people thinking his daughter was married to an unstable alien. It was bad enough she was married to him at all. A worthless foreigner, no good for Sophie, no good for anyone. Pointless threatening him if he was dead. Finn let his face fall between his knees, his hands covering the top of his head. He wanted to scream out loud. So loud that it would drown out the insidious voice that disturbed his brain. Nothing could stop those three words, 'I own you.'

The monster of his past prodded him. 'I told you so, didn't I?'

Finn shook his head refusing to acknowledge its return. He was stronger now, older, wiser. He had beaten it before and he would again, he just needed to try harder. He had promised Sophie. Only a couple more weeks.

What could that witch do to him? It was her game, nothing more. Her silly game. He would treat it as such and play along. He would cope. She couldn't really hurt anyone, not without cause. What reason would she give to go after Carl? He didn't teach her. He had no contact with her. What about Sophie? No, she was protected. The Commandant wouldn't go against her father. He was too powerful. Tim was part of the Albian Leadership. The Commandant's dreams of a position within the inner circle would end. No, Sophie was protected. The only person she could truly hurt was him, and he would let her. After all, there were only a couple of weeks left.

The crying hit him the minute he opened the kitchen door. Her wail finding him, propelling him to the sitting-room. On the floor the shaking body clutched her half-finished piece of embroidery. Silk threads twisting and knotting with her rocking. Back and forth, names chanted out between sobs, 'Anna, Christopher'

Finn didn't need to hear the explanation, there was only one event that could possibly cause such sorrow: death. Her tear blotched face lifted to see her husband, bending down to carry her to the sofa.

'They're dead, Finn. Anna, Christopher, they're dead. They're dead.'

What words of comfort could he give her? He kissed her face, his lips moistened by her salt tears. There were no words.

'It was a bomb. They didn't stand a chance. It wasn't even meant for them, Finn. It was meant for Dad. They should have been safe.'

He held her, stroked her hair, kissed her and held her some more. His sadness edged with bleak hope. In death may they find freedom from the misery of life.

Finn whispered loud enough for the device to respond, 'THEO play soothing music.'

The inanimate spy replied with perverse beauty. The sitting-room filled with the contralto voice laden with sadness. *'He was despised and rejected.'*

Finn was indeed a man of sorrows and well acquainted with grief. He thought to tell THEO to stop, but emotional exhaustion had overtaken Sophie. Her body had become heavy in his arms. She was asleep. He kissed her once more and closed his eyes and allowed the music to anaesthetise his own grief.

The final silence was enough to stir Sophie.

'Shall I make you a tea?' he asked.

She nodded to Finn's offer and followed him into the kitchen. Sat at the table, her fingers drew around the flowers on the cloth. 'It was meant for Daddy, you know. The bomb, it was meant for Dad.'

Finn handed her a chamomile tea. 'I thought so, is he OK?'

'Yes, he was in the house. Anna forgot something in the village; Mum told Christopher to take her back to get it. He was supposed to take Dad to AZ One later. It exploded. There was nothing anyone could do. By the time the guards got to the car, it was too late. Daddy was the target, not Anna and Christopher.'

She was crying again. Fear and loss overwhelming her. The man and woman who were her parents' constant companions. Her godparents, their best friends. Hidden in plain sight from the complexities of Albian life. Protected by her father from rules enacted by the legislation for which he had freely voted.

It was the early hours of the morning before they made it to bed. Sophie slept curled up against his body, while Finn remained awake, thinking, worrying. Would the terrorists try again? Would they kill Sophie too, just as they had done with the Keeler girls?

Sophie was given the day off to see her parents. The Albian Security Service sent a car with an armed escort to take her home. Finn hugged and kissed his wife in the privacy of their bedroom before Sophie descended the stairs to the awaiting officer. She would be gone for the night. There would be no funeral. That was not a privilege granted to DIAs, but he knew the Smith family would sit together and drink to their friends, talk about the funny stories and cry. Christopher and Anna were free.

The knock at the kitchen door was followed immediately

by the squeak of it opening. Finn didn't need to look up to know exactly who had entered the room. 'Hello George, Sophie's already left.'

'I saw them outside,' he said. 'You can't miss that sort of car. How is she?'

Finn knew it would be too complicated to tell George she was mourning her godparents. 'She's frightened for her father. Do they suspect a group yet?'

'No not yet, no one has claimed responsibility. Someone will though. Nearly getting the Foreign Minister, that's a big deal for the terrorists. They will be celebrating in their cave somewhere.'

'Foreign terrorists?'

'Oh definitely, it's always the Outer Worlders. They're never happy to let us live in peace. What have we done to them, eh?'

Finn drank in silence. George, accusing the Outer World of a heinous crime, to the Outer Worlder who lived in perpetual misery, due to the laws set down by George's government. Who hurt who first? That was long forgotten. Finn knew that with every terrorist outrage came vicious reprisals against the DIAs.

'I have something for you.' George placed a package on the table with Finn's DIA number clearly printed in the middle, no name, just a number. Below it was written, 'Repatriation Request Form'. 'I had to tell her, you understand, don't you?'

Finn nodded. 'It's your job. We've discussed it. I tried to explain everything and it's the fairest thing I can do. She is young enough to start a new life. She could have children. I think we both realise we missed our chance. I can't father children.'

'I see.' George looked away, uncomfortable with Finn's confession. 'But she does love you very much. It will be hard.'

'Hard for us both.' His voice was breaking. He wiped his eye with the back of his hand and cleared his throat. 'What do I need to do with this?'

'Read it, check all the details are correct. They usually are. These people have access to all sorts of information. Once you're ready, go to the Repatriation Centre on the form. That's where you sign the 'Consent for Forced Removal', and that's it. Your bangle is removed, and you go to the airport. They say there is a central sorting facility on the Outer World side. If you have relatives alive, they are contacted, and you are sent to them. I'd better be off. Are you going soon?'

'Not sure, I haven't decided yet. Can they take me without the consent?'

'No, nothing happens without consent. Right, duty calls. You up for chess at the weekend?'

'Why not?'

THE ESSENCE OF FREEDOM

What constitutes freedom? Humanity's gift of choice is a despot's nightmare. Shackled by insecure powers, they fear the consequences that freedom imbues within the people. They in turn must shackle the people and steal away choice, leaving that tyrant free to luxuriate in their own confected world, paid in full through the misery of others.

LAMBS DON'T GET NAMES

MELBOROUGH MANOR ESTATE, AGED FIVE

Saturday morning is our time, and no matter the weather, Daddy always finds me at breakfast and says the same thing, 'Come on my Lazy Bones, I want you to help me count the sheep.'

Before he finishes his sentence I am sliding off the seat and searching for my welly-boots, dashing back to Daddy and Piper before they change their minds and go without me. Mrs McManus hands me a chocolate cookie and a bag of seeds for the geese at the pond. Daddy tells her not to say anything to Mummy, and Mrs McManus laughs.

'It's our secret, Mr Sheehan.'

I stand on a rung of the wooden gate, peering over the top to watch the newborn lambs. Daddy's arm surrounds me, his large hand on my tummy. I hold it. His wedding ring is cold against my skin. I like the way its smooth hardness makes me feel safe and wanted.

'What shall we call them, Daddy?' I say, looking back up at him.

He chuckles and bends down to me. His kiss is loud and wet. 'They don't get to be named, darling. We tag them with their number.' Daddy winks at me as he pushes my glasses back into place, finishing with a hug. 'We have too many. You can't name all of them.'

I try to prove him wrong, pointing to the sheep closest to us. 'That one's Apple, and she's Barbara,' I say. I bounce on the rung calling out the sheep's names, 'Mint, Cheese, Bongo, Jenny and that little one is Bobby'. I turn back and grin at Daddy. 'Now they have names, just like Piper.'

Daddy laughs and lifts me off the gate, holding me in his arms. 'And what happens when Bobby goes to market? It's easier if they are a number.'

I don't understand and tell him they will still have their names at market. It's theirs forever.

Daddy holds me closer, comforting me as he tries to explain. My face is hot, and I wriggle out of his arms. 'I am never eating lamb again!'

Daddy kneels down before me and says, 'That's OK, you don't have to eat lamb if you don't want to.' He lifts my chin with his fat and rough middle finger. It scratches. 'Tell me which one is Bobby. I'll not sell Bobby at the market. We'll let the lads know she has a name and is loved by my little Finn.'

FINN

He had brought the Repatriation form with him to the graveyard, intending to spend some time going over it in case there were any mistakes. Officialdom could be so intransigent when it came to minor errors.

He nibbled at his sandwiches, but his eyes were fixed on his bag and the tiny corner of the envelope peeking out. It held him. The release order that would send him home. His sentence complete. The prospect of freedom was constricting his throat, and he returned the sandwich to its box. He stood up and wandered among the tombstones. His mouth was dry, so he gulped water down from the bottle. Yet behind him, the envelope called. He remembered the time he received his exams results. That same dry mouth and strange excited fear within him, desperate to rip open the brown envelope which might change his future. He couldn't do it, his hands shook uncontrollably. He must have stood in the school hall for half an hour, staring at it. His parents had been waiting outside, and in his pocket his phone had vibrated with their persistence. In the end, the head had sat him down and opened the results for him.

The dead resting beneath his feet were no help, their ghostly vibrations travelling up him, making him cold despite the warm evening. There was no friendly face to carry out the task for him. Finn resigned himself to the fact he was alone, and it was time to go home. He returned to the bench and fingered the flap on his bag. A blue tit swooshed past him and darted to the top of the cherry tree. Its tiny talons curled on the twig, and a round glossy ball of an eye stared back down at him. Then it was gone. Free.

Finn flipped over the flap and pulled the envelope out. On the white rectangular label, bold and clear, were the letters and numbers that identified him, '568216/2/MI'. A number ingrained within him. Identification imposed on him by strangers, denying him a name, an identity.

It was a slender document, just four pages. He expected that. Tim's scheming had ensured his son-in-law's public life would be dull and uneventful, despite the constant scrutiny of the authorities. The first page clear enough, number, aliases, addresses, place of work. It also included the tutoring in that section. Over the page, personal details, his profile pictures, with and without glasses. 'Status: Married'.

Had his public file been changed? He was sure that was left blank. Immediately below, next to the word 'Spouse', was his wife's full name. 'Sophia Elle SMITH'.

Then he saw it. The one detail that he thought the State refused to acknowledge. They called her a miscarriage, despite being alive at birth. They refused to register her, she never existed. But on that document, she did. There in black and white.

'Issue: One.

Name: Molly Eve SMITH, deceased.'

He rapidly scanned the rest. DNA result: no evidence of criminality. His punishment beating was recorded, all expected. The next page detailed his Medical Records. The illness at Christmas and the health check with Captain Enright. Mumps aged thirty-four. However, the 'accidental' injuries to his wrists was omitted, instead his medical details went back beyond his marriage. Tim's expensive clerical error had been corrected. All his records before marriage were supposed to have been erased, Tim had assured him no one would ever know. But there they were staring back at him, his therapy sessions with Dr Hargreaves whilst a student at the University of New Albany. Back further. In-patient at the private Saint Dymphna's Hospital. Lacerations to left and right wrists, aged eighteen years and six months. Everything. The various consultants his mother dragged him to see, from speech therapists to hypnotists. A medical history of a terrified life laid out to entertain the bored guards. His catalogue of mental illness, his anxieties, his panic. His suicide attempt, the treatment to help him cope and live with the anxiety, the drugs that made him feel so unwell. Everything. Absolutely everything. Tim had lied, nothing had been erased, merely temporarily hidden from the public view.

Oh God, what had he done. If the guards have seen it, then chances are she has a copy too. Ammunition for her daily onslaught. He would be in her sitting-room in less than two hours. No amount of breathing exercises could stop the growing panic. He pushed himself off the bench, but his legs buckled beneath him with pins and needles. His heart was pounding, and his chest rose and fell with rapid short breaths. He was hyperventilating. He felt the graveyard draw into him, malevolence where once he found peace. The tombstones had become an impenetrable wall, trapping him. His breaths became shorter and his sight distorted by sweat and tears. Panic was consuming him, devouring all semblance of logic and reason.

Finn slumped onto the ground, giddy and nauseous. The nightmare of his past clawed at him, returning him to the monsters who delighted at his distress. Eventually he found his way back to the present, back to the graveyard. He vomited. No matter how bad he felt, the lesson had to be given. If he missed it, she would set the guards on him again. Merely remembering his duty threw him into a second panic attack. Deep inside him, he dragged out a memory of a hospital psychologist with neatly crossed ankles, spotty tights and pink highlights shining in her short brown hair. She spoke gently of acceptance, of the promise of happiness, and of healing that comes through music. And there had been music, not there, not in the hospital, but outside, his sister's favourite piece.

'Put some Mozart on for me, would you darling?' she was saying.

The graveyard was gone. He was safe and sound, his subconscious had deposited him back in Evie's bedroom. He was delicately removing their great-grandfather's record from its cover, the edge of the disk pressing into his palms as he lowered it onto the ancient record player.

He was sleepy, she said it was the tablets. He lay on her bed guarded by her old teddies and Carol-Ann, her favourite doll, with curly red hair drooping off the plastic head and a blue bow hanging off a lock. The ribbon was frayed. The doll had a smell of vanilla about her, like fresh sponge cake and seaside ice-cream. Cradling Carol-Ann, he relaxed into the strings, oboes, percussion and bassoons.

Finn wallowed in his creative imagination; the music playing in his head bringing a semblance of cohesion to the confusion encompassing him. It played on repeat until he was transported by the unseen force requiring his presence in her sitting-room. The door clicked behind him, lifting the needle from the record. In place of Evie, lounged Cat, snarling back at him. Her top lip curled and in a voice snarling with disgust, she asked, 'Did you run here?'

He looked down at his shirt. It was damp from perspiration. 'Yes. I was delayed.'

'Then you ought to leave more time.'

She was still talking at him, something about lessons

learnt through carrots and sticks. He wouldn't listen. Instead he'd switch her off and press play on the symphony in his head. The beautiful music would drown her out. He had re-entered his own world and she wasn't part of it. All he could hear was the orchestra resonating deep inside of him.

Finn neither knew nor cared what Cat thought. He was unconscious of the words slipping off his tongue. He did not respond to her toying with the choke chain and leash, wrapping them around her wrists. That instrument of torture was not part of his imaginings. The only real things he heard were those nine chimes of release.

SLAYING MONSTERS

TOLBRIDGE UNIVERSITY, AGED EIGHTEEN

I prop myself up against the bathroom door, holding my wrists out in front of me and watch the deep red tracks trickle down my arms and beyond, to my elbows and then, the soft, almost velvet-like blood dropping onto my jeans. A dark circle on each leg radiates out with each additional drop. I am tired. Too tired to keep my arms up, so I rest the backs of my hands on the cold tiles. The blood switches direction and pools within my palms, searching for the easiest route of escape. Three trails have appeared on my left hand, I wonder which will win. Which one will join the little puddle developing on the cream tiles?

I expected the pain to flow out, but it stays within me. The blood inches along the lines between the tiles. It is supposed to remove the hurt, instead it merely stains the grout. I am making a mess of the bathroom. Marcus hates mess, we are both tidy and organised. He'll be forced to clean up, keeping the flat tidy is a stipulation of the accommodation rules. He'll hate it. He can't stand the sight of blood. Another failure. I should have chosen a different method. A cleaner method.

The pain is stubborn, clinging onto me like a terrified child. It pleads to stay with me, but I want to let it go. I want to be free of its control.

Behind the bathroom door another door slams shut. That's not right. It can't be him. Today is Wednesday. What if they've had another row? It must be him, who else could it be? No, I timed it so that he would be at rugby. But it is Marcus.

370

'They've only gone and cancelled, bloody lightweights. Scared of humiliation more like,' he shouts from his bedroom.

If I stay quiet maybe he'll think I'm out. There is a sharp knock at the unlocked bathroom door. 'You in there Finn? Hurry up, I need to go, Katie's waiting for me.'

I hear Marcus head towards our little kitchen. Christ, the letter. I've left the letter in the kitchen. No, he won't open it. It's addressed to my family. He just wouldn't do that. He respects my privacy.

'Finn? Finn?' The bathroom door is being pushed. It barely moves. 'Can you hear me Finn?' I hear the panic in his voice. He is talking on the phone, jumbled words mixed with crying. The flat door bangs and there is more pressure against my back. The left-hand trail won. There's another voice, Katie? The blood has congealed, our bathroom floor is heated. It's cooking my blood. Katie's crying too. I didn't mean to frighten them. They aren't supposed to be here. I don't want them here. A siren wails in the street below, and now there are voices I don't recognise. My body inches forward, sliding on sticky blood beneath me. There's a hand gripping my shoulder, I rest my cheek on it. It is cold and soothes me. I'm tired and I want to sleep now.

FINN

Normally he'd avoid the river path, taking a slightly longer route, but having survived the lesson, he just wanted to get back to the cottage. There had been heavy rain a few nights previously and the river was in full flow, hissing alongside him like a black snake slithering through the tall grass. He slowed, then stopped, captivated by the river. The last time he had stood on its banks was nearly seven years ago, August to be precise. Perhaps Sophie would come out to the riverbank to remember their anniversary. He wondered how he would celebrate it as a single, free man. Maybe take a ride up Cairn Top and watch the clouds, visualising those same clouds drifting over the love of his life.

He leant the bike up against a tree, then crouched by the edge to watch the debris carried along by the flow of the river. Finn removed his socks and shoes and lined them up neatly next to him. Dangling his feet over the edge, he touched the blackness below him. It was so cold. A shiver ran through his body as every part of him sensed the snake writhing between his toes. As he leant forward to peer over his knees, his glasses slipped down his nose. Instead of pushing them back up, he took them off, carefully folding the spectacles before tucking them inside one of his shoes.

The earlier heat of the day was giving way to an approaching thunderstorm. Growling grey clouds had gathered earlier that evening keeping the moon and stars from view. A distant burst of light made him look up. He counted the seconds, 'One, two, three, four, five.' The rumble was low and far away. There was plenty of time before the storm would be over him.

Finn could barely see the river now, but he could hear it. Unwanted detritus hurled into the water by unthinking patriots, collided noisily. He could smell it too, grimy filth, destroyer of life. The river held so much terror for him. A terror that needed breaking, then perhaps he would be normal, able to face his fear and fight back for once. He edged further forward, soaking the edge of his trousers, the bitterly cold dampness wicking up the fabric. His feet were already numb from the chill water. And forward again. The snaking river swirled around his knees. This was wrong, dangerous. He wanted to live. He tried to move his legs, but they had become lead weights, pulling him down, too heavy for him to lift out. And within him, pernicious monsters delighted in their taunting, 'They'll never let a madman back into the country'.

What if they were right? It had been nearly twenty years since he last lived there, and the Outer World's views may have changed too. They would see his medical file, perhaps refusing him entry back home. The bolstering symphony in his head was being drowned by clashing thoughts and burgeoning panic. Finn fought with his noxious theories, repeating to himself, 'If I beat the river, then the monsters will go. They won't be able to fight me. Just a little more and I will have won, I will swim away from this misery and those monsters.'

The water rushed up to his face making him gasp. His arm was caught on something, preventing the flow from taking him away. No matter how much he tugged, it held onto him, dragging him back. Back onto the bank. There was someone there. Someone was saying his name. Not a number, his name, his real name.

'Finn? Finn? Can you hear me Finn?'

Why? Why now? He was going to win. Finally, those monsters would be destroyed. His sister was on the other side. Evie was waiting for him.

'Finn, it's Sergeant Mason, George. Can you hear me, Finn?'

Handcuffs locked on to his wrists, he was being hauled up and pushed into the car. The door slammed shut, his bike tossed into the back along with the rest of his stuff. Arrested again, it must be after curfew. What was the punishment for that, he wondered? More broken ribs?

George manhandled Finn into the kitchen, dragging out a chair.

'Sit! Don't move or I'll cuff you to the bloody radiator!' he ordered. He was flustered, cheeks puffed out and hands running through his hair.

All Finn could think of was how this was the strangest arrest he had ever encountered. George frantically searched the cupboards, mumbling to himself. He slammed one shut then opened another. Eventually he stopped banging the cupboard doors, his search proving fruitless. Finn was relieved to have the silence back, a brief respite from the encroaching headache.

George patted down his wet jacket, pulling out a mobile from his uniform pocket and immediately began texting. 'Thank God, for waterproof mobiles,' he said, more to himself than Finn. The message sent, he stood hand on hips and examined his shivering prisoner. Beneath the chair, little puddles of river water were forming on the kitchen floor. 'Hmm, best you change, you're soaked through.'

Finn looked up at the equally wet officer unsure as to who was the one who had lost touch with reality. 'That's what happens when you fall into a river. I take it I'm not being arrested.'

George shook his head. 'There are a hundred and one things I ought to be doing, and one of them would be charging you with attempted suicide, but at the moment I am more concerned about you catching pneumonia again.'

He lifted Finn up by his arm and directed him out of the kitchen, picking up his mobile on the way out. Once in the bathroom he unlocked the handcuff and ordered Finn into the shower. 'You should get that gunk off you. You're covered.'

A trail of black slime snaked down his clothes. Finn looked in the mirror, it was in his hair and on his face as well.

George was back on his mobile when he came out of the shower. He tossed him a towel and indicated towards the bedroom. While maintaining one eye on his prisoner, Sergeant Mason kept the mobile pressed against his ear, uttering an occasional 'uh huh' to whoever was giving out the orders. With the call ended, he slipped the phone back into his pocket. 'You should get into bed. Try and get some sleep.'

Finn didn't need asking twice. Chattering teeth reverberated in his aching head and all he wanted was the peace and comfort of his bed. But before he could snuggle beneath the duvet, George grabbed his left wrist and handcuffed him to the bedstead.

'There, that's better, I can think now. I'm going to fetch something from downstairs.'

Alone in the bedroom, Finn yanked his cuffed arm in fruitless protest. Downstairs he could hear George searching the sitting-room. There was no note, not this time. There was no evidence.

'You'll not be getting out of those cuffs.' George had returned and was standing in the doorway with a glass of water. 'I saw a programme about the materials they use to make them, clever stuff.'

'If you haven't arrested me, why have you cuffed me?

Not to start a conversation about new policing technologies, I presume.'

George approached the bed and put the glass on the side table. 'No.' He opened up his right palm where a little white tablet was nestled. 'You need to take this, it's a sleeping pill. You gotta sleep now.'

'You didn't answer me.' The handcuff clattered against the metal bedstead. 'One sleeping pill isn't going to change anything. I'm still your prisoner. I'm still subject to the restrictions of this prison camp.'

'Guess you are right. And as the arresting officer, either you take the pill willingly, or I shove it down your bloody throat, your choice, but you are taking that pill.'

There was menace in the way George spoke that Finn had rarely heard. With his free hand, he picked up the pill and popped it in his mouth. He drank the water, gagging as the pill journeyed down his throat.

'Have you swallowed it?'

Finn nodded but George was taking no chances. Without permission, he prised open Finn's mouth and ran his fingers around the gums and under his tongue, assuring himself that the pill would soon be doing its job. That kindly sergeant, keen to help with a smile and a joke, was above all an Albian guardsman, jailer and persecutor, used to forcing unfortunates to do as they are ordered and aware of all the tricks of deceit.

Reassured the pill would do its job, he pushed the bedroom chair closer to the bed, snatching up a book from the bedside table.

'Anne of Green Gables, any good?'

'I think you'll like it. It's my sister's favourite book,' replied Finn. His parting gift to New Albany – instruct one of their sergeants in the delights of idealism, imagination and the capacity for love by, and for, an outsider. Closing his eyes, he pictured iconic scenes from the book, where familiar faces from his home inhabited the characters he loved so much.

The sun on his face and the rattling of curtain rings woke him. His hand was uncuffed, it was sore with red welts. He rubbed his wrist and turned over, expecting to see George. But he had gone. Sitting on the chair, was his wife, arms crossed in angry defensiveness and a headmistress's stern glower hardening the features of her face.

'I'm sorry Soph,' he said, before she had the chance to lay into him.

'I'm going to make you some breakfast.' Her terse reply highlighted her fury. She stood, handed him his glasses, then locked his hand back in the handcuffs.

'Oh, come off it, Sophie. I mean it, I'm sorry.' He tugged at it again, as he had done with George, but like the sergeant, she ignored him and walked out of the room, slamming the door behind her.

She returned ten minutes later with a breakfast tray. The milky smell of porridge mixed with the sweet herbal odour of the tea turned Finn's stomach. 'I can't eat this.'

'Tough!' she said, putting the tray on the bed. She scooped up a spoonful of porridge and held it to his lips.

He moved his face away and rattled his handcuffed hand. 'Is this really necessary?'

'I didn't want you sleep-walking while I was downstairs. Who knows what you might have done?' Finn saw her eyes flick to the little box above the dresser, and a finger rise to her lips before saying, 'We were lucky George found you before you got too far.'

377

It was obvious, George, Sophie and Tim had already devised a story to accompany the need for sleeping pills and handcuffs. Undoubtedly, the previous night's discussion had been miraculously wiped from the records by a skilfully placed bug.

'You probably ate something dodgy while I was away. You know how a bad prawn can affect you.'

Falling into a polluted river as a result of food poisoning was a bizarre ploy but he wasn't about to argue. No doubt there would be a raft of official documents to support his sudden prawn-induced somnambulism.

'You are to rest today, don't worry the school know.' She stretched over him and unlocked his wrist from the handcuff. 'There,' she said, placing his arm on the bed, 'you'll be fine now. I'll put some cream on that sore, if you want.'

Her anger appeared to have been brushed away, and the Sophie he loved was gently rubbing the welts on his wrist with the lightest of touches. She had always been his glue, but as he enjoyed the warmth of her touch, he wondered who would be his glue once he was back in Melborough?

SOPHIE

The branches of her apple trees were full of fruit, it would be a good year. Fruit they would not see ripen. Sophie really didn't care about the apples or anything else in the garden. She had thought the cottage garden the love of her life, except it wasn't. Finn was. As far as Sophie was concerned, all her plants could wither and rot as long as he was safe. Showered and looking slightly more human, Finn sat back in the deepening shade of the trees. He hadn't said anything since getting out of bed and there was a blankness to him that Sophie had never seen. It frightened her enough to decide it wasn't safe to leave him alone, not even for a minute. She handed him another cup of chamomile tea, which he placed straight on the ground without so much as a sip of the yellow liquid.

Like all other medics in New Albany, Sophie had no training for mental health. *'A waste of valuable resources,'* they said. *'It's not a medical matter.'* Those unfortunates who manifested their problems publicly, were decried as seeking a chosen path, one that a true patriot, with the iron will of an Albian would never follow. There were more pressing demands on the country's finances, namely security, especially of the leading politicians and elites. Sophie thought back to the days when she and Finn first met. He admitted he found living so far away from home challenging. He told her about his regular therapy sessions with Dr Hargreaves. She vaguely remembered the pills he took, although he complained about headaches. She sympathised, she supported him as he came off the pills, she made him fall in love with her. His plan to return home, forgotten. Sophie had become his home. She was his safety net. He relied on her and shared his life with her. There was nothing left to discover about the foreign student before their marriage. Finn was an open and well-read book for Sophie, but she kept her own story hidden far away from him.

In many ways they had been fortunate. Together, Sophie and Finn had managed to control most of his anxiety attacks. Outside the family, he was just a very shy man prone to frequent colds that occasionally meant time off work. Tim helped where he could, securing a job at School House 87, and ensuring that Finn's medical history appeared remarkable by being completely unremarkable. Ever an optimist, Sophie made the best of the situation. It was her optimism that had been his saviour. However, Sophie now understood her world differently and no amount of false optimism could sugar-coat the danger awaiting him.

Finn slept on and off most of the day, occasionally watching her embroider, although he said nothing. Sophie persuaded him to eat some fruit, but he refused to drink anything except plain water. By the time George reappeared in the late afternoon, Sophie was exhausted, her temper ready to explode with Finn's stubbornness. On George's insistence, she hauled herself upstairs for a quick doze, relieved that someone else was watching over Finn.

A PROMISE FOR EVIE

MELBOROUGH MANOR HOUSE, AGED TWENTY-ONE

I wake to the gentle strains of a quartet of voices rising and falling in harmony as they sing the 'Benedictus'. Do I feel blessed to be here? I do. Now I can see a future for me. The prospect of an anonymous life in New Albany where I can hide from my past. Somewhere I can start afresh.

'Hello, Sweetie. Good sleep?' Evie puts her book down and wanders to the bed. Her perfume filling me as her lips brush my forehead.

'Yes, thanks,' I lie. My dreams had been populated by the monsters screaming, waiting and clawing behind closed doors. I had to open the door and destroy that nagging doubt that had crept in the previous night. 'Evie?'

She curls up on the bed next to me, stealing a pillow from under my head to make herself comfy.

'Do you think you will always love Maya?'

'Why do you ask?'

'It's just...' I hesitate, I don't want to upset her, but I have to know, 'you were arguing?'

Evie picks up my hand, playing with my fingers. 'Things are busy at the practice. She's a little stressed, that's all. Loving someone doesn't mean you never argue. It's healthy to have the occasional blow out.'

'Does she want you to go back?' I ask, guilty about being the cause of their argument. 'You really don't have to stay, as lovely as it is to have you here, but—'

'No, darling. Maya understands why I need to be with you

right now. She'd be here too if she could. It won't be so easy when you go to New Albany. We're fine, honestly darling. Don't worry about us, in fact, can you keep a secret?'

The burden of secrets is something with which I am well acquainted. Those vile monsters run through my veins. I could say no, no more secrets, but I don't. 'Shoot, I won't tell, cross my heart.'

Evie snuggles into me, excitement fizzing from every pore. 'She's asked me to marry her. What do you think of that? Your big sis is going to get married, bet none of you thought that would ever happen.'

I hold her, the joy of her happiness rebuking my unspoken jealousy.

'You are happy for us, aren't you?'

My silence had lasted too long, the truth of my feelings seeping into the embrace. 'Of course, I am.' I kiss her cheek. 'Do Mum and Dad know?'

'No, not yet.'

'Then let me be the first to congratulate you. Maya is a very lucky woman.'

'Oh, I think the lucky one is me.' She laughs and I hide my feelings with a smile.

'When will the wedding be?'

'Ages away. We want the practice to be fully up and running first. Get some savings behind us and then I want the whole caboodle, all bells and whistles.' She jumps off the bed and spins around in her imaginary white dress. This time I smile for real. 'Didn't think you'd be up for all that fairy tale wedding stuff.'

'A fairy tale life, happily married, two point four children and the dog sleeping by the AGA. Perfection.'

I laugh. 'Hmm, I thought vets are supposed to know about reproduction.'

She bounds over to the bed and thumps my arm. 'Cheeky sod, we'll use an agency. Maya is more maternal, so she'll do the hard bit.'

'You're maternal,' I say, remembering the times I'd call for Evie ahead of my own mother.

'Maybe.'

I hesitate before saying it, the possible repercussions bouncing off my idea. In the end my brain declares it a sensible offer, everyone will be happy. 'Don't go to an agency, I'll do it, call it my wedding present.

FINN

'Checkmate!' George was pleased with himself. Third win in a row.

'Why were you following me?' Finn was collecting up the pieces for another one-sided game.

'I wasn't following as such, it's just, well you know. I come off duty about the same time you leave the mansion and I caught you riding down the hill. I spot you on your bike fairly regularly and...' he started lining up his pawns, 'well it struck me as rather strange when you went towards the river. You always turn left and suddenly you were going straight on. I am a guard, Finn, I am a curious creature, suspicious. So, I did what came naturally, I followed you. I knew something was wrong when you stopped by the river. Sophie said you were scared of the place. It just didn't feel right.' George turned a pawn in his fingers while talking, 'We are all pawns of this State to some extent. I am a sergeant. I follow the rules but there are times when my conscience wins. I break rules too, just as the elites do every day. Last night was another broken rule to add to all the others.'

Finn did not expect that answer. He thought George was as patriotic as any of the others who made his life a perpetual misery.

'Not many know this, but my wife's brother was married to a foreigner, one like you. Such a lovely lady. They had a son the same age as mine. More like brothers than cousins. They did everything together. Abe was quiet, shy, again, a bit like you, and so clever, top of his class. A couple of years ago his mum got breast cancer, she had a choice, stay and die with her family by her side or get repatriated, treated and live a life devoid of the ones she loved. There was no competition for her. She loved her husband and son more than anything in the world.

'Abe took her death badly, there was no one there to help him through his grief. It wasn't my brother-in-law's fault; he was struggling himself. Abe was the son of a DIA, doors were being shut to him. There was no prospect of university, nor any recognised profession, even guardsmen are a restricted occupation. He had lost his mother and there was no meaningful future for him.' George turned away from Finn, talking to the plants instead of his charge. 'I was the one who found him. Finding a body in that polluted, disgusting excuse for a watercourse is a regular occurrence. Usually patriots, usually the child of a mixed marriage but not always, never properly reported. Depression, despair, suicide, these are not patriotic traits and do not happen in New Albany.' He turned back, his eyes glistening with pain. 'There are no suicides here, just tragic accidents. We have so many tragic accidents.'

Finn stretched out to hold George's hand, knowing how impossible it would be for George to admit his grief publicly.

'When you started getting into the water, I had a good idea of what was happening. I couldn't let you do it, could I? You're both my friends. How do I explain it to your lovely wife? "I let him drown because it was easier to stay in the car". No, I had no option. Nearly gave me a heart attack running down that slope.'

'You brought me home though, not to a medical centre. Not to the Treatment Centre.'

'Instinct, I suppose. I'll get into trouble if anyone finds out. You won't tell, will you?'

Finn shook his head. Part of him was cross at George

385

for being there, for stopping him in his battle against the monsters, but at least he understood. He would have done the same.

It was dinner time when Sophie re-emerged from the house. George refused the offer of a meal and said he would return the next day.

Sophie insisted Finn ate a small amount of dinner. Yet again she offered chamomile tea and yet again he refused it, the smell making him feel giddy and uncomfortable.

'Please stop trying to get me to drink that stuff. I'd probably feel so much better if I wasn't being force fed a poison every hour.'

'It has a calming effect.'

'It certainly does have an effect on me, it turns my stomach. I'd go as far as saying I get anxious whenever that hideous stench comes near me.'

'OK. But you should drink something. I have some mint and fennel, or rosehip.'

There was no way he'd let mint anywhere near him. Mint meant Cat. Cat meant agony. Agony meant panic. At the merest thought of her, he sensed his pulse accelerating. He had to control it, Sophie was monitoring him, noting every change.

'Are you OK, darling?'

He took a deep breath and smiled back. 'Yes, I'll be fine, just a bit tense that's all. I'm fine now, honestly. I'll have rosehip, thanks.'

'You'd better come back to the kitchen then.'

'I think I might just head up to bed.'

The fine crow's feet by Sophie's eyes deepened. 'Then I'll come upstairs with you and I'll give you your sleeping pills while we are there.'

'I don't need sleeping pills. I'm fine now.'

Sophie stood to leave, snatching up her sewing. Her deliberate actions a sure sign of her irritation with him. She stopped and faced him. 'They are so I can get some sleep or, would you rather I stay awake all night again, watching you pretend to sleep, waiting for me to succumb to my own fatigue, just so you can break your promise to me, because that is what you will do. You can't lie to me, Finn Sheehan. Right now, I can't trust you. In the absence of a better idea, either you take those damn pills, or you spend the night handcuffed again. Your choice!'

SOPHIE

She didn't go to sleep straight away, watching him from the bedroom chair. He had fallen asleep quite quickly; he always did. It was staying asleep that was Finn's perpetual problem. She was tearful, desperate for someone to hold her and tell her it would be all right again. That they would survive this, and they would survive the escape. She was terrified of what they were about to do, yet unable to share her fears. There was no one to confide in, no one with whom to share her secret. Sophie didn't want to think about Monday. There would be no avoiding it. He would have to return to work. There would be no George to bring him home if it became too much for him. Most likely a call to Captain Kendrick. His fate sealed. There would be no holiday, there would be no escape. He would be taken to The Treatment Centre. One more lamb to the slaughter. She had failed and could no longer protect him.

'I'm not doing it! You know they don't suit me.'

Sophie dropped her head back down into her hands, the discussion was going nowhere. He was adamant. 'Darling, if we had another option, I would try that. This is all we have, please try again.' She left her chair and knelt by Finn, prepared to beg if necessary. 'Please, Finn, I need you to do this, it's important.'

'No, I'm not going on them again. It's pointless, they don't work straight away. I'll be back home by the time they show any effect. I don't want my last few weeks spoiled with headaches. I promised to go on the holiday with you and I will. You shouldn't worry, I won't do it again.'

'I want to believe you. I truly do.'

'But?'

Sophie was going to have to tell him. He still believed he would be sent home. 'You must stay well, Finn, the antidepressants help, you know that. I can't risk you being taken away to the Treatment Centre.'

'It's only a few more weeks, I'm sure I'll cope.'

'No, Finn, you don't understand, this is far more serious than you are making out. You're going to leave me, I understand why, but if you believe you'll happily cope with a decision like that, then the man I've loved for over seventeen years isn't the man sitting in front of me. I can't risk them taking you away.'

Finn remained silent, then moved forward, his cold cheek touching hers, his face in her hair. 'Then let me go now, why wait any longer? I could go this afternoon, be back in Melborough by tomorrow. Oh God, Sophie, I know it will be hard, but you will be free to live a life and I promise you, Soph, I absolutely promise to live a full life too. Just say yes and I'll go and pack.'

'No.'

'No?' Finn pulled back, confused by her refusal. 'No, you won't let me go, or no, I won't live a full life? I'll get help, I promise I will.'

'No, you won't live a full life. I'm sorry, Finn, if you go to the Repatriation Centre you won't live any life at all. The only thing that will happen is transportation to the Treatment Centre.'

Sophie had begun to cry, the emotion of their situation too much to bear. Finn touched her tears, tenderly wiping them away. 'Why would they do that? It makes no sense.

Why treat me when it is cheaper to repatriate me? No, it makes no sense.'

Sophie had tried calm, she had tried reason, nothing seemed to get through to him. Her heart was thumping with the knowledge of what she was about to reveal. Her eyes filling up each time she pushed the tears away.

'They transport you to the Treatment Centre, not to care for you, but to dispose of you.' Her shoulders were lifting and falling as her crying turned into full sobs. 'Don't you get it Finn? They terminate you, kill you, dispense with you like some piece of unwanted rubbish. It is an extermination camp!'

Finn sat back in the seat, all colour draining from his face, turning him into a bloodless wax work. Sophie lay her head on his lap, her breathing interrupted only by her weeping. Either they escaped, or he would die, by his own hands or the State's. Wasn't that what he said when he requested the repatriation form.

Finn lifted her head up. 'I don't believe you. Why are you saying this? No state would do that again. You are lying to keep me here.'

Perspiration was gathering on his forehead. Sophie, fearing his reaction, held onto his wrists. 'Finn, I am not lying. If I thought I could save you from this by letting you go home, then I'd be taking you to the Repatriation Centre myself. I know the truth. Please, you've got to believe me. There is no easy return trip home. The prisoners don't get parole. This is a life sentence.'

Finn pulled back, getting off the chair and moving away from her, his whole body shaking with shock. She knew her words had extinguished his last hope. He was hyperventilating, his arm flailing about to prevent her from grabbing him. There were trails of perspiration running down from his forehead and his legs wobbled, unable to withstand holding him up. She watched him fall to the ground, grief overwhelming him.

Sophie scrambled across to hold him. 'It's OK darling, we'll figure something out, I'm sure we will.'

The morning sun filtered through the apple tree as she held him, keeping her voice quiet and calm, as she repeatedly told him she loved him. But she knew he was no longer shaking in the beauty of his eternal prison. He had escaped and was elsewhere, somewhere calm, somewhere safe, somewhere deep in his past.

It was late morning by the time Sophie managed to get him to drink some herbal tea. Exhausted and with the help of the valerian root in the drink, Finn fell asleep. Not even George's noisy arrival woke him. Sophie put her sewing down and kissed the sergeant in welcome relief. 'Oh, George, what would I do without you?'

'How long has he been sleeping?'

'Not too long but if he wakes before I get back, then there's some food in the basket. Help yourself to anything you want. You know my kitchen better than me.'

'I might be a decent cook, but I haven't a clue about all your herbal stuff. How did you find out about it all?'

'A friend, George. A dear, dear friend.'

Sophie hid her emotion as she remembered Anna. Her godmother would be advising her against her next course of action. Acutely aware she had no idea what she was doing, there was no one to ask and no help available, only what could be figured out for herself. Cobbled together, D.I.Y mental health plans had been part of Sophie's routine for years, but now there was no room for herbal tincture and calming music. Finn needed help, and she would lie and cheat to keep him alive until they were free of New Albany's shackles.

Finn was awake when Sophie returned, chatting to George about his childhood. She kissed her husband, hugging him tightly. 'How are you feeling?'

'Much better, I needed that sleep. Back to normal really.'

They smiled at each other for George's benefit. Normality would never again be an option for the couple.

Sophie, the well-practised actress, turned her manufactured smile to George. 'And what stories has this reprobate been telling you while I was out?'

'It's been very interesting. I didn't know Finn grew up on a farm. It all sounds so rural and peaceful. No wonder you two live out here. Your little Eden. Right, is that the time? I'll drop by tomorrow if you need me, just text. Bye Finn.'

'Bye George.'

Sophie snuggled onto the steamer chair with Finn. 'How are you really feeling?'

Finn lay his head on her shoulder. 'As good as I can ever expect to be. I'd better get used to it. This is it. At least I am imprisoned in a Little Eden with the woman I love.' Tears welled in the corners of his eye, his heart breaking at the sudden realisation of the most painful consequence of Sophie's revelation. 'I'll never see my home again, will I? My parents, my brother, Evie, I have lost them all.'

Sophie relished the evening breeze on her face, quivering the apple tree leaves above her. She relaxed back into her chair and opened the flask of lemon balm tea. 'It's going to be cooler, we might get some decent sleep tonight,' she said, topping up his mug before snuggling under a blanket, warm and ready to continue the debate from this morning. 'We need to talk about the pills, Finn. We must do it now.'

'I told you, I'm not taking them. I don't care what happens to me. You remember how they make me feel. Standing in front of those girls, nauseous, my head throbbing. No, I'll pretend. I've done it before. I became an expert at it. There wasn't a therapist I couldn't fool. Who knows how long I will be able to endure this prison but the days I have, I want to be pain free, so that at least my time with you is unspoilt.'

Sophie desperately tried not to bite her lip. Her words might give him hope, but she would also be breaking her promise to her father. 'The reason you must appear well is because I need to keep you safe until an alternative route is found.'

'What alternative route? The smugglers? They'll take the money then slit our throats. You've heard the stories.'

'I don't know, they might just be that, stories. I've heard of escape routes.' At that point staying vague seemed the better option to Sophie. 'We just have to be careful. It might take some time, so you have to help me.'

Finn remained defiant. 'I'm still not taking them.'

Sophie screwed up her face in frustration. Why did she have to marry such a stubborn man? 'Please hear me out. I did some research while you slept and found out about a new drug. It's in testing and not easily available. I called Dad and he'll arrange everything. He knows about your fall into the river and he wants to help. It's OK, this one has fewer side effects, hardly any in fact. It may take a while before you feel the benefits but at least you will. In the meantime, practise those breathing exercises you learnt, and you'll need to stay on the sleeping pills. A good sleep always helps. By the time we return from the holiday you'll be able to see things differently. You can spend the summer in the garden.

It's only two more weeks of teaching. I know we can get through this.'

Sophie studied his face, had she convinced him? It was hard to tell. She wondered whether he had sufficient hope to cling onto until they arrived at the beach house.

'OK, but if I start to get headaches, I'm coming off them.'

'Fine, agreed.'

FINN

The School House chatter on the Monday morning was all about his father-in-law. No one was interested in the chauffeur and housekeeper, who were the actual victims. There was no taunting, no giggling, no snide comments from Mr Harrison. Finn's fear that everyone would know about his previous health problems were unfounded. His ride home was undisturbed. No one spat at him, no one laughed at him. On his way past Mrs Carter's house, he saw her wave out of her window. He slowed to stop, expecting a tirade of abuse.

'Mr Michael, dear. So glad to catch you. I heard about poor Miss Sophia's father. I do hope they are all well. Such a shock, and what a lucky escape, eh? You must be so relieved.'

'Um, yes, very relieved. Sophie spent some time with her parents over the weekend. She was very upset about Mr Christopher and Mrs Anna. They had been with the family for many years.'

'Well it's a relief it was just them and not her father. Send her my love will you.'

Finn didn't reply, mounting his bike and focusing on his breathing one more time. DIAs were disposable, that was the current view. They were of no more consequence to a patriot than a plastic bottle, useful but ultimately disposable.

Sophie was right. There was no confusion, no dizziness and thankfully no debilitating headaches. There had also been no change in his perpetual state of unhappiness, but she said it would take a while for the pills to work. Going to the mansion still caused palpitations, but he would wait outside her sitting-room and do the exercises he had been taught after his first attempt. Those monsters of his teenage years had never been truly exorcised. Not content with lingering in the background of his mind, they had become bolder, mocking him when he stood obediently in the doorway, laughing when he stammered his way through 'Tess'. He was convinced they would go eventually, falling back into the background, just as they had done before, taking with them the penetrating voices that screeched out his inadequacies. It just required some more patience.

The bells called the faithful to the ten o'clock service. There was quite a congregation outside the church, Albian patriots delighting in the pleasant weather and chatting about nothing in particular. There were too many ears for anything even mildly controversial.

They spotted George standing by the door talking to Dr Thatcher. Finn was reluctant to approach the doctor, but Sophie insisted. 'He won't bite, and it might seem odd if we don't.'

They headed towards the chatting men.

'Shall we go in together? My wife is here with the boys,' said Henry, having spotted them approach. His hand was out for Sophie, grinning broadly at her while ignoring the husband at her side. Sophie took his arm and walked through the carved oak doors to the gloom of the building, her every step watched by Finn.

'Don't normally see you at this service,' George said, getting Finn's attention.

'No. Sophie let me sleep in.'

'Thought so, you need to get plenty of rest and that wife of yours knows what's what. I tell you what Finn, you're one hell of a luck—'

'Dr Thatcher usually goes to the early service, seems he was sleeping in too,' interrupted Finn.

'Seems so. He's a man who likes to be seen with the right people.'

'Hmm, obviously.'

George was turning to go in when Finn stopped him. 'George, who else would have seen my repatriation file? It was open when I received it.'

'Well, I suppose I see it first as your guardhouse sergeant, but I brought it straight to you. No one else in the guardhouse saw it.'

'You didn't tell them about me.'

George shook his head. 'Like I said, I think you're a decent guy. You're my friend.'

'A friend you would have arrested or have beaten if required,' replied Finn.

George shuffled his feet. 'You know what, Finn, sometimes I've got to make choices and they're never easy, but I've got to live with that.'

'Sorry, I shouldn't have said that.' He touched George's arm in apology. 'So, the only people who know about my file are the two of us and the clerk who printed out the report.'

'The Commandant's office gets a copy of everything, every file, every note, even copies of memos. Can't imagine the Commandant would have read it unless there were a note attached. It only has your number on the envelope. He would have to know that off by heart to recognise it. There are over seven thousand DIAs in this AZ alone.'

'I teach his daughter. He may have been interested in that particular file.'

George snorted out a half laugh. 'Believe me, he would have known all about your illnesses long before he employed you. Those people have access to all sorts of information which they keep hidden from the little folk like us.'

Finn pondered George's words as he found a spot to stand on the balcony. Did she already know? Had she known, from the beginning? He closed his eyes, only one more week. Only one more week.

The Reverend Peters droned on in his monotonous voice, a stark contrast with the beautiful melody of the choir. It struck him as odd that a place so evil, so vicious, was capable of making music that could lift him, transport him to peace and tranquillity, and take him home. He noticed how the teenagers' eyes were firmly focused on the music director. Her hands communicating in its own language, every wave, every gesture followed by her young disciples. A soprano's voice sang the Agnus Dei. Crystal clear, gaining height, reaching for the cupola above the heads of the congregation. He imagined the purity of her voice shattering the glass, her music released into the cloudless morning sky, willing his soul to rise up with her angelic voice, escaping the misery of his existence.

'Agnus Dei, qui tolis peccata mundi, miserere nobis.'

Was God even listening? Was he enjoying the misery pressed onto Finn's mortal body? The soprano sang of a merciful God, whose mercy graced those wise enough to be born to the right family in the right country.

'Agnus Dei, qui tolis peccata mundi, dona nobis pacem.'

Where was Finn's peace? Their God had allowed peace to be stolen from the perceived unworthy. The peace he sought in her music, in her voice, it was all an illusion, a disappearing mirage.

Finn peered through the tiny holes in the screen, searching the nave below for Sophie. He saw Henry first, sitting with a blond lady and three children sitting alongside her. Each a carbon copy of their father. Henry leant forward to speak to one of the boys, revealing Sophie next to him. His height had hidden her petite frame from Finn's view. He loathed the fact he was not allowed to sit with his own wife, digging his nails into his palms. The self-inflicted pain momentarily distracting him.

The reverend began his liturgy of boredom, followed by prayers for the Foreign Minister, his wife and daughter. The congregation were invited to say prayers in thanks for his miraculous escape from the terrorists that plague their beautiful country, offering up support for the security forces who work so diligently to root out the evil in their midst.

The congregation bowed their heads to pray to their Albian God for protection from their psychotic housekeeper, or murderous gardener.

Finn could see Sophie slightly better when he leant to the right, much to the annoyance of the man next to him. The doctor's wife had her head bowed; her eyes closed in prayer. A quick glance at his wife, then Henry whispered into Sophie's ear before resting his hand on her lap, smiling smugly. Finn stared down at the deep red indentations across the middle of his palm.

After the service Sophie thanked the reverend while other well-wishers caught her eye, giving her sympathetic nods. Meanwhile Finn waited by the wall, picking at some loose mortar. He doubted any of them cared about Christopher and Anna. Finally, released from the Reverend Peters' dreariness, she started back to Finn, only to be intercepted by Henry and his wife. She kissed Mrs Thatcher on the cheek and talked to the tall boys, the eldest, already far taller than Sophie. After his family left for their car, Henry hung back to talk to Sophie. Finn scrutinised his every movement, his every posture. That self-satisfied grin on his face and his relaxed arm draped over her shoulder, pulling her into him for an embrace. Pushing himself off the wall, Finn started down the road towards their lane. She could catch up with him, but he wasn't going to wait any longer.

'Why did you go off like that, I thought I had lost you? Given what has happened recently I really didn't need another fright.' Sophie was out of breath from running to catch up with Finn, but he was in no mood to slow down.

'You were talking to so many people; I was tired, I wanted to go home.'

The day continued, like any other day, Sophie getting ready for the week ahead and Finn, in the shade of the apple trees listening to Mozart. At bedtime she handed him a sleeping pill and sat on the armchair by the bed, waiting for him to swallow it.

Finn held the pill in the palm of his hand, making no movement to pick it up. 'Why are you still forcing me to take these?' His voice was sharp, confrontational.

'You need to sleep, and it will help.'

'Who will it help?'

Sophie sighed. 'What are you babbling about? You of course.'

'Is that your excuse? I am fast asleep by the time you say you come to bed, and you are always up when I wake. The perfect alibi.'

Sophie shook her head and handed him a glass of water. 'Finn, you're being irrational, it's late and I'm tired, take your pill and let's go to bed.'

'And whose bed will you sleep in tonight? Henry's?'

Sophie stared back at Finn, aghast. 'Isn't it enough that I spend my days with him, now you want me to spend my nights with him too!'

'You know exactly what I mean.'

'Yes Finn, I do.' She stepped away from the bed, her back to him, picking up discarded clothes on the floor.

'Is that all you have to say to me?'

'Yes.'

'I don't believe you. There's something going on between you, isn't there?'

There was a childish moodiness about the way he shoved his hands under the cover. If she hadn't been so annoyed, she would have laughed. 'Oh for goodness sake, Finn, I don't even have energy to contemplate an affair let alone with someone who makes my skin crawl.' She perched on the edge of the bed, grasping his hand. 'Darling, I love you and you alone. When you sleep, it's me beside you and I'm not going anywhere without you. Come on, sweetheart, take the pill. I'll get ready, then we can cuddle up.'

CORRUPTING LOVE

Forbidden fruit lies abandoned on the ground, its faint scent rising, ripening the air with sweetness. That once precious gift, caressed by Venus and a temptation for Eve, now fallen and bruised. A welcoming host to invading disease, its fine skin is pocked, and its tender flesh alive with crawling scavengers. It rots into oblivion.

FINN

* * *

Tuesday 22nd June

Daddy said yes. I can't believe it. Called it my wedding present. I can't wait to tell him. I'm so happy. I'm actually getting excited about the blasted wedding. The sooner it happens the sooner we'll be together.

* * *

He had barely entered her sitting-room when Cat snatched up his wrist and yanked him to the sofa.

'I have wonderful news. It's very exciting.' She was virtually jumping on the spot like a child at a birthday party. 'You won't guess. I'm sure of it. Try and guess, go on, try!'

Finn couldn't help laughing. All these months torturing him, and yet again she was a child standing before him, excited to reveal her secret news. 'Is this to do with your wedding? Are you going on honeymoon to AZ Eight?'

'That's too obvious. There's nowhere else to go. No, guess again. You have two chances left.'

Of course, she would be going to AZ Eight, just as he would at the end of the week. The playground for Albian elite. She would be photographed entering restaurants, sitting on yachts. The beautiful Commandant's daughter being shown off by her fortunate husband. 'Your fiancé has been given an amazing promotion and you are leaving AZ Five.'

'You are getting close, he will be promoted to major when we marry, and he will need a personal assistant. You

403

have one last guess, have you got it yet?'

'Has your father bought you a new house as a wedding present?'

'You failed.' Cat dropped on her sofa, deflated. 'And I so very nearly gave it away. You won't make a good personal assistant if you can't second guess your employer.'

Finn's smile disappeared. 'I beg your pardon, I'm to be employed as your husband's secretary?'

'Isn't it fantastic? I'll see you every day. Except Sundays, of course, not unless there is an important deadline or crisis. Albian morality rule apparently.'

Finn thought of the countless DIAs who laboured seven days a week, serving their patriot families. New Albany didn't have a problem with the morality of Sunday work when it came to DIAs. The invisible workforce, harvesting the food for other nonentities to prepare, cook and place on the table for the Sunday lunch.

'Daddy approved it. As an MI you get special privileges, so you can serve my husband. Isn't it wonderful? Aren't you happy?'

As genuine excitement fizzed around Cat, Finn tensed with indignation, his staccato reply pulsating with anger. 'I am an English tutor, not a major's assistant.'

'Well you are now. You start as soon as we return from honeymoon.'

'I have no intention of res–.'

The speed of her attack left him winded. She swung the leash again, whipping him on his cracked ribs. She drew her arm bask for another assault, but instinct propelled him to defend himself, catching the leash before it lashed him. He jerked it from her hand, unbalancing her. Cat stumbled.

'How dare you?' The exhilaration of confrontation widened her eyes and threw back her shoulders. Defiance met with provocation. 'Go on then, hit back.'

'I won't hit you, just as I won't be working for your husband. After your exam on Friday, I'll be finished for the summer and I will take immense pleasure in knowing I'll never see you again.'

She sniggered. 'God, you're stupid. You think you can just leave me. Shall I tell you a little secret? You will never leave me. I know you too well.'

'I will leave you.' He jabbed her back with his finger, an unknown force imbuing him with the capacity to fight back, vanquishing the fear that had controlled his life. 'Once I am gone, you will never lay eyes on my face again.'

Cat retrieved the leash from his shaking hand and sulked on her sofa. Her lips pouting, and huffs of rage adding to the almost comical teenage tantrum. But Finn knew that Cat's tantrums were far from an amusing game. He rubbed his side. It was still stinging but defiance was worth the pain.

Finn stomped to the table and slammed an envelope on it. 'You have three lessons left before your exam. You might want to look at the questions.' A guard had come into school earlier that day with the envelope. He had a good idea what it contained, but he was not going to be party to her cheating. If she wanted to look, she could but he would not be answering them.

'You are an ungrateful wretch. Why they gave you special MI status is beyond me.' She pointed to the opposite sofa. '568216, come here! Read to me!'

Finn did not move. The clock ticked past the minutes, the sound echoing through the room.

Cat rose from the sofa, hissing her threat as she approached him, 'I insist. I am your mistress and I will bring you to heel.'

'How? By whipping your disobedient whelp? Go ahead

if that's how you derive happiness. It's what you do, isn't it?'

'I have that God given right.' Her fingers were twiddling with the snake like leash. 'I own you.'

'Then tell me, Miss Fry, what happens when a DIA fights back?' He was fully aware of what happens, they are shot in the head, with the accompanying charge, 'A suspected terrorist'. Her silence betrayed her. She wanted him alive, her living breathing pet. 'You won't have me then, will you? I can't work as your husband's lackey if I am dead. I will be free, and you'll have to find another DIA to punish.'

The glint in her eyes sent a spine-tingling shiver through him. She had read him well, he did not have to hear her to understand the malice of her words. 'The punishment does not have to be carried out on you, for you to receive it. You just have to watch someone else suffer. You forget who I am.'

Defeated, he sat down and opened "Tess". They would soon be finished, and Tess would meet the inevitability of her death.

With exams ongoing, the school was a place of monastic calm. Finn sat marking by an open window, the gentle summer breeze lifting the edges of the papers. Just three days left. He knew nothing of the place where they were going. He hadn't left AZ Five in six years. Tim had rung Sophie early that morning, the Interior Ministry had granted his application. They would be going on a family holiday.

A commotion outside halted his progress, and he craned out of the window to see what all the fuss was about. Below two guards were shoving a pleading Carl into a van. Finn shuddered.

He raced down to the reception, nearly colliding with Mr Harrison coming in from the lawn. A group of girls followed in behind their teacher, all eager to get their questions answered.

'Is he a saboteur?'

'Is he one of the terrorists?'

'Are we in danger, Sir?'

Finn overheard one girl as she carried on along the corridor.

'Always hanging out with those DIAs. Bet he was radicalised.'

Mr Harrison gave Finn a self-satisfied smirk. 'Guess we all knew why Mr Farnborough never married.'

In a place like that rumours could destroy a person and rob them of their life, quite literally leave them choking from the gallows. Carl never spoke of his private life. Their conversations centred on school, Finn and Sophie, or New Albany, ridiculing any new law so as to prevent despair. Finn had never even visited Carl's apartment. The only thing he knew for certain, Carl despised cheese.

Carl was never far from his thoughts throughout the rest of the day. Teaching, riding home, pushing food around his dinner plate. He didn't tell Sophie, for what reason? She would only worry that it would darken his mood. That was already black. He knew who bore the responsibility for Carl's arrest, an innocent victim punished for Finn's act of defiance.

* * *

Wednesday 23rd June

Who is he to disobey me? We are bound together and when he tugs, then our unbreakable bond tightens.

* * *

'Did you get my message?' Her voice was so even and dispassionate that Cat could have been talking about a picnic or a simple errand.

'You really don't care who you hurt, do you? What has Mr Farnborough done to you?'

'He's guilty of being your friend. There've always been rumours, so I made an official complaint. The guards will question him, but I expect he's too careful to have any evidence. That sort are a secretive bunch.'

Carl's interrogation, the beating, the threats, all Finn's fault. She had warned him, defy her and condemn an innocent person in his place.

'Who will you hurt next? Sergeant Mason? He's been known to play chess against me. What about old Mrs Carter? I tiled her bathroom last year. I'm sure you could find some form of subterfuge going on there. You will run out, and then who do you hurt?'

'You forgot to mention your dear wife, Sophia Elle.'

He watched her revel in her threat, before giving his reasoned reply, 'Your father is too ambitious to allow anything to happen to my wife.'

She tipped her head to the side as though that thought hadn't occurred to her, then she laughed and headed back to the sofa. 'I feel like a drink and you are going to join me?'

Finn went to the cupboard and brought out the caramel vodka and two glasses. He would have preferred not to drink, wanting to keep his wits about him. However, he wasn't about to risk another person's arrest for his refusal to comply with her demands. He put the bottle and glasses down on the table while his mind tried to figure out how best to deal with the situation.

'I want you to sit next to me tonight.' She patted the seat beside her. 'Now pour the vodka, and I will tell you a story of love and betrayal.' From beneath the fur cushion she pulled out a photograph, and placed it face down on the table.

Cat gulped down her vodka while Finn swirled his drink, watching the sweet liquid sticking to the side of his glass before dribbling back.

'Hurry up, 568216, finish your drink. I assure you, once you hear my story you are going to want more.' She was already pouring out another generous measure into her glass. 'What sort of music do you like?'

He looked up from the glass, baffled. 'Classical mainly, Mozart, Chopin, Mahler, Handel.'

'Really? I'd have put you down for the wild erotic pop songs from your liberal student days.'

His siblings' rooms were always full of music. His brother in particular favoured the latest releases provided they were cool enough. Finn wasn't bothered about who was in or not, he just liked the music. It would be another reason for Andy to yell at him and make fun of his inability to fit in properly, so Finn pretended to only like classical.

She picked up her tablet and located her private list of music, songs banned for their provocative lyrics. Songs accused of promoting licentious behaviour. Songs about passion, about freedom, about rebellion. Cat moved forward as though to kiss him. Panicked, Finn flung his head back.

'You're such a prude.' Laughing, she shuffled position, lying her legs across Finn's lap, trapping him. 'Anyway, it's time for my Othello to learn the truth about his Desdemona.'

Catherine returned her empty glass to the table. Finn could see she was ready for her attack, but he would ignore it all. It would all be baseless lies. Sophie was his glue.

Cat poured another drink, then picked up the photograph. 'My father wanted your Sophia to notice him when he was around.' She twirled it around in her fingers. There were glimpses of the picture and then it was gone. 'He loved her. He wanted her. She was promised to him. She was his, but she ran away.'

Finn saw glimpses of a nurses' uniform. He squinted, straining to focus on the spinning picture. It wasn't just Sophie, her parents were in it too. He leant forward to snatch it off her, save the family from her clutches, but her reactions were too quick for him and she held it aloft, tutting at the tutor's audacity. 'Now, now, that's not how we do things, is it? Ask nicely and I'll let you see.'

Finn sat back in the seat. He didn't want to play her games, and the photo was another part of her torturous routine. But he did want to see it. He needed to see it, just to be sure. 'May I see the photo, please.' Each word rasping through his throat before they were released into the air between them.

'I want you to finish that drink first.'

He swallowed the vodka, only for the glass to be refilled.

'It's not right for a gentleman to make a lady drink alone.' She topped up her glass and held it up to him in a toast.

Finn stared at the photo still in her other hand and the crystal tumbler hovering in front of his face. He picked up his glass. 'Cheers.' The glasses chimed and he felt the vodka burn its way down to his stomach.

'You do have beautiful manners, don't you?' she said, flipping over the photo.

He wasn't listening. There they were, Sophie, standing stiffly in her new uniform. Uncomfortable and impractical, it emphasised her shapely body. Her father next to her, all smiles and pride with his arm across her shoulders. The embodiment of a proud father. Michelle was standing apart from the others, studying a map. This was not a staged photograph. It was a picture taken by someone watching them. Someone spying on them.

'Did your father take this photograph?' he asked.

Cat was already tipping the bottle towards his glass. Finn hadn't felt like eating dinner, upset about Carl, and the alcohol was already making him feel woozy. He put his hand across it, signalling he'd had enough, nonetheless she removed his hand. 'Questions come at a price. One question for each glass you finish.'

'I don't think we should drink too much. You are not used to it; you might make yourself ill.'

She sloshed more vodka into their glasses. 'I think it maybe you who's the lightweight. Drink up.' She lifted the glass for Finn to take. 'And no, my father is no peeping Tom. He has others to do that sort of thing. People who watched Sophia for him. They kept him informed of her behaviour, which lectures she attended, who she spoke to on the wards, where she went to relax and who bought her drinks.'

The permanent knot in Finn's stomach tightened. Had he been spied upon, investigated? Had they watched him kiss her for the first time? Photographed them lying in the shade of a tree talking, holding hands. Was he followed each time he went to his appointment with Dr Hargreaves? Did they know why he saw the doctor? Was he employed by the Commandant purely because he was married to Sophie?

Finn didn't notice the vodka in his mouth or sliding down his throat. Thoughts were jangling through him, colliding with each other, Liam, the bar, meeting Sophie, drinking with her, dancing with her, kissing her. Paralysed within his memories, Cat reached across and took the empty glass from his hand. She was still talking accompanied by the glugging liquid filling his glass.

'So many friends and such a gregarious girl according to Daddy. Until she met him. Besotted, that's what he said. Stopped meeting her friends, just spent time with him. Daddy was so jealous. Why him and not the dashing Captain? What did he have to offer the beautiful Sophia?'

Cat untied her blue silk gown and slid her hand inside. Her white lace and silk night dress was so fine it was almost translucent. She leant forward allowing her hand to search behind her back. The gown slipped off her shoulder with her movements, sliding down her bare arm. Finn did not avert his gaze, captured as he was by his own thoughts.

'There, found it. Holding the second photo, she pulled at her gown, re-tying it. 'It's bit chilly tonight, isn't it?'

He ignored her but she did have his attention. He was gripped by the photo in her left hand.

There was no playing or teasing, she just flipped it over in one quick action, like a bar mat game. Finn recognised Sophie immediately. The short pixie haircut and her head tipped back. She was naked. And there he was, under her, one hand on the small of her back, the other on her breast.

'That man doesn't look like you. He's taller, yes definitely taller, and with dark hair. You are quite fair. Shall I tell you all about him? He lives locally.'

Finn awoke from his horrified trance. 'That's not real. You've made this up. It's a doctored picture. She wouldn't do that!'

'"Doctored", I do like your use of words. Looks like she's enjoying being "doctored". Maybe she is being "doctored" right now, while you're here with me.'

Finn refused to acknowledge the infidelity laid out before him. Sophie was at home. It was all imaginary. None of it was real, the pictures were fake. It was all fake, lies devised to further Cat's control over him.

'It seems you have something in common with my father. You have both been betrayed by the beautiful Sophia Elle.'

Finn left the sofa, his trembling limbs requiring him to

cling onto furniture as he made his way to the window. In the evening light he made out a small flock of birds that had landed on the Commandant's carefully tended garden, black silhouettes against the setting sun, the white feathers glowing with a golden tinge.

Cat was behind him, her hand resting on his lower back as though to prevent him from stepping back from the window. 'Look how many we have today! One, two, three, four, five, six, oh and there's one in the tree. Seven magpies. Seven, for the secret never to be told. Isn't that exactly what I said? All married couples have secrets.'

They both stood side by side staring at the magpies below. Her hand rising up and down his back. After a moment or two of silence, Catherine yawned. 'I'm tired, read to me.'

Without a word Finn followed her to the sofa, picking the book off the table as he passed.

Catherine had fallen asleep before he finished the first page. He didn't attempt to leave early, just in case she woke. Instead he watched her gown rise and fall with her steady breathing. The belt had loosened, and the gown was slipping open. The soft white muslin swathed over her, like the folds of cloth covering a Greek goddess. Finn reached for the blanket folded at the end of the sofa and covered her with it, before continuing his vigil over the sleeping teen.

The minutes ticked by and soon the little clock chimed the hour. She did not stir. Finn was uncertain what to do. Should he wake her to get permission to leave, or just go, leaving her on the sofa? In the end he decided to go without waking her. He pushed the bell by the mantle then listened carefully for the door to click. In his hurry to leave, he stumbled on the stairs. Once in the kitchen, Mrs Fran grabbed hold of his arm. 'Sit down, I'll make you some tea. You leave like that and the guards will know you are drunk.'

Her intervention took Finn by surprise. In all the times he had passed through that kitchen, she had barely looked at him let alone spoken.

'Drink!' she handed him a cup of mint tea, 'Vodka doesn't have a strong smell on the breath, but the mint will help.'

She stood over him until he finished the whole cup. 'Do you think you can walk in a straight line?'

He nodded. 'Yes, I think so. Thank you, Fran.'

'Good luck, Michael.'

He was amazed he deceived them. In the guardhouse a screen flickered, meaning the young guards were more interested in the local derby than questioning a drunk tutor.

Finn decided not to say anything to Sophie. Ignore it, another ridiculous conspiracy by his pupil. A means to control him, to keep him by her side. Just two more days and then he would escape Cat Fry. Whatever happened next he would not be returning to be letter opener to Catherine's Major Harper.

There was a note propped up on the kitchen table. *'Emergency with Mrs Greeley. Baby coming early. Back when you see me.'*

He was used to the occasional emergency, but this time he couldn't stop the jealous monster poking him. Was Cat telling the truth? He paced around the kitchen, increasingly bewildered by his own thoughts. He could trust nothing and no one, his world a confection of lies to keep him in his place, that of the unworthy immigrant, the Immi, the alien, the DIA. Eventually, with a bottle of wine and a glass in front of him, he sat down to wait for her, she would tell him the truth. Sophie would not betray him, she was his constant, she was his glue.

SOPHIE

It was one o'clock in the morning by the time she tiptoed into the cottage. The kitchen light had been left on. The thoughtfulness of a caring husband. Heading to the kitchen to switch the light off, she saw Finn through the partially open door. He was slumped across the kitchen table. Panic shot through her. Had he found the sleeping pills? No, that was impossible, they were in her bag. She double-checked, yes, the little tin was in the pocket. It was the smell of elderflower wine that allowed her to begin breathing again. The two bottles, one empty, the other with only a couple of inches left, told her exactly what was ailing her husband.

'Finn! Wake up Finn!'

He did not respond. She tried again and this time his eyes opened. His speech was slurred and incomprehensible with the only word she could make out being 'Henry'.

'Finn, you need to wake up. You're drunk. Come on Finn, wake up!' Annoyed, she had anticipated bed, not babysitting a drunk in her kitchen. Her stern voice and prodding eventually paid off and he opened his eyes, only to shut then again and mumble into his sleeves. He made no sense.

'Come on Finn, you need to drink some water. Finn! Stop bloody talking and drink some water.'

Sophie spent the next hour coaxing Finn to sip water between his intoxicated ramblings. He rarely drank, in fact she couldn't remember him ever being drunk, tipsy yes, but never drunk. After a Herculean effort, she manhandled him upstairs. Sophie struggled to undress him, constantly replaying the alcohol fuelled monologues in her head. He was definitely talking about Henry and university. Her confusion kept her awake most of the night listening to her husband snore. This was not what she needed, but it's what she got.

Sophie was awoken by Finn's groans. He attempted to get up but immediately lay back down. It was gone four by the time she had fallen asleep, dreaming fitfully of her student days. Finn's pathetic efforts to get out of bed made her chuckle, and with his strange whining noises, it was a comical reward for her own lack of sleep.

'Whatever else you learn today, the first lesson is what happens to your body when you drink too much.'

His hands covered his face. 'Tell the room to stop spinning first.'

Sophie laughed and guided him to the bathroom, fully prepared for the consequence of her father's experiments. Her teenage years littered with friends swearing abuse, followed by swearing abstinence. Finn sat back against the side of the bath, soothed by the cool enamel.

'You're not teaching today, are you?' she asked handing him a damp flannel to place over his face.

Finn shook his head slowly. 'I have to go in at lunchtime for an end of term meeting this afternoon, otherwise no.'

'How fortunate.'

Finn didn't hear her. He was too busy emptying what was left of the contents of his stomach down the toilet.

By eight o'clock, Finn was outside on the steamer chair under the apple tree.

'Breakfast for the idiot called Michael Finlay!' called Sophie. She was carrying a tray of tea and toast with her gardening gloves dangling off the edge of the tray, intending to wage war on the weeds before neglect and abandonment took charge.

'You are joking. I'm never eating again or drinking for that matter.'

'Wrong answer. It's mainly a breakfast of pills to be honest. The toast is so you have something to line your stomach.' She handed him the paracetamols and the Albian substitute antidepressant. 'Are you going to tell me what possessed you to drink nearly two bottles of Dad's wine?'

'You said I was your first lover. Was I really?'

Sophie's mouth gaped open, his question taking her by surprise. After a moment to consider her answer, she replied, 'Finn, what on earth is the matter with you? We've already had this conversation. You are the first man with whom I have ever made love. Satisfied? Can we get on with life now?'

'You're lying to me. I know that's not true. Unless you started the affair after we were married.'

'What affair?' Sophie was becoming frightened. She knew Finn had a jealous streak, but he had always controlled it. He had never accused her of infidelity. He trusted her.

'Henry! I saw a photo of the two of you. Looked like you were enjoying yourself, fucking Henry senseless.'

This definitely wasn't Finn. He would never speak to her like that. In fact, he would never speak to anyone at all like that. The man before her was not the man she had spent years loving and trying to protect. She rapidly rehearsed her response before replying to Finn, 'Are you saying you saw a photograph of me having sex with Henry? Really, you believe that do you? We both know how easy it is to fake photos, any child can do it on their laptops. One fake photo and suddenly you think I am capable of adultery. Listen to yourself Finn!'

'I know what I saw, and it looked pretty real to me. Is that where you were last night? Fucking Henry. Does he help you deal with the time you have to spend with your imperfect husband? The beautiful Sophia Elle shackled to a failure. When was the last time we made love? Can you even remember that far back?'

'You are not a failure.' Sophie stroked the back of his hand, tracing a line where prominent veins criss-crossed. 'You have been very ill, and it has just taken time to get back on your feet. This holiday is just what we need. You'll see, you'll be fine by next week, I guarantee it.'

'Is that why we haven't had children?'

'Sorry Finn, what are you talking about now?' Sophie snatched back her trembling hands. Genuine fear deposited at her feet.

'You made me believe it was all my fault. Poor Sophia Elle married to an infertile man, but all the time he's been fucking you. You must have been taking something to stop having his child. He's a doctor, for goodness sake! I bet he has all the right contacts to avoid embarrassment.'

Sophie turned away, picking up the gardening gloves and pulled them on with unnecessary force. 'I don't know what that girl has said, or what ridiculous pictures she has shown you, but you really have to stop now. You know me, you love me. We trust each other. I would never ever do anything to hurt you, but right now, you are in danger of hurting me.'

'Like you hurt our daughter. Was she a mistake, just like me? The unwanted arrival.' He was standing behind her, his hot breath on her neck. 'Unlike my mother, you succeeded in ending the pregnancy.

Anger flared within her, she spun round to confront him. 'You know that's not true. That was a bastard thing to say.'

'Was it? How many of Anna's herbal remedies do you make for women fed up with constants births and screaming children? You know exactly where to look in the garden to sort out any unwanted problem. Just make it look like another unfortunate premature birth. New Albany must hold the world record for neo-natal deaths.'

Her hand stung from the slap across his face. She could see the red mark emblazoned across his cheek. His eyes were sparkling whether from hurt or his mania, she couldn't tell. She was not going to wait to find out. 'I am going to go inside. I have nothing more to say to you.'

Sophie picked up the tray. Her fingers so tightly wrapped around the handles that her knuckles turned white. Everything appeared to be pounding, her heart, her head and her ears all burnt with rage. Globules of tears balanced precariously on her lower eyelashes. She blinked hard, forcing them back determined not to cry in front of him. Storming her way back to the house, she threw off the gardening gloves, leaving them to land by his rose. Once in the kitchen she allowed the tears to fall. Each searing tear branding a track across her face.

Upstairs in their bedroom, she shut the door and turned the key. There would be no apologies this time. Sophie sat at her dressing table and took hold of the tear drop handle of the centre drawer. It felt bitterly cold against her hot hand and she let go. She tried again, this time tugging at the handle. The drawer was stiff from lack of use. There was a squeaking of wood passing over wood as she jerked it open. In the drawer lay the small box, a pink fairy embossed on the top. Sophie lifted it out the drawer, her fingers pushing up the lid to reveal her secrets; a dried buttonhole flower, Finn's; her trainee nurse badge; a birthday card signed by her fellow trainees and an expensive looking card, topped with a neat gold bow, the wedding invitation, her emerald engagement ring sewn onto it. Too valuable to wear given the environment where she chose to live. She held each memento, each carrying scenes from a past life. Underneath lay a tiny parcel. Tears marked the tissue paper, forming little dark circles on the pale blue paper. At first Sophie hesitated, then she unfolded the tissue, inside lay the tiny baby's bonnet, embroidered with miniature daisies at the side. Like a curator handling a precious relic, she placed it on her hand and brought it to her face, her tears watering the flowers. It was meant to be worn by a bonny baby, loved and wanted. Molly was too fragile for it, swamping her tiny head. The scent of Molly had gone, but that memory persisted. Nothing had been erased as her sobs grew in intensity.

At the bottom of the box was a photograph. She was so tiny, even more so cradled in his hands, alive and crying in that brief freezing of time. In the absence of paternal joy, sat grief with red rimmed eyes and an ashen face. He had been gently rocking his dying daughter. Father and daughter captured together for all eternity. Some pain is so sharp, so visceral that even seeing that image made her feel faint from heartache. Not some fictional heartache of a lost romance, but stabs of pain shooting across her chest. She couldn't look at it any longer and returned it to the box along with the other treasures. The lid was closed, and the drawer pushed shut. She had stopped crying. Sophie stood to leave, glancing out of the window. His arms were tightly crossed, and his foot tapped nervously. After a few moments his hand raised to his face, pushing tears away from his glasses.

It was an hour later before she returned to the garden. Finn was where she had left him, uncertainty written across his face.

'I've made you a tea. It will help settle your stomach.' Sophie had made her decision. It needed to be said, otherwise she feared the coming days would leave her floundering. 'You made me hate you for the first time ever. I swear it took every sinew in my body to stop me walking out of that gate, straight into the guardhouse and have you arrested on trumped up charges. No one would question my story. I am the unfortunate Foreign Minister's daughter lumbered with a DIA. You would be dead within twenty-four hours of my complaint.'

'Am I supposed to be grateful you didn't?' Finn put the cup down. He looked back at her, earlier sorrow replaced with anger. 'Death is infinitely more preferable to this miserable life. Death is my only escape from hell.' He grabbed her arm, pulling her in close. His grip pinching her, hurting her. 'Time for Sophia Elle to have a new, proper husband and become an elite Albian once more. It's a wonder you're still standing here. Or is it because that is precisely what you don't want.' His grip was tightening, she picked at his fingers, trying to free herself. 'Oh no you don't,' he slapped her hand away. 'I know why you want me. Keeping me means you are free to continue your affair with no risk of pregnancy. You chain me to this hell, so that you can live a guilt free life.'

Sophie bit the inside of her lip, her mouth filling with the taste of blood. She was going to stick to her decision regardless. She dug her nails into his flesh. He retracted his hand, three curved marks evident on his skin.

'Do you to know what's really happening, Finn Sheehan? Do you want to know why I didn't report you?

'Go on then, tell me,' he shouted back.

'Because we are leaving this place. We will be leaving New Albany forever. This isn't a holiday to celebrate Dad's seventieth, this is the escape. We are returning you to safety. Can you comprehend what risks I am willing to take to get you home, can you?'

Finn stood in shocked silence. Eventually, in a faltering voice he asked, 'Am I going alone?'

'No, we are both going. That's the plan and we are sticking to it.'

'Why, why now? I have been living this nightmare for six years. A prisoner of your father's design.'

'He didn't devise the programme, you know that?'

'He did vote for it, though. He used me. The convenient poster boy, the Foreign Minister's son-in-law, happy to be the first in the Digitally Interned Alien Programme. Show the others there is nothing to fear, it's for your own protection against the evil terrorists.'

Sophie was well aware of her father and Finn's role in the acceptance of the programme. A safeguarding law turned into a weapon of terror. She thought of Ryan, how it was just a job for him, a pay rise and a promotion. For the DIA it was genocide. It was guilt that now made her cheeks flush. 'He regrets everything.'

'Regret?' Finn tossed his head back in mocking laughter. 'Regret is the most impotent of words. It is meaningless. Does he care about the humiliation, the pain, the death? Does 'regret' change any of that? Does he 'regret' our dead child, my destroyed career, our doomed marriage? So much regret but no courage.'

'He is risking everything to try and save you. There are rumours about his loyalty. If we make it, I will never see my parents again. Both of my parents will be tried for treason if we are caught. This is the sacrifice we are making for you. There is your courage. Do you understand? If we are discovered, we all die!'

In the hush that descended on the warring couple, she turned her back on him, unable to look at the man who believed their marriage doomed. She felt his hand on her once more. A gentle squeeze instead of a jealous grip. Then came his finger, tracing across her face. His touch always meant so much more to her. Where words would fail him, his gentle affection did not. There were a thousand apologies in that single, delicate movement. It was not enough.

'I'm sorry Sophie. I love you. You know that don't you. I don't know why I said those things. We can work this out, I'm sure we can.'

Sophie spun round to face him, fury rampant behind her hazel eyes. Her reply was speared by sobs, 'I never once doubted you. I trusted you implicitly, but how can you even conceive I could kill my own child? You've changed, she's changed you. You broke us.'

'I'm sorry, I am, Sophie, truly.' His head bent as the penitent husband pleaded forgiveness. 'We can fix this. I was angry, I believed her, I'm sorry, please Sophie, I am so sorry.'

Sophie heard the desperation in his voice, his need for forgiveness. Finally, she interrupted her considered silence with a command, 'You must do everything as normal. No one can know, Finn. You were not supposed to know until the day of the escape. My parents' necks, our necks, they are all in the noose if we are discovered. We cannot fail.'

He nodded. Behind them, the hall clock struck the hour. There was no more time for further questions or accusations. 'I'd better get a shower and change. I need to get to the school for the meeting.'

FINN

He had hoped to get news about Carl from the others. The rumour mill run by the girls was pretty reliable. After all, what was the point of a guardsman fiancé if they couldn't be used to secure valuable gossip?

However, Finn was surprised and somewhat relieved to see Carl in the meeting. He had been beaten, evidenced by the black eye and swollen lip. A sneaky wink from his good eye signalled that they would talk later.

The meeting about the next term's timetable and curriculum seemed never-ending. Finn ignored the arguments and allowed himself to daydream about the future. Relaxing in the garden at Melborough, sitting on the terrace with his parents and having a cool drink. They'd be telling him about all the grandchildren, his nephews and nieces. The farm, the guys that worked there, who had retired, married and moved on. Evie and Maya would fly back to see him.

'We'll be sad to lose Mr Michael next term. He's leaving us to take up a post in the Commandant's office with Captain, soon to be Major Harper. I am sure you'll all join with me to wish him luck.'

Finn was hurled back from his blissful reverie. He stared at the head in disbelief. Cat had done it. No resignation required. He was a slave to the system which would decide where and for whom he would work. Well, she'd get a shock. He would not be turning up for work. He intended to be free again, free to make his own decisions, free to be an adult once more. She no longer had control of him. In fact, he'd even miss her last lesson.

Finn sat on the graveyard bench they had so often shared, a place where he liberated himself of the agony and torment of his life in New Albany.

'I haven't got long. I am probably still being watched.' Carl looked about him anxiously. He was slightly out of breath from his trot across the school playing field.

'What happened?' Finn had his head in his hands. He was queasy and with a pounding head, compounded with the guilt for his part in the terror perpetrated on his friend.

'I could ask the same about you, you look awful.'

'Self-inflicted injury with a couple of bottles of Tim's wine,' was his quiet response.

'Christ, surprised you even made it in. Do you like my new look?' Carl moved his head about like a preening peacock. 'It's the black eye, cut lip style. De rigueur for the fashionable man about town this season. Especially popular with those ageing bachelor teachers, with neither wife nor girlfriend.'

'Why did they take you?' He wanted to know the justification the guards gave. He already knew the true reason.

Carl raised an eyebrow, putting his hand on Finn's knee, tapping it gently. 'You don't really need to ask that question, do you, laddie? I hang out with a DIA. One that doesn't have children to boot. There were questions, there are always questions. A few punches too, for good measure. There was no evidence, so I was released, and they advised me to marry before the end of the summer holiday. We are all slaves to the system. We are men, but we lack the God given gift of freewill.'

Finn sighed, uncertain whether it was just coincidence or part of her plan. 'Who'll be the lucky recipient of this whirlwind romance?'

'Do you remember a Charlotte Daviny from six years back? Young widow now. Husband killed in a skirmish up in AZ Twelve. Already has three children, doesn't want any more. The head is going to fix it. Hope you'll be my best man.'

'Of course, I'd be delighted.'

SOPHIE

Sophie was upstairs packing when Finn returned from school. Her father had told her to pack warm clothes as well as the normal summer holiday wear. In the wardrobe hung the unworn blouse she bought with her mother back in the autumn. The long sleeves and soft cotton would be perfect, a new blouse for a new life. She wrapped Molly's box in the blouse and placed it in the suitcase.

Finn stood in the doorway watching her. 'Apparently I have a new job.' The bedroom wall was illuminated by green light as he spoke.

'You can tell me about it downstairs, I'm parched. You'll have to help me pack, I've no idea what you want to take.'

They drank tea in the garden and Finn told her about Cat's plan for him to be her husband's secretary, Carl's arrest and his forced marriage. 'I've decided not to go back tonight. I want to spend it with you.'

'No, you can't.' She saw him taken aback by her answer.

'We can get through this, I'm sure, I didn't know what I was saying, please forgive me.'

'No Finn, you misunderstand me. You can't stay here. Carry on as normal, we can't allow any reason for suspicion. You have to see her tonight as usual. You must take the lesson.'

'Tell me you have forgiven me.'

Sophie contemplated what to say next, Finn's eyes never leaving her face, urging the answer he needed to hear. 'I'm not ready for that.' She watched his body visibly shrink before her. Finn was crestfallen but that was all she had to offer. 'I need more time. I doubt you could ever know how much you hurt me. I can't just forget that now because you say you're sorry. I'm not saying never, just not right now.'

'I see. I'll go and pack then.' He got up, picking up the cups. 'There is something I want to take back with me.'

'What thing?' She couldn't imagine what he might have from his time in New Albany that he would want to keep.

'Kitty, I brought her with me when I first came as a student. She has been everywhere with me. I'm not going to abandon her now. She deserves to go home too.'

FINN

* * *

Thursday 24th June

*It's all planned. Fool the man that thinks that he can
defeat me. They play me, their living breathing chess
queen, lining me up for the attack, blind to the fact that
my own strategy will win out in the end. Isn't the queen
the most valuable piece, the one to treasure? Even an
impotent king still requires a queen.*

* * *

Finn savoured the delightful pleasure that every part of the
journey to Cat's sitting-room was a last. The last ride up the
hill. The last indignity of the sullen guards checking him
with a sniffer dog. The last wordless encounter with Mrs
Fran. The last climb of the stairs. The last time he would
force himself to relax before entering her chamber. The last
time he would have to stand by the door waiting for a child
to give him permission to sit.

For a seventeen-year-old girl who had drunk six glasses of
vodka the previous night, she had recovered remarkably well.
Cat was wearing a new nightdress. One he hadn't seen before.
It was made of the darkest of green silk, almost black, but as
she walked towards him, the silk shone brightly highlighting
the contours of her body. The front and back were attached
by a series of criss-crossing silk ribbons made of the same
dark green, tied in a bow halfway down her thighs. A pair of
thin gold straps held the dress on her shoulders, with little

bows flopping down, their jewelled ends resting just above her breasts. Finn could see her flesh through the ribbons, her hips, her waist, the curve of her breast.

'Miss Fry, I think you might get cold, perhaps you would like to change?' He was embarrassed, yet he was powerless to avert his gaze, captivated by the shimmering green fabric and the curves it hardly hid.

'I lit the stove, we will soon warm up, don't worry.'

Finn finally broke the trance and glanced apprehensively at the coffee table. There were no photographs tonight, instead, an ice bucket with two bottles of champagne. One had been opened. Next to the ice bucket, two champagne flutes, brimming with rising bubbles, hissing pops bursting on the surface.

She was smiling, not her usual one, all teeth and insincerity, this was gentler, almost pleasant. 'We are going to celebrate tonight.' And with that, the softness was gone.

Finn looked down to the rug, avoiding her face. 'Given you have your exam in the morning, is that wise? Shouldn't we go over some last-minute revision?'

'I'm not going to sit the exam. It is unnecessary. We will continue our own little book club in private. Don't worry, my fiancé will approve. I can be very persuasive.'

Cat opened the stove door and forced in a couple more logs into the chamber. She closed it and watched the fire rage inside, rapidly heating up the room.

'Come, sit by me,' Cat ordered, slapping the floor next to her. 'If you are worried about me getting cold, then we will sit here on the rug.' She stretched out her long legs in front of her and held up the glass nearest to her. 'Let's toast?'

Her glass hovered in the air, waiting to touch his. There was going to be no avoiding it. He picked up the other glass, the chink of the toast making his spine shiver. Cat leant back.

Her emerald eyes studied him, almost daring him to disobey. He lifted the flute to his lips, took a sip then returned it to the floor.

'Finish it, but make sure you savour that champagne. I had the bottles smuggled in especially.'

The Catherine of a few moments ago was but a mirage, the controlling girl was in charge. Finn didn't want another fight. Cat observed him until the glass was drained then pulled the chilled bottle from the ice bucket, refilling their glasses. 'Did she deny it?'

Finn was not going to answer her. He would not give her the satisfaction.

'I expect she told you it was fake. It's all in your head. Your poor, poorly head.'

She knew, he was certain of it. Finn got up and retreated to his usual corner of the sofa, hugging his arms in comfort. Of course she knew. A copy of his file was sent to the Commandant's office, that's what George had said. The Commandant's daughter would make sure there was nothing about Michael Finlay Sheehan, 568216/2/MI, that she didn't know. The power of knowledge, chains to hold her prey captive.

'Your silence is very loud. Is she giving you pills to make you better? Ones to make you happy, and ones to make you sleep.'

Stunned by what he was hearing, Finn glanced up to see her smirking face. How could she know? That was not on his repatriation file. She was guessing; an educated assumption.

'She mothers you, doesn't she? Always looking after her darling Finn.'

Cat had said his real name, his nickname. It was Finlay, his mother's maiden name, that was the name on his file, not Finn. Evie was the first to call him Finn, preferring it to Michael. How could Cat possibly know his real name?

'I have video you know. The two of you at home. I have spent hours watching you. Daddy has spent years watching her betray you. When was the last time she let you touch her, when was the last time you actually fucked your own wife?'

'You are making all this up.' His fist tightened around the stem of the crystal flute. He wanted to hurl it at her. He wanted to put his fingers around that elegant long neck and squeeze until her smirking face was no more.

'You only moved back into your own bedroom a few weeks ago, or are you going to contradict me?'

Not content with listening, Finn realised there must also have been cameras in the house monitoring them. Spying on the couple live out the monotony of their life, their arguments, their tenderness, their lovemaking. Always on. Always watching. 'How long have you been spying on us?'

'How long have you been married? I told you, Daddy likes to keep an eye on his property.'

'Just us, or everyone? Are we all an amusing reality show for the Albian elite?' his anger barely controlled.

'No, just you, the two people he is most interested in. Well one person really, you just happen to be there most of the time.'

On the table next to the champagne was a small gold dish with a glass lid. She lifted the lid releasing a minty aroma from the little pale blue diamond shaped sweets. Cat carefully removed one and placed it on her tongue, allowing the sweet to dissolve. 'Would you like a sweetie too?'

She bent forward, her lips virtually touching his. He could almost taste the foul-smelling mint coming from her mouth. He didn't want a sweet or anything else.

'Open wide, time to take your pills!' She put two sweets next to his lips, but he did not open his mouth. 'I insist, 568216!'

It was just a game, that is what he kept telling himself.

Yet another game, one that would soon be over. He opened his mouth and let her place the sweets on his tongue. Mint infused his mouth. One dissolved to nothingness while the other remained stubbornly on his tongue. He pushed it to the side and crushed it between his teeth. There was no mint this time, but a strange and vile bitterness. Cat held up her champagne glass to his lips. He drank it. He would have drunk anything to mask the taste of that strange, bitter candy.

'There, you'll be all better now!' She drank what was left of her champagne. 'Tell me, Finn, do I remind you of your wife? Do you prefer me to her? Am I more attractive, more enticing? Be careful how you answer!'

How could he? If he said yes, she would know he was lying, if he said no, then she would become spiteful, vindictive. He couldn't risk her anger, not tonight. He only had to survive for another thirty minutes in her company.

'You are a beautiful woman. Your fiancé is a very lucky man.'

Cat picked up Finn's glass from the table and handed it to him. 'But I want to hear about the things you admire about me.'

His glass was still full, so he sipped the champagne slowly, desperate for some moments to think of a way out of her questioning. 'You're intelligent, perceptive,' he said after a long pause.

She had made herself comfortable on the sofa next to him. There was no space for him to escape her. 'I see you are getting into the spirit of the occasion. Tell me more.'

Finn looked over to the stove, the flames burning intensely, the heat almost suffocating.

'Aren't you going to talk to me, whisper those sweet nothings, just as your wife does with her lover?' Red fingernails stabbed into the soft flesh beneath his jaw, tipping his head back, forcing him to see the face before him. His

433

glasses had slipped, and she was blurred, her hard lines softening into the background.

'I don't believe you. Sophie wouldn't betray me. She loves me, no others. Sophie loves me. You are playing games again.' Finn's words slurred, the champagne already having an effect on him. Another barely tasted dinner, this time anxious about his final lesson with Cat.

'She really has you in her thrall, doesn't she? You believe her lies and she makes you feel like the guilty party when you accuse her of betrayal. Did you apologise to her? Did she make you beg for her forgiveness?'

Finn thought back over the earlier row. His accusations followed by pleas for forgiveness. He felt dizzy, his face hot, perspiration beading on his forehead. He was confused. Who betrayed who? Was it Sophie? Yes, no, he had said unforgivable things to her. Accused her of killing their child. No, he was at fault. Their argument bent and twisted with his disorientated recollections. 'I don't know what happened. We had a fight.'

'A fight? She was the one deceiving you. What could you have done to her, you're my sweet harmless creature? She was the one being fucked in your kitchen by her doctor friend while you fought for your life upstairs. Did you know that?'

Cat was straying into the preposterous. Sophie would never have betrayed him in their own home. No, she was lying. Everything she said was untrue. Lies to make him jealous, lies to make him injure Sophie. 'She wouldn't do that. She loves me.'

Finn lay his head on the back of the seat, staring up towards the ceiling rose. It reminded him of his favourite flower. Sophie can't have betrayed him. She was for his eyes only. Around him he could hear the room echo with music, not her usual repertoire of banned lyrics, but the one piece that relaxed him. The strings, oboes and trombones that sent him to the safety of Evie's bedroom. He shut his eyes allowing himself to briefly escape the claustrophobia of that stifling sitting-room.

Her silk nightdress caressed his skin as Cat curled up close to him. Her fingers tracked a bead of sweat rolling passed his eye. Her touch gentle, relaxing. He felt the weight of his glasses lifted off his face. He did not attempt to stop her.

Cat refilled their glasses and passed one to Finn. He was so hot he would have drunk anything to cool down. She left the seat to add more wood to the stove, moving like her namesake, a cat, a pedigree cat, long limbed, graceful. Each gesture considered, so bewitching, so enticing. He squeezed his eyes shut again, desperate to bring back Evie's room, but this time it was Cat sitting at the desk, facing the boy on the bed, grinning at him, tugging him back to her. Evie's bedroom was lost. He tried to focus his vision on Cat, but all he could see was the silk gown, green and flowing across her body. So hypnotic, so mesmerising.

'It's so green, so beautiful,' he slurred in a slow carefully considered manner.

'I'm glad you like it. I wanted you to see it. It's for my wedding night. Pull the ribbons and it is undone. It just drops away.'

She stood up and twirled around to the music. Wherever the gown flowed his eyes followed. Finn reached out to touch the fabric. The tips of his fingers stroking the silk, sensing the luxurious threads of the expensive duchess silk satin. So similar to Sophie's wedding dress, cut on the bias and moulding against her body. He could still see the wedding night bedroom and his new wife standing before him. He had been transfixed by the whole ritual, the unzipping of her dress and watching it fall off her shoulders and float down towards the floor. The rolling down of her stockings, so fine they almost disappeared in his hands. Then standing to kiss her, tasting her lipstick with his tongue. His cheek resting against hers, the musky perfume intoxicating him. His inexperienced fingers travelled along her back locating each hook on her handmade basque. She was a goddess standing on the cloud made of lace and silk. A dream too soon flicked away when Cat scratched her fingernails across his cheek, demanding his attention. 'More champagne?'

Finn shook his head. 'I don't think I should drink anymore.'

He wanted to go to sleep, escape outside and throw himself onto the cool grass. There was a jug of water on the table. He stood, intending to pour himself a glass of water, instead he stumbled, sending the champagne flute flying from his hand. It smashed on the floor. He gazed at the shattered crystal, bewildered, unsure if it was real or imaginary.

'I think my creature is a little drunk, whatever shall we do with the drunken teacher?'

Finn sat back down and giggled at the thought of the poor mistreated drunken sailor of sea shanty fame. 'I could never be a sailor.'

'Why ever not, my sweet?' Cat lifted his legs off the floor, lying him across the sofa. She undid the laces on his shoes and removed them.

'I'm terrified of drowning. I nearly drowned as a small boy. I knocked myself out on a rock.'

'I'm so glad you didn't. What would I have done without you, Finn Sheehan?'

She had used his surname. She knew his surname. His mind was wondering, freed from the monsters of fear.

'I'm not Mr Sheehan, I'm Dr Sheehan. I would have been a professor too if I had stayed. Professor Sheehan. I like the sound of that.'

'I've never met a professor before, are you any different from any other man?'

Finn didn't answer her, he was back at the university, driving to the faculty. Talking to students, walking into his office, sitting at his desk, opening an email from Evie.

'Are you too hot?' she asked.

Cat unbuttoned his shirt. Finn followed her movements, watching each button released from the grip of the buttonhole. She helped him out of the shirt and blew down his chest to cool him. He didn't think about the impropriety of the situation. He could only think how good it was to have her cool breath on his chest.

'Are you really that different from the others? Do you feel more intensely, do you hurt more profoundly?' She picked up his left arm, where the scars were more prominent, and kissed the inside of his wrist.

Finn played with the end of the strap off her left shoulder. That sensual sensation of the silk between his fingers. So light, only just there, but he was sure he could feel each and every thread. Fascinated, he pulled it towards him, watching one side of her nightdress drop away. Her breast was uncovered, young and full. Cat bent down to kiss his neck allowing her naked breast to brush against his chest.

It wasn't Cat whispering in his ear, it wasn't the Commandant's daughter he could feel on him. It was Sophie. Sophie's champagne lips on his. Sophie's breast touching his cheek. It was Sophie's firm nipple tickling his lips. It was Sophie's fingers on his waist. He put his hand on her thigh, sliding it up through the ribbons. He was holding her again. So long, too long. The silk was moving; he was the one pushing it away. He lifted his head to meet hers and opened his mouth to taste her. She was releasing him. She was guiding him into her. His secrets revealed. He could trust her, his fear evaporating. He loved her. Her hands caressed him, and her lips kissed him. It was Sophie loving him, and he was free to love her back. They had waited so long, too long.

* * *

Friday 25ᵗʰ June,

I am Catherine. I am Regina. I am Victoria. The King is dead, long live the Queen.

* * *

Seven bells echoed through his head, each more excruciating than the previous. Finn moaned with wretchedness, determined not to wake to another hangover. He covered his ears with his hands, but even touching his skull induced agony rippling through him. His left arm slid down onto Sophie's side, and with faint whispering, he called to her, 'Soph?' But her side was empty. He could feel her warmth lingering and stretched out his fingers, lying his palm flat where her body had been. The electric shock of awareness pulsed through him, he jerked his hand back. Fresh lavender infused cotton was replaced with deep, musky perfume ingrained within the silken sheets that rucked beneath his naked body. He was not in his bed.

Though the breach between the unfamiliar drapes came the harsh brightness of morning, piercing though him, stabbing his retinas with unrelenting energy, while to his left came the tinging of metal on metal. He inched his head around towards the jangling and saw the golden tag glinting back, hanging triumphantly from the plaited leather leash that curled around the bed knob. From the other side of the room came a hushing of a door opening over thick piled carpet.

'I thought you might be thirsty.'

He recoiled with her voice, slinking below the sheet to make believe the nightmare was not happening.

'Are we playing hide and seek?' Cat peeled back the sheet. She glistened with tiny droplets of water and her blond hair was slicked back. The mattress depressed slightly with her weight and a dribble of water rolled off her, falling onto his chin. She touched it, tracking with her finger as the trickle continued down into his morning stubble. She continued its trajectory, drawing down his chest and onwards to his stomach: The executioner's dissection line.

'Oh God, oh my God, what have I done?' Finn doubled up, knocking away her hand with his rising knees. 'Oh God, they are going to hang me. What have I done?'

'You worry too much.' She lay down, tessellating into his position, whispering, 'I'll keep you a secret, just as she keeps her doctor a secret from you.'

He wriggled out from her grasp. 'No. No, it's impossible, the servants, Mrs Fran, what about the guards? They will all know?' Fear of imminent arrest blocking the pain receptors. He could only cope with one terror at a time.

She reached out, clasping his arm. 'No one is going to arrest you. You think I cannot plan for their interference.' Chasing back into him, she gently pushed his hair from his eyes, speaking soothingly, 'I called down to the guards while you slept. *"Mr Michael has been taken ill. He is sleeping on my sofa. No, I'm sure he'll be fine in the morning. Yes, I'll lock my bedroom door, just in case."* I am quite the actress when it pleases me. No one came up to check, and no one witnessed you in my bed, making love to me throughout the night.'

The inevitable consequences were all too apparent to the former university lecturer. Regardless of her words, the law considered intimate relations between a DIA and an unmarried patriot girl as a violation of her father's property. All guilt was his, and the sentence mandatory: death by hanging. The Foreign Minister's son-in-law, the DIA poster boy, a disgrace, not only betraying his daughter, but the system put in place to protect the alien. There would be no holiday by the sea. There would be no celebrating Tim's seventieth. There would be no escape for Sophie and Finn. All hope was destroyed.

'I read on your file that you are going away today. AZ Eight?' She was pushing down on his knees, unfurling him. 'I hate that you will be leaving me.' She bent to kiss his stomach, but he thrust his hand at her, stopping her.

The controlling witch that resided just below her love-sick persona burst forward. 'Why did you do that?' Then she was gone, and coquettishness returned. 'Oh my sweet, don't tell me you've gone shy on me, not after everything we did last night?'

Finn was grateful for the amnesia that blocked out the previous night's activity. 'No, not shy. I...I...I mean we mustn't. This is wrong.' His brain had been whirling, and with her strange behaviour, he had gleaned a slight glimmer of hope, of survival. Catherine Fry believed she in was love.

'Have you forgotten your fiancé? He'll realise,' he said, more in hope that she would come to her senses and send him away without another thought.

Cat got off the bed and shrugged on a gown, tying it with irritated vigour. 'Not until after the marriage and then it doesn't matter. And he if he does have the wit to notice, he's the sort who'd rather be cuckold in private than lose his position and respect through scandal.' She snatched up snowy white towel that was folded next to the chair. 'Do you want a towel?'

'Thank you.' He edged off the bed and wrapped the towel around him. Unexpected heat flamed through him and he slumped back onto the bed, dizzy from the brief exertion. 'I need to go home. My wife, she'll be worried.'

'I doubt it,' she said sulkily, adding, 'Anyway, I told a guard to ring her and let her know you were sleeping here.'

'Well I'm fine now,' he said, attempting to stand again. He held onto the chair where she was sitting.

'Really?' Cat hooked her finger into the towel, drawing him closer. 'You don't look it. Perhaps I should put you back to bed.'

'Just tell me where my clothes are?'

Cat stood up her naked body radiating even more heat into him. 'Where you left them.'

He turned around to see a trail of hastily removed clothes that led from the sofas to the bed. Rivulets of sweat raced down him. He broke free of her, and stepped back, wiping his face.

'I suppose you should shower.' She nodded to the door behind her. 'Use my bathroom.'

Catherine was basking in the morning light, drinking her tea by the time Finn emerged from the bedroom. She crooked her finger, ordering him to her side. He ignored her and headed to the double doors of the sitting room.

'Where do you think you are going?'

The steely timbre of her words was not enough to cower him. He had figured out she was as trapped as him. 'I have to leave. I am expected at school later, but first I must explain what has happened to my wife.'

She remained impassive, as though weighing up her options. Finally, she stood and approached him. 'No you won't, not if you love her as much as you say.'

There was no need for her to elaborate, he understood the threat perfectly well. His grip tightened on the crystal doorknob. It was cold against the heat that still raged through him. Behind him, Catherine's hands slipped around his waist and he felt the weight of her head on his back.

'My darling mouse. My precious creature. My 568216.' Each phrase was interspersed with a kiss, her breathe filtering through his shirt, prickling his skin. 'Remember my sweet Finn, we were always meant to be together. There are no laws that can stop the inevitable. You are mine and I am your queen.'

He felt her slip something heavy into his pocket before going to the mantle to press the release button for the door. He put his hand in to retrieve it. It's unmistakable shape and weight crushing him. He opened the palm that concealed the gold name tag.

'I own you, Finn Sheehan. Don't you ever forget that.'

SOPHIE

The moment Sophie heard the garden gate she flew out of the kitchen. 'What happened? A guard rang. He said you were ill. I was so frightened.'

Finn avoided looking at Sophie's worried face, giving her a whispered excuse on his way past. 'She wanted to celebrate the end of tutoring, we drank champagne, it must have reacted with those pills. I passed out again.'

Sophie kept silent. It wasn't the pills, she knew that, but if she questioned him, he would discover her lies. She grabbed hold of his arm forcing him to look back at her. 'How do you feel now, you look awful?'

Finn recoiled, dumping his bag on the floor. Sophie had enough experience to guess this was not an alcohol induced hangover. His pupils were dilated, his hair was dark damp and he was grabbing the back of a chair to steady himself. The other hand was firmly hidden in his pocket, yet the slight tremble in his arm was still visible.

'Do you need me to help you upstairs? Maybe you should lie down.'

He winced when she spoke, as though even the quietest of voices was like a loud hailer in his face.

'No. I'll be OK. I have to go into school. A few last-minute things to sort out. I'll get showered and change first.' He was barely audible.

Sophie decided to join Finn in the garden while he ate his breakfast. Her hands on his shoulders, she brushed against his cheek kissing him. He let out a quiet murmur as though relieved.

'We'll be OK, I'm sure of it. Just a few more days,' Sophie whispered into his ear. She opened her hand and gave him his tablets. Once they got to the beach house, she would tell him, but for the time being, pretence was more important.

I WON'T TELL

MELBOROUGH MANOR, AGED SIX

It hurts so much, but he doesn't stop. Andy forces my head underwater, holding me there. My glasses are lost. I tried to catch them, but now they are gone. Andy pulls me back out of the water. I can hear him shouting above my cries.

'You fucking pervert, you're a weirdo, do you know that? A perverted weirdo that should never have been born!'

He pushes me back under the water. I am struggling to hold my breath. I need air. He drags me back out just in time and I gasp, 'I'm sorry, please Andy, I'm sorry.'

'She only kept you to cheer up Grandad Mike, you were born to make a dying man happy. I heard them. They didn't want another child. You were a mistake.'

My arm hurts so much. I want it all to stop. I'm so cold. 'Please Andy, I promise, I won't say anything.'

He hauls me in and out and I open my mouth. Water fills me. I stop squirming, Andy is in control. I want Evie.

Andy drags my head out one more time to hear my brother's insults, 'Do you know what Trevor does with the runts in Puss Cat's litter? He tosses them in a bag and throws them into the lake. That's what should have been done to you.'

He shoves me away from him. Free of Andy, I try to scramble out of the water, I want Evie. I can't get out, my legs crumple beneath me and I fall.

'Finn! Oh fuck! Finn, wake up. Oh shit, shit, shit! Don't you dare do this to me!'

I am on the bank and Andy's is shaking me. I feel sick and I want to go back to sleep. Why doesn't he just leave me? 'I want Evie, where's Evie?'

'Oh my God, thank you, God. Thank you.' He pulls me up and holds me in a hug. 'I thought you were dead.'

'My arm, let go, you're hurting me. I want Evie.'

'God, you're a fucking ungrateful brat. I should have left you to drown.' He grips my arm squeezing it.

'Please Andy, let go. It hurts. Please let go.'

He squeezes it harder, 'I'll let go when you make me a promise.'

'My arm, please, yes.'

'Say you promise.'

'I promise. Please Andy, please let go.' I feel dizzy and I know I am going to be sick.

'Promise you will never say anything about this or about me and Jas.'

'OK.'

His grip tightens even more, 'Say 'I promise' or I'll fucking well make sure you don't ever come up for air, do you hear me, weirdo?'

'I promise.' I throw up over his top. Disgusted he lets go and I fall back onto the grass. I can hear Evie calling. I can hear her feet thundering towards me.

'Christ Andy, what happened? Is he OK?'

She has me in her arms, but I can't see her. There's blood in my eyes and I am shivering.

'Dunno. Honestly, I just saw him running past, next thing I know he's in the brook. Looks like he hit his head on a rock. Think he may have broken an arm too. Thank God I got to him in time. I tell you Evie, that fucker is not right in the head.'

'Call Dad.'

She is rocking me, softly murmuring, 'You'll be just fine, Baby, just fine.'

'I haven't got my mobile,' says Andy.

'Then run and get him, you twat.'

I hear him run back up the slope, calling out for Daddy.

'Can you tell me what happened, Sweetie? Did you fall?' He's not there to hear if I tell the truth but I promised. I could never break a promise. That would be wrong. I shake my head and cuddle Evie, her warm cardigan wrapped around me.

'It's all right, Sweetie, you'll be fine. You'll be just fine, I promise,' she says and I believe her.

FINN

Finn walked around the gravestones fingering the gold tag.
He had meant to throw it away on his bike ride back to the
cottage, but worried someone might find it, so he kept it.
Once back, there was still the risk Sophie might spot it in
the bin. He couldn't risk disposing it where there was even
the slightest possibility it could be found. He took it out of
his pocket and read it once more, *'If found please return
to owner, Miss C Fry.'* The hot sweat that had plagued him
since waking, flared through him again.

He headed to Eloise's bench and with the heel of his shoe
started to kick away some dirt. The ground was hard, and he
scarcely made an indentation.

'What you doing, lad? Are we looking for buried
treasure?'

Finn jumped, quickly thrusting the tag back into his
pocket. 'Er, no, not treasure. I thought I saw a snake, but it
was nothing.

They sat on the bench, Carl occasionally glancing at his
silent friend, while Finn agonised over how he would tell his
friend about his betrayal. In the playing field behind him, he
could hear girls squealing with laughter; mocking laughter,
manic laughter.

'You must leave. Get away from here. It's too dangerous
for you now.' There, he had said it.

Carl laughed. 'What? Oh God, if you mean my faux pas
with ASSU, that's all been sorted. I marry at the end of the
holiday. They won't bother me after that. I'll be the patriotic
Albian husband and step-father.'

Finn shook his head. 'Your sexuality was not the reason you were arrested. It was my fault and it's about to get a lot worse. Believe me Carl, you have to escape for your own safety.'

'I don't get you. What are you talking about?'

Finn perched on the edge of his bench and faced Carl. He was smiling, but behind those bright, mischievous eyes he knew so well, was a growing tinge of anxiety. Impatient to know the news, Carl held Finn's arm.

'Come on, you can't leave me hanging like that. That's the job of the Executioner General.' But his subsequent laugh did not hold its usual confidence. As Carl scrutinised Finn's expression so his own wry smile evaporated. 'Why do I need to be scared, Finn? What's happened?'

The betrayal needed to be completed. It was Carl's right to know the truth.

'Catherine Fry, the Commandant's daughter, she did this to you.' Finn waved at Carl's face. 'She's mad, I didn't want to be her plaything, so she attacked my friend. Made sure I'd witness what she is capable of doing when I refused her demands. I'm sorry, I can't go on anymore. I have to get out and not come back.'

Carl appeared confused, 'I know, the head told us, remember, yesterday. You're going to the Commandant's Office. Isn't that what she wants? There's nothing to worry about.'

Frustrated, he pulled away and stood up, 'You don't get it, do you? I slept with her. Last night, I spent the night with her. I am a condemned man. Allowed to live while it pleases her, and then, disposal. An unwanted and broken toy. Anybody I love or care for, subject to her tyranny, a means to control me. I'm not coming back, Carl. I can't come back, this is it. When she realises it, she'll lash out? You'll be in her direct line of fire. Don't you see? You must escape, there's still a chance for you. You don't have a movement control order on you. Start a new life, get a new job. Find a new sham marriage. Please Carl, she will hurt you, and hurt you badly.'

Carl bent over, head in hands. 'You fucking idiot. What possessed you?' He looked back up. His face pale with the consequences of Finn's confession. 'Why did you have to tell me? If I don't report this, I will be guilty of the same crime by association. Everyone knows you only talk to me. They'll just assume. I'll be hanging from that gallows right next to you. You complete and utter fucking idiot.'

'But you can escape,' he said. Finn was certain there existed a possible get out, for both of them. 'Look, she can't tell anyone about last night, not yet. She's about to be married and the Major's family will annul the contract if they find out about us. No high-ranking officer will ever want her. Her future will be ruined. No, she'll be angry because of me. She wants to keep me but I'm going to escape. She won't have me, and she will lash out, targeting my friends. She knows we are close. You see, you've got to escape while you can.'

Carl sat in silence, contemplating his fate, periodically taking a sideways glance at Finn. After a while he sat up and asked, 'Are you going to try to kill yourself again?' He grabbed Finn's wrist and pushed up his sleeve. 'I see your good days and your bad days, and these scars area permanent reminder of where those bad days can take you, lad.'

'No, I thought about it, but no. I want to live, Carl. I want to go home, I want to see my parents, my sister, I want to see all my nieces and nephews. I am going home.' He grinned with the thought. 'We are going home. Sophie and me, together. We are going to escape.'

The man who had been his friend and confidant throughout his time at School House 87, embraced him, a reassuring bear hug that could only come from Carl.

'And you must go, both of you,' said Carl, releasing the

embrace. 'Escape while you can. Get out of this godforsaken country. Fuck, I would jump at the chance if I could. I'll miss you, you know; I'll miss you so fucking much. I've loved you like a brother. And it's because I love you, love you both, that you must take this chance. Stay safe, bro.'

SOPHIE

Sophie had been struggling to maintain her composure all morning, but the slam of the car door was the crack in her dam. She dropped into the chair by at the kitchen table, the pansy design of the oil cloth blurring under her falling tears. Their cottage, their home for nearly seventeen years, with each room holding a treasured tale telling of the lives of Sophie and Finn. He stood beside her, his hand on her shoulder. In the other hand, he held out his handkerchief, one she had embroidered with his initials years ago.

'Probably not a good idea to let the guard see you crying, we're supposed to be going on holiday, not a funeral.'

Sophie laughed and wiped away the tears. 'Give me a sec to wash my face. Why don't you take the bags out, before he thinks to come in?'

Refreshed and lipstick re-applied, Sophie left the cottage, locking the kitchen door behind her. She faced her garden, her beautiful garden, in glorious full bloom. That rose by the door, the woodland flowers on the bank and those steamer chairs under the apple trees. Sophie's garden, the child she nurtured with love. Her creation.

'We'll have another one someday. I promise you.' Finn took hold of her hand. 'You'll have another one soon.' He picked a rose bud from the bush by the door and threaded it through her top buttonhole. 'You are for my eyes only. No one can compare with you, my darling. I love you so much, Mrs Sheehan.'

He let go of her hand and walked out of the gate to the waiting car and to the Albian Elite Protection officer, who would be their driver for the long journey to AZ Eight.

Pretence is Not Enough

We deceive ourselves and believe the pretence of normality is enough. How can we be saved when we allow evil to wear that cloak of normality? We are guilty of creating our own monster. Only the bravest will uncloak that evil and fight that which seeks to destroy truth.

FINN

It was late when they arrived at the beach house. He had sat in silence throughout the journey. Lost in his thoughts, he was too afraid his voice might betray the fear lurking in his head.

Finn watched the countryside pass by from his seat in the back of the bullet proof car. What did the people on the street think as that car drove past? Its sinister blackness with its little flag displaying the Albian insignia flying from the grill. Would they see the physical emblem of their patriotic pride or a symbol of the daily oppression by the shadowed occupants hiding behind dark tinted glass? Except he wasn't an elite, he was the oppressed, he was their prisoner.

To break the journey, it had been pre-arranged they would stop at the Commandant's mansion in AZ Four for a late lunch. Tim and Michelle had travelled there separately and were waiting with Commandant Greyson when Sophie and Finn arrived. Sophie kissed her parents and Tim made the introductions.

'Commandant Greyson, may I introduce my daughter, Sophia Elle Smith and her husband, Michael.'

Finn, after being politely welcomed, sat in a side chair and remained quiet throughout the brief visit. He could feel his bangle lying heavily on top of his wrist. He nudged it back up his arm. He wanted it out of view despite the fact everyone knew what he was. His family chatted happily, the plans for the week, hopes for fine sailing weather. Neither Commandant Greyson nor his bored looking wife directed any conversation towards Finn. He was always the unwanted guest at the table.

The family travelled in convoy for the final leg of the journey, with outriders from the Albian Security Detail, ahead and to the rear of the limousines. New Albany affording them every protection from any further terrorist attacks.

By the time the sun was setting, they were crossing the border into AZ Eight, its exotic vegetation giving hint to its balmy weather. In the distance Camellia Sinensis covered the terraced hills. Further down the slopes, he saw the silhouetted watch towers and the high security fences. Labour camps to give the likes of Finn and Sophie their morning cup of tea. He turned away, ashamed. The deeper they drove into AZ Eight the brighter the towns became. Relaxed couples enjoyed al fresco dinners. Music blared out from clubs and bars. Black cars lined the curbs, their chauffeurs patiently waiting for their partying employers. In brightly lit shops, multiple assistants fawned over a solitary customer, tempted by the latest imported fashions. This was no place for ordinary patriots. These patriots were the beneficiaries, the chosen few. Leaving the bustle of the night life, they passed grand entrances to luxury villas, each surrounded by high walls and security lodges. The protection required by the cosseted occupants from their own invention.

He could smell the distinctive sea air coming into the car from the vents. Something he hadn't smelled since his last beach trip with Evie when he was twenty-one, almost exactly twenty years ago, happy memories he would soon repeat.

The car slowed, the outriders already dismounting their motorbike beside a large security gatehouse. Fiercely white lights shone down from metal towers behind the cream stucco walls. Running along the top, circles of razor wire glinted in the light. Two black uniformed guards approached Tim's car. Finn could see them joking with Tim's driver. One moved to Tim's opened window, nodding and shooting looks back to their car. The guards stepped aside and the wooden gates to the beach house slowly swung open. The car accelerated up the long drive and Finn expected theirs to follow suit, however their car only crept forward, stopping by the gatehouse. Their driver lowered the windows at the back allowing the guard to peer in. Sophie smiled and greeted the head at her side.

'Welcome back to St Maximilian's, ma'am.' said the guard.

Finn turn to the one waiting at his window, expecting a similar welcome.

'Wrist to the window and remain facing forward.' The guard's lip curled in disgust.

'Oh, you don't need to do that, do you?' Sophie was leaning across Finn. 'He's my husband, Minister Smith's son-in-law.'

'It says on my file he's a DIA with a Level One Controlled Movement Order.'

'A what?' replied Sophie.

Finn shrugged his shoulders, also confused.

'My husband's CMO has been suspended by order of the Interior Minister. It should say that on the file.'

'Hmm, I'll check.' The guard glared at Finn who was watching him from the opened window. 'I told you to face forward.' He pulled out a small pocket tablet. While his fingers swiped and tapped, Sophie unbuckled her seatbelt and squeezed the door handle to open the car door.

'Sorry, ma'am,' said their driver from the front, 'can't unlock the doors until I've been given the all clear.'

The security guard bent back down to her window. 'Your DIA's Area Zone Five CMO is suspended for seven days, however the Level One CMO has not. You must know about Level One CMO's? Came in after bombing in Bees' Bay last year.'

'No, I don't. Enlighten me.' The charm Sophie offered a couple of minutes earlier had disappeared. Finn recognised that sharp tone. She was irritated, teetering on the edge of angry and that guard's surliness was fanning the flame of her ever-shortening fuse.

'Well, ma'am, AZ Eight is a Level One security area. Non-domestic DIA's are prohibited from wandering unchecked. It would offer too many opportunities for terrorist activities. It's for our safety, ma'am. Surely you of all people can't object?'

Sophie's shoulders lifted and her chin jutted forward. Finn, realising she was about to vent her objections loudly, poked her gently in her ribs to catch her attention and with an almost imperceptible shake of his head warned her against arguing. She got the message and threw herself back into her seat.

'Absolutely, no, sorry, it's been a long journey,' she said with bitterness.

'Not at all ma'am. Always happy to help.' He smiled at Sophie, before returning his attention to Finn. 'Bangle!'

Finn put his arm out of the window. He was always their prisoner, no matter what.

With the drivers and personal bodyguards retired to the guards' house in the garden, the family were able to slump into the comfy chairs and relish the heightened privacy of an Albian Government property. AZ Eight was as popular with ASSU as it was the elite, and the last thing an Albian spy wanted while on holiday, was for another spy to be watching and listening.

Tim let out a sigh of relief. 'At last, I know it's late but who's up for some wine? I asked that there should be a couple of crates brought down first. We are going to enjoy this week.' He reached up for his wife's hand, 'A holiday to remember. Much better idea than a party don't you think, darling?'

'If you say so, but the September party is still happening.' Michelle wedged herself in next to her husband.

Finn watched his in-laws kiss, relaxed in each other's company. Michelle had no idea what was going to happen that week. She would lose her daughter, and in all likelihood, she and her husband would be arrested for treason. Her blissful life would be over. Painful reality was about to set foot in Michelle's home.

'Do you want some tart?'

Finn turned to his wife who was helping herself to the apple pie. 'No, thank you, I'm not hungry.'

'Are you sure? You hardly ate anything at lunch. Why don't you at least have a thin slice? It looks delicious.' She had picked up a plate expecting a change of heart.

'No, I'm sure.' Finn got off the sofa and headed to the door. 'I'm rather tired, I think I might go to bed.'

Sophie put down her plate and joined him at the door, kissing him goodnight, she held him close and whispered in his ear, 'It will be OK, darling, trust me. We will be just fine.'

SOPHIE

Michelle went up shortly after Finn, leaving the father and daughter alone in front of the fire, warming crystal goblets of cognac with their palms. Sophie had been irked by the incident with the guard and was determined to say something to her dad. He was lost inside the swirling of amber liquid like a fairground fortune teller delving inside the crystal for the answers to impossible questions.

'Dad?'

'Hmm, what darling?'

'If Finn is under a Level One Order, won't that make things difficult.'

'Oh, yes, sorry, I should have warned you.' He finished the drink and put the glass down before continuing. 'It was a stipulation of the Interior Ministry. I tried to get it removed but they insisted. It was that or not allow him out of AZ Five, which would have definitely made things difficult. And you won't need to leave the grounds, so don't worry.'

'I suppose, but it would be good if they could at least treat Finn with some dignity, you should have seen that guard's face. I just wanted to slap him.'

'I don't suggest you do that, it wouldn't be helpful, but I'll have a word with them and maybe get that guard transferred to night security.'

'Yeah, that would be good.' Sophie chuckled, pleased that there were still some advantages to being the daughter of an elite.

He reached into the inside pocket of his jacket to retrieve a small envelope. 'I have something for you.'

She took it, examining the postmark. It was unfamiliar. 'Do we know anyone in AZ Seven?'

Tim shook his head. 'No, nobody you know. You should open it.'

She opened the envelope and took out the short note.

* * *

'Dearest Tim, Michelle, Sophie and Finn,

Wishing Tim all the best for his birthday. We are sorry we will not be able to attend the party in September, but hope your holiday is everything you wish it to be.

All our love

Angus and Caroline'

* * *

She recognised the handwriting instantly. Decades of birthday cards and loving notes when she was away. Anna and Christopher were safe. Sophie returned the message to her father. He left his seat to squat in front of the open fire, stabbing the burning logs with the poker. Some embers flew up like tiny fireflies. In the light of the flames, her father seemed to lose his wrinkles, and she saw the rejuvenated father of her childhood. He held the envelope and card in a flame waiting for it to catch light, dropping it into the fire only after the words had disappeared behind a charred veneer. He returned to Sophie, sucking his burnt fingers.

'Who were the bodies?'

'I don't know. They were already dead, there was nothing we could do for their poor souls, but they allowed Christopher

461

and Anna to get to the border to escape. The smuggler was to post this note only after he had seen them across.'

'Will we be using dead DIAs again? How did you get them here?' Sophie was both excited at the prospect of freedom but equally disgusted by how easily she accepted other people's death to achieve her goal.

'No, it wouldn't work again, they'd be suspicious. Tomorrow you are going to teach Finn to sail.'

Michelle joined Sophie on the terrace and handed her daughter a steaming cup of hot chocolate.

'Looks like no-one could sleep,' said Sophie, warming her hands against the cup and blowing the milky froth to one side.

'Hardly surprising, why would you want to sleep when there's all this beauty to admire? I had forgotten how much I love this place.' Michelle made herself comfortable on the lounger next to Sophie.

The view was stunning. Sophie watched the birds dart to and fro from the nests in the cliff above the cove. The earth was rich with iron. That mineral, along with the morning light, making the cliffs glow blood red. Below, lay the little cove. It was shingle rather than sand and as the sea lapped onto the shore, the tiny stones rang out their own peculiar song. Sights and sounds of a happy childhood.

'Where's your dad?'

'Down on the beach getting the boat out. Finn's with him. I'm supposed to be taking him out sailing later.'

'He's very quiet at the moment, is everything alright?' Michelle was running her finger around the rim of the cup, collecting the froth before sucking on her finger.

'Mum, he's always been quiet. He's fine, there's nothing wrong.'

She pulled her finger out. 'Now, why don't I believe you?' Her accusatory finger pointed towards Sophie. 'What were those pills you were giving him this morning?'

Sophie had intended to stop the charade as soon as they arrived, but the incident with the guard made him so uncomfortable and anxious. It was ridiculous, she knew that, but also given his strange behaviour over the previous few days, it didn't seem wise to admit he had been taking multivitamins for the past fortnight.

'They're vitamin pills, Henry recommended them after he was ill, he just hasn't stopped taking them.'

'And how is Henry?'

There was something in the way she said it that made Sophie's cheeks redden.

'Does Finn know, is that the problem?'

Sophie decided there was no point lying anymore. These would be her last days with her mother. 'No, I lied to him. He has found out I was seeing Henry before I met him. I was a teenager, away from home. I made a mistake.'

'I knew you were sleeping with someone back then; I thought it may have been Henry. You were besotted with him when we came up to visit. To be honest I was cross, I wanted to bring you home, but your father said we shouldn't interfere. Next thing I know you're engaged to Finn. What happened?'

'Henry wasn't right for me, we didn't share the same views, or hopes for the future. He would have stopped me working. All I ever wanted to be was a doctor, but that path was blocked by our own dear government, the closest I could get was being a nurse. I wasn't about to let someone else steal that from me too. Finn came into my life just when I needed a man like him. Gentle, kind and who understood I needed to work too.'

'You work with Henry, what are you going to say if Finn finds out you lied?'

Sophie stopped admiring the view and turned to face her mother. With her eyes narrowing in anger, she hissed back, 'I supposed you are itching to tell him, just like you told him about the Commandant?'

She denied her daughter's accusation, huffily turning her back on Sophie. 'He must have heard it from someone else, because it definitely wasn't me.'

Certain her mother was to blame, Sophie decided not to pursue the matter. In her heightened emotional state, she feared she'd make a mistake and it wasn't worth the risk.

'I'm going to find the boys,' she said, leaving Michelle to stew on the terrace.

The little boat was already moored on the east side of the cove. Steps from the house brought Sophie directly to the wooden pier. Her father and Finn stood next to each other, hands on hips, staring down at the boat, Evolo. Next to it bobbed another, even smaller boat.

'Hello darling, just trying to convince Finn that this little boat won't sink. He's not so sure.'

'Who does the other boat belong to, I don't remember it?' asked Sophie as she gave her dad a hug and Finn a kiss.

'The guards will use it. They won't let you two go out alone. Another stipulation of the CMO, apparently.'

Sophie took hold of Finn's hand. It was cold.

'Don't worry I picked these two guards myself. They have been told to give you two some space.' Throwing his arms over the pair, Tim squeezed them in his embrace.

She pressed her head against her father's chest. 'Thanks Dad. It's going to be such a gorgeous day.' She pointed to a small island in the distance. 'Do you see that little island over there?'

'I do see something. Not sure you can describe a big rock as an island.'

Sophie elbowed her husband. 'That big rock has a stunning beach which is completely private.' She winked at him but standing at the end of the pier were the two bodyguards. Thoughts of romance and passion would have to wait until they had escaped New Albany's censure. 'Really darling, it will be great. We might have to row a bit, there's hardly any wind today, but once we are clear of the cove it will pick up and you'll understand why I love it so much. No one can keep up with me, you'll see.'

'She did love her sailing when she was younger, Finn.' said Tim. 'Honestly, there were times I was tempted to change her name to Stephen Smith and let her enter the sailing competitions. She would have beaten those amateurs, no trouble.' He gave her another hug full of paternal pride.

'Yeah, well I'm a girl, so no competitions for me.' She sighed and returned her attention to Finn. 'There are a couple of life jackets, so you'll be perfectly safe. I promise.'

Hopeful he would trust her ability and she was finally rewarded with a smile. 'OK, but only because you promised.'

The afternoon was hot with the lightest of breeze, but enough to fill the sail. The boat was designed to be handled by a single person, so she instructed him to enjoy being on the water without getting too wet. His lesson could start later. Taking her eyes off the destination for a moment, she saw him with his eyes closed and his face tipped sunwards. Finn appeared uncharacteristically relaxed, probably due to the fact he couldn't see anything, having left his glasses behind, just in case.

Sophie controlled the sail, occasionally telling him to move to the other side of the boat. It took an hour to get to the little island. They rowed up onto the beach and laid out their picnic rug on the white sand, beneath the shade of a large boulder. In the distance they could see the bodyguards. Fortunately, it looked like the guards had heeded Tim's advice and were eating the picnic lunch on their boat, but close enough to continue their surveillance of Finn and Sophie. Always visible, always watched.

For over an hour the couple were content to lie on the blanket, eating and drinking. Finn lay his head on Sophie's stomach, peacefully dozing while she tenderly caressed his head, her fingers combing through his hair. For a moment she even convinced herself that they were a normal couple enjoying a beach holiday. With that happy thought wandering around her head, Sophie closed her eyes and fell asleep.

The late afternoon brought with it a drop in temperature and the clear blue sky had disappeared behind clouds. It was Sophie that woke first, she gently nudged Finn. 'We ought to head back, this sort of weather change happens frequently around here. You think it is going to be fine, then it all changes. It can be nasty at times.'

'Sounds like my life.'

They packed up and pushed the boat into the water. The onshore wind was blowing them back towards the cove, it wouldn't take them as long to return to the pier.

Finn was gazing into the distance. Sophie wondered what must be going through his mind. The people beyond that horizon, probably.

'Finn?'

'Yes?' he mimicked back her questioning voice.

'You know those pills?'

'The sleeping pills or the antidepressants?'

'The antidepressants, well you see, and don't be angry, I was desperate, I thought it would help, but, well they're not.'

'Not what?'

'They're not antidepressants, they're multivitamins.'

'Yeah, I know.'

'You do? How?'

'Lack of side effects. I have always reacted badly. At first, I thought it must be some miracle cure, but this is New Albany, keeping up to date with scientific progress is not their favoured position. Why would they invest in drugs when they think we make it all up? Just being dramatic, as your mother would say.'

Sophie shrugged in agreement. 'Logical I suppose.'

'I wasn't one hundred percent certain, but with everything else you said, I realised I needed to pretend again so we could get here and have a chance of escape. Letting you believe that I was starting to feel better was part of that plan. I'm good at make believe. Perhaps I should have been an actor.'

Sophie laughed. 'No, I don't think that would have been the profession for you darling.'

'Oh, I don't know, my parents, schoolteachers, therapists, psychologists, all of them were subject to my bouts of make believe. Tell them what they want to hear, and I'd be allowed to go out and amuse myself.'

'So, are you angry with me for deceiving you?'

'Depends, if that is the only thing you are deceiving me with?' Finn had turned to look back at her.

Sophie lost concentration, letting go of the tiller. 'Damn it.'

'Well?'

She regained control but did not look up. 'No Finn, there is nothing going on between Henry and me, if that's your question. I've told you already. You're just not yourself at the moment, we both know this happens and when I get you back to your parents, you'll be able to get proper treatment. All this Henry stuff, it's just a symptom of your illness. That's all.'

'If you say so.' Finn stretched his arm out to run it through the water, pulling his hand back suddenly after touching it. 'Christ, I didn't expect the water to be so cold here.'

'Only because you're not used to it. It can make you feel alive, swimming in these waters. I remember coming out here with Dad. He'd take the boat and I'd throw myself off the side to swim. I loved those days so much. Everything seemed possible.'

'Didn't you worry about drowning?'

'It didn't even cross my mind.'

'I wasn't intending to drown myself that other night, you know. I was curious, that's all.'

'Somehow, I don't think it was curiosity, was it?'

'Maybe not.' He crunched up in his seat, his toes tapping. 'It's just, well I'm not sure what I wanted. Maybe I wanted to feel something other than fear. I wanted to remember what it felt like to be so cold that your entire body goes numb.'

'And so you thought you'd throw yourself into a fast-flowing river when you can't swim. Well I think we can agree that is probably one of the dumbest ideas you've ever had.'

'What do you think it's like, drowning I mean? Do you really think you see your whole life flash by? Everyone you have ever known, in front of you, even for the briefest of seconds? Do you think I would have seen Evie again?'

Sophie was concentrating on the boat and not really listening to Finn. 'Don't know, you're going to have to change sides. Watch the picnic basket.'

The boom swung across and he slipped under to the other side, carefully avoiding the basket. He was watching the accompanying boat with the guards trailing behind them. 'I know why I have this new CMO, but you'd think they'd leave us alone out here on the water. I'm hardly a risk to the public out here.'

'Oh, I suppose they are being extra careful, what with the terrorist attack on Dad, and all that. Dad did try and get it removed but the Ministry insisted.'

'Except there wasn't a terrorist attack. It was fake wasn't it?'

'Um, what? OK, yes, how did you guess?'

'I may be mildly insane, but I'm not stupid. If we manage to escape, then your father will likely be under suspicion, putting Christopher and Anna at risk. He'd want them safe first.'

'He thought if there was a threat against him it would make it easier to convince the authorities that our disappearance was terror related and not a case of a DIA and his wife sailing over the horizon.

'Especially given this DIA can't even swim.'

'No, especially given that.'

Sophie remained silent, thinking how they would possibly escape. It seemed crazy that it involved boats and water. She had to trust her father that there was a plan.

'Christopher and Anna are safe, that's all we need to know. As for you swimming to safety, that is the worst plan imaginable. That really is insane. These waters are freezing. You'd be dead in minutes. No, that cannot be the plan. Can you cross over again?'

Sophie was unsure what happened next, whether he tripped or went over on purpose. All she knew was one minute he was in the boat, the next he was in the water. Panic filled her, quickly followed by instinct. She searched over the side to see where he had gone and spotted him about ten metres from the boat, the life jacket keeping him afloat. He was thrashing about. Sophie dived in. The shock of the cold made her gasp. It had been a very long time since she had swum in these waters. Once she got her bearings, she headed towards Finn.

'I got you, it's OK. You need to calm down, Finn. Finn, listen to me, you're safe.' Afraid he was going into shock, she waved frantically at the bodyguards' boat. 'It's OK, Finn. We're going to get you out. Finn? Speak to me Finn?'

'Fr..fr..fr..frigging freezing.'

The afternoon clouds had cleared as quickly as they had arrived. Sophie joined her father on the terrace to watch the sun set behind the cliffs. Dusky pink grass waved along the cliff edge, like gaudy fringing on a little girl's party dress. Snuggled under a soft blanket on the lounger she took the glass of wine from her dad's hand.

'Shall I fetch the bottle then?'

'Yeah, it's good stuff.'

'So, how's Finn?' He topped up her glass and filled another for himself.

'I left him watching a daft comedy in the sitting room. Anything to distract him from boats and water.'

'Probably for the best. Where did Mum go?'

'The housekeeper's about to leave and she wanted to talk about tomorrow's dinner. Does she know?' Sophie asked, unable to look up from her wine.

'No, I couldn't tell her. You know, the woman you see today is very different to the girl I married. She was so angry about the injustice back then, but New Albany has become a religion to her now. A Damascene conversion, you might say. She didn't see New Albany as an opportunity back then. But I said it would be the new Utopia, the example to other nations of how to do things differently. I thought we would have a fairer, kinder world. I was deceived just like so many. I thought we could change things from the inside, but I became just another cog, wound up to carry out other peoples' deeds. I am Faust to New Albany's Mephistopheles. But after you were born, your mother became part of the cult, blind to everything around her. Said it was to ensure your protection from the terrorists, but I don't know. Your mum loves you, but maybe she loves New Albany more.'

Sophie thought back to her infant days, when her mother was fun. How she'd run around the garden, pretending to be an injured elf so Sophie, the fairy doctor, could fix her again. And laughing with Anna, always smiling and laughing with Anna. That never changed. Why couldn't she love her as much as she loved Anna? Her best friend, closer to her mother than her own daughter.

'Does she know Anna is safe?'

'No, I couldn't risk it. To her Anna is dead. I honestly thought she would die of a broken heart. The doctor gave her something to calm her down. He can usually get his hands on something to make her happy, make her sleep, make her want to live another day longer. She has far more in common with Finn than she would like to admit.'

'Odd how a doctor can prescribe all sorts of drugs to Mum, but then again she's a patriot. A true Albian. Finn is condemned to suffer, all because of political prejudice. It's so stupid, so illogical.'

Tim laughed, but it was tainted with sadness. 'My dear girl, logic will not be found in the corridors of power. It is the mortal enemy of authority.'

'Well that's true.' She held out her glass for a refill. Her father duly obliged.

'Dad?'

'Yes, dear.'

'Why didn't you have more children? I was happy to be

your only one, but I did wonder why you didn't want more?'

'Just one of those things I suppose. Your mum found pregnancy difficult, but we love you beyond words. We just didn't want to risk having any more.'

Sophie got onto her father's chair to cuddle him.

'I'm glad, that way I haven't had to share you. You've been all mine!'

Tim put his arm around his daughter to bring her in close, his heartbeat evident on her cheek. The pain was almost too much to bear. She hugged him even more tightly, sensing his whispering lips on her head in response, 'I received the message just before we left. The escape route is open. It will be the day after tomorrow.'

Sophie pulled back. He seemed so calm, while she was trying to contain the bag of nerves that was once her stomach. 'How? Where?'

'You and Finn are getting back into the boat. Do you remember Angel Cave about four miles to the west of here?'

'Sort of, you took me when I was little, you wouldn't let me steer, too many rocks you said.'

'It is dangerous, and you'll have to keep your wits about you. The weather is going to change in the late afternoon, they told me we could expect a severe storm, but the earlier part of the day will be perfect to go sailing again. You will need to time it carefully. Get to the rocks before the worst of the storm starts, but it needs to be fairly choppy. You must give the impression of getting into trouble, get the boat to the rocks. Once you get to Two Fingers, you'll need to jump out and swim through to the cave. They will find you there.'

'What about the guards? We'll need to distract them somehow.'

'It seems we've been fortunate with a pair of landlubber guards. They'll never keep up with you. By the time they get to the boat and raise the alarm, the storm should be raging enough to make a rescue difficult.'

Sophie was horrified. The plan was worse than she thought. 'Are you crazy? You are talking about suicide. If I am very lucky, I might make it, but what about Finn. He'll die for sure. Hasn't today shown you, he can't do it. How on earth is he supposed to swim to a cave in a storm? No, it's too dangerous, there has to be another way. He'll die.'

'He will certainly die if he stays. When it comes to survival, we sometimes do things we never thought possible. It's his only chance. But you must promise me one thing. Whatever happens, you keep swimming. You must get to that cave and you have to escape, with or without Finn.'

Sophie was shaking her head, incredulous at the suicidal plan. 'No, Dad, it's too dangerous, I'm not sure I can do it.'

'You must. I love you with every fibre of my being, you're the only good thing in my life. Do you think I'd put you in extreme danger if I thought staying here were safer? No, this is your only chance to live. Stay and they will kill you. Promise me you'll keep swimming, no matter what.'

She could see the sadness in her father's eyes. 'I promise, Daddy.'

Getting Finn to agree to go back into the boat was harder than she had expected. After a day of stubbornness, sulks and frustration, Sophie stormed off to swim out her anger. When she returned, an apologetic Finn was sitting on the beach holding up a towel. He wrapped her up, kissing her as she cuddled him for warmth.

'Sorry about earlier, the thought of getting into that boat again fills me with terror. I just don't think I can do it. You understand, don't you?'

Finn moved to get up. Looking around she saw her bodyguard was already sauntering back to the guest house. 'Stay awhile,' she said, tugging him back down onto the shingle.

'As long as you want me.' He kissed her salty neck.

'I love you, you know that don't you?'

'Of course, an—'

She stopped him talking with a finger to his lips.

'I wouldn't ask you to do this if we had another option.'

'Do what?' His hug loosened and she saw uncertainty cloud his eyes.

'Look, either we stay here, and you die, or we get back in the boat for a chance of survival. This isn't me saying you'll get used to it and I promise if we get out, I will never make you sail again. Please, Finn, we have no other alternative. This is our last and only chance to escape.'

He was smiling again, almost laughing. His arms tightened around her.

'It had to be a watery escape, didn't it? Why couldn't your dad have picked some barbarous smugglers instead!'

'Because that option wasn't available. You'll just have to put up with your barbarous wife.'

'I can think of lots of reasons to put up with you.'

Sophie pushed him back onto the shingle to sit astride him. Not caring who was watching, she knew there was enjoyment to be had in the last few hours of blind optimism and blissful ignorance.

The beach house terrace glowed orange with early sunshine. Out on the water, Sophie saw Evolo, the breeze bringing her back to the pier. Her father had always enjoyed early morning sailing trips and when she was young, they would

474

get up before dawn, armed with blankets and flasks of hot drinks. A couple of bars of chocolate were always hidden in her father's jacket. Then they'd escape, just the two of them. Alone on the water, listening to the symphony of nature crescendoing with the sunrise. A memory that filled her at once with both joy and intense sadness. She didn't want to think what would happen to her parents after their escape. It would be better to create her own happy story than imagine the likely outcome. In her fairy tale, Tim would continue to sail out on Evolo, contemplating the distant horizon and imagine his daughter and unseen grandchildren, safe and fulfilled just beyond his limited view.

He must have seen her on the terrace and called up to her as he tied up the boat. Sophie watched as one of his bodyguards left their boat to help her dad. She felt irritated for her father, his independence already being eroded, however kindly meant by the guard.

Her father joined her on the terrace, and she wished him a happy birthday, kissing his cheek.

'I sincerely hope you are right. I want this to be the happiest birthday of my life,' he replied returning her kiss.

'There you are!'

The father and daughter turned to see Michelle, champagne bottle in hand. 'Happy Birthday, darling. You left before I woke.'

The Smith family returned to the house, hand in hand to the table laid out for a champagne birthday breakfast.

Sophie noticed Finn's reluctance to drink the champagne, he was nervous, and so was she. Conversations were going on around her, but she could only catch the occasional word, her brain mentally rehearsing what she would need to do, how and when.

'Sophia, did you hear me?'

She looked up. Her mother was staring straight at her. 'Sorry, what?'

'I said, there might be a storm later, the cook told me. Perhaps you should put off your trip until another day. Given what happened to poor Finn last time, a sailing trip in a storm will definitely put him off for life.' She giggled, before refilling her glass. 'What do you say Finn? Do you fancy sailing in a storm?'

'I… it's not…'

'Leave him alone, Michelle.' Tim's voice was firmer than usual. 'There isn't going to be a storm and you will be perfectly safe, Finn. You need to do this. Believe me it will be good for you.'

Finn smiled at his father-in-law but made no reply.

'I've asked the housekeeper to prepare a special picnic. Plenty of wine for the two of you and the guards too. They should be allowed to celebrate as well,' he said rising from the table.

Sophie wondered if her mother noticed the croak in her husband's voice, the tears waiting on his lower eyelash, or the tremble in his hand as he laid it on Sophie's shoulder, before leaving the room.

The sky was crystal-clear when they departed from the little pier. Her father waved her off while her mother sunbathed on the beach. She blew them both a kiss. Normality, always normality. To do otherwise would be to court suspicion. New Albian normality, breaking a little girl's heart.

Beyond the small island, the wind began to pick up strength. Clouds were forming on the horizon.

'I hope you know what you are doing. It looks like it might get rough,' said Finn.

476

'It is going to get very rough with any luck. I see the guards have already started on the wine.'

Finn threw a glance back towards the bodyguards' boat. One of them had his head over the side. 'What did your father give them?'

'A bottle of peach liqueur and two bottles of elderflower wine with some extra bite from my pharmacy.'

'Oh, was he trying to kill them?'

'It might be useful, but it will make them a bit unwell, shall we say!'

Nearing the group of rocks out towards the west, the increased swell made the boat sway. Sophie remained focused on her task, but noticed Finn had begun to pale, unused to the movement beneath him.

'Look out towards the horizon, it will help.'

'That's not the problem, it's this escape. I'm not sure I can do it, Sophie.'

Horrified, Sophie glared at her husband. It was their only option, he must not give in. Not when they were so close. 'Finn, we'll be fine, just hang onto that thought. We will make it.'

'What if you get hurt, or worse? I can't let you get hurt.'

'We're already hurt, we're damaged goods. Returning to our old life isn't going to happen, Finn. We escape together, or we die together. This is it, judgement day.'

Evolo bounced over the growing waves. Its occupants silent. She watched her husband, his hand clinging onto the side. The boat needed her attention, but she was certain she saw him drop something into the water. 'What was that?'

'Sorry?' He twisted to look at her.

'That thing you had in your hand, you threw it into the water. What was it?'

'Oh that. Nothing really. Just a little leaving gift from

teaching, I don't want to be reminded of life here, not once we are back home, so I thought, let the sea have it.'

'I think that's the best place for it.'

The storm was heading in from the West and the dark purple sky merged with the horizon. There was little time left.

'Finn, grab my life jacket, would you? It's in the basket over there and get a knife. I want you to cut one of the ties. Not all the way through, just enough so I can rip it off once I'm safe. They might think I lost it caught on a rock.'

Finn did as he was asked and handed it to Sophie. Slipping the jacket on, she noticed him cutting the ties on the one he was wearing. 'Stop it! You need yours, otherwise you'll drown. It's too dangerous.'

Finn ignored her, continuing to cut his tie. 'We have to convince the guards that we've drowned, don't we?'

'Yes, we need to make it appear we have, but it would be preferable if we didn't actually drown. You can't swim. You need the life jacket. This isn't up for discussion.'

'I can swim, I just don't like swimming.'

'Really? I think you need to explain that one.'

'It's another of those "It will be good for you!", I hated it then and I hate it now.'

'And the other day? Are you saying you were faking?'

Finn grinned at her. 'Didn't I say I should have been an actor. It was cold though, that wasn't an act.'

'I don't understand, why keep it a secret?'

'That was your dad's idea. When I was staying at your parents, your dad kept on asking me about school and sports, what I played, teams and stuff. It was odd, but no odder than him insisting I stayed behind to recover. Have to say your mum wasn't thrilled.'

'Yeah, well that's Mum for you. What else?'

'That was it really, he was mostly interested to find out

about me being in the swimming team.'

'The swimming team?' Sophie was shocked by Finn's admission.

'Actually won some medals too. As I said, falling into the sea was your dad's plan. He said it was important that everyone should be convinced about my inability to swim. I never asked him why.'

Sophie remained silent, unresponsive to his admission. After a few minutes she looked up. 'And the river, was that all an act too?'

Finn turned away from her before speaking, 'No, like I said before, I wanted to numb the pain. I wasn't thinking straight. I don't believe I wanted to die, but even good swimmers drown sometimes. Isn't this what it's all about. A tragic accident. You are going to try to save me, but it will be too late. We'll just be two more bodies that get whisked away by the currents and washed up on the shores of the real world.'

'We've got to make this work, Finn. I don't think I can live without you. Do you understand? We have to make it to safety.'

The grey clouds were rolling into place above them. Sophie had interspersed her sleepless night praying for the fine weather to turn and for once, her prayers were being answered. A growing squall splattered their faces, heralding the storm. By the time they got to the rocks, controlling the boat had become difficult. It would be impossible to swim to safety if they didn't make their escape soon. The other boat was a considerable distance behind them. Sophie's sailing expertise, added to the guards' amateur efforts to control their own boat, had given Evolo the advantage. It was the snatch at hope that Sophie was after. She managed to manoeuvre the little boat behind a group of rocks, and once out of sight of the guards, she tried to get as close to the cave as possible. The opening was wide, but she remembered that the roof of the cave entrance was low. By the time the gale was lifting the waves up high, the mouth of the cave would be virtually invisible, especially for those guards unaccustomed to the area.

'Do you see those two stacks over there?' Sophie shouted to Finn, pointing to a pair of rocks that stood tall and thin. 'You need to swim between them, then you will see the entrance to the cave ahead. It's not far. Go to the very back where there is a little beach, that's where they will find us.'

He nodded, blew her a kiss, then mouthed, 'I love you.'

They hurled themselves to the side of Evolo, deliberately making it tip. The sail touched the water and as one, they jumped into the sea. Finn's new glasses flew off his face and disappeared below the surface.

Tentacles of rope twirled around Sophie's arms and legs, trapping her. Sustained by the occasional gasp of air, she untangled herself and once released, powered away from Evolo.

Floating on the surface like driftwood, she rose and fell with the swell. With each rise she scanned the water, turning her head side to side, searching for his yellow life jacket. And there he was, just a few metres away, clearly visible within the murkiness of the turbulent sea. Sophie tugged at her jacket snapping the ties, freeing her to dive below the surface. Her fingers were outstretched to capture him and lead him to safety. With each kick she expected to touch him, but the current was dragging her back. She kicked harder.

In among the rocks, the waves had started to break over her, buffeting and tossing her one way then the next. Her vision blurred with salty foam. She dived under again, forcing her eyes open, only to see green-grey bubbles. She could feel her body freezing with every moment spent in the water. It was no good, Sophie was running out of breath and had to return to the surface. Two Fingers was just ahead. Another wave slapped her, knocking her sideways into a barnacle encrusted rock. The sharp edges sliced into her side, each wound smarting with brine. With weakening arms, she clambered onto the rock. Cold fingers and toes sought foot holds, gripping through adrenaline alone.

Above the maelstrom of the storm came a cry. Sophie risked craning her head away from the rock, hoping to catch a glimpse of Finn, but it was only a gull. How long had she been in the water and how much time was left before the guards would reach Two Fingers, ending any chance of escape? What if they had already found Finn? Sophie was within touching distance of the cave entrance, but she daren't let go. Not yet, not while there was even the slightest chance of spotting her husband. Her fingers struggled to stay inside the little crevasses. Every wave that slammed into her sucked her backwards, demanding she return to the depths along with the boat. Another wave struck her, harder, more determined than the others. The muscles in her fingers contracted to resist the pull. The force was too strong. Sliding down, her hands slapped at the rock, desperate to find any hollow, but it had lost all its cragginess. Underwater again she turned and twisted, unsure what was up and what was down. She was confused. She was cold. Heavy legs weighed her down and moving her arms required more effort than she could muster. The odds of reaching the beach were shortening with her dwindling strength.

Pain roused Sophie from increasing torpor as her back collided with another boulder. By some miracle the current had carried her onto the cave beach, its gritty sand rubbing into her sores. She pushed the palms of her hands on a flat rock, lifting her shoulders and head out of the shallows. It was so dark, she wondered if she were inside the cave at all. Sophie attempted to stand but collapsed back down, exhausted. Undeterred, she dug her elbows into the sand and commando crawled out of the sea.

'Finn, Finn are you there?' Only the waves replied. She pushed forward, grit embedding itself beneath her nails, calling and listening but there was nothing to hear except the wind.

Rain was filtering down from the cracks in the rocks above and landed where she sat cuddling her numb limbs. Sophie moved to the very back of the cave, bumping into a box, and realised it must have been the supplies left by her father on his early morning trips. She was in the right place. Fumbling inside, she felt for a blanket. Wrapped up but still shivering, she returned to the waters' edge to cling onto hope, but there was no sign of him. He was gone. She had failed him.

The waves taunted her from the entrance, its echoing noise berating her stupidity. Sophie covered her ears and resumed her mourning. She argued with herself, debating whether to even go on if it was without Finn. That promise made to her father seemed futile without her husband beside her. Sophie wailed out her sorrow against the deafening tempest, emptying herself of the agony within. Finn's long held desire for freedom had been granted. Once the storm had abated, she would swim back to the rocks and await rescue by Albian guards.

Weak splashes and indistinct moans came from the direction of the cave entrance. Whatever it was, it was getting closer. It could only be the guards, proving themselves to be more capable than anyone had imagined. Flashes of an Albian future edged her closer to the cave wall. Her parents could not and would not protect her liberty. To return to New Albany would be to imprison herself, just like all other

Albians. Her father was right. With the shadows surrounding her she made the decision to keep her promise. Sophie Smith would be free. Free to pursue her dreams, liberated and with autonomy over her own destiny. Crouching low behind a rock, Sophie held her breath and prayed that Finn's soul was watching over her.

'Soph, Soph, are you there?'

It was like an electric shock. Every hair on her body stood on end, paralysed both by fear and joy.

'Finn? Is that you?' she called back, her voice distorted and croaky.

'Yes.'

Sophie leapt from her hidden cover onto his collapsed body, babbling out her relief and happiness, all thoughts of caution abandoned. 'Finn! Oh God, you made it! You made it! We are going to be free. God, Finn, we've made it!'

All they needed to do was to stay quiet and wait for Tim's contacts to find them. They would come after the search had been called off for the night. Albian forces would not waste resources on a DIA and a nurse, regardless of who her father was. Their life together could finally begin.

Free of their wet clothes, the couple snuggled up inside more blankets, their cold bodies touching and warming each other up. It had been such a long time since Sophie had felt her husband's naked skin. Her head rested on his chest and she listened to his heartbeat.

'Am I still alive?' he laughed.

'I think so.' She kissed his chest. 'If not, I shall kiss you better. I'm a nurse, remember.' She kept on kissing him, moving from chest to neck to lips. Finn lifted her on to him. Neither could really see the other in the darkness, but they knew each other so well that it was of no consequence to them. They were together, they were alive, they were going to be free. They needed each other. His hands caressed her back and her fingers walked through his hair. She arched backwards when Finn's lips travelled across her skin. With each kiss her body was rediscovering the man she had lost. The noise from outside the cave muffled her joyous cries of passion driven through tenderness and enduring love. She loved him and he was loving her back. Nothing could compare to his love. Without him she was a mere human fulfilling a natural process, but with him, she was Sophie. She needed to be with him forever, for better for worse, for richer, for poorer, in sickness and in health. Sophie would obliterate all guilt through this ceaseless love.

Dressed in the warm, practical clothes provided, they devoured the food. Neither of them knew how long they would need to wait, but rescue would come. Sophie thought of her father, everything he had sacrificed for her. He was wrong, Hope was still at the bottom of Pandora's box. She was sure of it.

'My old glasses, your dad thinks of everything.' He put them on, 'Nope still can't see a thing, too damn dark.'

Sophie mockingly shushed him just as she would do with the small children in the surgery. 'It's only for a little bit longer, darling.'

'I can't wait to get back home, Soph. It's Evie's birthday next week, she'll be so surprised.'

It was Finn who heard them first, nudging Sophie. 'Someone's coming,' he whispered.

They peered into the distance, straining to listen to the voices, unsure whether the language was right, it was so hard to hear clearly. Finn stood up, just as Sophie remembered her father's words.

'They will be silent. You won't even know they've arrived.'

She shot her arm up to pull Finn back down, but it was too late, his accent proudly evident in every syllable called out, 'We're over here!'

A search light was directed to the back of the cave, bathing the couple in a dazzling light.

The dinghy arrived, silent as death and laden with soldiers bearing night vision goggles. All they found was an empty picnic box, a bag of wet clothes, a little box with a painted fairy and a dishevelled toy cat. They departed as silently as they arrived.

MICHELLE

Michelle stood on the terrace, her bare feet curling up from the bitter chill of the stone paving. Apart from her rising toes, the rest of her barely twitched. A gust of wind, the fading remnant of the previous night's storm, whipped her unkempt hair from her face, Mother Nature compelling her to bear witness. Her silk dressing gown flapped about her legs, so she grabbed the material and clutched it shut. She had done everything asked of her. She had been dutiful. She had fulfilled the promise. Once so beautiful, now she did her best to stay, if not a beauty, then at least handsome. Weekly appointments for hair and nails. Clothes that enhanced her toned and starved body, jewellery that underlined the sacrifices she made for her husband's career. But despite it all, there she was, standing, waiting, devoid of the adornments of privilege. The grey light allowed her to view the emerging cove, and in the distance, she could just about make out the ghostly black silhouettes of boats coming ashore. Waves broke on the shingle, like an orchestra of rain sticks, the unnerving composition disrupted by the dissonance of the male chorus shouting out instructions. Then she saw her. Her daughter, so little next to the guards. A constricting pain gripped her heart. She remembered that little child with fairy wings, running towards her, smiles lighting a cherubic face, her dark hair tousled by the sea air and that sweet voice calling across the cove, 'Can pixies live in the sea too, Mummy?'

Turns out they can't.

A guard grabbed her daughter's arm to help her out of

the boat. Michelle watched Sophie snatch it back and part of her soul died. The guard took it again, roughly this time, yanking her off the dinghy. Another two guards had come to join him, dragging Sophie's protesting body up the beach. Rising above the men's shouts, she heard her daughter cry out for Finn, swearing at the guards and fighting against their controlling grip.

Another dinghy came to the shore. He was in that one. Far calmer than Sophie. He wasn't protesting, it was as though he had already accepted his fate. The sun had just risen above the horizon. A glint of dawn light reflected off his glasses. Could he see her from down there? Would he even look up? Michelle looked across to her husband. When did his face become so wrinkled, so old? That mane of black hair, just thinning grey strands. He was sobbing. This was all his fault. The indulgent father. If she had relented and given him other children, would he have been stricter with Sophia? Would he have kept a tighter rein, stopped her reckless adventure? Kept her little pixie safe from the reality of their world?

Two of the guards were holding Sophie up. Her spindly legs buckling beneath her. A third guard clamped Sophie's head between his hands. He was a large heavy-set man. Michelle shivered, imagining the terror her daughter must be feeling with her head, so tiny, so delicate in that man's massive hands.

Finn was placed in front of his wife. His hands bound behind his back. If he said anything it was drowned out by the noisy guards. One of them pushed him down onto the beach forcing Finn to kneel before Sophie. He tilted his face up towards his wife. He had always been that gallant knight who swears undying allegiance to his lady.

Michelle didn't hear the solitary shot. It must have

487

happened, but her brain refused to register it. She only heard the blood curdling screams from her daughter, reverberating off the blood red cliffs surrounding the cove, echoing and prolonging the pain. The noise woke the roosting sea birds, their black silhouettes peppering the red of the dawn sky. After a while she realised someone was holding her arm. Looking to her left she saw her husband's tear stained face bringing her back to the terrace and to what had to happen next. She gave him no words of comfort, calmly repeating her old mantra, 'This is your fault, all your fault.'

A man behind Michelle placed his hand on her shoulder. He had been there all along, watching, checking that correct procedure was being followed. He had promised Michelle that the guards would be respectful. Sophia Elle would not be harmed. Taller than Finn and with his dark hair showing signs of age. He had an unnerving smile, insincerity mixed with sycophantic zeal.

'Don't worry, my men will deal with...' his arm waved towards the cove.

Michelle looked back to where he was pointing and saw her daughter collapsed on the beach. The trail of blood was glowing beneath the rising sun. It led away from Sophie and back to the corpse of her son-in-law. Guards were dragging him to the shoreline for disposal; no ceremony, no dignity, no respect.

Her arm was touched, and she looked back to the man beside her.

'It's time to leave now. Would the two of you like to travel in my car?'

She nodded and followed Commandant Fry back into the house.

A DISTANT CRY

'Come to me in the silence of the night;
Come in the speaking silence of a dream;
Come with soft rounded cheeks and eyes as bright
As sunlight on a stream;
Come back in tears,
O memory, hope, love of finished years.'

from 'Echo'

Christina Georgina Rossetti

Evie

You invade my thoughts. I am chopping vegetables for our evening meal, a mundane activity, but you don't care. I know it is all in my head, I know it is my imagination, but the need for it to be real makes me yearn for every second you interrupt my life.

There you are, across the island, eating chocolate cookies, with your mischievous smile reserved solely for me. You have that summer holiday glow about you. Tanned and carefree, your freckles highlighting your innocence. It's too painful. I squeeze my eyes shut, reluctantly forcing you away, before grief grabs me again. When I reopen them, it is to gaze upon the other loves of my life, Maya and Mikey discussing school and weekend plans. Cara, headphones firmly in place, locked in her own world, her feet keeping time to the unheard music. My precious wedding gifts. My constant reminder.

Mikey has more of Maya's colouring, but Cara, she is fairer, more like you. If only you could see them too. Everyone comments on their likeness, Mikey's mannerisms, his sensitivity and kindness. Cara's stubbornness, the cause of so many rows. She also has fiery passion. It reminds me of Andy. Then again maybe we all have a bit of Andy's fury in us too. Grandad Mike's genes run deep through all our veins.

You should see Mikey, he's so excited. He's off on his first residential, an adventure camp. Talking so frantically, all the while pushing his glasses up his nose. You'd always be doing that; poor optician, forever fixing your glasses. I'll take Mikey in tomorrow, get his glasses adjusted before his trip.

There's an old photograph of Grandad Mike on the island. Mikey has printed it off for a school project on ancestors. Grandad is smiling out of the picture directly at me. You don't remember him, do you? Mum always says that you and granddad seemed so alike. Maybe that picture is you, a traveller through time and space. A forty-one-year-old man lying on a beach, relaxed and happy with a battered book on your lap. Your fringe covers one of your eyes. Of course, your glasses have slipped down your nose, did I expect them to be anywhere else? You are lifting your hand, a well-practised movement, pushing up your specs and then, your fingers splay out, combing the lock of hair away from your face. You realise you are being watched and look up from your book to give me a smile and blow me a kiss.

My phone rings, it's Andy. Why is he ringing this evening? It's Tuesday, he never rings on a Tuesday.

Mum's not well again, a fall this time. Andy says I have to go home. Maya and Mikey are worried, so I tell them she'll recover, she has to. I don't tell them about the pain in my chest. The tightness that grips me, momentarily holding my lungs in a vice. It has happened before. And like Mum, I too will recover, I have to.

I am such a coward. I can't face the thought of going back. It is just about bearable here, but there, in Melborough? The ache in my chest intensifies with the reawakening of memories. Happy reminders that only bring despair.

Mikey no longer asks me about you, directing his questions to Maya instead. She says it upsets him when I cry. Cara rarely says anything, although she does have a picture of you, the one Dad took when you were on Cairn Top. She made the frame when she was six, purple feathers and smiley faces. Maya has suggested buying her a new frame, silver, like the one by our bed. Cara isn't keen, she thinks you'd prefer to be surrounded by googly-eyed smiles.

This is ridiculous, I return to preparing the vegetables. The surreal blade takes on the task, chopping away. Have I lost control? I watch it as it comes down onto me, slicing my skin and I hear a distant cry. Was that really me? I lift my finger to examine the wound. The blood flows freely out of the cut, rolling down and gathering at the base of my finger.

Mikey looks up, concern written across his young face.

'You OK, Mum?'

'Yes, Sweetie, no need to worry. I'll live.'

But I am transfixed by the blood. It slips off the tip of my finger, a fat tear, dropping onto my chest and staining my white blouse.

NEW
ALBANY

THE HOSTILE ENVIRONMENT

Faced with the dire prospect of living in a hostile, alien environment, we seek to distance ourselves through the unpleasant compromise of survival. But we are individuals within the greater body of existence and every decision, every choice, every compromise, must surely affect those of others and the direction of their solitary lives. The time has come to enter into the depths of our souls and touch the agony of hell. Compromise must stand aside. Our intelligence must be fashioned into swords for truth, and our perseverance, the shield against insults and falsehoods.

SOPHIE

It was a windowless box with four grey walls, grey floor, grey ceiling and grey door. An existence in permanent night, a perpetual nightmare, oblivious of the sunrise, ignorant of the sunset. Her days had no beginning and no end. A life on hold, a life in limbo, dependent on the whims of others.

Periodically she was blinded by the strip light above her head. Invisible faces watching her, judging her. The door would open, and a silent guard would bring her food and water. His task complete, her restricted world plunged back into darkness. Her fingers felt the ground for the plate and cup, which she propelled with meagre strength against the wall. Starvation, her route to salvation.

She mourned, she cried, she remembered and wept again. His DNA in the bloodstains on her blouse, her fingers gently locating each hardened spot of blood, his blood. Her husband's blood, all that was left of him for her to touch. Her face and hair harbouring his remains. He was there, still with her. She shut her eyes to visualise him before her, imagining his touch, his body on her, recalling with agonising pain their lovemaking in the cave. However hard she tried, reality thrust itself forward and there was only the beach and the shingle. Those tiny red glistening stones that became macabre ruby jewels at her feet. She longed to see Finn in her kitchen, in the garden, reading an essay, anything except that cove bathed in the red light of dawn. The guard held her head too firmly, obliging her to be a witness. Finn kept on repeating that he loved her. Her vision an explosion of blood. She reached out to touch him one more time. Even through that darkness, that memory persisted, the stones, sticky and wet with blood. She tried to defeat that memory by recalling the cave, her hands sinking through the cold grains as he made love to her. But those miniature stones had implanted themselves beneath her fingernails. Each as sharp as a knife. A constant reminder of love, a constant reminder of evil.

Sophie expected the same treatment as the Keeler girls. Dragged up to the house, she scanned the opened doors for her parents' bodies. There was nothing, nothing at all. She screamed out for them. Silence the only reply. Handcuffed and shackled, a patriot no more. She was Sophie, the saboteuse, the insurgent, a terrorist, an enemy of the state, the enemy of New Albany.

The light switched on and the door unclicked. The same guard entered. It was always the same guard, he never varied. The food was placed next to her. The same food with each visit. Nothing to distinguish whether it was breakfast, lunch or dinner. She couldn't even be sure if they were brought at regular intervals. This time he didn't leave. He slid the gun off his shoulder and pointed the barrel at her. The tip flicking between the food and her chest, as though being asked to choose. She had chosen. Sophie stared back at the guard, willing him to shoot. Starvation or execution, the destination remained the same. It was the guard who blinked first. Picking up the untouched food and drink, he left the cell. Sophie was free to sink back into her despair.

She was not free for long. The light was blinding her within moments. Three silent guards entered the cell. The largest of the three lifted her off the floor, the second guard pulled her head back by her hair, the fingers of his right hand pushing into her mouth, forcing it open, making her gag, while the third guard poured a liquid down her throat. Sophie tried to close her mouth, shaking her head. The first guard pinched her nose shut. She gasped as the cold liquid filled her throat. The vile poisonous water preventing her desire for death. They wanted her alive. Salvation through starvation had been stolen from her. Death denied.

And so it continued, the blinding light, the three guards, the ice-cold water poured into her weakening body. With each visit so her fight diminished. Strength and memories being flushed away from her.

She was woken by the sound of metal falling onto the hard floor. Her wedding band abandoning her frail body. Sophie scrambled to her knees, scrabbling in the darkness until she was reunited with the hard coldness of the gold band. Guiding it back onto her finger, she was Mrs Sheehan again. Sophie bent over her ring finger, determined to make her fragile body hold onto the symbol of their marriage.

The strip light above her head no longer disturbed her thoughts. The Trappist guards were just shadows. The cold water was replaced with a thick creamy liquid, forced into her. Throughout it all, Sophie struggled to hold on to remembered conversations with Finn, listening to his silent replies in her head. Unaware of the stench of the cell, she was lying in the shade of the apple trees, the air sweet with the scent of a multitude of flowers from her fertile garden.

The guard lifted her to her feet, manoeuvring her towards the cell entrance. Her legs dangling beneath her, their purpose forgotten. They edged forward, shackles jangling with each step. Propelled along the corridor, she saw only blank walls and grey doors.

Another guard waited for them at an open door, yet another grey windowless box, but this one had a table and two chairs. The second guard helped his companion to seat her onto the chair, her shackles locked to the floor and her handcuffs chained to the table. A hood was placed over her head and there she was left, the door closing behind the exiting guards.

The door clicked, and footsteps approached her. The room filled with the unmistakeable scent of peppermint and the sound of a liquid poured into the bell like vessel that could only be the finest bone china. Whoever had entered the cell was standing behind her. She felt hands on her head and his breath on the back of her neck making her skin prickle. Instead of removing the hood, the firm hands moved over her, feeling her hair through the course material. Gentle, caressing touches. Sophie flinched, she didn't want gentle, she didn't want soothing. The hands grabbed her shoulders, forced her back in the chair, and pulled the hood from her head. Unveiled, Sophie faced her inquisitor. Tall with dark, tired eyes and closely cut black hair speckled with grey. The gleaming silver insignia on his black uniform announced his identity. Commandant Fry could only smile at his Sophia Elle.

There was so much she wanted to scream at him. Sophie opened her mouth, but her voice failed her; a scream held hostage.

'Can I pour you some mint tea, it really is refreshing?'

Sophie met his offer with a blank stare. The enemy of the state, detained and awaiting her punishment, being treated as though she were still the honourable daughter of New Albany's Foreign Minister. She needed to seek deep within her to find what was left of her voice.

'Are my parents dead, too?'

'No, my dear. Of course not. Why would they be? They are recovering well in one of our best hospitals. We should have known the terrorists would not be content with a botched assassination attempt. The fact their own son-in-law was one of the assailants has left them quite traumatised. They trusted him. Goes to show, you can never trust an Immi. It was fortunate you were found before he drowned you.' He touched her hand with his fingers. 'So fortunate for all of us.'

Her lost voice found strength with the help of disgust and anger. 'You liar, you fucking liar! You know that's all lies. The only terrorist here is you. You're the fucking terrorist, not Finn! Your guards made me watch. You forced me to watch, you fucking bastard. You made me watch. Why did you shoot him? Why did you kill him?'

Tears streamed down her face and into her mouth. She swallowed, lubricating her arid throat while she screamed abuse at the man sitting before her. He let her, saying nothing, his bitter chocolate eyes watching her while he softly blew across the minty drink. Her profanity was halted by the sound of his chair scraping the floor. He stood close, examining her face. Unbuttoning his jacket, he removed a white handkerchief from his inside pocket, and proceeded to dab the tears from Sophie's cheek. He smiled and she glared. Revulsion filled her when he held the cloth to his lips. He had begun to pace the room, leather soled shoes quietly tapping the concrete floor. He stopped behind her, and she braced her body for impact. He did not hit her, it was worse. Fingers tickled the nape of her neck, gentle circular movements massaging her. Sophie flung herself forward, snarling at the hidden vileness behind her, 'Don't you dare touch me. I don't want any man to ever touch me again.'

'You are not well, Sophia. Don't worry, I will ensure you recover,' he said before leaving the room.

Her unfriendly guard returned and unlocked Sophie from the floor and table. The hood back on, she was guided back to her cell. There were no sounds other than footsteps and the turning of keys in locks. A prison of solitary silence, its residents waiting for unknown faces in unknown places to sign a document. They were no longer human. They were the names that needed sorting. A number with evidence of imperfection according to the arbitrary rules of dictatorship.

The floor of her cell was wet, the smell of chlorine stripping the back of her throat as the stench of faecal waste was hosed away. The door shut behind her, rewinding her day, ready to press play and repeat the whole process, over and over again. Lights, sticky liquid slipping down her throat, darkness, rewind and repeat. One torture exchanged for another. The Commandant, his fingers massaging her, the absurdity of his interrogation, followed by the cold stinking cell. Rewind and repeat.

The Commandant's interviews followed the same predictable pattern. After caressing her head, he would pour a cup of mint tea and place it before her. Her hands remained handcuffed and chained to the table. Sophie pondered his stupidity. He treated her as his equal, polite conversations informing her of her parents' health, the fine summer weather, society weddings and the insidious problem of the DIAs. Government plans to crack down, the need to eradicate them, the scientific evidence showing it was pointless to try and integrate a flawed species. The inherent failures of the DIA programme. Even so-called trusted MIs were a risk to society. He told her about prayers said for her in church services, hoping for a miracle cure for the unfortunate daughter of the Foreign Minister. Sophie listened in apathetic silence until she found the strength to end the interview with the same insult.

'Go fuck a horse!'

Time could only be counted by her interviews with the Commandant. She dealt with each torturous session in the same way, silence. He would talk about Finn, his role as an insurgent, who were his friends, who were his associates. Her reply, silence. It must have been during her sixth or seventh session that the Commandant abruptly stopped his questioning. He prodded the pitiful creature that sat before him with dull and matted hair. Her soft skin stained with her own filth and her clothes stiff with dirt, sweat and blood.

'You stink! I want you clean before I see you next, new clothes, clean hair, clean face.'

Tears rolled down Sophie's cheek. If they took away her blouse, they would be taking away what was left of her husband. She broke her silence, 'I want to make you gag each time you see me. I want you to be disgusted. I want to revolt you. I want you to put me out of my misery.'

'Then I suppose you'd want me to 'Go fuck a horse'?'

'You can do what the fuck you want. I'll be dead.'

He left the table and pressed the button for the guard. The session was over.

Returned to her damp clean cell, she expected the usual routine to begin again. The light switched on not long after she was brought back. It wasn't her guard this time, but a medic. The Rod of Asclepius on his breast pocket reminded her of Ryan. Like Ryan, this guard was young, but the similarity ended there. There was no toothy grin, no chit-chat full of innuendo. This guard had a job and carried it out efficiently. The hypodermic pushed into her vein, the clear substance flowing through her body.

She woke in a bed. Her handcuffs and shackles replaced with clean white dressings where the bondage had cut her skin. Clothed in a white cotton nightdress, she had been bathed and her hair washed. Sophie felt the weight of the invisible wedding ring at the base of her left ring finger. The physical band, stolen from her, but she clung onto her fading memory.

This cell had a large window across one wall, wire criss-crossing within the glazing. Outside it was grey and overcast. Sophie struggled to her feet. Her hands stretched out to catch the windowsill for support. Below, several floors down she could see a garden, trees and a river running alongside. No longer in a prison, Sophie was an inmate. A suitable asylum for wayward Albian women. There was no means of opening the window. Apart from the bed, the room was bare. As before, the door had no handle on her side, just a button next to it. Sophie delighted in repeatedly pushing it. No one came in. No one checked on her. They didn't need to. Sophie was their captive, under observation. Perpetually filmed, perpetually watched.

The herbaceous border tempted her out of bed. The flowers that opened, withered, then died. Sophie no longer cared about life. Her fight was neatly tucked away in its narcotic box. Interviews with the Commandant had ceased. Her world, three guards and a bare six square metre box with a view.

It was the pain that woke her. Blood radiating out, staining the sheets and nightdress. Despite the drugs, her mind was vaguely aware of the early signs of pregnancy. Her daydreaming filled with fantasies about the baby developing in her womb. Would she be clever, ambitious, courageous? Would he have blue eyes, be kind, gentle and loving? They were only ever dreams, and reality must vanquish such frivolity. There was no room for such pleasant imaginings in her world. Her womb belonged to an official. A man who would determine whether the death of an unborn child was murder. Arrest and execution, the ironic punishment. Or, as in this case, a means of ensuring only the right unborn child should have the privilege of birth into its incarcerated world. Irony was not a word that featured in the New Albian dictionary. Sophie touched the blood stain, desperate to hold onto him, but all she had left was nothingness. Finn had been exiled from her body.

They came for her seven days later. Handed clothes to wear, Sophie meekly obeyed their command. Their guns pointed to the floor, their eyes inspecting her naked body. A wide navy skirt with a white blouse, stockings and neat navy court shoes. Dowdiness personified; Sophie had been transformed into the epitome of a patriotic Albian. All she needed was the summer hat and white gloves to complete the look. Dressed to face her kangaroo court, she would be an example to the others. No one is exempt from punishment. Her crime, birth in the wrong land, love for the wrong man and a desire for freedom in both mind and action.

Neither handcuffed, nor shackled and her head free of the coarse hood, Sophie took her first opportunity to see this new prison. The carpeted corridor, lined with cream walls and decorated with generic landscapes of New Albany. The blandness of a businessman's hotel rather than its true purpose, a prison, where the crying behind the doors spoke of the unhappiness being wrought upon its captured guests.

There was no court room, there was no jury. Sophie was ushered through double doors at the end of the corridor. The guards remained outside the room, the latch clicking as it was locked behind her. He was waiting, seated on a pale green sofa. Opposite was another smaller one, upholstered in a coordinating floral fabric. Beautiful dark blue irises reminding her of the ones in her garden, *'Daughter of Stars'*. Even stars must fade and die. He indicated to her that she should sit there. On the coffee table stood a silver pot and two china teacups. The smell of mint rose from the teapot's spout as Commandant Fry poured out the pale green liquid.

He passed the delicate cup to her, smiling at his treasured prize. 'You look pale, the medic said you lost a considerable amount of blood. I hope you are feeling better.'

If the Commandant thought Sophie would respond to his civility, then he was left disappointed. She looked away, his outstretched hand shook. Sophie was not going to accept the cup.

There were paintings covering the cream expanse, swirls and splotches, greens, blues, purples and greys. She fixed on them, trying to make pictures out of the strange shapes, deaf to the Commandant's chatter.

'Sophia, darling, are you listening to me? I said we have arrested Dr Thatcher. Are you not interested?'

Sophie was inside an abstract hanging over the fireplace. It had become the cove. Marine odours lifted her spirit, and she swayed to the music of waves breaking on the shingle.

'Do you want to know why he has been arrested?'

She was back on Evolo, sailing to freedom.

'He has been supplying contraception pills to married women. A black marketeer, an abortionist, but you knew that, didn't you? Henry was your supplier, wasn't he? Kept you baby free for all of those years.'

Her eyes were closed, and her flesh was cooled by the easterly wind against her face.

'Did 568216 know? Did he know how you paid for your supply? Would you like to watch?'

Two taps and the tablet on the table sprung to life. There was always a payment to be made. She didn't need to look to remember the humiliation of succumbing to his blackmail. How could she tell Finn that they would be bringing a child into a world where it would be born a prisoner? A child born in the wrong land, a child loved by the wrong father, a childhood devoid of freedom, her thoughts and actions the possession of others. It was Henry's idea; people believe mumps in adulthood always causes infertility. Go on the pill and let Finn believe it's all his problem. He didn't tell her about the price she would pay for the deception. She wanted to stop, but only felt safe once there was the possibility of escape. Henry refused, demanding further payments. She owed him, time off to care for her unstable foreigner required satisfaction. There were other ways to ensure she didn't fall pregnant by him. Henry had no interest in destroying his career by fathering an illegitimate child.

'It must be a relief to know you are clear of Henry's child. It would have made things difficult in the future.'

Sophie flicked her stare back to him. A black monolith sipping tea. There was no emotion from Sophie as the Commandant told her about Henry's fate. Sentenced to a labour camp, his wife given permission to annul the marriage and remarry. The three boys removed and sent away to an Albian Military school. Their mother too emotional to care for them, but not to worry, New Albany would ensure their well-being. Future guardians of Albian ideals, their father permanently erased from their lives. It didn't matter if you were an alien or an Albian. All the souls beneath Albian skies, dutifully praying to the Albian God, were prisoners of that vicious and vengeful omnipotent who sat in his palace counting his money and playing with the lives of others.

The Commandant had moved on from the fate of the Thatcher family and was enthusing about his own child, Catherine.

'Did you know I am to be a grandfather? I shouldn't really say, not yet. He'll be my first grandson.'

Sophie was returned to her room. Her clothes taken away, a

clean nightdress awaiting her on the bed. From the window she saw three magpies in the tree opposite, watching her. It was reminiscent of one of Finn's recurring nightmares. Three magpies attacking him, pecking at his throat and eyes.

Every day, after lunch, the guard collected her and escorted her to the shower block. He afforded her no privacy. Sophie showered while her guard blatantly lusted over the forbidden fruit in his care. Then began the beauty routine inflicted on her according to one man's fetish. She was a pixie no more. The fairies had retrieved their sprite and returned her back to the safety of a faraway woodland.

Once in the Commandant's sitting room, Sophie would ignore his offer of tea, meditating on the abstract while he recounted the events of the day. Her parents had returned to their home. He informed her of the increased security surrounding her father. A terrorist attack was always possible.

He showed her pictures of his daughter and her growing bump. Sophie did glance at the screen then, curious to see her husband's tormentor. A proud father showing her the wedding pictures. His daughter, elegant in her fitted dress. Her blonde hair pinned up into an elaborate hairstyle, a tiara of emeralds sitting majestically on her head. Major Harper resembled Henry. A haughty man with soulless eyes, looking down at his young bride. The groom's smile was not one filled with pride. Her bored face only conveyed inherited prejudice. Sophie hoped he was as controlling as Henry. Give the cold teen a taste of her own medicine.

She rarely uttered a single word in her daily sessions with the Commandant. In fact, Sophie had barely spoken in months. Was she even capable of speech anymore? The conversations that she heard in her head were wonderful exchanges of passion, affectionate reproaches of a man's stubbornness, pillow talk of desire and love. Commandant

Fry's inane jabbering was just interference, white noise, and through her silence, she tuned him out.

The view from her window became her calendar. Trees in the distance delighted her with a regal display of reds, burnt orange and gold. The days were shortening, and the sky had lost its vibrancy, reverting to the neutrality of grey. The colourful summer annuals that had been dotted among the perennials, were long since dead. Victims of the purifying frost. Nature always left her the clues. Nature cannot be halted or denied. Nature, ever triumphant against fickle humans. The regime would not confuse her, and Nature would not abandon her.

It was time.

'It's nearly Christmas, I would like to ask for a gift from you?'

He did not flinch, or even look surprised, but his face betrayed delight. He took her pale hand. 'It depends what you ask for and whether you deserve it.'

'I want to see my parents.'

The delight was gone, if not the smile. His fingers combed through her growing hair, pushing the dark locks away from her face. 'My sweet Sophia Elle, you have made remarkable progress, but you are still very ill. We must care for you. I suggest a compromise. You may see one of them for ten minutes. Who do you wish to see?'

Sophie almost said 'Daddy' straight away but stopped short. It would be too painful. It would hurt her father too much. No, it had to be her mother. The woman who placed a twisted regime above love for a daughter. A traitor.

They hadn't told her when to expect her mother; she was just there, sitting on the sofa. Thinner, her skin was pale and tissue paper delicate. It made her wrinkles more obvious. Grey hair crowned her fragility. Michelle as she truly was, an aged woman and the frightened wife.

She used the arm of the sofa to help her stand, before taking uncertain steps towards her daughter. Sophie allowed her mother to hold her close but did not reciprocate.

Music started playing on THEO and the door behind Sophie re-opened. Her guard entered carrying a tray of tea and cakes. 'Thought you ladies might like some background music.'

Sophie gaped blankly back at him, that low, tender voice was not what her mind had assigned to the young silent man.

The music rolled out of the wall speakers swirling its way around the room as he laid out the cups. 'Shall I pour, Ma'am?'

Her eyes were glistening with unhappiness, and that pleased Sophie, there could be no forgiveness for the woman sitting opposite.

'Is that Chopin?' Michelle asked when the guard had finished pouring.

'Yes, it's a favourite.' His face was alight with his smile. 'I love the etudes, the 'Revolutionary' is the best one in my opinion but perhaps not restful enough for you ladies.'

'I hate Chopin. Please switch it off.' Michelle leant forward to pick up the cup as the crestfallen youth stared at her.

'As you wish, Ma'am.'

The room returned to silence with the closing door. While Sophie contemplated how to confront her mother's treachery without alerting the guards, Michelle offered up polite comments about how well she was looking all things considered, complimenting her clothes and hairstyle. 'I'd quite forgotten what you looked like with longer hair. Do you prefer this more feminine look?

'Don't know, I'm not allowed a mirror.'

Michelle persevered with stilted gossip of life outside Sophie's prison. Auntie Emma was celebrating her tenth grandchild. Her father was well enough to return to work, the Commandant's own son-in-law had been assigned to him and was proving to be very helpful.

Sophie wasn't listening. No one would suspect a daughter embracing a mother. She placed her arms around Michelle and pulled her in close. Her face buried deep within her mother's hair. 'I know it was you, I know you were the one who told the guards about our escape plan. You betrayed your own daughter. You are responsible. You murdered my husband. You killed your grandchild.'

Sophie sat back, her goal achieved, she had avenged her child by breaking its grandmother's heart. She expected her mother to leave, their relationship at an end. Instead Michelle pulled off her gloves.

'You can't imagine how it gladdens me to hear that. I worried he had radicalised you against me, but we can start over now, can't we?'

Sophie was confused, how could her mother misinterpret what she had said?

Michelle's fingers surrounded Sophie's face, slipping a bare hand around the back of her head and drawing her daughter into her. Sophie felt lips brushing her ear.

'I could never betray you. You are my everything. I knew just how to behave to protect you. I endured that pretence to prevent your sadness. I'm sorry I failed. I'm so sorry, my darling, the act took over, and I lost control. Despite everything, believe me, I love you and I love your father. He gave us safety. I'll protect him as best as I can, and I'll let my watchers believe I am their dedicated follower. If you love your father, you must do the same. Once his purpose has been served, he'll be eliminated, unless you can give him a stay of execution. We are each of us living on borrowed time, but we can fight back. I gave up my values to protect the people I love, just as you were able to deceive and commit adultery to protect Finn. There can be no boundaries when it comes to protecting the ones you love.

'Use your love, my darling. It is your greatest weapon. Understand him, let him trust you. Make him believe he is your everything.'

Michelle kissed her daughter's cheek and sat back in the chair. Sophie just gawked, opened mouthed and baffled.

'You know, Daddy told me a funny little story the other day. You'll love it. Now, what was it again?' Her mother pondered before looking straight into her daughter's eyes. 'Ah yes, The Sun and Wind had a bet. Whichever could force an old man to remove his coat would be the greater of the two. The Wind went first. He blew, but the old man buttoned up the coat. Angry, the Wind conjured up the rain and hail. The old man flipped up his collar and held the coat close to his face. The Wind had failed. My turn, said the Sun. She pushed the clouds aside and threw light upon the man. He stopped, closed his eyes and turned his face to her. She caressed his body with warmth and smiled as he unbuttoned his coat, removing it and tossing it over his shoulder.'

Before Sophie could question her mother on her bizarre little fable, a buzzer sounded, and a guard entered. Michelle kissed her daughter, put on her gloves and departed.

It wasn't long before her own guard returned, ready to accompany the confused captive back to her solitary existence.

Sophie lay on the bed. Her mother's words holding her motionless. Had she really committed adultery? How can it be adulterous if one is the unwilling participant? Henry had used her. And as for Ryan. She had to do it, for Finn's sake, no other reason. No, she was not guilty of adultery. Deception was another matter. She permitted Finn's unhappiness to prevent hers and that of any children they may have had.

Then there was that strange tale and her mother's advice to use love and understanding. Were they giving drugs to her mother too? Was her brain as addled and confused as Sophie's?

She forced herself off the bed and wandered to the window. The ground was covered in fresh snow, the garden, hidden by its pristine white coat.

The daily session with the Commandant had changed from interrogation to inane conversation. He would chat about plants, show her pictures of beautiful gardens, ask her opinion as to which flower would be best in a particular position. Sophie limited her answers to as few words as possible.

'You are such a taciturn woman, not typical at all but at least we have found a topic on which you will talk. This is progress. We will design the garden for my new mansion together. I expect promotion to Interior Minister by the Summer. My son-in-law will be appointed Commandant in AZ Five. Catherine is thrilled, she does love that house. It holds happy memories for her. Of course, I will keep a substantial apartment there. I cannot be too far from my grandson. Not long now.'

For a society that put so much emphasis on producing sons, Sophie wondered where their wives would come from. She was aware of how the elite society ladies aborted their female foetuses, so they could *'get it right next time'*. Was that the crying she could hear in the adjoining rooms? At some point, someone would realise the absurdity of the whole venture. An elite society facing extinction.

'I think we should set our wedding ceremony date. I have waited long enough. I thought April. Your parents tell me you love the Spring and the baby will be born by then. A double celebration.'

A wave of nausea engulfed Sophie as her brain absorbed the words, 'our wedding'. She must have misheard. It couldn't be right. He was her sentence. He was her punishment.

'I will kill myself at the first opportunity. You know that, don't you? I will not be yours, ever!'

'Don't worry, my darling. I will never allow you to hurt yourself. We will keep you safe.'

'I refuse. I will not be yours. I will not be anyone's!' Sophie cried back at him.

The Commandant picked up her hand, playing with her left ring finger. 'Technically, you are mine already. Your consent is not required. Your father has signed the contract and the dowry payment has been made. I came to a very satisfactory deal with your father. He gave me his loyalty. You are legally mine.'

Sophie tried to pull her hand away, but his grip was too firm.

'Your fingers are so slender. I think a delicate ring would suit you best. I will call the jeweller this afternoon. Emeralds, that is what you will have. Only the best for my wife.'

SOPHIA ELLE

Sophie counted the emerging flowers, each new bud heralding her forthcoming execution. Sophie Sheehan, nee Smith must die. Sophia Elle Fry would step into that corpse and assume her new role.

She had been moved to a new prison. Her own rooms within the Commandant's Mansion. The windows were sealed, doors were locked and cameras blinked from every corner. Perpetually on, perpetually watched. A large window looked out beyond the town. Searching the distant view beyond the security wall, Sophie could see the trees and fields of Hanbury Common. Nestled below, lay an abandoned cottage and its neglected 'Little Eden'.

The buzzer at the door announced the arrival of yet another official paying court to the honoured prisoner. Her days had been filled with appointments, dress designers, architects, chefs and wedding planners. Each armed with folders of designs and decisions to be taken by her legal jailer. Only the best would do for his Sophia Elle.

Her personal guard opened the door and showed the officers to the sofa. Sophie obediently sat down opposite, sighing at the array of buff coloured folders placed on the coffee table. She had not met these men before but recognised their clothes. Black uniforms, a white shirt glimpsing from behind the sombre jacket, silver buttons on the epaulettes and cuffs denoting their high rank. The files held by these men were of other people's lives. A cold shiver ran through Sophie as each file was opened to her. A photograph and its accompanying obituary, murdered by terrorists, died from natural causes or a tragic accident. She read the obituaries of 'Auntie' Emma and her family. The annoying but harmless woman's throat had been slit by the housekeeper. Her grandson's neck had been broken falling off his pony. Adam, that creepy man-child had been killed in a drunken brawl. She spotted the names on two more files, held in the hand of the more senior officer. Michelle Smith and Tim Smith, their obituaries waiting to be announced. Her parents, her friends and colleagues, all dead, but still alive. The choice to wield Death's Scythe dependant on her actions and choices. Sophia Elle Fry must perform to maintain the lives of others.

Her personal guard helped Sophie into the new dress for the final audience before the wedding ceremony. The dress was tight around her torso, the skirt full. Made of pale green silk, it was embroidered with a multitude of coral rose buds. It reminded her of Finn's favourite rose bush, 'For your Eyes Only'. He never strayed far from her thoughts, no matter what threats were placed before her. The guard had finished his task. Her make-up applied, her hair arranged and the wide ribbons on her high heeled shoes tied into beautiful bows. He held her arm as he escorted the mannequin from her cell to be admired by her owner.

She was taken to a different sitting room. The room was warm, too warm. The stove opposite burnt intensely. There was a round table basking in the Spring sunshine coming through the bay window. Next to the table stood the Commandant, champagne in hand. In front of Sophie, on one of the two sofas sat a young blonde-haired woman, cradling her newborn child.

Her fiancé stepped forward, handing her a glass. 'Sophia Elle, let me introduce you to your stepdaughter, Catherine, and here is our gorgeous grandson, Michael.'

Taken aback at the name she looked up, surprised. 'Michael?'

'Named after his father, of course. Don't worry my darling, we will soon have our own Charles.'

Sophie shuddered at the thought of her forthcoming life sentence, preferring to scrutinise Finn's tormentor as she took her seat opposite the teenager. Catherine looked different in real life, maybe it was motherhood. She expected to see a confident, almost calculating, young woman, indifferent to her husband's child, but she only saw a face filled with love, gazing adoringly at the infant cradled in her arms. There was nothing cold about the way she hummed lullabies to her baby. She was in love. Catherine did not greet Sophie, instead she placed her little finger near the infant's mouth. The newborn turned his face towards his mother's finger, instinctively sucking. She unbuttoned her blouse, exposing her breast for the baby to find her nipple and feed.

The proud grandfather sat by his daughter, admiring the suckling child. Sophie did not know what to say or do. Was she supposed to congratulate that maternal witch before her? The girl that destroyed her husband. Despite her attempts to remain impassive, Sophie was still drawn by the young woman's devotion to the child. It was so at odds with her expectations. She stared at Catherine's face. There was something strange about it. It was the make-up. Lots of it, far more than you would normally see on a patriotic woman's face, especially one who was only eighteen. Catherine possessed the advantage of youth. The more she stared, the more obvious it became. During Sophie's work in the surgery, heavily made up women, girls wearing sunglasses, even on the rainiest of days, bruises from unusually clumsy mothers, these had been a regular occurrence. The physical manifestation of a husband's disappointment at their wife's imperfections. New Albany believed in the rights of the patriarchy above anything else and it seemed to Sophie, that this was a lesson being imposed on Catherine by Major Michael Harper.

The baby had stopped feeding and was sleeping contentedly in his mother's arms. The Commandant smiled across to Sophie, lost in his make-believe world of dutiful wives, obedient brides and genetically perfect sons.

'Would you like to hold your grandson, darling Sophia?'

Her silence proved sufficient for the Commandant although Sophie was certain she caught a flash of anger pass across Catherine's face when her father delicately removed the child from his mother's grasp. The movement woke the sleeping baby, and his infant blue eyes opened as the Commandant gently laid the child in her arms. The urge to cry out rocked her entire body with each recognisable feature of the baby's face.

'He's so beautiful, so very beautiful,' she whispered, unable to release herself from the baby's unfocussed gaze. Her eyes were warmed by the emerging tears as she rocked the baby in her arms. She placed her finger by the child's tiny hand and felt the electric shock of pleasure and pain as his tiny fingers curled to grip her with all his newborn strength. She ran another finger along his downy cheek. All things she had done during the short beautiful moments she shared with her own daughter. Molly resembled her father so much, the same fair complexion, the same shaped nose, the same round eyes. Michael, the image of Molly, and both the image of their father.

'He has your fair colouring, Catherine,' said Sophie, after what seemed hours of admiring the baby, but had only been a brief moment.

'I know, my husband is darker, but this little boy is my blue-eyed darling. Such a beautiful innocent little mouse.'

If Catherine knew of Sophie's anguish, then there was no sign of it in her words, but those green eyes burnt into Sophie when she looked up at the girl.

Later, back in her prison room, Sophie could not remove the image of the child from her mind. She could smell that unique infant scent on her silken dress. The confusion and dread of the past months obliterated from her mind. She did not dwell on Finn's infidelity, remembering the morning Finn returned home professing a hangover. She had been certain he was lying and now knew why. Finn was no more an adulterer than she was.

Sophia Elle Fry was fully born. The loving wife, the devoted grandmother. She would use every skill in her arsenal of deception and manipulation to fulfil the task handed to her by her dead husband. The child would be her world and every decision she'd make would be with his protection in mind. She would become the sunshine in Commandant Fry's life. Each fawning smile and mocking kiss, ammunition to make her torturer wither beneath her control. He would burn beneath her ice-cold retribution. The time needed would be irrelevant; only the outcome was of any importance. Her final revenge, reuniting Michael with his father's family.

C.K HAMILTON

Mr Hamilton held back a few steps to observe the young officer knocking at the door. The officer's head tipped forward, listening for the permission to enter. He was young, well-spoken from what the guest could tell from their brief conversation. He figured the lad must be the son of 'somebody' given his elevated rank and teenage pimples. From beyond the mahogany door came the sharp command, 'Enter!' The boy turned the handle with all the confidence of an inexperienced bridegroom.

From where he stood, Mr Hamilton got a clear view of the spacious office. To the rear he saw the Interior Minister sitting at a carved desk, his face ghoulishly illuminated by the screen before him. Without averting his attention from the file, the Minister impatiently bent his fingers to and fro, harrying the young man to speak. He was comfortable in his role, a man who revelled being both judge and jury. Names and photographs flickered on the screen, and that was all they were, names and numbers, to be shuffled and dealt with according to his prevailing view of morality and justice.

Timorous, the officer squeaked out his message, 'The new Chief of Security and Surveillance has arrived. Shall I send him through?'

'Yes, yes. Bring refreshments, Mr Hamilton is a man who likes his food and drink.'

The visitor strolled into the room with arrogant self-assurance, sporting a broad smile for the Minister who was already out from behind his desk, arms wide for the warm greeting that quickly followed.

'This is such a wonderful surprise. It must be nearly two years since we last met. How are you?'

The chill climate of fear dispersed with the Minister's welcome. Another watcher might ask who was the imposter, the jovial Minister greeting his friend or the cold killer of contentious thought? His friend knew and kissed the Minister's cheek while holding him in his manly bear hug.

'So good to see you too. It's been an age. I think you're right. God, has it already been two years? Shit, that was a long case, glad it's over.'

The Minister put a guiding arm around his Security Chief's back, directing him to a couple of ample armchairs. The pair united in common cause, excited to see each other after a prolonged absence.

Their opening chatter of the blustery weather and expected deaths was interrupted by the young officer knocking at the open door. In his other hand he carefully balanced a tray of miniature sandwiches, cakes and a pot of tea. The Minister scowled at the boy for his failure to divine his wordless requirements.

'Not tea, you idiot. What do we want with tea? Bring the whiskey.' The officer turned to exit the room, enraging the Minister further. 'What are you doing, fool? Leave the sandwiches and fetch my whiskey.'

The Minister leant back against the leather of the chair, a beaming smile dominating his face. 'The whiskey is a gift from the new Foreign Minister. A particularly fine one, with smoky peatiness; it's a thank you for my support during his selection. I think you'll like it.'

When the contraband arrived in the finest of crystal glasses, Mr Hamilton momentarily lost himself within the liquid and all it represented. He inhaled the aroma, throwing his memory back to faces betrayed. He did not regret his actions. He was proud of his expertise, and his work had provided him with a lifestyle of an elite, if not always for him, then for his first priority, his wife and sons. Family was everything.

Behind the Minister's left shoulder stood the polished framed photograph of her. Beautiful and enticing, her long hair loose over one shoulder, verdant eyes beckoning, daring him to speak.

'My condolences on your loss. She was a beautiful woman, a true asset to you,' said Mr Hamilton as he looked back at his friend.

The Minister glanced over his shoulder to view the photograph and for a second, he appeared diminished as if weighed down by self-doubt. Mr Hamilton had his own concerns about his friend's ability as a minister. He would perform precisely as expected of one in high office, and together, they had cultivated an excellent working relationship over many years, but he could not sway his fear that this Minister might let personal issues dictate his actions. He let those thoughts filter through his mind while he waited for the Minister to return his gaze from the picture.

'Thank you, I still miss her, such a devoted mother, we do our best for the child. It was an accident you know.'

'Yes, tragic. I received the report. There was no doubt, a dreadful accident.'

Mr Hamilton smothered his internal chuckle, while the Minister shuffled in his seat to look out towards the river that stole his daughter's life. His moment of grief passed, he attended to his guest once more.

'We should talk of happier news. Congratulations on your promotion. I suppose you will be moving to AZ One now you are the Security Chief.'

'Thank you, your support made all the difference to my

appointment. I'm being provided with an ample apartment in the secure district, but the family will remain at home. Mary loves AZ Eight, and the children adore their freedom. The boys are quite feral to be honest. Mary won't mind me being away, I was always undercover before my promotion, so she is used to my occasional visits. We try to make the most of the time together.'

The Minister chortled at the innuendo and raised his glass to his friend in a toast, 'Number seven, I hear. Many congratulations.'

'That's right, a girl. For Mary really, she always wanted a girl, so I thought I'd let it proceed this time. Your first son must be due shortly.'

'Another girl, although the next ones will be boys I have been assured,' replied the Minister, as though his statement were not shocking and alien to their society.

'Are you intending to corner the market in young brides, Charles?'

'Well, even the most eligible of patriots needs a wife. Only the most loyal and wealthy need apply!'

Mr Hamilton noted Charles' phony laughter. He had his files and understood the truth. She was the one who had made the decision, keeping the girls because it suited her. That woman could tutor Machiavelli in the art of subterfuge, the Lady Macbeth of New Albany. The next generation of New Albany leadership will vie for their favours. Minister of the Interior, Charles Fry might think he was in charge of the girls' destiny and seek to trade them for ever greater power and wealth, just as he had done with his first daughter, but it would be his wife who would guide him, manipulating each decision to suit her own strategy. He would say nothing to Charles, not yet. There was much to be gained in understanding the rationale behind his enemy's secrets.

Mr Hamilton stood to admire the view, ensuring his presence could not be seen from the garden. 'Your grounds are looking spectacular, so much colour.'

The Minister acknowledged his wife's skill in garden design. It was a stunning view. A small army of gardeners at her disposal, every whim catered. In the distance, close to a newly planted orchard, Mr Hamilton could see the Minister's wife, holding a small blonde-haired child, her own expanding womb visible under the black crepe of mourning. Her widowed mother walking alongside, pushing a pram with her eldest granddaughter.

Few would understand the public transformation of the woman in the garden. Her apparent devotion to her husband, and ability to entertain simpering ministers with grace and wit. She possessed the skill of a masterful agent, extracting information out of those mesmerised officials in order to strengthen her husband's hold within the Albian Leadership. Mr Hamilton never doubted her power over men.

The spy had a lifetime of watching her, from child to woman. He had stood in the shadows noting the names of teenage boys who gave up their virginity to her charms. Hidden behind garden walls, she was a girl more interested in the woodland plants than paying attention to her conquests lost in lust. Sophia Elle, mistress of her world, intent on moulding her destiny until that day, when he would force her to stand face to face with reality once more.

Sophia spotted her husband at the window and waved to him. The Minister's guest stood back, secrecy paramount. One day he would re-enter her life and then the battle would commence for real. He sniggered as the besotted Minister blew his wife a kiss. Charles Fry was completely enslaved by her skilled portrayal. Yet one more weakling bewitched by the enchantress, that beautiful dryad who once sat on a wall, posing for a photograph, dangling her sandal at the captivated Captain Fry. He had been there. He was always with her. Eternally there, eternally watching.

'You're such a lucky lad,' said Mr Hamilton, retreating to the darkness of the comfortable chair.

'Yes, Carl, I think you are right. A very successful man indeed.'

THANK YOU

They say, 'Everyone has a novel in them', but getting that novel out is hard work. I began writing 'The Third Magpie' back in 2017, and I had no idea the effect it would have on me - I was a daydreamer who was about to become a writer.

Characters and situations developed through the hours I spent writing on my phone. By October 2017, I thought I had completed it, except I hadn't. What I had was a first draft. That draft was the beginning of a very long process of re-drafting and editing. Each stage led to more editing, after the first beta reads by willing friends, after listening to advice from my writing companions and of course, after consultation with my copyeditor, Joanna Barnard.

Going from the spark of an idea to seeing it on sale is wonderful, but also exhausting. Now it is out of my hands and in yours, the reader. It is the public who determines the fate of a book through word of mouth, writing a review or by leaving a rating.

I hope you have enjoyed Finn and Sophie's story. By leaving a review you help others discover and enjoy it too. I look forward to reading all your comments.

You can find me on Twitter, @msclementsbook

ACKNOWLEDGEMENTS

A heartfelt thanks to the many people who have assisted and encouraged me to write and publish this story. My dear friends, Alexa, Marian, Gaye and Clare, who read the first drafts and whose positivity helped me to keep going. Joanna Barnard who helped me shape the story. My proof-readers, Kate Galley, Kate Stuhldreer and Sarah Foster and the many beta readers and my fellow #vwg writers who have given me unlimited support and advice, especially Daniel Aubrey, Fíona Scarlett, Michael Ellison and Pushpinder Kaur.

Thank you to Gill Storr of Go-Design who produced the cover for 'The Third Magpie'.

I would also like to thank The Gefffen Playhouse, whose decision to put on 'Constellations' by Nick Payne, ending up with me reading the play, falling in love with the structure and waking up the next morning with ideas for 'The Third Magpie' filling my thoughts. If ever there was a sliding door moment, then surely that was mine.

Finally, to my husband and daughters who always believed I could write a novel, despite my many protestations. You were right and I apologise for being somewhat distracted over the past two and a half years.

ABOUT THE AUTHOR

Of Anglo-Spanish heritage, M.S. Clements grew up in Exeter, Devon. After gaining her degree in Economics and Spanish, she moved to London. She trained for her PGCE at the Institute of Education and was later employed as a Spanish teacher at all boys' comprehensive in Surrey until 2000, when she left full time teaching to start a family. She continues to run a Spanish club for primary aged girls at a local school and tutors privately.

She has had short stories and poetry publishing both online and in print. She is also a founding memeber of the online writing group, @Virtwriting.

She lives in Buckinghamshire with her husband, teenage daughters and two cats.